Mel Campbell and Anthony Morris are both film critics, journalists and editors. Mel co-founded the award-winning poster-journal *Is Not Magazine* and online pop culture digest *The Enthusiast.* Her first book was *Out of Shape: Debunking Myths about Fashion and Fit* (Affirm Press, 2013). She is currently a columnist on writing at *Overland* magazine, a co-host of *The Rereaders*, and a frequent contributor on film, TV and media at *Junkee, Crikey, The Guardian, The Big Issue* and more. Anthony is a freelance film writer and editor. Since 2005 he has been DVD editor at *The Big Issue,* a magazine he first began writing for in 1997. He has been the film editor for *Forte* magazine since 1992, where he provides regular reviews, film stories and interviews. Anthony is currently a regular contributor to media outlets including *Empire, Junkee, Broadsheet,* SBS Online and the Wheeler Centre.

https://thehotguybook.wordpress.com
@incrediblemelk
@morrbeat

THE HOT GUY

Fuck me hard
with your steel
ploush,

MEL CAMPBELL & ANTHONY MORRIS

echo

echo

An imprint of Bonnier Publishing Australia
Level 6, 534 Church Street, Richmond
Victoria 3121 Australia
www.echopublishing.com.au
www.bonnierpublishing.com.au

First published 2017

Cover design by Alissa Dinallo
Page design and typesetting by Shaun Jury, with illustrations by
Alissa Dinallo

Typeset in ITC New Baskerville

Printed in Australia at Griffin Press.
Only wood grown from sustainable regrowth forests is used in
the manufacture of paper found in this book.

National Library of Australia Cataloguing-in-Publication entry
Title: The hot guy / Mel Campbell and Anthony Morris.
ISBN: 9781760406219 (paperback)
ISBN: 9781760406226 (epub)
ISBN: 9781760406233 (mobi)
Subjects: Romance fiction.

 bonnierpublishingau
 bonnierpublishingau
 bonnierau

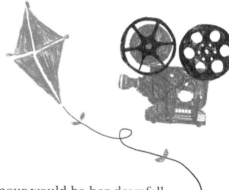

1

Cate always knew her sense of humour would be her downfall. But she never thought she'd be dumped over a joke.

'Get out,' Alistair said. 'I never want to see you again.'

It wasn't that she was inappropriate, or secretly racist, or overly fond of puns, more that she often found herself putting her own amusement first in situations where... well, perhaps 'inappropriate' was the right word after all.

'Are you even listening to me? Hello?'

As Alistair shouted, Cate thought back to five minutes earlier that Sunday morning, when she'd been lying in his bed trying to figure out if she really did have a hangover or just needed more sleep. She could tell Alistair was getting annoyed, but increasingly that had become the norm between them. Men always seemed to find her sense of humour attractive when they first met her, but once the relationship inevitably began to fizzle, Cate's jokes seemed to lose their appeal. When she'd started dating Alistair, she'd thought he was someone she could laugh with – now, the more she tried to lighten the mood, the grimmer it became.

For his part, the ambition that had made him seem so energetic when they'd first met was now looking a lot closer to snobbery. Why else would he be trying to drag her to a polo... game? Match? Race? He'd never even asked her if she wanted to go, and now he was striding around the bedroom, banging and clanging, trying to be annoying enough that she'd have no choice but to get out of bed. She was scared to look out from under the covers in case he was wearing jodhpurs and smacking a riding crop against his thigh.

When she'd said the night before that she was going to go wearing tracksuit pants and a T-shirt that said 'RUM PUNCH', he hadn't seen the joke. Instead, he'd rummaged through the wardrobe where she kept a few staying-over clothes, and when none of them had met his high standards he'd laid out an outfit for her – white shirt, blue blazer, baggy beige pants, all his own clothes – as if she were eight years old. Did he really want her to show up to this posh event in ill-fitting drag, as some Halloween-costume version of him?

'We've got to get going in half an hour,' he said loudly. 'It's a two-hour drive down the coast to the playing field.'

'Can we put the bed in the car and I'll sleep the rest of the way?'

He frowned. 'I told you not to have that second wine.'

'You didn't say anything about the third, fourth or fifth.'

'You knew this was happening,' he said. 'You know how important it is to me. I can't believe you'd act this way when –'

'It's sport,' she groaned. 'Can you even gamble on it?'

'Get up, get dressed, get going,' he said. 'George and the Quanty boys are going to be there.'

'I hate their music,' she said, then giggled. Something thudded against the doona she had over her head. *Wow*, she thought, *none of my jokes are landing. Maybe today's not the day to test out the 'Ali-Stair' gag about his social climbing.*

'This is serious,' Alistair said. 'This is serious to me. If we're going to make the start of the polo you have to get moving right now.'

'Forget the polo,' she groaned, 'I'm more about the YOLO.'

Silence.

'Wait,' she said with a giggle, 'I can do better: I might be about the YOLO, but I draw the line at polo!'

Silence.

Slowly, she pulled the doona down from her face and peered out from the bed's tangle. Alistair was glaring at her, eyes bulging. His always-hammy complexion had deepened to an intriguing corned-beef shade. He seemed literally too angry to speak.

'You do know what YOLO means, right?'

'Get out,' he said, his surface calm not fooling either of them.

'Of bed?'

'Of my house. This relationship is at an end.'

Cate rolled her eyes. 'At an end? Did I wake up in the 1890s?'

'Leave. Just leave.'

'What, you're dumping me over a YOLO reference?'

'It's not –' he stopped, and rubbed his face. 'Yes. Yes, it is. Why would you make a YOLO reference? No one's even said YOLO for, what, five years? What kind of person thinks that's something they should be saying?'

'I was... trying to be amusing?'

'You're always trying to be amusing! And you never are!' he spluttered. 'Everything is a joke to you all the time and –'

'That's hardly true.'

'You have spent the last month trying to come up with a joke about me being a social climber because my name has the word "stair" in it!'

'No I haven't,' Cate said in a small voice.

'I've found your notes! You've been leaving rough drafts all around the house! And it's a shitty joke in the first place! I am not a social climber, so it doesn't work!'

'Well, you have to admit you do look upon relationships as a way to raise your social standing...'

'Then what the fuck was I doing with you?'

Cate just looked at him. 'Yeah,' she said, 'I think maybe this *is* over.'

'Great. Glad we agree. Now get out.'

She pulled the sheet up to her chin. 'But I'm not dressed! And I put all my clothes in the wash last night because you wanted me to wear that horsey-set outfit today!'

'Get out!' he bellowed. 'You're not wearing my clothes because I don't ever want to see you again.'

'What kind of monster kicks someone out naked?'

'Get your clothes out of the washing machine and get out.' He folded his arms. 'Put them on, wrap them around you like bandages, whatever. Bye-bye.'

'But they'll be all cold and wet...'

'Hey, like they say, you only live once. Just do your living out of my sight.'

Cate's jeans were too wet to pull on. But at least she could wear the tracksuit pants once she'd wrung them out a couple of times. And layering all three of her T-shirts, one over the other, would largely avoid the transparent look that comes with soaking wet clothes. Defiantly, she chose RUM PUNCH as the topmost shirt.

'I'm fucking freezing here,' she said, shuffling for the front door, leaving puddles on his fancy tiling.

'Don't overreact.'

'To freezing?'

He sneered. 'I can tell you're putting on that shivering.'

'How do you fake shivering?'

'You should know,' he said. 'You're the one doing it.'

'I'm really, really going to miss our little conversations.'

'Just get out.'

'You're so kind-hearted,' she said, 'they should call you Alistairway To Heaven.'

'Crap joke.'

'If you were a real social climber, you'd be called Ali-Lift. Only servants take the stairs.'

'Get out.'

'You're such a massive snob, they wanted to call the TV show *Upstairs, Alistairs.*'

He slammed the door in her face.

Cate's sense of humour had first disrupted her love life at the age of twelve, when she was almost-but-not-really going out with a boy named Geoff. Geoff was the star of the school's under-fourteens football... club? Squad? Team? She'd never cared enough to pay attention to the finer details of sport; all she knew was that he followed her around a lot, and he had a lot of spare time because he'd injured his ankle and so couldn't play football, which was A Big Deal.

At first everyone wanted them to get together, then once they were together, everyone wanted her to be nicer to him. It was apparently a massive thing that he liked her, because he was basically going to be king of the school the second he was able to play again. But all he talked about was sport! Cate wasn't all that interested in boys yet, but all the cool girls had boyfriends and once she had one too they seemed slightly more interested in her dumb jokes. Going out with Geoff wasn't all that difficult either, especially as all it required was standing near him when he talked about football. And not yawning... though it took her a week or so to figure that out.

Then came the big day when Geoff's ankle was finally healed enough for him to play. Flags went up; special chants were written. The game was on a Saturday morning but the whole school was basically ordered to turn out and show their support for a promising young lad who was clearly destined for great things. Cate took a *Garfield* comic book with her to read during the boring parts, which she assumed would be all of them.

The crowd around the small suburban oval was three deep as Geoff and his teammates prepared to run out. They hadn't won a game without Geoff, and now the scent of victory was in the air. The parents had even made a slogan banner for them to run through: IF IT BLEEDS, WE CAN KILL IT seemed a little aggressive to Cate, but clearly the parents were passionate about their sport.

A huge roar went up when Geoff led the team onto the ground. Finally, his promise fulfilled! Finally, the months of suffering were at an end! Finally, they would see their enemies crushed before them! Finally – and then Geoff fell over clutching his leg. A stretcher was called. Slowly, funereally, he was carried from the ground to a dismayed silence from the crowd, broken only by the hysterical laughter coming from a small twelve-year-old girl.

She later tried to blame her reaction on the *Garfield* book. Sadly, no one believed that a fat lasagne-eating cat could possibly be that funny.

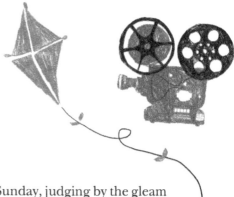

2

It was shaping up to be a beautiful Sunday, judging by the gleam of morning sunshine through the gaps in Adam's venetian blinds. He blinked himself awake, adjusting to the greyish light, and reached automatically for his phone on the bedside table before remembering it was still in the pocket of his jeans, which were in a heap on the opposite side of the room.

He gave himself a second before turning to see if she was still there beside him. Saskia, of the wicked laugh and imperiously tilted chin. Yes – she was quite asleep, her hair spilled across the pillow, the ghost of last night's lipstick still on her mouth. Adam supposed he was wearing the rest of it.

Listening to her soft breathing, watching the small movements of her eyes under their lids and the light striping her face in a vaguely noirish way, Adam felt... happy. He tried not to notice this feeling too much; he kept it at the edge of his mind for fear it would evaporate if considered directly. *Don't over-think this*, he reminded himself.

Over-thinking things was Adam's main problem. He worried about what people thought. He angsted about the significance of events. It was exhausting, living in a fog of possible interpretations. He envied people who could go about their lives without micro-analysing everything. Simple folk. Like his workmates Steve and Renton. They wouldn't be lying here all filled with feelings. They'd be nudging Saskia awake for another go-around.

Indeed, last night over knock-off drinks Renton had nodded coarsely at Saskia and said, 'I'd tap that bitch in a second.'

Appalled, Adam followed Renton's sticky gaze across the room, where a proud-looking girl with tortoiseshell-framed glasses and a mass of dark hair was sitting at the bar. She saw them staring at her and a look of vague distaste crossed her face.

But then she noticed Adam and her expression softened instantly. Did he know her from somewhere? Oh god, had he met her before and didn't remember? Adam couldn't just sit there rudely. He got up and went over to the bar, ignoring Renton's 'Fuck's sake Adam, I saw her first!'

'Hey.'

Saskia's eyes fluttered open, widening as she registered Adam's face on the other pillow. She frowned, looking adorably flustered without her glasses on. 'Hey,' she mumbled. 'What... what's the time?'

Adam pushed the covers aside and hauled himself out of bed. 'Let me see,' he said, padding over naked to where his jeans lay, bending to rifle through the pockets.

He found his phone – *Ah, shit, three texts from Renton* – and turned back to Saskia.

'It's only 9.13,' he said. She'd put her glasses on now, but she still had that dazed look on her face, which had turned quite pink.

'Okay,' she said in a funny, strangled voice.

'No need to get up yet,' Adam said. 'Just hang on a minute and I'll make some coffee.'

He pulled his jeans on and walked into the kitchen, busying himself with the stovetop coffee maker.

'How do you have it?' he called.

No answer from the bedroom. Maybe she'd fallen asleep again.

When the coffee was ready, he picked two of his better-looking mugs – plain, grown-up ones with no slogans or cartoon characters – and carried them, steaming, back to the bedroom.

'Here you – oh. You're going?'

She had her dress on already, and was sitting on the edge of the bed, pulling on her boots.

'Yeah, sorry,' she said evasively.

Adam tried to sound playful. 'Not even time for a cup of joe before you go?' He waggled the mugs up and down temptingly.

Saskia was shrugging her coat on now, lifting her hair over the collar. 'Yeah... No, thanks.'

She was looking everywhere except at him. She cast her gaze around the room, located her handbag on the floor under Adam's jacket, picked it up, and walked over to where he stood in the doorway.

'Listen... um...'

'Adam.'

'Adam,' she said, 'last night was... great.' She reached a hand up to cup his face, catching his eye at last. She stroked the side of his neck and over his collarbone, her palm lingering for a moment on his bare chest. She heaved a sigh. 'But I have to go now.'

He just stood there awkwardly, gripping his two mugs of coffee like a stupid dork.

'Can I get your number? I mean, I'd like to hang out with you another time, maybe –'

'I'm sorry,' Saskia said, 'but I, uh, *really* have to go. I... um... I've got to save the president.'

As he puzzled over this implausibly republican emergency, Saskia edged past him along the hall and swiftly let herself out of his apartment.

Adam slumped. He was dumbfounded, and bitterly disappointed. As he turned to head back into the kitchen, he noticed the framed *All the President's Men* movie poster on his bedroom wall.

He poured the coffee straight down the sink.

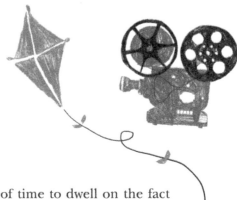

3

Heading home, Cate had plenty of time to dwell on the fact that she was now single. Alistair had picked her up the previous night, and he wasn't about to drive her home. She hadn't been able to find a taxi driver willing to pick up someone who looked like they'd just crawled out of a storm drain; then, when she finally found a bus, the driver told her she wasn't allowed to sit down.

Alistair lived in a half-empty McMansion out in the 'burbs; Cate's house was a crumbling inner-city terrace, and it took her two miserable hours to get home. She hadn't agreed to go to the polo with Alistair, but she hadn't exactly told him no, either. She'd just made a bunch of jokes and hoped he'd get the message. *Why am I always doing this?* Cate berated herself, as the bus trundled slowly down a side street.

Men always liked a funny girl at the start of a relationship, but when things got serious, they wanted her to stop joking. Not that Cate treated her relationships lightly; there'd been a time – there'd been a *long* stretch of time – when she'd thought Alistair could have been someone special. But being funny was just how Cate saw the world. It wasn't that she needed to be more serious; she needed a guy who could see the serious side of her. *Good luck finding one of them!* she thought, staring out the window.

Once she arrived home, she took some dry clothes off her back line. The idea had been to get changed outside rather than drip water all over her carpet. But now she wondered if any of her neighbours had seen her undress – especially the creepy dude who lived behind her. Oh well. Giving out a free show wouldn't be the worst thing that happened to her today.

It was lunchtime, and she hadn't even had breakfast yet. Her hangover was fading and her appetite was back, but there was nothing in the fridge. Fast food seemed like the best option. Comfort food – she needed it, she deserved it, and she was going to have it. For breakfast and lunch. And dinner. People with broken hearts shouldn't have to cook, she told herself. Or wash dishes afterwards. Plus, fast food was what defeated people ate. 'I should be with my people,' she muttered, and headed out to wallow in her misery.

Problem was, after she'd made the ten-minute walk to the Chicken Shaq outlet she'd decided to make her new home, the burger she wanted was no longer on the menu.

'We've got the Smacker now,' the bored teen behind the counter sighed. 'It's basically the same as the Clucker, only cheese is extra and there's a new sauce.'

'I don't want a new sauce,' Cate said, pretending she couldn't hear the whine in her voice. 'The sauce was the best bit.'

'Sorry. You want a Smacker?'

'I want a Clucker. The whole point of comfort food is that it doesn't change. Who thinks change is comforting? I mean, I guess homeless guys must; they're always asking for change.'

The bored teen sighed. 'Did you want anything from our current menu?'

'An emotional connection to a time when I felt loved and cared for?'

'Hey, just what you see, pal.'

Cate thought for a moment. 'Is there a food court anywhere near here?'

It turned out there was a shopping mall a short bus ride down the road. It was bound to have a wide range of fast food outlets to choose from. She just wanted to sit somewhere quiet, and eat something familiar, and not have to think so much about how everything in her life sucked. She just wanted a table she could stare at for hours on end without having to worry that something was going to remind her of Alistair, and of how he was rubbish, and of how she couldn't even keep a relationship going with a guy who was rubbish. At least a decent hamburger wouldn't judge her.

The mall was slightly dingy – a few too many empty stores, and a few more closed for Sunday – but the food court was open, and there were half-a-dozen sushi and Indian places to choose from between the burger joints and Chicken Shaqs. There were even plenty of empty tables to sit at; it wasn't until her third complete orbit around the court that she realised she was in no fit state to choose from a range this extensive. Nothing looked worthwhile. Nothing looked like it could fill the Clucker-shaped hole in her heart. Nothing looked like a meal she could stare at for hours wondering where it had all gone wrong.

The bottle shop was off to one side, near the exit that led to the car park. She wandered in as if drawn by an unseen force. So much alcohol! This was a far better place to grieve than a grotty old food court. She made a beeline for the white wine and started browsing. It took her a moment to figure out why the clerk was shouting at her.

'Lady, you can't just come in here and start opening bottles. You've got to pay for that.'

'But the supermarket lets you sample stuff all the time,' Cate protested. 'If you eat it before you get to the checkout, it's free.'

'Yeah, nah, I don't think so. You're gonna have to pay for that wine.'

'What wine?' she said. 'This bottle was empty when I found it.'

Her phone beeped. She checked the screen while the clerk glared at her. It was Vanessa: she wanted to know how the polo was going. *Didn't go. Broke up instead,* Cate texted back. The phone rang seconds later.

'We're down the park. Come join us,' Vanessa said.

'No, I've made plans. But thanks.'

'Lying on the floor under a blanket does not count as "plans".'

'I'm at the bottle shop.'

Vanessa gasped. 'Cate, no. Leave! Leave now, don't buy anything, and come join us at the park.'

'But if I don't buy anything I'm going to get in trouble.'

'Forget the booze – what you need is some bracing open air.'

'I'm too emotionally fragile to fly a kite.'

'What? You don't need to bring your kite, just come hang with us. See you in fifteen.'

Cate mumbled something noncommittal.

'Or we're coming to get you.'

Twenty-five minutes later and clutching an empty but paid-for bottle of wine, Cate was walking across the last oval before the cliff that led down to the river. Kirsty's orange bat-winged kite was rising off the thermals and Vanessa's remote-controlled drone buzzed around threateningly. She would rather have stayed at home and moped, but experience had taught her that the initial break-up debrief was best done as soon as possible – and during daylight hours, otherwise the boozing would get out of hand and she might end up having poorly judged rebound sex. Cate had made a promise to herself that she'd only choose her sleeping partners sober after spending the night with a guy who'd turned out to have football-themed bedsheets. Then again, if Alistair was the best she could do sober, bring on the booze.

Kirsty was the first to see her, waving excitedly as Cate approached. Kirsty was a little woman with big hair, a bigger smile, and an even bigger hip flask. As far as her hair was concerned, big was an understatement. She had the kind of thick, bouncy hair you saw in shampoo commercials where they'd brought in Hollywood special effects artists to animate it. But Kirsty was unaware of the power her hair had, barely seeming to notice the endless, grasping hands reaching out to touch it. And yet she had once drunkenly confessed to Cate that she had nightmares about creatures clawing at her hair every night; whether that explained her steady drinking was an open question.

Beside her Vanessa looked like an Amazon. Tall, thin and blonde, Vanessa projected an air of severity. Some might even call her ruthless. There were whispers she was really a robot. Vanessa was well aware of these rumours, and had done nothing to dispel them; sometimes she even walked jerkily around her office chanting monotonously, 'Does not compute!' and 'Kill all humans!' Coming from anyone else, this would have seemed funny. From Vanessa, it was deeply unsettling.

'Poor you!' Vanessa said, throwing her non-steering arm around Cate, who made a sad face. 'What did he do wrong?'

'It was the polo,' Kirsty said, not turning around. 'Am I right?'

Cate nodded. 'Uh-huh. He didn't like my joking about it.'

'Awww,' Vanessa said.

'I'd offer you a swig from my flask,' said Kirsty, 'but I can see you're way ahead of me.'

'Alistair is a total tool,' Vanessa said, bringing her drone buzzing over their heads. It was a metal X-shape with rotor blades at each end. Nudging the controls with her acrylic nails, Vanessa was good enough with it that she could make it hover at eye-level right in front of her face. Which kind of defeated the purpose of their kite-flying club, but Vanessa always did what she wanted.

They'd been friends since high school. At university, they'd all done business-related courses: Cate studied marketing, Vanessa and Kirsty did commerce. They'd managed to avoid taking on board the smarmy jargon and aggressive money-making ambition, but as they'd moved ahead in their respective careers, they'd found it harder to make time to get together. A shared hobby was the solution. Well, other than drinking – you could hardly talk in bars these days. They'd tried knitting, dog grooming, trainspotting, scuba diving, rambling, movie nights and going on television game shows, but nothing had stuck.

Kite-flying had been big a few years earlier, thanks to a virtual reality app where you attached your phone to a kite, and wore special glasses that turned your kite into a fantastical flying creature. The one time Cate and her friends had tried the app, Kirsty had thrown up within two minutes. She claimed it was vertigo; they suspected it was the pinot noir she'd had with lunch. Still, even without the app, kite-flying was great. It got them out in the fresh air and gave them some casual exercise. And unlike most indoor venues, the park wasn't full of sleazy guys trying to hit on them. A year later, they still hadn't got bored.

'You are much, much better off without that guy,' Vanessa continued.

'Are you sure it's over?' asked Kirsty. 'You're not going to get back together in a couple of days so if I tell you he's a fucking dickhead now you'll forever hold it against me?'

'It's over,' Cate said.

'Awww,' Vanessa said, giving her another one-armed squeeze.

'Well, the lesson is obvious,' Kirsty said, 'never date a fuckwit.'

'Or a dickhead,' said Vanessa, her drone whizzing around their heads.

'Such a fucking dickhead,' Kirsty agreed. 'He liked polo? Please.' Her hair was blowing across her face, and she tossed it back; even on a Sunday its volume was turned up to eleven. 'Strings, Vanessa,' she added loudly, her kite diving as she tried to avoid the drone. 'Watch the strings.'

'Get a real flying machine,' Vanessa said, sending the drone soaring.

'You are totally missing the point,' Kirsty said, her kite spinning in wide circles. 'Having a motor takes all the challenge out of it.'

'Sometimes you just want a sure thing,' Vanessa said.

'I'd settle for anything right now,' Cate said.

'You don't mean that,' Vanessa said. 'The only way for you now is up.'

'It sure doesn't feel like it. Alistair was the best of a bad bunch.'

'A rotten fucking bunch,' Kirsty said. 'Remember that guy who referred to foreplay as "saucing the pie"?'

Vanessa laughed. 'Or the guy who'd be feeling you up, and then he'd start singing the Bird's Eye Fish Fingers jingle?'

'What about the guy who farted in bed?' Kirsty snorted. 'He said he was revving the engine up.'

'It was barely a two-stroke.' Cate scrunched her face in disgust. 'Now you see why I thought I was onto a good thing with Alistair. He was a jerk. I knew he was a jerk, but he was a fun jerk. Sometimes.'

'More like, he was having the fun while you were doing the jerk,' shrugged Kirsty. 'Fuck, he wanted you to go to the polo with him. The *polo*.'

'He didn't want you for *you*,' Vanessa said. 'He wanted someone pretty to hang off his arm while he hangs around a bunch of horses.'

Cate's face brightened. 'So you think I'm pretty?'

'Ugh, shut up,' Vanessa said. 'We are your nearest and dearest and we think you are awesome. You get today to mope over this loser because breaking up with losers is hard – as soon as you break up with them all their loser qualities vanish. But let me list them once more: he is a snob, and a bore, and you never really liked him in the first place.'

'The sex,' Kirsty said, 'was rubbish. That's a direct quote.'

'But what does it say about me that I was going out with a guy like that?' asked Cate. 'And that he was the one who dumped *me*?'

Kirsty flicked her hair again. 'He dumped you because you, what, made a joke about polo? Wanting to go to the polo is the fucking joke here.'

'He's a loser *because* he dumped you,' Vanessa said. 'That's all there is to it. You're awesome, you deserve better, he's off looking at horses playing hockey and you're here with us and we're brilliant. So that makes you the winner of today.'

'The sex really was shit,' Cate said.

'Focus on that,' Vanessa said.

'I will,' said Cate. 'I'm sick and tired of spending time with guys just because they seem nice, or interesting, or even just show me some attention. I want what I want, and that's what I want. You know?'

'Absolutely,' Vanessa said, bringing her drone around in a triumphant swoop. But the effect was spoiled by a gust of wind that tipped it up on one side, digging an arm into the ground so it cartwheeled along, its rotor blades snapping off and flying away. 'Shit.'

'Well, what the fuck *do* you want?' Kirsty said, as Vanessa hurried off to the wreck of her drone. Flying was done for the day; the trio would be retiring to their regular hangout, Café Nom Nom, for the rest of the afternoon.

'That's the trick, isn't it?' Cate replied, watching Kirsty slowly reel her kite in. 'Finding out what I want.' She shrugged. 'Someone hot. You can't go wrong with someone hot.'

4

'So,' Adam said, turning up the cinema thermostat, 'how'd you go on Saturday after I left?'

'Shit,' said Renton, viciously dipping an ice cream cone in melted chocolate.

'Aww, buddy,' Steve Rogers laughed, 'did Adam cut your lunch again?'

'Women are people, not lunch,' Adam said. 'And Renton, you could totally chat them up if you want to. Just act normally. You know, rather than like a complete tool.'

Monday afternoon, the three of them were in the storage room in the bowels of the cinema, where the big chest freezer jostled for space with boxes of paper cups, straws, popping corn and wafer cones. The staff lockers were here. So was the lost property box full of black umbrellas, black scarves and single black gloves. Then there was the giant vat of chocolate, which was never, ever emptied, only allowed to solidify before being topped up if necessary and melted down again for the next batch of choc tops.

Adam, Renton and Steve were gathered now around the choc cauldron like Macbeth's three witches. Steve was scooping as Renton dipped and Adam packaged the choc tops that would be sold at the candy bar upstairs. They were all wearing black pants with the cinema's uniform shirts: sky-blue, embroidered all over with pink dots. Adam's shirt was half untucked. Steve's was preposterously tight in the biceps and rolled over his forearms. Renton's had a splodge of chocolate on the front. It was an old stain. Chocolate just never comes out properly in the wash.

A family-friendly movie about a dog was opening that week; all three were also wearing shaggy fake-fur tails clipped to the backs of their waistbands. Pinned to their shirts were large promotional button badges that read: I HAD A 'RUFF' TIME AT *WAGGIN'*! Adam didn't care if he looked ridiculous; it was just a lightweight kids' film. It'd be gone in a week. Steve didn't care, either. He never cared about the movies they showed; he was only working at the cinema to make industry contacts. But Renton hated the film. He'd slammed it on his review website BackedUpToilet.com: 'This dog of a film should be put down!'

'But hang on,' Adam had said when he read this review, 'wasn't it movie of the year on your other website?'

'Everything's movie of the year on BestMovieOfTheYear. com!' Renton had said.

'Why have you even got two websites?'

'I do BackedUpToilet for the cred, but the film publicists love BestMovieOfTheYear. I'm quoted on every poster; they send me free tickets and loads of swag. And then I rubbish their films on my other website. It's the perfect crime!'

'Yeah, a crime against your readers!' Steve had sneered.

'Why is it even called BackedUpToilet?' Adam had said.

'Because every real cinema's got a backed up toilet! All these sterile multiplexes with their clean bathrooms, freshly vacuumed carpets and bleached-out atmosphere – they're where movies go to die!'

'You'd rather a cinema where *people* go to die?' Steve had said.

'I want a cinema where movies *live*!'

Steve shook his head. 'More like a cinema where bacteria live.'

At this point, Adam had to put a stop to it. 'Speaking of which, maybe we should get back to cleaning now. The audience really took *Professor Pantswetter* literally tonight.'

Now, Steve was staring intently at Adam. 'So, did you nail her?'

Adam stared back.

'Did ya?'

Adam gave in and nodded. 'Not that it's any of your business, Cap.'

Steve howled and tweaked Adam's fake tail. 'Ahh-wooo! You dog!'

'I saw her first,' grumbled Renton.

'Did you do it...' Steve dry-humped the cauldron, making his own tail bounce, 'doggy-style?'

Adam squirmed away from Steve. 'I thought she was great,' he said. 'Well, I thought... ah, she didn't even know what *All the President's Men* was about! She thought it was about saving the president!'

'What a loser,' Renton said.

'*That* was your dealbreaker?' Steve said. 'I mean, if she didn't know what *Ant-Man* was about...'

'A guy who dresses up as an ant?'

'Oh my *god* Adam, he can become the *size* of an ant!' said Renton.

'No, dipshit,' retorted Steve, 'he can *control* ants.'

'Well, look, *Ant-Man* isn't really my thing...'

'It's not that hard to understand, Adam,' Renton said. 'He's a man! Who does ant-related things!'

'How did we even get onto *Ant-Man*?' said Adam, slipping another choc top into a cellophane sleeve.

'Hey, you should totally cosplay Ant-Man at the Christmas party,' Steve said.

'Haha, and tell people you came as Adam Ant!'

Steve and Renton both laughed and fist-pumped. 'Yessss!'

Adam did not laugh. 'Whatever, guys. I've got heaps of double choc here; better dip some more boysenberry.'

Steve punched Adam lightly on the shoulder. 'Aw, mate. It was just a joke. So you liked this one, eh?'

'Well, yeah. I wouldn't have slept with her if I didn't like her.'

Renton and Steve looked momentarily puzzled.

'Well, I wish I'd gone drinking with you guys,' Steve said. 'But, y'know, I had to get those headshots done.' He smoothed his hair back with one hand, leaving a smear of ice cream on his forehead.

Renton stifled a snigger. 'Yeah Cap, gotta think of your *acting career.*'

'Stop calling me "Cap".'

'Your fucking name is Steve Rogers,' Renton said, 'and you get mad when we make *Captain America* jokes.'

'I'm not mad,' Steve said, 'It's just unoriginal.'

'For once I agree,' Adam said. 'Why does everything have to come down to comic book superheroes?'

'Ask *Hollywood*, man,' Renton said.

'Superheroes or supernatural romance,' Steve said.

'Like that bullshit *Consumption* series,' Renton said. 'Teenage girls eat that up, but it's *shit.*'

'They *eat* up *Consumption*, do they?' Steve laughed.

Adam sighed and let the others rabbit on without him. He never wanted to discuss his love life with his coworkers; he suspected they would even mock him for using the term 'love life'. But because they insisted on dragging him to the bar across from the cinema for Friday and Saturday night knock-off drinks, they always noticed when Adam took a girl home, and then insisted on prodding him for the kind of gory details Adam didn't really feel like sharing.

He was only working the cinema job to finance his next short film, which certainly would not be anything like *Consumption*, or *Ant-Man* for that matter. It was a two-hander: a psychological drama set in a dystopian world where each citizen is assigned a government agent to spy on their every move. It raised important issues about the intrusion of the state into private life, the essential asymmetry of the panopticon, the spread of bureaucracy, and the intimacy that can grow between spies and those they surveil. If it came out well, Adam was hoping to seek funding to expand it into a feature. It was called *Metadata*.

Ever since casting his stuffed toy polar bear as Charles Foster Kane in his own childhood adaptation of *Citizen Kane* (which, he'd read in a library book, was the greatest film of all time), Adam had thought it would be fun to run a movie set. While other kids his age were renting *I Know What You Did Last Summer* and *Dumb and Dumber*, Adam was working his way through the French New Wave and the screwball comedies of Ernst Lubitsch and Preston Sturges. And while his peers worshipped Jason Akermanis and Gavin Wanganeen, Adam worshipped Akira Kurosawa and Michelangelo Antonioni.

He'd still played football – growing up in a country town, that was just what you did. It was pretty much all anyone talked about at school on Mondays. Footy was also a way to stop his parents from hovering in the lounge room doorway. 'You shouldn't be spending so much time watching old movies,' his mum would say. 'You'll get square eyes, love.'

He sensed she wasn't actually worried about ocular strain. A puzzled look had come over her face when, at age eleven, Adam announced he was using his family's camcorder to film a sci-fi drama in the vein of Tarkovsky's *Solaris*. It would star his polar bear in a clear plastic space helmet Adam had made from the top of a two-litre soft-drink bottle, its spout forming a futuristic spike. 'I'm calling it *Captain Horny*,' Adam told his mother.

To Adam it seemed ridiculous to ostracise one guy for liking fine cinema, yet treat another guy as a hero for kicking the winning goal. Which wasn't exactly difficult. Adam himself had done it once, and found himself hoisted on his fellow team members' shoulders on a victory lap around the oval. After the first lap he'd tried to hop down, but Robbo's grip on his left thigh was suspiciously strong, while Davo wouldn't let go of his other leg. And after fifteen minutes and six more laps, the opposing team had gone back to the change rooms while the crowd was still chanting 'AD-AM! AD-AM!' Footy was weird.

Well, that was how things were in the country, perhaps. But Adam had moved to a much larger town to study film and television production at university, and he'd been too focused on his studies to pay much attention to the people around him. Now he was living in inner-city bohemia, at the epicentre of screen culture, where all the action was, surrounded by far more sophisticated people.

As he bagged yet another choc top, Steve Rogers was doubled over in fits of tear-stained laughter at Renton, who was mincing about the room wearing a black beret from the lost property box and a goatee of melted chocolate. 'Ooh, look at me Señor,' he was shrieking, 'I'm Dirty Sanchez.'

Adam sighed.

5

Cate was the deputy publicity director at Sambo Stadium –
named after a local sportsman and not the racial epithet. As
publicity jobs went, it was… tricky. To begin with, it was a giant
building on the edge of the CBD: how much publicity did it
really need if a couple hundred thousand people could see it
just by looking out their windows? She'd actually made that joke
to one of the seriously high-up corporate types once, but he
was drunk and staring at her legs, so she managed to get away
with it.

That wasn't to say Cate wasn't serious about her work.
She'd spent her early career as a cog in a giant corporation's
publicity machine, and she'd reasoned that working at Sambo
Stadium would be a great chance to get more responsibility
on a smaller team. But it turned out that being on a smaller
team meant she had to do more of the nitty-gritty work: making
sure promotional offers were worded right, keeping the various
corporate box-holders happy with their sightlines, and so on.
And on Monday, slumping through the vast cavernous spaces
between the underground car park and the small office building
bolted to the stadium's side, she could no longer ignore her
job's biggest drawback.

'I hate sport,' she said to the protesters who were permanently
camped outside the stadium entrance.

'Yeah, well I hate racism,' said a stringy-haired man in a
buckskin jacket, carrying a sign that said, 'NO TOLERANCE
FOR PREJUDICE'.

'Fair enough, Gareth,' Cate said. 'See you this afternoon.'

'See you, Cate!' he said, as she drove in.

'I hate sport,' she said to Dave, the car park attendant.

He didn't look up. He was watching a replay of yesterday's game on his phone.

'I hate sport,' Cate said to Isobelle, the receptionist, on arriving at their beige, slightly out-of-date offices. Isobelle didn't turn around. She was hanging a framed football jumper on the wall behind the front desk.

'I hate sport,' she said to Mary, the office admin, when she stepped out of the elevator on the executive floor.

'Who doesn't?' Mary said. 'Coffee?'

'We have coffee?'

'You didn't bring me coffee?'

'Why would I bring coffee in to work?'

'I sent an email saying the machine was broken,' Mary said.

'I know. That's why I asked if we had coffee.'

'I sent the email so you'd bring me some coffee.'

'Oh,' Cate said. 'I got dumped on the weekend.'

'And your boyfriend has my coffee?'

'I'm going to go cry in my office.'

Mary turned back to her computer. 'Better look for my coffee while you're in there.'

And that set the tone for the day. Four hours of answering emails that had built up over the weekend – there'd been some kind of sporting event on, and generally speaking, everyone seemed happy with the result, but there was always that one little thing they figured she'd want to know about, which, really, no. Four hours of updating the Sambo Stadium social media feeds, and explaining to outraged Americans that 'Sambo' was the nickname of a successful Australian sportsman. And half an hour of staring out the window wondering where it had all gone wrong.

Not with Alistair, of course. He'd been half a jerk right from the start. But in general. Thirty was getting close, and she'd always seen herself at this stage as having, if not a giant ring on her finger, then at least a steady relationship with a steady guy. The kind of relationship that faded into the background a lot of the time – something you could rely on while focusing on your career. Or focusing on having fun on the weekends. Or just focusing on anything that wasn't finding a guy.

Apart from Alistair, the closest she'd come to male interest in the last month was a weirdo who'd tried to high-five her on her way through the stadium's car park. He was wearing a sports team scarf on a Tuesday, which ruled him out even if he hadn't also been wearing a team cap, jumper and tracksuit pants. She'd shaken her head and hurried past.

Behind her, the guy had bellowed, 'That's weak, lady. *You're* weak. You have *no* charisma!'

'I do have charisma!' she'd said. Just not loud enough for him to hear.

Ugh. All this stuff was boring. And yet, not quite as boring as the prospect of going home to an empty house and ordering something toxic for dinner. *Hmm, dinner,* she thought as she packed up for the day. *Guess I should probably try and eat healthy now that I'm back on the market.*

By Friday afternoon, there were four days' worth of pizza boxes piled up by her sink and she was sitting in a meeting still wondering where it had all gone wrong. Seriously – she worked at a sports stadium. If she couldn't find a smart, successful, halfway handsome man here, something was massively awry.

Even the boardroom where this meeting was being held seemed to mock her: three of the four walls (the fourth was nothing but floor-to-ceiling windows overlooking the ground) were lined with photos of famous sportspeople who'd played here. Wall-to-wall babes, Cate thought sadly. She was sitting with her back to the windows, along with a couple of other department heads. Facing her was a line of accountants and lawyers who presumably were useful in some capacity, though she never saw them outside of situations like this.

'So, what's the point of all this?' That was John Brunner, who ran the stadium. He had been hired, Cate was convinced, entirely on the basis of his incredibly thick head of hair. His pelt must have assured the shadowy institutional investors who owned the place that, if nothing else, he could maintain the ground cover essential for the smooth running of such an arena. Brunner didn't look happy at having been called to this meeting; anything that kept him away from the squad of groundskeepers Sambo Stadium employed displeased him.

'The point,' the tall, severe-looking woman on Cate's left said as she stood, 'is that we need to find new sponsors. Now.'

This was Ursula, Cate's boss. Ursula always gave the impression that she had a horse waiting outside ready to race her off to some windswept plain – though the only way to that windswept plain was via some kind of obstacle course where they handed out points based on style. One of the men around the office had tried to get everyone to call her 'Fate', as in 'Fate is a cruel mistress'. Soon after that he was gone. Cate liked to think Ursula had buried him under the centre square, but a few weeks later she'd seen him on a train heading for the beach.

Usually Cate wouldn't have been invited to a meeting like this – Ursula would have passed along anything she needed to know, which was usually 'Corporate wants more booze in their boxes for this week's game' – but Ursula had announced she was heading overseas for a vaguely defined, eight-week 'fact-finding tour'. Cate would be taking her place and Ursula wanted her to be up to speed. Cate was still trying to find someone she could high-five over this: Ursula had stared blankly at her when she'd raised her hand at the news, while Alistair had tried to turn her high-five gesture into foreplay. He'd had to stand on his head to line his groin up with her hand; she'd been so impressed by his determination she'd almost gone along with it.

'How much money are we short?' Brunner asked.

'Serious money,' said one of the accountants on the other side of the table. 'We spent a lot on payouts after that thing where the players' change room ceiling fell in.'

'Sounds serious,' Brunner said.

The accountant shrugged.

A small, balding man on Cate's side of the table spoke up. 'Obviously, what we need to do here is expand our sporting –'

'Oh, Isaac,' Ursula sighed.

'Shut up, Isaac,' groaned one of the accountants.

'Sport is for losers,' said Brunner's admin, Hugo.

'What were you thinking, Isaac?' Cate said, shaking her head.

'It's a sports ground!' Isaac said loudly.

'And you're an idiot,' countered Ursula.

'How does thinking a sports ground could earn more money by bringing in more sport make me an idiot?' he said, almost shouting.

'Calm down, Isaac,' Brunner said. 'You raise a good point.' He paused. 'Wait, did I say "good"? I meant to say "stupid".'

'Fuck this shit,' Isaac said.

'Why the hell would we want to put on more sport?' Ursula said. 'If anything, we want less sport here.'

'It's a sporting ground!' Isaac said. 'Sports!'

'Isaac,' Cate said, feeling briefly sorry for the deluded idiot. 'We've got all the sports we can handle. How many sports teams do we have based here?'

'Two. Three if you count the summer –'

'Three. And how many other stadiums of this size are there in town?'

'None.'

'So where else have they got to go if they don't like what we have to offer?'

'They could easily move towns, or finance building –'

'Where else could they go?'

Isaac looked at the surface of the table. 'Nowhere.'

'Nowhere,' Ursula said. 'Because they're sports teams. Where else are they going to play without us? A patch of dirt by the river? They need us, and we need more money. But if we try to squeeze any more money out of them, they'll run to the government and complain about how much they're being charged. And if the government thinks there's that much money to be made in sport, they might start thinking about building another sports ground to cut our lunch. So we can't screw over sport any more for a year or two. Which means, Isaac, that if we want to grow the business, more sport is out.'

Brunner shook his luxuriant head. 'Fucking sport.'

'Fuck, I hate sport,' Hugo said.

'It really is shit,' said Ursula.

'My boyfriend dumped me because I didn't want to go to a sporting event with him,' Cate said, hanging her head.

'Good on you,' Brunner said. 'He sounds like an idiot.'

'We work at a sporting ground!' Isaac said. This time everyone ignored him.

Ursula turned to regard Cate. 'That guy dumped you?'

'It's no biggie,' Cate said, not quite convincingly. 'I know you've been busy organising your fact-finding mission.'

'We'll talk after,' said Ursula. 'I have a proposal you might find... intriguing.'

6

Adam had first met his agent at a film festival, not long after moving to the city. A fat man had come up to him and pressed a business card into his hand.

'Clive & Letdie, Entertainment Representation,' Adam had read. 'Which one are you?'

'Clive,' the fat man said. His bulk was artfully draped in a tailored chalk-stripe suit that made him resemble a sweaty mob accountant.

'What happened to Letdie?'

'He died.'

'Do you represent directors?'

'Not if I can help it!' Then he realised Adam was talking about himself. 'Oh yeah, of course. Loads of directors. Stanley Scorsese, Woody Hitchcock –'

'I think you're mixing up names there.'

'No, Woody Hitchcock's a big name in the adult industry. You ever seen *Midnight in Paris? Hannah and Her Sisters? Blue Jasmine?*'

'Maybe…?'

'*Husbands and Wives? Whatever Works? Melinda and Melinda? Everyone Says I Love You? Hollywood Ending?*'

Adam couldn't argue with those titles. Clive signed him on the spot, then spent the next year trying to coax Adam into acting roles while ignoring his efforts to get a directing career going. Adam hadn't even seen Clive in person since that night. But he checked in every few weeks, and Clive never failed to offer him some completely inappropriate acting gig.

Glancing at his phone that night as he left the cinema, Adam noticed Clive had left him a voicemail. His initial jolt of excitement quickly gave way to annoyance at his own stupid optimism. Of course this wouldn't be his big break. Clive's phone calls never were. But still... maybe *this* time... maybe?

First thing next morning, he called his agent back.

'Got you a shampoo commercial!' Clive said over the phone.

'Am I directing it?' Adam said warily.

'Well... it is an onscreen role.'

'Not interested.'

'Wait, wait, hear me out. You won't even have to show your face... much.'

'Not interested.'

'Most of the action takes place on your abs.'

'What kind of shampoo is this?'

'A market-leading one, if *you're* in the ad,' Clive said.

Adam sighed. 'I've told you before, Clive, it's directing or nothing. I'm not an actor. Remember the time I agreed to be in that car commercial? They said the robot car gave better line readings than me.'

Clive laughed delightedly, remembering. 'It's a steal behind the wheel,' he said in a robotic voice. 'Heheh, that car was a natural.'

'Why didn't you get the car to sign a contract, then?'

'I tried,' said Clive, 'but it turns out a tyre tread print isn't a legal signature.'

'Seriously?'

'Who cares about the car? Last time anyone saw it onscreen, it was wrapped around a power pole on the nightly news. *You're* the one going places.'

'I'll be going to another agent if you keep offering me acting jobs,' Adam said. 'I told you, I only work behind the camera.'

'But how are they going to see your face behind the camera?' said Clive. 'Will they rig up a system of mirrors?'

'No one needs to see my face,' Adam said.

He could hear Clive making a choking noise. 'Are you crazy?'

'Look, I appreciate that you're my agent and it's your job to talk me up,' Adam said. 'But I really want to make a go of being a director. Directing's what I want to do. Get me directing work.' Was Clive yawning? Adam didn't care. 'Obviously features are my main goal, but I'm keen for other stuff, too. Shorts. Music videos. Commercials. Corporate videos. Web series. Ultimately I want to be successful on the international festival circuit, but I'm not ruling out Hollywood either. I just think –'

'Well,' Adam could hear papers rustling on Clive's end of the phone, 'I do have this gig where you'll be directing –'

'Yes…?' Adam said.

'Traffic. Hear me out!' he added. 'It's for a movie. It's called *Chocolate Highway.*'

'Why would I be directing traffic on a highway? And why's the highway chocolate?'

'I think it's… a metaphor?' Clive said.

'This is another acting role, isn't it?' said Adam. 'Stop offering me these shit onscreen roles. Any news about the Clear Ridge short film festival?'

'Well, they were interested…'

Adam brightened. 'They were?'

'… until they realised you weren't in the film.'

Adam was speechless. Down the phone line came the sound of a sad trombone.

Once Clive had finished his trombone solo, he sighed. 'I keep telling you – what you've gotta do is establish yourself in front of the camera, *then* move behind the scenes. Look at Kevin Costner. That watersports movie made a fortune.'

'That's the best example you can come up with? What about Clint Eastwood? George Clooney? Ben Affleck?'

'Those guys had to become directors,' said Clive, 'because they weren't half as good-looking as you!'

'He's right, Adam!' came a female voice from the background at Clive's end. 'You're so much better-looking than those guys!'

Adam shook his head sadly. 'Have you got me on speakerphone again?'

'I've got you on the PA!' Clive said. 'The girls insisted. They love it when you call.'

'Hi Stacy,' Adam said wearily.

'Hi Adam!' she called back.

'Hi Adam!' chorused several other girlish voices.

'I think we're done here,' Adam said.

'Look,' Clive said, 'let me be perfectly honest with you. At this stage in your career, no one's gonna offer you any directing jobs. You just haven't got the experience. Maybe if you can win one of these short film comps, I could work with that.'

'I've entered at least half a dozen,' Adam said in exasperation.

'Well, maybe that's telling you something,' Clive said. 'Maybe you should take some time off directing, focus on acting for a while. Make some contacts in the biz. You can always come back to directing in five... ten... twenty years. Whenever your looks have faded.'

'They'll never fade, Adam!' chimed in Stacy.

Adam was crestfallen. 'Is it even worth finishing the one I'm working on now?'

'Well, you're in this one, right?' said Clive.

'Yeah, but only because I don't have the budget to –'

'Then definitely finish it,' Clive said. 'Even if it sucks, it'll be great for your demo reel.'

'You think it'll suck?'

'Who said it'll suck? I said it'll *rock*! Now, I gotta go – my burger's ready.'

'No it isn't –' Adam heard Stacy say, before the phone line went dead.

For a minute or two, Adam stared into the distance, his phone hanging loosely in his hand. Then he reached across the table for the folder containing his *Metadata* shot list. He was determined that if he worked hard enough, thought it through carefully enough, this could be a good film. But then again, he'd thought the same about his previous films.

Adam wanted to make serious cinema that highlighted the injustices of today's society, but what was the point if nobody wanted to watch? There had to be *some* way to reach people, but right now he couldn't see it. *Maybe Clive was right,* he thought sadly. *Maybe I should give up.*

The phone buzzed in his hand. It was a text from Renton. *All set for Friday? [beer clinking emoji]*

Sure [movie camera emoji], Adam replied.

Jeez, Adam thought. There was more to life than just picking up chicks in bars.

7

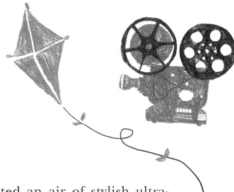

Ursula herself may have projected an air of stylish ultra-competence, but her office said otherwise. Cate would have wondered how her boss got anything done in this mess, but she already knew the answer: she got Cate to do all the grunt-work.

'Soon this shall all be yours,' she said as Cate lifted a pile of papers off the only other seat in the room. 'For the off-season at least. I'll be back in time for game one of the Turbo-Bowl.'

'I'll be counting the days.'

'You feeling on top of everything?'

Cate nodded. 'It's only the sponsorship thing that's stressing me out, and I'm sure we'll have people lining up once the word gets out. Plenty of big flat spaces out there for companies to put their names on.'

'And if you don't, I'll just fire you when I get back.' Ursula laughed, a harsh bark that cut off as quickly as it began. 'Just jokes. I'll be the one being fired for leaving you in charge.'

'That's not really making me feel better.'

'Relax! How hard is it going to be to find a bunch of chumps willing to give money to a sports arena? Men love sport. It makes them feel like they've been to war, only without the blood. Sport makes them feel part of something bigger, blah blah, tribalism, blah blah, big wieners... Now, speaking of sports-loving men...'

Cate gave Ursula the whole story. Actually, she must have given her more than the whole story, because her response wasn't anything like Cate had expected.

'And now you're crushed.'

'What? No! I'm fine with it. There are only so many times you can have someone put you down before it stops being attractive, you know? I probably wouldn't have minded being his show pony if he'd wanted to go to things that were, you know, actually interesting in any way.'

'And now you're crushed.'

'No! Well, you know, getting back on the whole relationship merry-go-round is a bit grim, but I'll deal.'

'Seriously darl, I didn't want to say anything when you started squiring your last beau, but he was well below your best. Money? Sure. Handsome? I guess, in that no-neck way. But you deserve a guy who actually likes you.'

'I know,' Cate said, sounding more exasperated than she'd meant to. 'But those guys are the guys everyone wants! And they know it! Even when they're not arseholes they've got women throwing themselves at them, so I've got to really, really *try*. And even then, they end up with some hot chick and it's just exhausting.' She shook her head. 'Exhausting.'

'You need a confidence boost,' Ursula said firmly. 'You are too good a catch to be doubting yourself like this.'

'I am not hitting the piss with you again. I think I have a permanent alcohol-related brain injury from last time.'

'Weak. Didn't you read the Surgeon-General's report? Brain injuries are the whole point of drinking. But no, I have something more... physical in mind.'

Cate groaned. 'Exercise? A guy just dumped me because I wouldn't go and *look* at people exercising – what makes you think I actually want to do any physical activity myself?'

Ursula smiled.

'Oh,' Cate said, finally getting it.

'This is the kind of exercise you'll enjoy.'

'I'm not paying for a hooker. You're not either. No one is getting hooked.'

'This,' Ursula said, getting her coat, 'is so much better than a hooker. Trust me.'

At first Ursula wouldn't say where they were going. It was on the other side of town, Cate could tell that much after ten minutes of slow crawl through the city's traffic. And as there wasn't anything sports-related happening there, Cate didn't have a clue what Ursula was up to.

'Can I at least call my friends, tell them where to meet us?'

Ursula looked out the window. 'Yeah, I guess you can't back out now. Tell them we'll be at the Rafferty Cinema.'

'You've made a big deal out of going to the movies? Can't I just download it at home?'

'I didn't say we were going to the movies. Just tell them to meet us there.'

Cate texted Kirsty and Vanessa with the address.

Fuck fuck fuck, C U when I get there, replied Kirsty.

Vanessa's text said, *On my way [fire emoji] [aubergine emoji]*. Cate frowned. What did that mean?

'So we're not going to the movies,' Cate said.

'No.'

'But we are going to the cinema?'

'Yes.'

'Are we buying drugs?'

'Why would we go to the cinema to buy drugs?'

'Aren't all the ushers drug dealers? Doesn't everyone go to the movies high now?'

Ursula looked at her. 'What kind of life are you leading?'

'I'm serious. Every time anyone I know actually goes to the movies, they're always saying they got wasted beforehand, and then someone told me you could just buy drugs direct from the cinema staff – the owners didn't mind, at least that way they got their cut. Plus,' Cate said loudly, remembering something that could bolster this increasingly unlikely story, 'cinemas make all their money off food and drink sales. And who buys more food and drink than people who are high? No one, that's who.'

'Well, you've convinced me,' Ursula said. 'But we're not going to the cinema, and we're not buying drugs. There's a bar upstairs where the cinema is, and that's where we are going. But I'm sure you can score drugs there if you want some.'

'I haven't heard anyone say "score" in years.'

'If you're going to call me old, we can go home right now. I'm about to do you the biggest favour of your life, and I expect the proper amount of gratitude.'

Cate kept quiet until they pulled up outside the Rafferty. It was inside a shopping arcade, and the only thing that indicated there was a cinema inside was a row of framed movie posters above the automatic doors. Inside, the building's ground floor was lined with clothes stores selling the kind of wispy skirts and shirts Cate would never wear, and the occasional jumper with buttons that indicated you put it on by laying it down on the floor first and rolling yourself up in it. There was a large escalator leading up to the first floor; Ursula headed straight for it as Cate trailed behind.

The cinema was at the top of the escalator on the right of the landing. To the left there were a few more storefronts, with massage centres or beauty salons inside, and past them, a dark hallway. Ursula made a beeline for it. It wasn't until they were inside that Cate realised this was the entrance to the bar.

The building itself was too new for the bar to look half as run-down and seedy as it was clearly meant to. But layered over the artificial sleaze – the old posters on the walls, the clearly decorative exposed brick, the gutter running along the base of the bar that occupied one side of the space – there was just enough grime in the corners, and sadness in the faces of the clientele, to make the place feel authentically dingy. It was a fake cool bar that was failing so badly it was starting to become actually cool; if the hipsters ever found this dive it'd make a fortune in a month, and be empty in two.

As it stood, there were just enough people scattered around the place to make Ursula and Cate seem like part of the crowd as they walked across to a corner table. This was clearly not the kind of place that had table service. *If we aren't here to drink*, Cate wondered, *what are we here for?*

'Should I get us some drinks?' Cate asked. 'The girls won't be here for a while yet.'

'I'll get them in a minute. You'll be needing a clear head tonight.'

'I'd have thought the whole point of coming here was to get as drunk as possible, as quickly as possible. What, do they have free cocktails here or something?'

'Or something. Something much better than something, actually. You see that guy at the bar?'

Cate looked over. There was a guy with his back to them, nursing a beer while looking down at his phone. 'Yeah. And?'

'That guy,' Ursula said slowly, making sure Cate heard every word, 'is the Hot Guy.'

'He doesn't look that hot.'

'Trust me. He's all that and a bag of chips.'

'I haven't heard anyone say that in a hundred years.'

'I can leave right now if you're going to start again with the "old" stuff. But you don't want me to leave, because this is going to be the most amazing night of your life.'

'How?' Cate shook her head. 'You've taken me to a dive bar on the far side of town, told me I'm not allowed to have a drink, and pointed out some guy with his back to me. Amazing doesn't seem to cover it.'

Ursula sighed. 'I was going to wait until your friends arrived because I didn't want them screwing it up. But here's the deal:

that guy at the bar is the Hot Guy. He's called the Hot Guy because he's really hot.'

'Good to know.'

'That is good to know, because tonight you're going to be sleeping with him.'

'What?'

'All you have to do is go up to him, say hi, make a little chat, and then suggest you take the party back to his place. He's a sure thing. Actually, I'm not sure why they don't call him the Sure Thing. Probably because he's so hot.'

'He doesn't look that hot.'

'Are you blind, woman? He's hotter than a thousand Hiroshimas on a sunny day. And that's the whole point: you need a circuit-breaker. You need to restore your confidence. You need to have a fun time with a great guy that doesn't mean anything. You need to tell yourself – you need to *show* yourself – that you can pick up the hottest man known to humanity because you are just that sexy and special.'

'You just said he was a sure thing.'

'For you, sure. He's not an idiot.'

Cate thought about it for a second. 'Have you slept with him?'

'Yes, and it was amazing. Totally got me out of a massive slump. I met Barry a week later and we've been together ever since. Seriously, it was life-changing. I felt...' Ursula looked over at the bar. 'I felt like I could do anything afterwards.'

'So why didn't you stay with him?'

Ursula laughed. 'Darl, no one stays with the Hot Guy. He's too hot. Seriously, look at him – he's a fucking god.'

'Yeah,' a voice said behind Cate, 'he's too hot to hold.' She turned: Vanessa was standing there, with Kirsty behind her shrugging off her coat.

'Don't tell me know you about this,' Cate groaned.

'Of course,' Vanessa said, sitting down. 'Once you said this place, I totally knew what was going on.'

'It's a good idea,' Kirsty said, settling next to Vanessa. 'I've heard nothing but good things.'

'But how do you all know about this Hot Guy?' Cate's eyes narrowed. 'Have you three been planning this?'

'Fuck, didn't you get my email?' Kirsty said. 'About a month ago?'

'I get a lot of emails,' Cate said, thinking of the seven thousand-odd unread emails clogging her inbox. It was getting pretty scary in there; these days she really had to psych herself up to look.

'It was the one with all the flame emojis in the subject line,' Kirsty said. 'It had a link to the Facebook page and –'

Cate cut her off. 'Wait, don't tell me you two have –'

They both shook their heads.

'I'm saving it for when I really need it,' Kirsty said.

'I have to be the best-looking one in any couple, even if it's just for one night,' Vanessa said.

'So why doesn't someone grab this guy?' Cate said, looking back at the bar. 'If he's so fantastic –'

'You would be spending the rest of your fucking life fending off other women trying to steal him,' Kirsty said.

'You need time on your own now anyway,' added Vanessa. 'This is way too soon to rush into a new relationship. He's just a bit of fun.'

'No one starts up a relationship with the Hot Guy,' Ursula said. 'He is a fun confidence boost, not marriage material.'

'Whatever,' Cate sighed, 'I'm just not interested. But, you know, thanks guys.'

'Fuck that,' Ursula said. 'We've come all this way; the least you can do for us is go up and say hello.'

Cate looked around the table. Everyone glared at her. 'Okay, I'll go up and get some drinks. If he says hello to me, I'll say hello back. That's it.'

'Fair enough,' Ursula said, taking a wad of notes from her purse. 'First round's on me.'

Cate took her time crossing to the bar. The Hot Guy didn't look up from his phone. Up close he didn't even look that hot; what were these women on about?

'Three gin and tonics, one...' her face fell as she consulted the scrap of paper on which Kirsty had written her order, '... Rick James Leg-Opener.' The bartender, a young woman who seemed a little too perky for a dive like this, did not bat an eye at this order. *Guess I'd be perky too if I got to stare at the famous Hot Guy every weekend,* Cate thought.

The drinks arrived. The Rick James Leg-Opener had the colour and consistency of tar, with chunks of white crystal floating on its surface. Cate took a deep breath. If she didn't do this now, the rest of the night would be hell.

'Excuse me,' she said in a rush to the man looking at his phone. 'Do you, uh, I'm guessing you must... come here often?'

He looked up. If this was a Hot Guy, then she'd been living her life all wrong. He wasn't ugly exactly, but he definitely wasn't model material. Perhaps he had a massive dick? But then wouldn't he be called the Big Dick Guy?

She blinked slowly, half hoping when she finished he'd have become the Hot Guy of legend. Nope.

'Not really,' he said. But he did have a nice speaking voice, and that had to count for something, right? 'Just came in after a film. Are you a regular here?'

'No, I'm here for, uh, the movies too. Are you a film buff?' she said.

'God, no – I work in product placement, I was here to check up on...' and away he went talking about his work. Which sounded solid and well-paid, so he had that going for him. Not that she cared about that, but at least he was trying to make his work sound interesting. And what else was hot? Kindness – kindness was totally hot. And respect for others. Treating people decently was totally hot. Maybe the Hot Guy was really the Nice Guy? And this guy seemed nice enough, and he was happy to be talking to her, so maybe this wasn't the stupidest idea they'd ever had – maybe this was going to work out and –

Ursula was standing behind her. 'Hi, sorry, I have to take my friend. Bye,' she said, twisting Cate around until her back was to the Hot Guy.

'What the hell?' Cate hissed, 'I was having a good –'

'That's not him,' Ursula said. 'He's not the guy.'

'But you said he was at the bar.'

'The *other* end of the bar.'

'What about this guy?'

'Forget him, he's nobody. The guy you want,' Ursula said, taking a step back so Cate had a clear view down to the end of the bar, 'is that guy.'

'Wow,' Cate said after a minute or so. 'That guy is *hot.*'

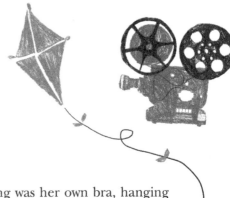

8

The first thing Cate saw on waking was her own bra, hanging from the bedside lamp.

It wasn't her lamp. It wasn't her bed. Then she remembered everything. 'Damn,' she said to herself. 'Hot damn.' Cate felt awesome.

The hype was true; the Hot Guy was easily the best-looking man Cate had ever bedded. He looked amazing without seeming vain like Alistair and his horrible, overly groomed buddies. And while he had a great body, he didn't look waxen and overstuffed as if he spent most of his time at the gym. What made him so good to look at was the completely unselfconscious impression he gave.

And he made Cate feel unselfconscious, too. It was like he could switch off that part of her brain that constantly made her embarrass herself, as well as the part that *felt* embarrassed. Being with the Hot Guy was easy. It was fun. It was a *lot* of fun.

The previous night, when they'd arrived at his place, she'd dimly registered framed artworks on the walls. (The finest work of art was right in front of her, removing his shirt.) Now, she saw they were movie posters. The only one she recognised at a glance was Uma Thurman in *Pulp Fiction*. Looking around the room, she was relieved to find none of the tedious paraphernalia of blokedom – no sports equipment, surfboards or guitars leaning against the walls. No collections of beer mats or souvenir shot glasses.

The bedclothes smelled tantalisingly of the Hot Guy, but he himself was nowhere in sight. Cate wondered if he had simply vapourised after his work was done. Then the door opened.

'Coffee?'

Oh my god, she thought. *Still hot.* His hair was sticking up in random tufts and he was wearing only a pair of striped flannelette pyjama pants, which sat lower on his hips than was surely decent. Cate felt a sudden urge to leap out of bed and dack him.

The Hot Guy was looking at her expectantly. Cate snapped out of her reverie, realising he'd actually asked her something.

'That would be amazing.'

The Hot Guy beamed. It was a smile of such artless delight that Cate couldn't help smiling back. 'How do you have it?'

'Um, with milk?'

'Any sugar?'

Cate, no, don't say it, Cate, begged the sensible part of her brain, *don't –*

'No, you're sweet enough!' she blurted.

To her immense relief, the Hot Guy laughed. 'Why thank you,' he said. 'Coffee coming right up.' He retreated, and Cate could hear rustling and clinking noises in the next room. She sank back and folded the pillow in half across her face. 'Fuck, fuck, keep it together,' she mumbled. Then she rolled out of bed, dragging the sheet after her.

Like a bedraggled ghost, Cate wandered through the Hot Guy's apartment. There were more movie posters. An art deco robot announced *Metropolis*; a giant cigarette-smoking man brooded over a busty blonde in *La Dolce Vita*. *Vertigo* showed a cartoon man leaping into a spiral. These were all old movies, Cate realised.

She entered the living room. Shelves and shelves of DVDs and VHS cassettes dominated an entire wall. Yep, the Hot Guy was a film buff. He had a large flat-screen TV opposite an equally large, expensive-looking L-shaped sofa. Cate's coffee table was currently cluttered with pizza boxes and forgotten, half-empty mugs; the Hot Guy's coffee table was stacked with fat, glossy books, and magazines with international air mail stickers. Cate picked up the topmost book: *Stamping on a Human Face Forever: A Century of Dystopian Cinema.* Good grief! Who *was* this guy?

The scent of fresh coffee drew her out of the living room. Cate shuffled into the kitchen, kicking the trailing sheet awkwardly out of the way with each step. The Hot Guy was standing at the stove, pouring coffee into two mugs on the benchtop. He was facing away from Cate, leaving her free to admire the graceful movement of his back and shoulder muscles. Truly, he was magnificent: as lithe as a panther.

He turned to open the fridge, and started back as he saw Cate standing there. 'Oh hello, you're up,' he said.

'I thought it was rude to lie there waiting for my coffee,' said Cate. 'I'm not accustomed to... bedside service.'

He cocked an eyebrow. 'Oh, really?' A smile spread lazily across his face. 'You know, it would have been my pleasure.'

Cate walked towards him until she was close enough to feel the heat radiating from his skin. 'I'm a busy lady,' she said, pressing the Hot Guy back against the kitchen bench. 'I usually order my coffee takeaway.'

The sheet dropped to the floor as they reached for each other.

'I think the coffee's gone cold,' she mumbled into his neck.

'Totally worth it,' he said.

They were still lying on his kitchen floor, tangled in a bedsheet. Cate raised her head and perched her chin on his chest. Her hair swung in her face and the Hot Guy brushed it back. Lightly, she kissed his hand.

'And you went to all the trouble of making it,' she said. 'You *are* sweet.'

'Yeah, people tell me that.'

She grinned, wickedly. 'Is *that* what they tell you?'

He looked so genuinely confused that she nearly laughed right in his face. Then in a flash, it hit her: *He has no idea he's the Hot Guy.* But all she said was, 'You're the loveliest man I've met in ages.'

He was silent, and Cate began to worry she'd put her foot in it again. *God Cate, why can't you be cool?* she berated herself. *You and your big mouth –*

'Hey,' said the Hot Guy, 'did you want to go out and get a coffee? Seeing as, uh, the one I made went cold?' He frowned, adorably. 'We could, um, have breakfast too. Unless... unless you've got something else on today?'

Cate grinned. 'Babe,' she said, 'do I *look* like I've got anything on?'

9

She borrowed some of Adam's clothes, rummaging through his drawers until she found a T-shirt she liked. It was red, with a motif of a green apple and a hammer cradled in a pair of disembodied hands. She looked unexpectedly cute in it, he thought. Pulling a pair of sunglasses from her bag, she shoved them on roughly. 'Let's go, hot stuff.'

The dusty cool of Adam's apartment building yielded to Saturday morning sunlight. Adam headed down the front path, but Cate lingered in the doorway. He turned. 'What are you doing?'

'I'm staring at your butt – wait, can you pretend I didn't just say that?'

He felt the blood rush to his face.

'Are you blushing?'

'I don't like the word "butt".'

She snorted. 'What?'

'It makes me feel vulnerable.'

The smile died on Cate's face. Then she frowned. 'Hang on... are you making a joke?'

'Maybe... *butt* you'll have to figure that out.'

She's like some wild creature, Adam thought. It was in the artless way she seemed to say whatever came into her head, and the carelessness of her gestures. Like the way she'd asked him for sunscreen, and then smeared it straight across her face as if hitting herself with a custard pie. Eyes shut, her expression was determined as she rubbed in the lotion with both hands.

Adam's neighbourhood had once been working-class, but now the little terraced cottages were mostly painted in neat, gentrified creams and greys, or stately Federation terracotta and bottle-green. Outside the houses were pot plants, roses and chained-up bikes. The shabbier ones were still clearly student rentals, with old couches sagging and fading on the porches amid jam-jar ashtrays crammed with butts.

'So, where are we going?' Cate asked.

'There's a newish place about ten minutes down the road,' Adam said. 'I went there once and it was pretty good.'

Cate caught sight of the cinema building. 'Oh, I know where we are.' She tossed her head. 'This totally isn't my scene.'

Adam had to smile; with tousled hair, sunglasses, her T-shirt sleeves rolled up, and ankles bare in her leather brogues below the turned-up cuffs of Adam's jeans, Cate looked much like the carefully insouciant indie chicks strolling past them, who'd clearly spent ages selecting and assembling their outfits.

'I'm serious!' she said, mistaking his expression for disbelief. 'Why is everyone so pale, and wearing so much black? When the sun goes down, it must be like trying to run an obstacle course through a haunted house.'

He laughed and grabbed her hand. 'Come on then,' he said. 'We'll get there quicker if we cut through the park.'

Salvos of urgent shouting, interspersed with whistle blasts, told them a local football match was in progress on the oval. A small crowd was leaning against the white-painted fence rail, slurping on takeaway coffees and yelling encouragement at their respective players.

Cate shuddered. 'Ugh, sport,' she said. Then she glanced worriedly at Adam. 'Unless you play, in which case... yay, sport?'

'God, no,' Adam said. 'What made you think I liked sport?'

Cate was silent for a moment. 'No reason.'

On the oval, a football player was jogging rapidly backwards, clapping enthusiastically. 'Come on, boys!' he bawled. 'It's all or nothing today, all or nothing!'

Adam and Cate both burst out laughing.

The footballer scowled at them so intensely he forgot to watch where he was running, and slammed into another player.

Adam turned to high-five Cate, and found her already lifting up her hand to meet his.

'Is *this* the place?' Cate sounded dubious. Done up like an old-fashioned barbershop, complete with candy-cane pole, the café was mobbed by fashionably dressed people trying their hardest to broadcast their dismay at being forced to line up for food. The queue was snaking down the street.

'Well, it wasn't quite as busy last time…'

'Are you kidding? Auberon's Moustache is meant to be the hottest new café in town,' Cate said. 'I'm always overhearing wankers talking about it on the train.'

'We can always go somewhere else if it's too hard to get a table –'

'Adam! Hey, bro!'

They turned to see a dapper waiter advancing on them purposefully. He was wearing a striped apron and had a truly extravagant moustache, waxed and curled up at the ends.

'Great to see you again, buddy,' he said, rubbing Adam's shoulder vigorously and nodding vaguely at Cate. 'Would you like your usual table?'

'Uh, sure,' said Adam. 'Um, Cate, this is…'

'Kent,' said the moustachioed waiter. 'Charmed to meet you, madame.' He caught sight of Cate's T-shirt. 'Ooh, Mnmskmo!'

'Bless you,' Cate said.

Adam stifled a snort. 'Your T-shirt,' he said. 'It's a film director named Mnmskmo.'

Kent laid a hand on Adam's bicep. 'Brilliant!' he said. 'Seriously, seven hours wasn't *nearly* enough time in that yurt.'

'Sounds… experimental,' Cate said, without enthusiasm.

'He can be a tough watch,' Adam admitted, 'but he's one of the most interesting Soviet auteurs. He got around official censorship by using symbolism. So the apple represents nature and religion, and the hammer represents industry and the state. His films always use these two motifs in different ways: the hammer can build something or destroy it, while the apple can mean both nourishment and temptation.'

Kent nodded. 'Yeah, totally.'

Cate frowned. 'What's his name again?'

'Mnmskmo.'

'How do you spell that?'

'That's the thing,' Adam said. 'Nobody knows. He refused to credit himself in his films or do any interviews in print. The only recorded interview that's survived is from 1981, on Ukrainian TV. It's pretty bad quality, and they sort of mumble his name. There are cinema studies academics and movie geeks still fighting about how to write it.'

'Is Mmski – Mossimo – whatever he's called – is he still making movies?'

'No,' Kent said. 'He died in, like, the '80s.'

'Well, the official story is that he died of leukaemia in 1987,' Adam said, 'because he was shooting *Second Star* in a Soviet nuclear waste dump. Most of the cast and crew died of cancer. But some film nuts have a conspiracy theory that he faked his own death to defect from the USSR.'

'Well,' said Cate, 'why didn't he come clean when the Soviet Union broke up?'

'You can't exactly come back from the dead. But the story goes that he's secretly helped direct some of the greatest works of world cinema since then. And you can tell because there's always an apple and a hammer somewhere onscreen.'

Cate laughed. 'Do *you* believe that?'

Adam shook his head. 'It's a great story, though, right? And I liked the T-shirt.' He slipped his arm around Cate's waist and murmured in her ear. 'I like it on you, too.'

She blushed. 'Thanks.'

By this time, Kent had ushered them into the café past the waiting crowd, who shot Adam and Cate dirty glances. 'Our favourite customer is back!' Kent announced to another moustachioed, aproned staffer – this one with gold bands holding up his shirt sleeves.

'Hey, Adam!' said the second waiter. 'Right this way, guys.'

'I thought you said you'd only been here once,' Cate hissed.

'I *have*,' Adam said. 'They must be pretty good at their jobs. Guess that's why this place is so popular.'

They sat in leather chairs and allowed the waiter to drape enormous linen napkins over their laps. He dispensed rolled-up hot towels with tongs and left them alone with the menu.

'Sorry to go on about Mnmskmo,' Adam said.

'That's okay. From your apartment, I gathered you were into movies.'

'You could tell?' he said with a grin. 'Yeah, I went to film school. And I've been developing a short film.'

'What, you have a darkroom too?'

Adam laughed. 'No, I mean it's in the planning stages. I've got the script; I'm just shooting it scene by scene as I finance the shoot.'

'By working at the cinema?'

He shrugged. 'The hours are flexible. And it's a great job for someone who loves film.'

Before long, the waiter was back with their breakfasts. 'Auberon's Special Googies for madame,' he placed before Cate a plate of scrambled eggs, saffron-orange and flecked with green, 'and for you, Adam, the brutalised avocado, with an extra slice of toast.'

They contemplated their meals for a moment as the waiter retreated. Then Cate leaned conspiratorially across the table. 'I can think of something *else* I'd like an extra slice of.'

He stared blankly.

'Sex. I'd like another slice of sex.'

'How do you even slice sex?' Adam asked. 'It's intangible.'

'Not if you're doing it right.' She wiggled her eyebrows suggestively.

'Well, eat your special googies and we'll see.'

'Sure, if you eat your thug-life avocado.'

As they walked back through the park, a breeze made the oak leaves whisper. Groups of students were picnicking on the grass inside rings of collapsed bicycles. A golden retriever chased a spaniel down the path and between the trees, barking in excitement.

'SPARTACUS!' shouted a middle-aged man helplessly after the dogs.

His female companion joined in. 'HERE, SPARTACUS!'

Adam couldn't resist. 'SPARTACUS! COME, SPARTACUS!'

The golden retriever perked up its ears, wheeled on the spot and lolloped towards him. First it nosed at his crotch, then, planting its front paws on his chest, it licked at his face, wagging its tail at top speed.

'Oh, there you are, boy!' said the dog's out-of-breath owner.

Adam and Spartacus turned their heads in unison; Cate giggled.

'Thanks for calling him back, mate,' the man said.

'He's such a bad dog,' the woman added as she approached, 'He just won't come – oh, *hello.*'

'Not a problem,' Adam said.

'Oh, Spartacus!' the woman chided as the dog began enthusiastically humping Adam's leg.

'Hey!' Cate said. 'That's my job, Spartacus.'

Adam started to laugh, too, as Spartacus was dragged off by the collar, whimpering.

'I couldn't tell if you were joking.'

'I never joke,' she said, 'about gettin' it *awn.*'

'And was that a joke?'

'This relationship isn't gonna go very far if you need to keep asking me that.'

Adam paused. 'This is a relationship?'

'Well, we've already had more sex than my last three relationships.' Cate's tone was flippant, but her face was anxious. 'Anyway. We should go for a walk,' she said, 'It's such a nice day –'

'Or,' Adam said, 'we could make like Spartacus and bone.'

The tension lifted from Cate's face. 'Now you're getting it.'

'Well, I plan to!'

'Maybe leave the jokes to me, Adam.'

'Wait,' he said, 'those were jokes?'

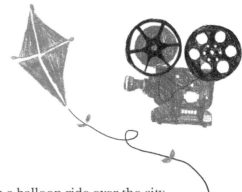

10

'And then,' Cate said, 'we went on a balloon ride over the city – we could see everything from up there!'

'Like what?' Kirsty said, taking another sip of her wine.

'Um, the water treatment plant? And the shipping terminal. It was so romantic.'

'Of course it was,' Vanessa said with a smile. 'The Hot Guy makes smearing sardines in tomato sauce on bread seem romantic. If by romantic,' she giggled, 'you mean "sex-ay".'

'Shut up, Vanessa,' Kirsty said, turning to Cate. 'Tell us more about your big date.'

'Well,' Cate said, 'then we got ice creams and he swiped his against my nose and left some ice cream there that he licked off, and then we went running through a field, and then we went on a paddleboat and then, uh, a mime gave me flowers and, er –'

Vanessa shook her head. 'You just fucked all afternoon, didn't you?'

'Yes.' Cate hid her face in her hands. 'And it was so good.'

Café Nom Nom was almost deserted, as usual. Back in 2009, the owners had clearly thought the name would never date. They must have had the same approach to the decor; the place was now an unintentional shrine to late-aughts pop culture, from the waiter's 'Team Edward' T-shirt to the Michael Jackson memorial mural that dominated the back wall. The mural depicted the late King of Pop with his arm around a bespectacled white guy in a bandanna, under the words 'REST IN PEACE 5EVER IN OUR HEARTS'. They'd thought the white guy was the café owner, but one of the staff had told them it was meant to be an author called David Foster Wallace. The artwork had never been especially accomplished, but repeated scuff marks where the door to the toilets banged open had, over time, eroded the paintwork on Michael's nose.

'You had sex the next day... after you had sex the night before?' Vanessa was tapping her fingernails on the formica tabletop. 'But when did you get time to fix your makeup? And do your hair? Did you stay indoors in the dark?'

'He's not like that,' Cate said. 'I didn't feel like I had to worry about that with him.'

'Of course not,' Kirsty said. 'It's not like anyone's going to be looking at you with him around.'

'Kirsty!' Vanessa said, shocked.

'What? It's true,' she said, her enormous mane of hair bobbing around her face. 'That's why he's the Hot Guy – you can be yourself around him because all the attention is on him. Being invisible can be really fucking relaxing.'

'I don't feel invisible around him,' Cate said. 'I've been with guys where I might as well not exist. He's nothing like them.'

'Good on you,' Vanessa said. 'It sounds like you're in a much better place than you were last week.'

'And yet, not as good a place as I was in last night,' Cate said. The other women stared at her. 'In his bed,' she sighed. 'I spent last night in his bed.'

'Wait,' Vanessa said. 'You slept with him again?'

'A second time?' asked Kirsty. 'A third time?'

'Well, I kind of lost track after a while, but last night was definitely more than the second time. What's wrong?' Both of her friends were shaking their heads.

'Fuck, this is bad,' Kirsty said.

'Very bad,' Vanessa said.

'The Hot Guy is a one-time deal,' Kirsty said severely. 'Done and run. It's about no pants, not romance.'

'You really shouldn't have gone back a second time – or however many it was,' Vanessa said. 'It's not right.'

'If feeling this good is not right, I don't want to be wrong,' Cate said. 'Wait, I think I got it wrong.'

'You sure did,' Vanessa said. 'The whole point of the Hot Guy is that you sleep with him once to get yourself back in the game, then you move on. He's not a keeper.'

'Well, I'm keeping him,' Cate said. 'He certainly didn't seem to want to let me go. Wait, is there a thing here? Is he a guy who says he wants you to stick around and then never calls you back, ever again?'

Kirsty shook her head. Her hair undulated like a field of wheat that had somehow congealed around her skull.

'I don't know,' Vanessa said. 'No one knows. Because no one's been stupid enough to go back for a second date with him!'

'This is a time for you to have some fun,' Kirsty said, slugging back the rest of her wine and signalling the waiter for another. 'You should enjoy getting to know who the fuck you are. Be single for a while, have fun doing things you want to do. You shouldn't be rushing into a new relationship. Not now.' She banged a tiny fist down on the table. Cate jumped.

'The whole point of the Hot Guy,' Kirsty said, 'is that he proves you're still a sexy woman, and then when you meet the right guy you'll have no trouble nabbing him. But the Hot Guy, he isn't that guy.'

'And seriously,' Vanessa said, 'do you really want to go out with a guy who is that hot? I mean, you're pretty hot stuff yourself, no one's going to say otherwise, but this guy is in a whole new league. How can you even leave the house with him? He must be pushing women away with a broom every time he goes out to check the mail.'

'Men too,' added Kirsty.

'It wasn't like that,' Cate said, 'he only had eyes for me.'

'It's not his eyes you need to worry about,' Vanessa said,

leaning forward to point a taloned finger right between Cate's own eyes. 'He is fending off women all day, every day, and it only takes one moment of weakness on his part and that's it. Game over. And what do you think it's going to do to you, having to be the one standing there as every single person who walks by is drooling over him and totally ignoring you? How are you going to feel when every time you go out with your man, every other person on the planet totally ignores you?'

'I'll just... I dunno.' Cate waved a hand around helplessly. 'Keep him on a short leash?'

'You don't need a relationship that's that much work. Not after the shit you've just been through,' Kirsty said. 'You need some time off.'

'I need some time *getting* off,' Cate said. 'I'm sorry guys, but when you're on a good thing, stick with it.'

Her friends were silent. 'And by being on a good thing,' Cate said, 'I mean his penis.'

'You're being an idiot,' Vanessa said.

'Vanessa!' Kirsty said.

'I'm sorry, but it's the truth.' Vanessa shook her head. 'This is going to end in tears. Stay close to the fire and you are going to get burned. And the Hot Guy burns oh-so-brightly.'

Kirsty nodded. 'He is the definition of too hot to handle.'

'I don't know about that,' Cate said, 'I've been doing more than my fair share of handling these last few days.'

'Well, don't come crying to us when you catch him in a foursome with a gaggle of fucking supermodels,' Kirsty said.

'You can totally come to us when that happens,' Vanessa said. 'And it'll probably be soon, he's so hot.'

'How's work going?' Cate said firmly. 'With you, I mean. How is your work? Tell me about work. Please.'

'Yeah,' Vanessa sighed, 'Fine, I guess. I got another promotion. Now I'm deputy VP of Corporate Restructuring.'

'How'd you pull that off?'

'Eh,' Vanessa shrugged, 'last week they sent me down to a bus stop by the waterfront. I had to be there by 11 a.m., let three buses go past, get on the fourth one, get off after two stops, walk back one stop, let two more buses go past, then get on the next one and ride it for three stops. If it was after 2 p.m. when I got off the bus, I was to come back to the office. It was, so I did, and the next day I got an email saying I'd been promoted.'

Cate shook her head. 'That seems... odd.'

'I know your little sports stadium seems like a big deal to you,' Vanessa sniffed, 'but you clearly have no idea how the corporate world works.'

11

The Sunday afternoon shift was one of the cinema's busiest of the week, so it wasn't until they'd closed the doors on the 6.15 session of *Go Hard Or Go Home* that Renton and Steve had a proper chance to debrief Adam.

'How'd you go with that babe on Friday night?' Renton said, absent-mindedly stirring the popcorn vat to bring the unpopped kernels closer to the surface. 'She was *niiiice.*'

'Yeah, she was nice,' Adam said, scrolling through the upcoming titles on the ticketing system database. It looked like they would be adding more screenings for the new *Consumption* movie; the only other film releasing that week was *Booty Shaker 2: Rump Roast*, and it would be lucky to get one session a day at this rate. That was a shame – Adam had a soft spot for musicals.

'Dude, that girl you were with Friday was *sweeeeet,*' Steve said, returning from the storage room with sheets of cardboard bundled under both arms. His skin-tight *Go Hard Or Go Home* promotional T-shirt was struggling to contain his bulging biceps. He dumped the pieces on the floor by the ticket counter then knelt down to slot them together; gradually, they became a display for the upcoming film *Deto-Nation: Lethal Impeachment*. From what Adam could see, it seemed to involve someone shooting a ballot box that had been thrown out of an exploding helicopter. Also, the ballot box seemed to be some kind of gun-toting robot with a screen that said 'Democracy: DELETED'. Maybe one for the political pundits?

'Yeah, she was sweet,' Adam said. 'Nice, and sweet.'

'What is up with your face, dude?' Steve said. 'I haven't seen you look like that since they accidentally sent us the print for that six-hour South American film about the native girl smuggling corn.'

'*The Maize Runner*,' Adam said. 'Such a great film.'

'Aw man,' Renton said. 'Don't tell us you're, like, falling for that chick!'

'I'm not falling for anyone,' said Adam. 'We had a good time, that's all.'

'Yeah, but are you going to have another good time with her?'

'I dunno,' Adam said with a shrug. 'I guess. We're going out for dinner tomorrow night.'

'Tomorrow night!' Steve stood up in a shower of cardboard. 'That's not right. That shit's not right at all.'

'Can't do it man,' Renton was shaking his head. 'Call her up, call it off. Right now. Rip that Band-Aid clean off.'

'What are you guys talking about?' Adam looked from Renton to Steve and back again. They both had identical expressions: faces creased in frowns, arms folded across their chests. 'Why wouldn't I see her again? She was –'

'Nice,' said Renton.

'Sweet,' said Steve.

'And that's fine for a night,' said Renton. 'Maybe even a weekend, if she's got a nice arse. But you don't – you do *not* – want to start making her a regular thing. Like it says on your T-shirt: go hard, then go home!'

Adam peered down at the fluorescent lettering on his shirt. 'I told you I didn't feel comfortable wearing this. Besides, it says, "Go Hard *Or* Go Home".'

'Nuh-uh,' Steve said. 'No way.'

'Why not?' Adam said.

He was trying to play down the whole Cate thing for his workmates, having guessed they'd react like this. Actually, Adam's thoughts were stealing back to Cate most of the time.

He was coasting through the day on autopilot. He'd be pouring popcorn kernels into the top of the machine and the sound would remind him of the smooth rattle her beaded necklace made as she laid it down on his bathroom vanity, which would remind him of the way she held her hair up, exposing the nape of her neck, which in turn summoned a vivid memory of the salty taste when he kissed her there, which made him remember…

'I like her,' he said now. 'She seems to like me. We get along great. She didn't jump out the window after the first night… I reckon she's a keeper.'

'Don't you get it?' Renton was almost shouting now. 'None of them are keepers.'

'It's true, dude,' Steve said. 'You have pussy on tap. Why would you want to turn the tap off? Most guys can't even get a hand on the tap, let alone turn it. You've got it gushing all over the place.'

'Adam, please,' Renton said, finally getting his voice under control. 'As your friends, we only want the best for you. And what's best for you is banging a different chick every night of the week for as long as humanly possible. You have years more of this to play out – *years*! Why limit yourself to just one woman at this early stage of your life?'

'Warren Beatty didn't get married until he was seventy-five,' Steve said.

Renton nodded 'Exactly. Jack Nicholson never got married. Not seriously. And he made a movie with Adam Sandler.'

'Who knows who you could bang if you just keep at it?' Steve pointed at Adam. 'You're going to be a famous director – think of all the big-name actresses you could be sticking your dick into!'

'Jessica Lange,' Renton said, 'Angela Lansbury, Katharine Hepburn –'

'I think some of them are dead,' Adam said.

'See!' Renton shouted. 'You're missing out already!'

'Listen,' Steve said, 'You've been granted a special gift here. Women like you. They want to sleep with you. Well, dudes want to sleep with you too, obviously. But women want you. Why would you want to give up saying "sure" to women and making them happy? Why would you want to make your life an endless procession of "No thanks, can't help you today"?'

'That sounds like a nightmare,' Renton said sadly.

'A nightmare! So many women being rejected, being neglected.'

'Ending up dejected.'

'From a lack of your jizz being injected.'

'I think that's enough,' Adam said.

'It's not about what you think,' Renton said. 'It's about what's right.'

'And what, dumping Cate –'

'Wait,' Renton said, throwing up his hands, 'you know her *name?*'

'I'm not going to dump Cate. She's the first girl I've met since I moved here who hasn't run out on me.'

'You're setting the bar pretty low there, bro.' Steve stood, the assembled *Deto-Nation* display exploding in all its glory behind him.

'You know what I mean,' Adam said.

'No,' Renton said firmly. 'No, we don't. You've got it all – the looks, the lifestyle, a bunch of cool friends here to set you straight when you're about to make the biggest mistake of your life – and you're going to toss it all away... for what?'

'A smart, funny, good-looking girl I really like. And I think she likes me back.'

'You're going to regret it,' Renton said, shaking his head. 'When has that shit ever worked out?'

Adam shrugged. 'Isn't it about time one of you went and checked on Cinema Two?'

'With pleasure.' Renton grabbed an ushering torch and then,

grinning, his own crotch. 'Go hard or go home, buddy!'

He was back unusually quickly. 'You won't believe this,' he said, 'but there's nobody in there.'

'Bullshit,' Steve said.

'I'm telling you,' shrugged Renton. 'I think everyone just went home.'

12

The biggest moment of Cate's professional life, and all she could think about was the Hot Guy. Adam, she reminded herself. Think of him as Adam, not the Hot Guy. He wasn't just some pneumatic sex toy now; he was the man she was seeing – seeing pretty much all of every chance she got – and she had to start thinking of him as an actual human being. Or better yet, she could stop thinking of him entirely and focus on the presentation she was meant to be giving.

But it was his fault she was so scattered, and not just because she hadn't spent the weekend preparing like she'd planned. She couldn't stop thinking about him. Yes, sure, fine, okay, his body was a major part of it, and she had no complaints whatsoever about that side of things. But he was kind, and nice, and listened to what she had to say, and didn't make her feel stupid when she made jokes that she kind of felt she deserved to be made to feel stupid for.

Obviously it could all go wrong at any moment. Kirsty and Vanessa both did kind of have a point with the whole 'he's too hot for you' argument. But, Cate thought wistfully, he did seem to be at least partly into her, and nothing had gone horribly wrong just yet, and it was all really just a bit of fun anyway, so why not just go with it, at least for a while? She was sick of always worrying away at every last –

'Cate? Are you ready to make your report?'

She blinked. Time to stop thinking about him now. She was standing at the end of the table in the main boardroom at

Sambo Stadium, about to give a presentation on why one half of the people there – marketing types from an investment bank – should give the other half of the people there – her bosses at the stadium – a truckload of money. Basically, she was there to sell them on the idea of purchasing naming rights to the stadium.

The bank was named Plaid, but it was so fusty and old-fashioned that everyone around the office called it 'Staid'. It was pretty much seen as a done deal, and 'Staid Stadium' was the new nickname doing the rounds.

'But isn't it pronounced "Pladd", rhymes with "dad"?' Cate had asked Hugo.

'I thought it was pronounced like "played sports",' Brunner's assistant replied. 'Shit, now the nickname doesn't even work.'

'Surely you know how to say our potential sponsor's name – didn't you set up this meeting?'

'I sure did,' Hugo said, 'by email.'

'Of course,' she said briskly now, then realised in horror she had no idea at all what was going to come out of her mouth next. She'd pushed Adam out of her mind. Unfortunately, he'd taken everything else with him. 'Ladies, gentlemen, uh, *this bank* has a long and proud history behind it. But as we all know, history is, um, in the past.'

Everyone nodded. *You can wing this,* Cate thought. *Everyone likes you. You're hilarious!*

'And if you don't want your bank to remain in the past, you have to move forward. Into the future. Like they say all over town: to avoid being *staid,* invest with…' She paused meaningfully.

'Invest with us?' one of the grey-suited, grey-faced bankers said.

'Is that really what people are saying all over town?' piped up his colleague.

'It sure is,' said Cate, with a conviction she didn't feel. 'Why, just last Tuesday I overheard a man on the train saying, "The future can't be *bad* if you invest with…" '

'Hmmm,' the banker said, after another lengthy pause. 'That's something new for us to take on board. It's very different to what our focus groups have been telling us.'

'Well, we've definitely got our ears to the ground here,' Cate said.

John Brunner nodded approvingly at this.

'That's why we approached you first,' she went on. 'Because, um, as we said to ourselves, when the future is being *made*, you'd better call...'

'And naming a stadium is the future?'

'A pretty cool future if you ask me,' Cate said. 'And, uh, if you ask the sports fans of this city – this entire state – I think you'll find they agree. Every lassie and *lad* –'

'But this stadium is over forty years old,' said another of the bankers.

'Tradition,' Cate said, 'stability.'

'Didn't one of your grandstands collapse last year?'

'No, that was the player change rooms.'

Cate noticed Brunner was trying to send her some sort of signal using only his eyes and eyebrows. He looked as if he was suffering a brain aneurysm.

'Still got tradition,' she said.

'Isn't tradition one of the things naming your stadium is going to get us away from?'

'You're going to have your name on a giant sign on the side of one of the biggest buildings in the city!' countered Cate. 'That's pretty cool, right?'

'We already have our name on a giant sign on the side of the biggest building in the city,' the oldest and greyest of the bankers said.

'Excuse me,' Brunner said, getting up from his seat, still rolling his eyes at Cate, 'but I think you gentlemen may have forgotten why we've gathered here today.' He paused dramatically. 'Free sports tickets.'

The bankers began muttering excitedly among themselves. Brunner glanced at Cate, his expression a mixture of relief and 'we're going to have a serious talk when this is over'. It was a pretty complicated look, and it gave Cate plenty of time to sweat.

Why was he so mad with her? Charm was always the way Ursula won over a crowd. It wasn't her fault these people were more excited about sports tickets than what she was saying. God, she thought, this was worse than the time her high school English teacher Mr Statham had ridiculed her poem *The Crying Clown Was Me*. It was even worse than...

And suddenly she was back to her university days and remembering a guy – Luca ('not Luke. Never Luke') – who hadn't exactly been the one, but had definitely been one-adjacent. He'd seemed so nice, but not in a wimpy way. He was nice to her because she was worth being nice to; not because he was a sap who bent over backwards to everyone. Which, when she thought about it now, was maybe the reason why she didn't really trust nice guys all that much. Because, well...

It had been at a party, some formal thing one of the other schools (nursing?) had put on, and so all the guys had looked kind of the same in their tuxes and all the girls kind of looked alike in big puffy dresses. They'd gone off to be with their respective friends for a while, and she hadn't realised his group had drifted back next to her group until she heard Luca saying loudly, 'Cate? Yeah, she's fun to be around, but –'

'But she's fun to be around?' one of his douchebag friends said with a sneer she could hear in his voice, and they all laughed. And not in a 'yeah, she's so cool and funny,' way either.

'Don't you call her your trashbag, mate?'

'I don't know what you're talking about,' said Luca.

'Yeah,' the douchebag friend said, 'she's your trashbag, cos that's where you put your junk.'

Just for an instant, she wanted to slink away and have a good cry in the bathroom. But fuck that; time to teach these losers the real meaning of 'fun to be around'.

She spun around dramatically. Maybe Luca and his friends gasped in astonishment; maybe she just imagined that part.

'Yo, Derek,' she said, pointing at the douchebag who'd called her a trashbag, 'I hear you're transferring to agriculture.'

'No,' he said, puzzled, 'I'm still studying nursing and –'

'Well, how'd you like *these* acres?' she said, and kicked him hard in the balls. He went down like a sack of rotten apples.

She smirked at his collapsed form, then a look of concern crossed her face. 'Wait,' she said. Luca froze, about to bend down to tend to his injured friend.

'I can do better.'

She kicked Derek in the balls again.

'Guess that nursing degree is going to come in handy,' she said. 'You know… for your junk.'

'What… what are you talking about?' Derek gasped.

'Shut up,' she said. 'Tragedy is when I hear your pathetic shit. Comedy is when I kick you in the balls.'

Cate's attention drifted back to the meeting. 'No man's gonna tell me I'm not funny!' she yelled. 'This presentation is over!'

She glared around the boardroom, waiting for a reaction. There was none. The room was empty.

After a dismaying few seconds, Brunner put his head around the doorway. 'Are you coming?'

They retreated down the corridor in silence.

'Looks like rain this weekend?' Cate finally ventured.

'Mmm, yes,' Brunner said. 'It'll definitely be good for the turf. Now, Cate,' he turned his magnificently coiffed head in her direction, 'I think I defused things back there with those free tickets. But you can't vague out like that in a presentation. You just sort of stood there, staring into space and occasionally clenching your fists. I like that determined vibe, but gotta keep it sharp, understand?'

'Yes, Mr Brunner.'

'John, please.'

'Yes, John.'

Brunner peered out a stadium-side window. 'We've got them touring the ground right now. Can't go wrong with that grass. I'll go out and schedule another meeting for a fortnight or so from now. But you've got to come up with something better. Take the weekend to brainstorm, then run it by me next week. Hugo has my schedule.'

'Yes, John.'

'Excellent,' he said and turned, rubbing his hands together as he strode off.

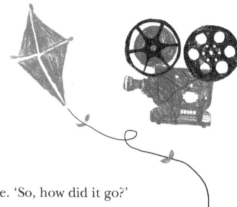

13

Adam handed Cate a glass of wine. 'So, how did it go?'

She drained it at a gulp and held it out for a refill.

'That good, eh?' He smiled and poured again.

'I really screwed up,' she sighed. 'Just like I've screwed up everything in my life.' She looked at him lustily. 'Except you, Adam. You I've just screwed.'

'I'm sure that's not true,' Adam said, stroking her free arm consolingly as she upended her glass again. 'Where's that smart, funny girl I fell for?'

She arched one eyebrow. 'Good question! Have you been cheating on me?'

'Seriously. You're great when it's just us two. You're spontaneous. But it's like you sort of... freeze when you get nervous. There's got to be a way to get them to see the same Cate I do.'

'What, should we fuck on top of the conference table in front of Brunner and all the bankers?'

'Sounds like fun,' Adam said. 'But seriously, this is what I mean. We're just talking, and you're really funny. You're great at speaking off the cuff.'

'I'm good at making *jokes* off the cuff,' Cate said, 'but this has to be serious. This presentation is really important to me.'

'Why?' said Adam. 'I thought you hated sport.'

''Course I do,' Cate said, 'but sport isn't my job. Public relations is my job. And while my boss is gone, this is my chance to step up and show I'm not just someone who does the grunt-work.

I can head up a team, I can attract sponsorship, I can run marketing campaigns. So when I move on after... I don't know, a year, eighteen months, I'll have the experience to get a top-level job working on something I *am* passionate about.'

'Sounds like you've got it all planned out,' Adam said. 'But I still think maybe you're over-thinking this. I do that sometimes. I get what it's like to feel paralysed by worrying about how you come across to other people.'

She laughed. 'Other people *love* you.'

'People are *nice* to me, sure. But I can't just relax and take it for granted. I'm always asking myself *why*. Second-guessing people's motives.'

Cate quietly studied Adam's living-room carpet.

'Trust me, I've thought a lot about this.' Adam sighed. 'Maybe I make life too complicated. But maybe we're the same in that way. You over-think things too, and you get all tangled up.'

'That's the first time anyone's ever accused me of thinking too hard,' Cate said.

'Well, you're definitely not stupid,' Adam said. 'I've worked with some people who seem allergic to the very idea of thought.'

'Those guys from the cinema? The one who was practically bursting out of his T-shirt? And the weaselly one, who kept mentioning trainspotting? Is that a hobby of his?'

'That's Renton. He meant the movie *Trainspotting* – the main character is called Renton.'

'Oh. Is it his first name or his last name?'

'You know,' Adam said, 'I'm really not sure. I've never asked.'

He reached across to the coffee table and poured a glass of wine for himself. 'Anyway, they're not bad guys. Just excitable, and a little too much into being fanboys.' He settled back on the sofa beside Cate. 'No, I've been having real problems with the DOP on my film.'

He noticed her blank face. 'Director of Photography. The cameraman. I met this guy at the Expressionist Film Festival last year, and he seemed really across the whole industry thing. His name's Orson Reich.'

Cate snorted. 'You reckon that's his real name?'

A faint look of dismay crossed Adam's face, as if a puzzle piece had just fallen into place in his mind. 'Well, who knows?' he said. 'Anyway, he's a fair bit older, he's directed six features. And I'd only just moved here. I hardly knew anyone. I was keen to have someone on my production team who seemed to know his stuff.'

'And it's not working out like that?'

'Well, on the first day of my shoot he was ninety minutes late. I decided to just start without him, and then he walked right into frame as we were rolling. We had to set up the shot all over again.'

'Get rid of him.'

Adam looked pained. 'I would, but he's working for free. It'd be ungrateful.'

'Yeah, but it sounds like he's actually costing you money.'

He rolled his eyes. 'It's worse than if I was doing it by myself. He's hopeless. He's not there half the time. He knocks off after lunch. He contradicts my directions to the cast. Once he ruined a take by shouting, "Imagine your uncle just died!"'

'Uncle?' said Cate, frowning. 'What an odd thing to say.'

'That's one of the more normal things. Another time I was looking for him everywhere and then I found him napping under one of the lights, wearing sunglasses and holding one of those foil tanning reflector things under his chin.'

He seemed upset, Cate realised. She felt a little guilty now for pouting about her dud presentation. 'How long has this shoot been going on?' she asked.

'Four months, on and off. We snatch a day here and there when we're all free. Principal photography is almost over... I hope. At least, after Orson's bullshit this week I'm pretty much over it anyway.'

'What comes next, then? Vice-principal photography?'

Adam laughed, laying a hand affectionately on Cate's leg.

'Shut up!' she protested. 'I don't know your industry jargon.'

'Well, there are a few shots we need to go back and get.'
Adam was now lazily circling his thumb on her thigh, just under
the hem of her skirt. 'Pickup shots, those are called. Things that
don't need the actors.'

'Like what?'

'Oh, there's this one montage I wanted to do about
surveillance. Lots of really stark, exposed spaces. But I'm still
looking for a location that really says "society of the spectacle".'
He slid his hand further up, caressing Cate's inner thigh.

She shifted on the sofa. 'Is this a pickup shot right now?'

'Maybe.'

'Well, look,' she said, scooting closer, 'why don't you come
and film in the stadium? It's empty most of the time right now.
And – ohhh – if you want stark and exposed, just film our busted
stand.'

That slow, gorgeous smile was blooming on his face. 'Seriously?
That would be incredible. But wouldn't it be a headache to
explain to your boss?'

'I'll think of – mmphh – I'll figure something out. Oh...
god...' Her empty wineglass fell from her hand, thudding on
the carpet.

'Thank you! You're amazing.'

Cate was unbuttoning his jeans. 'No, you're... *amazing*...'

14

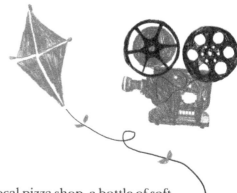

Cate was walking home from her local pizza shop, a bottle of soft drink tucked in the crook of her arm as she pulled a steaming slice of margherita from the box.

'I like my pizza like I like my men,' said Cate to nobody in particular. 'With a stuffed crust!'

Chuckling to herself, she crossed to her side of the street. A large, shiny black SUV was cruising very slowly on the road behind her. *Must be trying to find a park,* Cate thought, taking another bite of pizza. She tossed a half-chewed crust into the gutter, as the car sped up to overtake her and pulled in to the kerb a few houses down the street. She drew level with the SUV, rooting around in the box, trying to tear another slice free. As she lifted it to her mouth, the car door suddenly swung open and two sets of hands grabbed her.

She tried to call out but her voice was muffled by the slice of pizza. She attempted to spit it out, as a hood was roughly pulled down over her head. Cate was dragged into the SUV and shoved into a surprisingly comfortable seat. She heard the door slam shut. They were moving.

'You want to stay safe, you'd better stay quiet,' said a woman's voice from the front of the car.

'You *really* want to stay safe, you'd better do up your seatbelt,' said another woman's voice from beside her.

Cate had been too terrified to realise her hands were still free. Slowly, not wanting to anger her captors, she buckled her seatbelt, then raised her hands towards her head so they'd see she wasn't trying anything.

'Don't touch that pillowcase,' said the woman next to her.

'Is she still eating that pizza?' came a third voice from Cate's other side. 'Eww, she'll be getting grease all over it.'

'Can I get a slice?' said a fourth voice from up the front. Cate felt the box yanked from her lap.

'Did you kidnap me or the pizza?' Cate said at last, having swallowed her final mouthful. Some of her initial panic had gone down with it. All around her she could hear her pizza being divvied up and chewed on. The car filled with a delicious scent of garlic, basil and melted cheese. 'Take it!' Cate went on. 'You've got what you wanted! Now let me go!'

'Oh, we're only just getting started,' the voice up front said with an evil chuckle.

'Not my soft drink!' Cate shouted, struggling against the seatbelt. But it was no use; she heard the *pssst* of the seal being broken, and then satisfied slurps and swallows as the bottle was passed around. 'Damn you,' Cate sobbed, as the window buzzed down and she heard the empty bottle hit the road, *doinnng*, like a plastic bowling pin. 'Damn you all to hell.'

'You're the one who's put us through hell,' one of the women snarled.

'What are you talking about?' Cate said, 'what do you mean?'

'We're here,' the driver said. The SUV came to a sudden halt. Cate felt a stab of anger at her own stupidity. When you were kidnapped, weren't you meant to count speed bumps, left and right turns, and how many times you stopped, instead of trying to save your dinner? Now she had no idea where she was. And after these thugs had finished with her, the police wouldn't even know where to look for her mangled, chopped-up corpse...

'Welcome to Wine Hangar,' said a chirpy voice as the still-hooded Cate was led through automatic doors into a brightly lit space. 'Hen's night, is it?'

'Something like that,' said one of the women. 'We've booked the day spa.'

'Ooh,' Cate said excitedly. 'Day spa! Is this a work treat?'

'Not for you,' said the woman holding her left arm, pulling her forward.

They walked for what felt like ages, footsteps echoing first off hard surfaces then muffled by carpet, until finally Cate heard a door shut behind her.

'Took you long enough,' said a new voice.

'She was eating a pizza,' said one of Cate's captors.

'Tie her up.'

The room smelled pleasantly of lavender and geranium. On the stereo, an acoustic guitar twanged gently over a pad of soothing synthesiser chords and the sound of a babbling brook. Cate felt herself pushed roughly down into a chair, and her wrists bound to its arms with rope. A Celtic flute cooed. Then the hood was yanked away, leaving Cate blinking in the sudden harsh light of a beautician's lamp positioned to shine directly into her eyes.

Facing her were ten women, ranging from Cate's age to their forties. Standing around the walls or perching on a massage table, some were dressed in business attire. Others were hipster chicks wearing rock T-shirts and vintage dresses, and yummy mummy types in jeans and activewear. But in the warm flicker of the tea-light candles that dotted the room, the flinty looks on their faces were almost identical.

'Who are you bitches?' Cate burst out.

'We're your worst nightmare,' said a petite blonde, who looked to be in her mid-twenties.

'You want me to join your netball team?'

'Insolent dog!' said a woman in fluoro pink leggings. 'You'll beg for mercy before we're through.'

The blonde held up a warning hand. 'Jess, you know that's not our way.' She turned back to Cate with an air of ceremony. 'We are... the League of Icarus.'

'Who?'

The blonde frowned in irritation. 'He made wings by sticking feathers in wax. But he flew too close to the sun, the wings melted. Game over, Icarus.'

'Huh?'

'It's a story about how you only get one chance to get that close to something that hot,' chimed in an older woman with a severe bob haircut.

'I still don't get it,' said Cate.

'The Hot Guy!' said the blonde. 'The whole point is, you only get one night with the Hot Guy!'

On the soundtrack, a whale moaned.

'Right,' Cate said. 'So, since I'm dating Adam now, does that make me the president of your little club?'

'No!' shouted the blonde. 'You've ruined our lives – you jumped the queue, then you jumped the Hot Guy!'

'And you kept on jumping him!' yelled a woman in a floral dress.

'He's not a trampoline!' added a tall woman with silky black hair.

'What's it to you?' A horrified expression crossed Cate's face. 'So you've all slept with Adam?'

'No!' the blonde said. 'We were in the *queue* to sleep with him before you ruined everything!'

'There was a queue?'

'There was a whole Facebook group,' said the blonde.

She turned and waved forward the floral-dress woman, who ran over to Cate and held up a mobile phone, its screen displaying a Facebook page.

'Twelve thousand members!' Cate said, horrified.

'Well, a lot of those are inactive,' the blonde said. 'Rubber-neckers. Or veterans. Once they've had their night with the Hot Guy, posted a few selfies they took while he was asleep, they tend to drop out. The most active members are in the queue.'

'Just how long was this queue?' Cate said.

'You're looking at it,' the blonde said, nodding with grim satisfaction at Cate's dismay. 'That's right. Everyone here was in line to sleep with the Hot Guy when you pushed to the front.'

'I didn't even know there *was* a queue. My boss just brought me to –'

'Ignorance of the law is no excuse!' Jess shouted. 'The punishment for disobedience is death!'

'Probably not death,' the blonde said. 'But you can obviously understand why we're not happy. It was all organised – once a week, whichever member was at the top of the queue would go meet the Hot Guy, they'd do the deed, then step aside. But when Maria got her turn, who did she find cock-blocking her but you?'

'Guess that's how you solve a problem like Maria,' Cate said.

From the back of the room someone let out an anguished sob.

'Sorry, Maria,' Cate said, 'but I had no idea about any of this. And even if I had, what do you expect me to do now – break up with Adam so one of you can take a turn?'

'Yes,' the blonde said sharply. 'Exactly.'

'Sorry to disappoint,' Cate said, 'but I'm not leaving Adam just because you guys had a list.'

The blonde was silent for a long moment, regarding Cate stonily. 'We hoped you'd be reasonable,' she said at last, 'but we did anticipate this. You're not the first woman who's found the Hot Guy hard to let go.'

She reached into her bag and pulled out… a severed hand.

'Holy shit!' said Cate, 'Is that thing real?'

'Uh, yes,' the blonde said.

'No it's not!' Cate said. Now she looked more closely, it was obviously a mannequin hand, its plastic fingernails painted sparkly silver. 'Nice nail polish.'

'Thanks,' said the blonde. 'But you get what we're implying. You'd better leave the Hot Guy.'

Cate laughed. 'Or what? You've got nothing. In fact, if you don't let me go right now, I *will* see Adam again, and I'll tell him all about you and your list. And then none of you will ever have a chance with him.'

'That's if we *do* let you leave here alive,' Jess said. 'Murdering you would solve all our problems.'

'Sure, you could murder me,' said Cate, 'but what happens then?'

'You'd be dead!' Jess shouted.

'You don't know Adam like I do,' Cate said. 'He's a man of honour. A tenacious avenger of injustice. If anyone *dares* to kill his girlfriend, he won't rest until he's found the no-good scum who did it. Why, he'll scour every inch of this town, from the corridors of power to the darkest alleyways! And what do you think he's going to do then?'

The League members leaned forward excitedly.

'Not sleep with you!'

The League members sighed and slumped back.

'He's not even gonna hate-fuck us?' came a voice from up the back.

'No,' Cate said. 'Kill me, and you kill your chances with the Hot Guy.'

'What if we just... cut off your legs?' Jess said hopefully.

Cate rolled her eyes.

'Well, you've won this round, Cate,' replied the blonde. 'But we ladies of the League are very patient. We're good at waiting. Face it: a girl like *you* won't be with the Hot Guy for long. And if he doesn't dump you right away, we'll be watching, ready to... help things along a little.'

Cate snorted. 'Yeah, *sure* you'll be watching. You look like the kind of chicks who like to watch. But I'm a doer. You'd better believe I'm all about doing things... in the bedroom... with Adam...'

There was a knock at the door. 'Party pies!' came a voice

from the other side. 'And there's a wine tasting, starting in five minutes.'

A ripple of excitement passed through the ranks of the League. 'Party pies!' someone whispered.

'Well Cate, since you're such a woman of action, I'm sure you can find your own way home.' The blonde strode from the room, followed by the rest of the League. Jess was last; she paused in the doorway to glare balefully at Cate, drawing a finger across her throat.

'Uh, guys?' Cate said. 'I'm still tied to this chair?'

'And what happened next?' Kirsty said.

'Well, I had to walk back out to the bottle shop with a chair tied to my arms. One of the shop assistants cut the rope.'

They were sitting in Cate's lounge room. A replacement pizza was sitting on the coffee table, along with the baseball bat Kirsty had brought in case the League of Icarus returned.

Vanessa shook her head. 'I can't believe they took you to a bottle shop.'

'Not just any bottle shop,' said Kirsty. 'The Wine Hangar is the fucking best! It's my home away from home!'

'I thought the Dead Dingo's Donger was your home away from home,' Vanessa said.

'That's my holiday home away from home. But the Wine Hangar – that's something else! It's a full-service, female-friendly pampering centre. Alcohol is only the start of what they offer. You can get massages, manicures, get your hair blow-dried…'

Cate was twisting a strand of her hair around her finger. 'And they have torture rooms, too.'

'They usually use those for hens' nights,' said Kirsty, pulling a slice of pizza from the box.

'They seem pretty focused on wine, judging from their logo,' Cate said. 'It was an aeroplane with two wine bottles for wings, and the pilot was another wine bottle.'

'Hmmm,' Vanessa said, taking another bite from the slice in her hand.

'And it was being waved into a wine bottle-shaped hangar by an air traffic controller whose paddles were also bottles of wine. Now I think about it, that's a pretty busy logo.'

'Well,' said Kirsty, 'it's not called the Vodka Hangar.'

'More's the pity,' Vanessa said through a mouthful of pizza. 'Why did they bother to put a pillowcase over your head if they were just going to take it off? In a place that had its own logo on the walls?'

'That's just what you do when you kidnap someone,' Kirsty said. They both looked at her. 'I'm not speaking from experience, obviously,' she muttered.

'I don't know, guys,' said Cate, picking at her thumbnail. 'Should I be worried about these freaks? They made a lot of threats... and some of them sounded pretty scary...' She shivered.

'Of course not,' said Vanessa, putting her arm around Cate. 'You played it perfectly. They know you could bring down their whole communist sex scheme at any moment.'

Cate didn't look up. 'But they could turn Adam against me somehow.'

'They won't, though,' Kirsty said. 'Trust us, we know what real fucking threats look like.'

But Cate couldn't let it rest. For the rest of the evening she kept looking around the room nervously, and that night, she slept badly, tossing and turning. She hoped that when she woke, the whole silly League of Icarus would have melted away, like waxen wings in the sun. But the next morning the nasty, clammy feeling in her gut hadn't gone away. When Kirsty and Vanessa had warned her about all the women who wanted Adam, Cate hadn't taken them too seriously. But now she'd seen her enemy face to face. Anyone could be a member of the League. And if the League was willing to kidnap her off the street, who knew what they'd do to get to Adam?

15

It was noon. They'd been at the stadium since 9 a.m., and Orson was still nowhere to be seen. Adam looked fretfully at the sky, heavy with clouds. Cate was trying hard to limit her glances at her watch to one every minute.

'I can't wait for this guy all day,' she said. 'I've got to do my job.'

Adam shook his head. 'He said he was going to get breakfast and he'd be right back.'

'That was three hours ago,' Cate said.

'He's done worse,' Adam said. 'Last week he tried to get us to wrap early because he had a Tinder date. He said we were losing the light. But it was an indoor shoot! With lights! And he nicked off without helping us pack them up.'

Cate sighed. 'Once he gets here, how long is it going to take? We've got a game on tonight, and Brunner's going to be checking the turf at least four more times today.'

'Not long,' Adam said. 'It's just pickups – it'll only take a few minutes.' He smiled at Cate. 'Thanks so much for letting me film here.'

'No problem,' Cate said distractedly, scanning the exits, the muscles in her neck straining as she forced herself not to check her watch. It didn't matter; the clock at the base of the stadium's giant electronic scoreboard told her barely a minute had passed. 'Remind me what you even need this guy for?'

'I don't know,' Adam said. 'Basically I can't bring myself to fire him.'

'It's great that you're loyal,' Cate said. 'But at some point today I'm going to have to get back to work.'

There was an incoherent shout from the other side of the stadium.

'There he is now,' Adam said, clearly relieved.

'About time,' said Cate, looking at her watch.

She looked up to see what looked like a grizzled, inebriated Druid shambling towards them, wearing some kind of black poncho made out of carpet offcuts, and carrying a pair of plastic shopping bags that clinked as he drew closer. The skin of his face had the texture of a long-forgotten apple; its deeply incised lines appeared caked in immovable grime.

'Okay ramblers, let's get ramblin'!' said the mysterious stranger.

'Where have you been, Orson?' Adam said.

'I had to –' he burped loudly, 'go shopping!'

'At Bong World?' said Cate, reading off the side of the shopping bags.

'Yeah, dude, they were having a sale – 50 per cent off skull bongs!' He reached into the bag and pulled out a skull with a pipe sticking out of the cranium. 'This one looks like Hitler.'

'Looks more like my career if we don't get this movie going.'

'Guys, chill, it's just a few shots,' said Orson.

'I think someone may have already had a few shots,' Cate said.

Something seemed to snap in Adam, who set off wordlessly towards the middle of the arena.

'Where's he going?' Cate said to Orson.

'Oh... man... and this bong looks like Stalin!' He held the two skulls up and made them kiss. 'Look, it's world peace!'

'I said, where's he...' Cate rolled her eyes. 'Never mind.'

After a while, she noticed Orson had turned his attention from his new purchases and was staring at her intently. 'So, you're the girl,' he said.

'Last time I checked,' Cate replied. 'What's *your* role in all this?'

Orson leaned in confidentially. 'Adam's going to be in my next film. It's gonna be huge, man.'

'Is it about Hitler?' Cate said. 'Or bongs?'

'Better,' Orson said. 'It's a Hemingway adaptation.'

'Ernest Hemingway?' she said, surprised. 'Is he back, in bong form?'

'Of course not,' said Orson. 'This is a serious adaptation of one of the master's greatest works.'

'Is it *A Farewell to Arms? Snows of Kilimanjaro?*'

'No,' Orson said. 'Better than all those.'

'Really?'

He held up his hands and dramatically spread them wide, as if imagining his words up in lights on a cinema marquee. 'I'm going to adapt *For Sale: Baby Shoes, Never Worn.*'

'Is it called *Never Worn?*'

'Oh, that's a better title. I was going to call it *Baby Shoes.*'

'Six words doesn't seem like much to base an entire movie on,' Cate said.

'Well, I've had to expand on it a bit. Adam is going to play Bruno "Baby" Shoes, a mob enforcer whose baby gets killed in the crossfire.'

'Why is he called Baby when he *has* a baby?'

Orson ignored this inconvenient question. 'Yeah, he has to go on the run, but his running shoes have never been worn. And that's pretty bad when you're on the run from the Yakuza.'

'I thought it was the mob.'

'It's the mob and the Yakuza. And al-Qaeda.'

'Are they all babies?'

'There's a whole bunch of babies. Maybe it could be like *Bugsy Malone* but with babies.'

It was at this point that Cate realised he was making it up as he went along. 'Have you even asked Adam if he wants to star in your movie?'

Orson looked offended. 'Why wouldn't he? I've already had offers for the role from some big names.'

'Would I have heard of any of these names?'

'No, they're up-and-comers.'

'Have they even been born yet?'

'Fuck off!'

He stormed away, to where Adam was standing in the centre of the arena. Cate could see them having an animated conversation. Well, Orson was certainly animated, waving his arms around wildly. She could hear the faint clinking of the bongs in the bags he was carrying. Eventually, Adam walked back over.

'Maybe you should go back to your office for a while,' he told Cate.

'Is it Orson's nap time?' she said. 'Is he overtired?'

'That baby movie is going to be pretty autobiographical,' Adam said with a smile.

Cate smirked. 'Okay, sure. I'll be back in an hour.' She walked across the stadium to where her jacket was draped over the boundary fence. 'See you soon!'

Adam waved, then watched as she shrugged her jacket on. She pushed one arm into a sleeve, then, unable to find the second armhole, twitched around as she fumbled for it. Eventually she thrust her arm into the sleeve, nearly overbalancing from the follow-through.

Adam laughed.

As she headed towards the exit, she turned to check if her jacket label was sticking out. Simply reaching behind her neck didn't seem to have occurred to her. She twisted her head first one way, then the other, trying to see it from the corner of her eye, then began to turn her entire torso. As Adam watched, astonished, Cate's twisting sent her stumbling into a sprinkler nozzle, which she promptly fell over.

From behind him, Adam heard a shout: 'And *this* bong looks like my grade three teacher!'

He glanced away, then back to Cate. She was sprawled on the ground, her gaze darting around to check if anyone had witnessed her lapse in dignity.

Something dawned on Adam. Cate looked *relieved* that he didn't seem to have noticed. It only served to remind him of the fact that she was never usually this self-conscious. Indeed, Cate's unselfconsciousness – her talent for living in the moment – was one of the things he liked most about her. Adam realised she was the opposite of him that way. He expected to be watched all the time.

Maybe he was going about this film all wrong. Or, more precisely, perhaps there were other, better ways to express what he wanted to say. He'd envisioned *Metadata* as a story about oppressive surveillance, but what if there was a better angle? Wouldn't it be much worse for his character to be an exhibitionist who never has an audience? Someone who thought they were being oppressed, but really nobody gave a shit?

He became excited as he realised how his film could turn the usual idea of surveillance on its head. He'd been so pompous before! It was embarrassing how seriously he'd been taking this film. Maybe it wasn't even a thriller. It was a comedy.

'Cate!' he shouted.

She walked over, still looking flustered. 'Hey, is the tag sticking out of my jacket?'

He reached behind her neck and tucked the label away.

'Thanks.' She smiled sweetly. 'What did you want to say?'

'I've had a breakthrough,' Adam said. 'About the film, I mean. It's actually about how the expectation of surveillance changes how we act. We're not hiding from being watched. We've *chosen* to become exhibitionists.'

'And that's... good?'

'No! It's terrible. We've forgotten how to forge real connections with people. Our emotions become performed, rather than lived. What we do,' he waved his hands around helplessly, 'it isn't even interesting.'

He was expecting Cate to share his enthusiasm, but instead, she frowned.

'Is that what's going on here? Are you saying our relationship is just a performance?'

'What? No! It's the complete opposite. I love that you're always so... natural. I never get the feeling you're trying to put on an act just to impress me. We *do* have a real connection. You're always right here.' He tapped a finger against his broad chest.

She looked sad. 'So I don't impress you much?'

'Of course you do,' he said. 'You're the most impressive person I know.'

'It's not just an act?'

'If I were just putting on an act, I'd wait for an audience to do... *this.*'

He scooped her into his arms and kissed her on the mouth. Behind them came a cough.

'Mr Brunner!' squeaked Cate. 'Uh, I mean,' she said, struggling to sound calm, her voice dropping at least an octave, 'John.' She disentangled herself and straightened her jacket.

Brunner's gaze was discreetly fixed on a patch of grass a metre or so to their left. He shook his head in immense disappointment. 'This is a disgrace,' he said.

'John, I'm so –'

'A dead patch. On my turf.' His eyes narrowed. 'Someone else is gonna die tonight.'

'That doesn't sound good,' said Adam.

'And you are...?' Brunner said.

'This is Adam.'

Adam looked at Cate. She looked back at him, wild-eyed. He could practically see the gears turning. He clearly had to explain why they'd been kissing, but he didn't know what looked worse: Cate kissing a random cameraman, or her bringing her boyfriend to work.

'I hope you don't, uh, mind,' Adam said. 'We've just been filming –'

'Ah,' Brunner said, clearly already bored. 'The promotional video thing. Carry on.'

'Promotional video?' Adam mouthed to Cate as Brunner strode away.

'I had to tell him something. Having you filming a puff clip to win the bank over seemed more plausible than a sex tape.'

'Do you want to film a sex tape?' he said with a smile.

She shook her head firmly, glancing at Orson, who was trying to sniff his own armpit. 'No!' Then she looked at Adam. 'Well, maybe later.'

'But doesn't this mean that now I actually have to film a promotional video?'

'Uh... yeah, I guess you do.'

'Any ideas?'

'Yeah – don't film the toilets. Or the stand that collapsed. We're still waiting for the funds to renovate them properly. Maybe don't film anything to your left. Or your right.'

'That basically leaves the turf.'

'Yeah, great. Film that!'

'Don't worry,' Adam said, 'I think I've got this covered.'

She raised a lascivious eyebrow.

'Oh, come on,' he said, 'what's sexy about being covered?'

'Nothing,' she said. 'That's the problem.'

'I think the real problem is that you just committed me to making a promo video about something I know nothing about.'

'Yeah, I guess I can see how you'd think that.' She gave him a quick peck on the cheek. 'But all you have to do is film a bunch of interesting stuff this afternoon and – can you stay tonight? There's a game on, that'll be full of things that will make this place look like less of a death trap.'

'Sure,' he said, 'I can always use some more crowd shots for my film too.'

'You're the best,' she said. 'And not just in bed.'

'Lunch first?' he said.

'It's on me,' she said. 'And no, don't say it.'

'I wouldn't dare.' They walked off towards the exit.

'And *this* bong,' Orson said, taking yet another skull-shaped smoking device from the plastic bag, lifting it high to display it to the empty stadium, 'looks like Hamlet.'

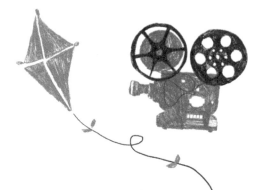

16

With a series of heavy thuds, the lights snapped on one by one around the stadium, illuminating row after row of empty seats, their geometric precision interrupted by the occasional sleeping drunk or cluster of half-sloshed women.

'Bring on the stuuuuuuuds!' someone yelled forlornly.

'I'm not sure I should be filming this,' Adam said, pointing his camera up at the rows of empty seats. 'It's kind of depressing.'

'What do you mean?' Cate said, puzzled. 'This is our best turnout in weeks.'

'Seriously?'

'Most of them are still in at the bar. It's buy one, get seven free for ladies.'

'Isn't that a bit... irresponsible?'

'Well, once we water them down, eight of our drinks work out to one regular drink.'

'Still...'

'Look,' she said, putting a hand on his pleasantly firm bicep. 'Mmmm...' she sighed, distracted.

A minute passed in silence.

'Yes?' said Adam.

'Sorry.' Cate shook herself alert. 'This is the off-season, so nobody is coming in. But all our running costs don't magically vanish just because all the –' she shuddered, '*sports fans* are off at the track or the tennis or the... argy-bargy finals or whatever. So we have to come up with ways to get people in the gate, and if it takes cheap booze for the ladies then I'm ready to get my sisters all liquored up.'

'But surely if you put on sport, guys will come?'

'Nobody likes sports!' she snapped.

'So,' Adam said carefully, sensing he was on thin ice, 'what kind of game is on tonight? I mean, if things are that grim, maybe you don't want me filming it...'

'No, it'll be fine,' she said. 'It's just the land swimming finals.'

'Land swimming?' said Adam, perplexed. 'Isn't that just... running?'

'Running in Speedos,' Cate said firmly. 'It's quite eye-catching in the groin area. Plus, the blokes have to be bent over when they run, so it kinda looks like they're swimming.'

'Do they have to flail their arms around too, like they're doing strokes?'

'Only in the heats.'

'Why do I think someone's just made this up as an excuse to get a bunch of topless guys running around?'

'You are very perceptive.'

'So is this going to be part of your piece to camera?'

'Oh, right,' Cate said, fishing out a sheet of paper from her jacket pocket. 'I've spent the whole afternoon on this, so make sure I'm in focus.'

'Sure.' He swung his camera around on the tripod to face her. 'But maybe reading off a piece of paper isn't the best look?'

'I can't memorise all this,' she said, a touch of panic in her voice. 'It's three thousand words! I've got six paragraphs on the new plumbing system!'

'Maybe you could just... be yourself?'

'Arrgh!'

'It's just going to be a bit at the end telling people what a great stadium it is.'

'And six paragraphs about the new ball-flush mechanisms in the toilets is how I will do that.'

'Maybe – and it's just an idea – you could record that as a voice over? That way you can read off the paper without people seeing you, and the bit with you on-camera will seem more natural.'

'But… I tried to be me at my last presentation, and it almost got me fired! What if I make a dumb joke? Lots of dumb jokes? Or start grabbing your butt? What if I grab all the butts?'

'That seems unlikely.'

'Does it?'

'Okay, it might happen. But I'm going to be here, and the moment you start getting shaky we can stop filming and give you a breather.'

'All right, let's go for it,' she said.

'Full script?'

'Three thousand words ain't gonna read themselves.'

Three minutes in, even Adam was bored shitless by Cate's speech, and he'd sat through all nine hours of *Turnips: A Season of Dirt*. At least that had been a rich, earthy drama – though a little undercooked for his liking.

'And with these newly installed, synchronised ball-flush mechanisms,' Cate was saying, 'we've been able to cut our water use by up to 7 per cent on non-game weekdays. Which, I think you'll find, puts us firmly on the list of the most environmentally friendly stadiums in the forty to sixty thousand capacity for the state.' She paused theatrically. 'Try beating those stats, Derek van der Brufen Memorial Hockey Rink and Skate Park!'

He zoned back out. It was hard to reconcile the robot talking into the camera with the exuberant woman he'd begun to fall for. Maybe she was more like a zombie. A robot zombie? That would be closer to a Terminator. It'd be cool to work on a *Terminator* movie, he thought, though the last few instalments of the franchise had drifted away from what made the original (and to a lesser extent, the first sequel) such classics. They needed to play up the love story more, the idea of a guy who loved someone so much he'd travel across –

'Adam?'

'Huh?'

'How was that?'

'Oh... yeah, great. Are you done?'

'Well, I read out everything I wrote down, so... should we do another take?'

'*No!*'

Cate took a step back.

'I mean,' Adam said, this time more gently, 'no, that'll be fine. But we should really get a shorter take where you say all that in your own voice.'

He saw her frown. 'Just a shorter version,' he added encouragingly. 'A summary. For editing purposes.'

'Oh, okay. I can manage that.'

'I know you can. All you have to do is look into the camera, smile, and just tell people why the stadium is such a great place. Imagine you're telling me what you like about it.'

'There are so many quiet corners where we can bone?'

'Well, maybe not that. But something like, "It's a great place to make new friends – and to get to know old ones better"?'

'Sounds good.' She squared her shoulders, looked down the barrel of the camera, smiled that smile only Adam saw, and said, 'I...'

17

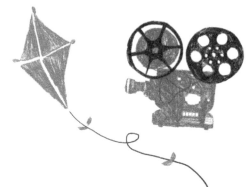

Meanwhile, Vanessa and Kirsty were sitting in a corporate box on the other side of the stadium, taking full advantage of the cheap drinks.

'Didn't Cate say these drinks were meant to be watered down?' Vanessa said.

'They taste watered down to me,' Kirsty said, 'watered down *with more booze!*'

They high-fived each other. Behind them, the waiter shook his head sadly and quietly let himself out.

'Where's Cate?' Kirsty said. 'I mean, what kind of girls' night out is this?'

Vanessa snorted. 'She doesn't care about her friends now that she's got a *maaaaan.*'

'You've got a man,' said Kirsty. 'All I've got are my romance novels, and they're mostly about cats.'

'He's not my *man.* Scozza's just my root. I hit it and quit it.'

'Isn't he a drummer? Surely *he's* the one hitting it – hitting the skins, if you know what I mean.'

Vanessa sighed dreamily. 'He is a fan of the butt bongos.'

'I'm surprised he has the energy,' Kirsty said. 'He looks kind of scrawny.'

'Thin is in,' Vanessa said defensively.

'He should be in,' Kirsty nodded '– in *rehab.*'

'He only uses recreationally.'

'What does he do professionally? Sleep?'

'You can't talk, Kirsty! Your last boyfriend was a sex pest.'

'I dropped those charges.'

They stared out towards the field, sipping their wine in silence.

Kirsty shook her head. 'It's all changed.'

'She should never have stayed with the Hot Guy,' said Vanessa. 'He's too hot.'

'It's not right,' Kirsty agreed. 'He's gonna break her fucking heart. It's only a matter of time.'

Vanessa nodded. 'If only she had some really good friends. Friends who were willing to act in her best interests.'

'Yeah, but who?' Kirsty said.

Vanessa swirled her drink ominously.

'Ahhhhh,' said Kirsty.

'That was great,' said Adam.

'Really?' Cate said. 'Did I even say any of the good stuff?'

'You said everything you needed to. When we go through it in editing we're going to have more gold than we know what to do with.'

'I'm worried I didn't say enough about the tile regrouting in the G-level underpass.'

'Uh, yeah,' Adam said. In fact, she'd gone on about the tile regrouting so much he'd turned the camera off after she'd said 'regrouting' three times in the one sentence. 'Anyway, we'd better get moving – this place is starting to fill up.'

'Oh shit,' Cate said, 'I was supposed to meet up with Kirsty and Vanessa.'

'Didn't you say you'd stashed them in a corporate box? They'll be fine.'

'If by "fine" you mean "completely wasted", then sure.'

'Okay,' Adam says, 'I can finish up here. You go meet your

friends, and I'll –' The stadium sound system blared into life, playing a jaunty yet copyright-free slice of upbeat dance-pop that signalled this was a venue where people came to party. Adam waved her off. She gave him a thumbs-up and headed towards the corporate boxes.

Like a pair of evil queens surveying their ruined domain, Kirsty and Vanessa looked out over the rapidly filling stadium.

'Man,' Vanessa said, 'those chicks are drunk.'

Behind them the waiter silently exchanged their empty wine bottle for a full one.

'Yeah,' Kirsty said, 'if they got ahold of the Hot Guy they'd tear him apart.'

They looked at each other, then out at the stadium. Directly across from them, a five-storey high Jumbotron screen was showing random members of the crowd necking cheap booze from plastic cups.

'Are you thinking what I'm thinking?' Vanessa said.

'That we should get some plastic cups for this fine wine?'

'Well yes, obviously. But also, that we should get them to put the Hot Guy up on the big screen.'

'But this crowd would go crazy if they... ahhhhhh.' Kirsty nodded happily. 'Didn't we pass the control room on the way up here?'

'No,' Vanessa said, 'we passed the announcer's booth. Which is where I'm going now, to organise a suitable soundtrack for the Hot Guy's big-screen debut.'

'Soundtrack?'

'Look at those drunk skanks,' slurred Vanessa. 'If we don't do something to get their attention, they're not even going to know this place has a Jumbotron. And while I'm doing that, you go find the control room for the big screen and get the cameraman to zoom in on the Hot Guy.'

They laughed in unison, clinking their wine glasses.

18

Cate was fighting her way through an increasingly rowdy crowd. 'Watch it!' a bleary-eyed woman shouted, stumbling backwards. Cate surveyed the scene. A few spectators had made some effort to wear sporty gear, but as land swimming was a relatively new sport and the only official uniform was extremely skimpy Speedos, they'd plumped for the kind of tracksuit that hid stains. Others were dressed as if for a nightclub, in tight jeans, sparkly tops, slinky mini-dresses and high heels.

Someone threw up; the surrounding women cheered. A few plastic cups went flying, and Cate felt a light spray of watery gin and tonic on her face.

She pushed past a homemade banner that read I HEART BREASTSTROKE and looked up. From here she could see into the corporate boxes: the one she'd left Vanessa and Kirsty in was empty. Bugger. She could keep searching, but in this crowd the chance of actually locating them was close to none. She could wait in the box by herself, but who knew when they'd find their way back? Or she could rejoin Adam and hang out with him.

'I'll take door number three,' she said to herself, and turned to head back the way she'd come.

Kirsty burst into the cramped room where the Jumbotron camera was set up.

'Who are you?' the startled cameraman said. He was fat and balding – his gut was the main reason why the room was cramped – and his headphones had half-slipped off his sweaty head.

'That doesn't matter right now,' Kirsty slurred, steadying herself against the doorframe. 'Why does it smell so weird in here?'

'Um… we're by the garbage chute?' he offered, his gaze flicking nervously to the bin at his feet filled with crumpled tissues.

'People have sex in the garbage chute?'

'Sure,' he said. 'Um, get out?'

'No! I've got a request.'

'We don't take requests.'

'Then it's an order. I want you to –' Kirsty burped. 'Want you to find Cate's boyfriend!'

'Who's Cate? And why should I know her boyfriend?'

'He's the only guy in the crowd – find him!' she demanded.

Cowed, the cameraman frantically panned across the crowd. Kirsty looked out at the Jumbotron. The big screen filled with an image of a really ugly man sprawled in his seat, knees spread lavishly. Between bites of a meat pie, several oily gobbets of which reposed on the front of his shirt, he was picking his nose and scratching his balls.

'That's not him!' Kirsty said. 'Wait…' She leaned forward. 'No, it's not him.'

'But it's a guy!'

Kirsty sighed. 'Just zoom in on the hottest guy you can find.'

Above her she heard the stadium speakers begin to broadcast a new song; Vanessa's work in the announcer's booth was clearly going to plan. Outside, all heads turned towards the Jumbotron. *Aw yeah*, Kirsty thought, *this is going to be good.*

Vanessa flipped through the stacks of old eight-track cartridges that made up the stadium's sound library. 'Don't you have anything more recent than the '80s?'

'That's all we got,' the stadium announcer said.

He was a skinny guy barely out of his teens, with sad, liquid eyes and the kind of moustache that looked like he'd forgotten to dust off his top lip in the morning. It was very strange to hear the sonorous voice that ushered burly men onto the field issuing from this scrawny throat.

Vanessa scowled. 'Make that the 1880s.'

'Yeah, I got it the first time,' he said. 'Look, this system pre-dates the stadium itself. It was here when this used to be an air force base.'

'A Nazi air force base?' retorted Vanessa, having noticed the swastika stamped on the side of the case.

'I think it was a war trophy. The Nazis built things to last.'

'Wasn't the Third Reich still under warranty when it fell apart?'

'Well, maybe not systems of government. But their PA systems were great.'

'I guess I should be grateful this place even has a PA system. Can you even still get parts for...' she peered more closely at the speaker cables, 'Düfdüf speakers?'

The announcer shrugged. 'You can get anything on the deep web.'

Vanessa stared down at the weird little dude. 'So, do you have any songs with "hot" in the lyrics?'

Over the noise of the crowd, the PA was now blaring some song Adam didn't recognise. Whatever was going on in the stands, he thought, was driving these women nuts. He looked up, and his own bewildered face stared back at him from the Jumbotron.

Cate must be in the control booth, he thought. *Cute.* He smiled and waved and then turned away, bending over his half-packed camera gear.

For some reason Cate wasn't cutting away from him. The Jumbotron camera lingered on Adam as he gave up trying to pack away his gear and gazed up into the crowd.

The spectators roared, leaping out of their seats. Thousands of women were now chanting and stamping their feet. The song seemed to be building to a peak, bringing the crowd along with it. They weren't looking up at the screen any more, he noticed casually. Now they were staring directly at him.

Slowly, he began to back away. The crowd surged forward. The ones in the front rows were clambering over the railing, their gaze fixed upon him. The women behind were shoving each other in their stumbling rush to get closer to him. They were almost upon him when he finally started to run.

In the stands Cate noticed that, unusually, the stadium PA had switched from its regular background soundtrack of cheesy instrumentals to a song with actual lyrics. But why were they playing a kids' jingle? She listened harder. 'Hot cross buns?' she said to herself. 'It's nowhere near Easter.'

Nonetheless, it seemed the crowd was hungry. The stand began to tremble beneath Cate's feet as women around her clapped and stamped, turning the nursery rhyme into a war chant.

She tried to look at the Jumbotron, but a banner reading I'M WET FOR LAND SWIMMING was blocking her view. She continued to struggle towards the playing field, and then all at once the crowd was moving with her, surging down towards ground level. She looked for Adam, but she couldn't see him; the Jumbotron was back in view, but all it was showing now was an indistinct blur, as if the camera was struggling to track a moving object.

Borne along by the mob, Cate was so relieved she was no longer fighting against them that she didn't stop to think where they were going. By the time she reached the playing field, the scrum of spectators had moved on, leaving her behind like jetsam. They stampeded across the pitch and vanished into the tunnel that led under the stadium on the opposite side.

Adam's gear was sitting at the same spot where they'd been filming. He must have seen her coming; he wouldn't have left it unattended without a very good reason. Perhaps there'd been some kind of competition going on over at the other side of the arena, and Adam had joined the crowd rushing for a prize. She couldn't imagine what they could possibly be giving away that would make anyone get out of their seats, let alone run across the stadium. Free baked goods, perhaps? That would explain the bun song. Cate made a mental note to ask around on Monday.

She noticed the stadium lights were making the turf glow with a lush texture it rarely showed during the day. While she was here, she might as well get a few shots of it to edit into the corporate video. That'd make Brunner happy.

'This grass could sell the place better than I can,' Cate said, lifting the camera to her shoulder and pointing it at the ground.

Vanessa was cursing the stadium's ancient tape player. 'There's something wrong with this Nazi shit. The sound keeps dropping in and out.'

'Hot... buns!' the stadium speakers were now blaring. 'Hot... buns! Hot... hot...'

The sound kid rolled his eyes. 'I told you, that cart's from, like, 1967,' he said. 'The tape's probably all scrunched up inside. I'm surprised it's playing at all.'

'Put on something else, then!'

'If you don't want to go back to the pre-game playlist, there's not much else. I've got the team songs?'

'That'll do!' Vanessa said. 'Anything!'

The announcer shoved a new cartridge in.

'Where did he go?' shouted Kirsty, hitting the camera operator across the back of the head. Grimacing, she wiped her hand on the back of his T-shirt. She inspected her hand again, then squatted down to wipe it on the carpet.

'I followed him across the field, then he vanished into the tunnels,' the camera guy whined.

'What's under there?'

'I dunno,' he said. 'They never let me out of here. The change rooms, some toilets... half of it's still being repaired after the collapse.'

'Are there any cameras down there?'

'In the toilets?' he scoffed. 'No, of course not.'

She pointed to a bank of monitors. 'What about those screens labelled "toilets"?'

'That means something else,' he stammered. 'Not toilets.'

She turned on one of the monitors. It showed the inside of a public toilet.

'That's a... special training room.'

'Toilet training?'

Kirsty turned on another monitor. This one showed Adam standing in the middle of a men's bathroom, looking around frantically.

'There he is!' She tapped the tiny screen with a finger. 'Put this on the Jumbotron. *Now!*'

A bizarre combination of mariachi brass, hillbilly banjo and military drums erupted into the stadium, accompanying an all-male choir who bellowed jolly clichés about victory and sportsmanship. The crowd began to shriek in delight.

The land swimmers must be entering the arena at last, Cate thought as she panned Adam's camera methodically over a patch of grass in extreme close-up. About time, too.

Squinting through the viewfinder, she hadn't noticed what was really driving the crowd wild. Just as the team song had begun playing, a new video feed had come on the Jumbotron. It was in grainy, low-resolution black-and-white, but the man cowering in the bathroom was undeniably hot... and unmistakably Adam.

Having lost sight of their quarry, the women who'd chased Adam into the tunnel had given up and returned to their seats to rest and refuel. Now that he was again within reach, they dropped their drinks and sprinted for the men's toilets.

They wove around the security staff who were gamely trying to block their passage; the team song was gradually speeding up, growing increasingly garbled as it soundtracked this demented steeplechase. The music was playing at almost double speed, the blokey choristers now sounding like chipmunks underwater. One security guard made a determined last stand in the tunnel entrance, feet planted and arms spread wide like a soccer goalkeeper. As he was bowled aside by the mob, the remaining spectators let out an almighty roar.

'Stupid tape player!' Vanessa shouted up in the booth, dealing it a mighty blow with her fist.

'Hey!' the announcer kid said mildly. 'Don't hate the player, hate the game.'

Seriously shaken, Adam had taken refuge in a toilet cubicle. What the fuck was happening? He could still hear the roar of the crowd outside. At least he was safe here, cocooned in the comforting ammonia stench of his fellow men. Perhaps the land swimming had begun, and distracted them.

An ominous clip-clopping sound began to echo through the tunnel outside. It sounded for all the world like a pantomime horse – like two hollow coconut shells being clapped together. But as the sound multiplied and amplified, a cold dread flushed through Adam's chest. This, he realised now, was the sound of many women running in high heels, their footsteps echoing off the freshly regrouted tiles Cate had been so careful to describe.

He stood on the toilet and peered over the cubicle partition. There was no way to lock the door to the bathroom, nothing to barricade it with, and no other exits. He'd cleverly chosen a dead end.

As the women's shrieks and giggles grew louder, Adam slumped despairingly against the toilet cistern. He was surprised when it lurched to one side. Now he could see that the wall behind the toilets wasn't even a proper wall, but a sheet of plasterboard installed in a hurry – there were still builder's pencil marks showing where to cut the holes for the pipes.

Adam gripped the cistern in both hands and began to shake it violently.

'There he is! In that cubicle!' came a booze-thickened voice.
'Oh my god! Oh my god!'
'So fucking hot!'

More women began shouting. Adam couldn't tell how many; a cacophony of voices reverberated through the bathroom. Their urgency was almost palpable: a thick, choking fug of desire. Fingers were curling over and under the cubicle door – a thousand searching tentacles tipped in cherry-red, candy-pink, glossy black and glitter.

He redoubled his efforts. There was now a sizeable tear in the plasterboard around the pipe. Adam kicked at it, uncovering a damp crawlspace. The toilet pipes led into darkness.

He gave the cistern one final wrench, and it came apart in his hands. A jet of water from the broken pipe gushed into Adam's face. Wiping his eyes, he summoned his courage and scrambled into the hole.

Cate was still filming the grass, mesmerised by the play of light and dark across its velvety surface. She was finally beginning to understand why Brunner was so devoted to it.

An odd thumping sound came from behind her, seemingly from beneath the turf. She smirked, recalling the office legends of under-performing groundskeepers summarily interred beneath the centre square, nourishing the turf in death as they had failed to do in life. Maybe the zombie uprising would begin at Zombo (formerly Sambo) Stadium.

But then she heard a scraping sound of metal on metal, and a rusty drainage grating popped open. From it, like a bedraggled jack-in-the-box, climbed Adam.

'Oh, there you are,' Cate said. 'You left your camera behind, so I've been filming some... thingamawhatsits... oh yeah – pickup shots.'

'You weren't in the control booth?'

Cate looked puzzled. 'No, I've been down here the whole

time.' Something occurred to her. 'Why are you all wet? Not that I'm complaining…'

'Too hard to explain.' He reached for Cate and drew her close. 'I've just had the most bizarre and traumatic experience.'

She smiled, tenderly stroking the side of his face. 'Well, you're here now.'

'Thank god,' Adam said, and kissed her.

All the air was seemingly sucked from the stadium as the crowd gasped as one. Then the stands burst into electrifying applause, punctuated by lewd hoots. The Jumbotron was broadcasting Adam and Cate's kiss in a heart-shaped frame, spangled with graphics of stars and roses.

In the control booth, Kirsty raged, 'Who put that fucking love heart up there?'

The camera operator wiped away a tear. 'We keep those effects on file in case any sports fan decides to propose,' he said.

Grimly, Kirsty offered him the tissue box to mop his porcine face.

'They look so happy together,' he snuffled. 'I wish I could find someone to be happy with.' He cast a moist, meaningful look at Kirsty.

She tossed her head. 'Don't even fucking think about it.'

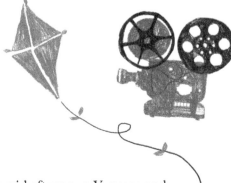

19

The next day was a Saturday, so by mid-afternoon Vanessa and Kirsty were down at the oval chilling out until it was late enough to start drinking. Vanessa had left her drone at home, so she was sitting on the grass while Kirsty flew her orange bat-winged kite. She was meant to be watching out for Cate, but instead she was daydreaming about Scozza. Would she still like him if he had a job that didn't require him to steal money out of her purse? Maybe she could find a guy who needed her in more of an *emotional* way...

And then Cate was tapping her on the shoulder. She didn't look happy.

'I thought you two would be trying to hide,' she said, doing a squinty thing with her eyes that only she thought made her look steely and determined.

'Nup,' said Kirsty, though the way her kite twitched in the air suggested that her hands were shaking from more than a lack of alcohol. 'Why would we be?'

'Because now I know,' Cate said. 'I found out everything.'

'Everything?' Vanessa said, her voice cracking. She looked down at the phone in her hand: seven unanswered texts from the announcer guy. Why couldn't he see it was a one-time thing? Anyone would have been swept away with all those love hearts flashing on the big screen.

'I know you two were trying to break me and Adam up! What were you thinking? Did you losers even stop to think about how this was going to make me look at work?'

'Losers seems a bit harsh,' Kirsty said. 'I mean, fuck, our plan didn't work, but –'

'No buts!'

'That's not what the ladies at the stadium were saying,' Kirsty said, unhelpfully.

'Shut up! I managed to smooth this debacle over, thanks largely to the record-breaking alcohol sales, but I can't believe you two were trying to destroy my relationship! Aren't you meant to be my friends?'

'We are your friends. That's why we did it,' Vanessa said. 'We're not going to apologise for trying to help you.'

Kirsty nodded, not looking around from her kite. 'You needed to see the truth: Adam is a Hot Guy, and only chaos can come of it.'

'It's true,' Vanessa said. 'It wasn't just the alcohol that drove them into a frenzy. There must be dozens of women out there waiting to get a load of the Hot Guy.'

'What? The League?' said Cate. 'Do you think –'

'More like a load *from* the Hot Guy.'

'Kirsty, *please*,' said Vanessa. 'I'm serious.'

Now she'd said it out loud, Cate couldn't shake the thought. What if it really *was* the League? No, it couldn't be – this farce had Kirsty's and Vanessa's names all over it. But what if Kirsty and Vanessa were *part* of the League? They were there on the night she'd met Adam, and they already knew he was the Hot Guy. And they'd been pretty clear that they wanted her to break up with him. All the pieces fitted together. But what kind of friends would side with a bunch of evil kidnappers? It was one thing if they were just drunkenly screwing around; it was something completely different if they were part of an organisation that was cold-bloodedly trying to ruin her happiness...

'Cate,' Vanessa said loudly, bringing her back to the conversation, 'what are you going to do if a lust-crazed mob chases after him every single time you take him to work?'

'I'll just...' Cate waved a hand around helplessly. 'I'll never take him to work, ever. Hey, look – this sounds silly, but I've gotta ask. Are you guys part of the –'

'D'you reckon Adam would even *want* to come back to the stadium?' Kirsty said, ignoring her.

'He has a kinda sporty bod,' Vanessa said thoughtfully.

'Who cares?' Cate said. 'He hates sport. Listen, I really need you to tell me if –'

'Everyone hates sport,' Kirsty said. 'But you do still work at a sports stadium.'

'You don't understand,' Cate said sadly. Were they even listening? 'That footage of them chasing him around the stadium went viral. It was on the news! Well, the late news that's just cute dogs and people being beheaded. But still.'

'You should be thanking us,' said Vanessa. 'This is the best publicity your stadium's had in years. Aren't you meant to be the publicist?'

'I'm publicising a stadium, not some kind of... sex brothel!'

'Well, when you met him he was pretty much just...' Kirsty stopped herself just in time.

Cate glared at her. 'It was never like that. Money never changed hands.'

'I hope *you* did; RSI is a real problem,' Vanessa said.

'It sure is,' said Kirsty, flexing her wrist. The kite whiplashed out of the sky to crash a few metres away.

They both looked at her. 'Is there something we're missing here?' Cate said.

'Just been doing a lot of... reading.'

'Whoa,' said Vanessa. 'You've got to lay off the cat porn.'

Kirsty tossed her head. 'It's not cat porn. It's *The Fur Chronicles*.'

They both stared at her silently.

'Shut up! You're so mean to me. It's just as good as *Consumption* – only it's for mature adults.'

'Lots of boning doesn't make something adult,' said Vanessa.

'I don't know about that,' said Cate.

'Nothing's better than *Consumption*,' said Vanessa. 'It's all-consuming.'

'You know what's all-consuming? My concern about the League,' Cate said. 'They're a real threat, not some crappy book about old-timey diseases and stuff.'

'Oh, there's *so* much more to it,' Vanessa said, warming to her subject. 'The disease is a metaphor for love. A love beyond love. It's a warning about how powerful physical desire can be.'

'Yeah, like the League's desire to steal my boyfriend,' said Cate. 'Can we talk about that, not some creepy anti-sex book written by a nutcase?'

'Chastity Horniblow isn't a nutcase! She understands the dichotomy between base, physical emotions and the higher, purer spiritual love.'

'What,' Cate said, 'you're saying that because we have a lot of sex, my relationship with Adam is meaningless? It's not. I care about him. That's what you've never understood. That's what those bitches in the League don't get. Even I didn't understand at first. That love is… you know…'

'But that's what the books are about,' Vanessa said excitedly. 'I'm not telling it right.'

'Here we go,' Kirsty said, taking out her hip flask.

'Back in the nineteenth century,' Vanessa said, 'Lucinda is a young, comely maiden, from a family of means. Then, a mysterious disease wipes out everyone she holds dear in a fevered night of carnal delight.'

'Sounds good to me,' said Cate, 'so they all die in some kind of giant orgy.'

'It was awful,' Vanessa said.

Behind her, Kirsty gave Cate the thumbs-up.

'Only Lucinda has the moral strength to resist those lethal, lascivious urges. Cut to a hundred years later –'

'Is it a real hundred years,' Cate interjected, 'or does it just feel like it without bonin'?'

'A real hundred years, and she hasn't aged a day. Her moral purity fights the disease to a standstill, and now she'll never die... unless she gives in to those unholy urges that torment her every day.'

'Do they describe these urges in detail?'

'No, but you get the idea. Anyway, after a hundred years she's living in the servants' shack – she's never gone back into her family home after that horrible night when they were all...' she leaned forward dramatically, '*Consumed* –'

'They died from sexxxxxxxx,' Kirsty drawled, taking another swig from her flask.

'Then this boy who's moved into the area after his mother died finds her and asks if she's going to be at school and she has to say yes but she doesn't know why.'

'Is she dead by page fifty?'

'No! She goes to school and she learns about the modern world, and makes this great group of friends, like –'

'Don't start with the best friends; they always suck,' Kirsty said.

'And they give her the courage to go back to her family home, where she discovers –'

'A lot of naked corpses?' Cate giggled.

'No, she discovers an ancient book that tells her about a hidden world – the world of the Consumed!'

'Is it a sexy world?'

'Shut up! No, it's full of strange and wonderful characters, but it's a world full of dangers. And while Lucinda's being swept away, her friends and Chunk –'

'Chunk?'

'It's his nickname. Anyway, Chunk and her friends start investigating the world and they realise there's a war coming – a war that might Consume humanity.'

'Is it a battle of the sexes?'

Vanessa glared at Cate. 'I'm not telling you any more.'

'Yo Chunk, what's crackalackin'?'

'Stop making fun of my favourite book!'

'It deserves to be made fun of!' Cate protested. 'It sounds like some creepy prudish tract designed to tell young girls that having sex is bad.'

'Just because her parents died in a sex ritual gone wrong, and the Consumed walk the earth, draining the life from everyone who has sex with them, doesn't mean the book is saying sex is bad!'

Cate raised an eyebrow. 'These kind of books poison you against normal human relationships. They're why you think me and Adam shouldn't be together. But me and Adam are awesome! And not just because we have sex... but sex is a big part of it.'

Kirsty laughed. 'Yeah, a big part sure helps.'

Vanessa's phone rang. 'It's Scozza,' she said. 'I've gotta go. I totally forgot we were hanging out tonight.'

'What,' Kirsty said, 'does he need a driver while he goes to buy drugs?'

'No comment,' said Vanessa.

'That's okay, I've got stuff on tonight too,' Kirsty said.

'You do?' Cate said.

'Totes. I've got loads of stuff on. You don't know everything about me!'

'You don't even have time for after-kite drinks?'

'Nah,' Kirsty said, beginning to reel in her kite. 'I'm really busy. Maybe during the week.'

Vanessa shrugged. 'Yeah, Scozza's taking up a lot of my time. Aren't you guys going away soon?'

'Next weekend,' said Cate. 'But we'll catch up before then, right?'

'Sure,' Vanessa said unconvincingly.

By now Kirsty had finished packing up her kite. 'You're giving me a lift, Vanessa?'

Vanessa nodded, slinging her bag over her shoulder. 'Let's go.'

'Wait!' Cate said. 'Aren't we going to talk about the League?'

'Pfft, what's there to say?' Vanessa said.

'Yeah,' Kirsty said. 'If a riot couldn't break you guys up, what else could they be planning?'

That wasn't exactly reassuring. The League could be up to anything, and the longer that thought was in her head, the more Cate wished they were all going to Café Nom Nom together. Couldn't at least one of them stay behind with her, just for a while, until this sense of foreboding passed? But by the time Cate thought to ask, her friends were too far away to hear.

20

Across town Adam was trying his best to keep his head down at work. The news stories had focused more on the crazed mob of women than on him, but there'd been enough shots of him cowering in the toilets to keep the phone calls and texts coming. There'd even been some from the few women in his past who'd actually wanted his phone number. *You missed your chance, ladies,* he thought sullenly, checking for the third time this shift that everything was plugged in inside projection booth number two.

'Man,' Renton said, appearing in the doorway, clearly having nothing better to do in a seven-cinema complex than follow Adam around, 'bitches be cray.'

'No, Renton,' Adam said, pushing past him and walking out into the cramped service corridor. 'Can we talk about this later?'

'You already said that.' Renton hurried to keep up with Adam as he strode away towards the storage rooms. 'This is later.'

'I was thinking more "after I'm dead" later.'

In the dingy storage room, behind a stack of old posters and promotional materials, Steve was getting changed into his costume for the evening's theme, which was 'submarine movies'. They'd had a bunch of classics to choose from – *Das Boot, U-571, The Hunt for Red October, Crimson Tide* – but Renton had lobbied hard, and successfully, for one of the genre's lesser lights.

'Don't forget *K-19: The Widowmaker!*' Renton had said.

'More like *K-19: The Sleepmaker,*' Steve had retorted.

'The punters are gonna flock to this movie! On

117

BackedUpToilet, my oral history of it got two thousand hits!'

'Oral history?' Steve laughed. 'That was just you reminiscing about how you got caught beating off to it when it first came out, and then the guy sitting in the row behind punched you in the head.'

'Wasn't all that traffic coming from some bondage website?' Adam had said.

'Nah, SubsAndDoms.com is obviously a submarine enthusiast website. And we got loads of traffic from GoingDown.com too.'

Steve had smirked. 'Guess they came for the "oral history".'

Now, Adam was looking at Steve with some disquiet. 'Jesus, Steve,' he sighed, 'put some clothes on.'

'Not my fault the girls are hogging the break room,' Steve said, striking an ostentatious muscle pose. 'I'm guessing they'd let *you* get changed in there though, now that you're a celebrity.'

Adam groaned.

'Still not happy with your fan club?'

'They're not my fan club. Those women were so drunk they would've gone after anything in trousers.'

'Even Renton?' said Steve.

'Hey! I'm right here!' Renton said.

'You would have had to tell them that,' Steve said.

Adam shook his head. 'They were a pack of raving lunatics and I'm never going back there.'

'Bet the girlfriend's not happy about that,' Renton sneered. 'She won't be able to parade you around the office now.'

'She's cool with it,' Adam said. 'She knows I hate sport.'

'Everyone hates sport,' they replied in unison.

'Seriously, Steve, put your Captain America costume on. We've got to get back out there.'

'This *is* my costume,' he said.

Adam raised an eyebrow. Steve was wearing nothing but a pair of green, sequined swimming trunks with a gold-painted belt and matching wrist cuffs.

'I'm the Sub-Mariner,' Steve said.

'The Sub-who?'

'More like substandard!' said Renton. 'I've seen better cosplay at LoserCon.'

'That's not a real convention!' Steve said hotly.

Adam began to realise. 'Is this another comic book character?'

'Yeah,' Steve said, 'Prince Namor, the Sub-Mariner. He's the hot-headed ruler of the deep.'

Renton was pecking away at his phone, bringing up pages from comic books. 'See!' he said, thrusting the screen at Adam. 'It looks nothing like him!'

Adam peered at the illustration on Renton's phone of an over-muscled man wielding a trident. The Sub-Mariner had slicked-back hair and looked vaguely pissed off.

'He looks like he's made out of bunches of carrots,' Adam said.

'He's got some muscles that they must only have under the sea,' Renton agreed.

'Screw you guys,' said Steve. 'I'll have you know this costume is 100 per cent accurate.'

Renton laughed again. 'They're not gonna cast you in the movie.'

'I never said they would,' Steve pouted. 'You're the ones going on about that Captain America shit. I want to be a serious actor.'

'That's good, because Adam's the one who should be wearing those Speedos.'

Nobody answered.

Renton turned to Steve. 'Come on, you know what I mean,' he said.

Steve stared back at him stonily. 'Are you saying Adam's better-looking than me?'

'Well... yeah?'

Steve frowned and looked away.

MEL CAMPBELL AND ANTHONY MORRIS

'Who cares about how we look?' Adam said. 'If you ask me, Speedos are for the pool... Or Steve's submarine costume.'

Steve refused to look back. Renton began rummaging in his bag. He pulled out a white bedsheet and draped it over his head.

'Um,' said Adam slowly, 'what the fuck?'

'Dude...' said Steve, turning around, 'it's not Ku Klux Klan night.'

'I'm not a Klansman; I'm a *ghost*,' said Renton, muffled by the sheet, 'the ghost from *Below*. You know, the movie about the ghost submarine.'

There was a pause.

'In World War II.'

The pause dragged on.

'With ghosts.'

Steve shook his head. 'You look like a Klansman!'

'Did the Klan have submarines?' added Adam.

'I'm not a Klansman!'

'The periscope could be a burning cross,' Steve mused. 'But you can't burn crosses underwater.'

Adam laughed. 'Was the sub the KKK-19?'

The front of the sheet sucked in and out with Renton's angry breath. 'Well, what's *your* costume, Adam?'

'I'm wearing it,' Adam said. He was clad in a roll-neck jumper and a navy-blue peacoat. 'Oh, wait.' From his pocket he retrieved a crumpled captain's hat, and settled it on his head.

'Looks good,' said Steve, but Renton was not mollified.

'When are you gonna dump your girlfriend?' he said aggressively.

'Whoa, where did *that* come from?' Steve said.

'Answer the question!' said the grumpy ghost.

'Jesus, Renton!' Adam said. 'I'm not going to! And I wouldn't tell you if I had.'

'So you have!' crowed Renton.

'What do you care?'

'Dude, you're totally wasting your potential.'

'Not this again,' said Steve. 'If he wants to throw the best years of his sexual life away, then more babes for me, I guess!'

'That's big talk from a man in Speedos!'

'You've gotta be a big man to fill these Speedos.'

'What size are they – extra small?' said the ghost.

'Big enough for your mum.'

'Gentlemen,' Adam said, 'this is neither the time nor the place.'

'It's never the time to discuss your sex life, according to you,' Renton said.

'Why would we?' said Adam. 'What's it got to do with you?'

'I just don't want to see you get hurt.'

'Why do you even care?'

Steve interjected, 'Because he was getting all the women you were too classy to hook up with.'

'That's not true!' Renton said. 'Lots of them wouldn't go out with me, either.'

'But you have to admit you were getting more action when Adam was single,' Steve said. 'Adam was the chum in the water... you were just the chum's chum.'

Renton nodded sadly. 'I was so chumpy you could carve it.'

'You got the chump part right,' said Steve.

'Well, this has been illuminating,' said Adam, turning towards the door. 'I've got to get back to running this cinema.'

'But I bet you're meeting up with her after work, right?' said Steve.

'I am meeting Cate, yes.'

Steve smirked. 'Not at the stadium?'

'No way!'

'Hanging out with her friends?'

Adam was silent.

'Have you even met her friends?'

'What's your point, Steve?'

'Are you sure she's not keeping you on the down-low?'

'No,' Adam said. 'We just spend a lot of time one-on-one.'

'C'mon, have you *ever* gone out with a girl who didn't want you to meet her friends within the first week?'

Adam still didn't say anything.

The sheet rustled as Renton cackled. 'Yeah, looks like her friends don't like you.'

'They don't even know me.'

'Doesn't sound like they want to,' said Renton. 'And you know what friends are like – always trying to ruin any good thing you've got going.'

Adam looked pointedly at Renton.

'Hey, I know of what I speak. Right now, her friends are talking you down, trying to get her to break it off.'

'Why would they do that?' Adam said, a note of worry entering his voice.

'All I'm saying is that you've been going out with her for, like, *a thousand years* now,' Renton said. 'And you haven't even had *one* boring friend get-together? Sounds like you're more into it than she is.'

Steve nodded.

Adam looked disappointed. 'And you agree with him, Steve?'

'All I know is, if her friends don't like you, they're gonna want you guys to break up.'

Adam shrugged and walked silently out of the storeroom. But as he checked tickets for *K-19: The Widowmaker*, and watched from the back of the cinema as the Russian submarine crew struggled to contain radiation from the leaking reactor, his mind kept returning to what Steve had said. All those women, all those one-night stands... Once they'd got what they wanted, they just pushed him away. Wasn't what he had with Cate meant to be different? Wasn't she supposed to make him part of her life? Maybe there was something poisoning his relationship. Was it about to sink to the bottom of the sea? Was he the Harrison

Ford character, or that other guy whose skin was peeling off?

Could he even bring this up with Cate? He could hardly ask her straight up if her friends liked him, but if he didn't, was it just going to fester, like the radiation from that movie? Adam walked out into the foyer. Jeez, *K-19* was a real drag.

21

It was lunchtime as Adam drove into Ladbroke, his home town. He and Cate had left early in order to allow plenty of time to get settled in ahead of the Ladbroke Film Festival, in which his short film *Metadata* was premiering. The drive had seemed even longer – Cate had insisted on cracking jokes about the names of the towns they'd driven through on the way.

'Tumescence? What kind of dick names a town that?'

Kilometres down the road, she sniggered again. 'Stud?' She turned to Adam with a smirk. 'Are you sure *that's* not where you grew up?'

Later still: 'Angel's Bottom! That can't be real!'

Adam replied defensively, 'It was named by some explorer. Those were more innocent times.'

'Basically, it sounds like this whole region was settled by sex-crazed perverts.'

'It just means they thought the land was fertile,' he said mildly.

'More like the land was up for it!'

Adam sighed. 'Are you getting all this out of your system before you meet my parents?'

'I'm just nervous,' she said. 'Meeting your parents is a big deal. Plus all your old friends. It's like I'm diving headlong into your past.'

Adam thought about how little he knew about Cate's past. He'd never met her parents, and her friends were still a mystery to him. But all he said was, 'They'll love you as much as I do.'

Cate didn't reply. Had she even heard him? *Shit*, Adam

thought, *why did I blurt that out now, when she's not even paying attention?* He was about to say something more when Cate started laughing at a mildly suggestive tree stump. 'That looks like a penis!'

'Do you want us to stop so you can take a picture?'

'Can we?'

'No.'

'Aww.'

Now, the car was crawling down Ladbroke's main street, which oddly enough was named Main Street. The shops were busy with locals getting their Saturday groceries. Plastic strips fluttered in a bakery doorway as a burly farmer walked out, eating a pie.

On the grassy median strip was a war memorial topped by a bronze statue of a soldier in a slouch hat. The face under the hat looked familiar.

'Why is there a statue of you in the main strip?' Cate asked.

'That's not me,' Adam said. 'It's an unknown soldier from World War One. After some sleep-deprived truckie ran over the old statue a few years back, they got me to model for the new one.'

They'd done a pretty good job, Cate thought. This Unknown Soldier filled out his uniform nicely… and the lower half of the statue looked very well polished. As Cate watched, a teenage girl laid a wreath at the foot of the memorial.

'It's not even Anzac Day,' she said. 'What's the wreath for?'

He shook his head. 'Kids can be pretty silly.'

As they drove past, Cate was close enough to make out the inscription on the wreath: ADAM.

'Hey, was that wreath for you?'

'No.'

'Was that wreath made out of underpants?'

'No.'

'You didn't even look.'

'We're nearly there,' Adam said.

They turned down the drive of Adam's parents' home. Cate had been expecting... she wasn't even sure. A raw timber farmhouse with a verandah on all sides, standing isolated in a sun-bleached paddock? A mangy, three-legged dog chained up in a dusty yard, in which flies swarmed around a ram's skull? That was where Cate's mental-image repertoire of rural houses ran dry. So she was surprised to discover Adam had grown up in an Edwardian house, the sort you'd see in the nicer suburbs. Weathered red brick, surrounded by hydrangea and agapanthus bushes. Cream paint on the gables, window frames and decorative wooden verandah posts. Lichen on the terracotta roof.

A woman in her fifties came down the front steps to greet them. 'Hello, darling!' she called.

'Hi, Mum,' said Adam.

'You've got to stop giving hitchhikers a lift,' Adam's mother said, winking at Cate. Her smile reminded Cate of Adam's.

'Mu-um!' he said, rolling his eyes. 'This is Cate. I've told you about her.'

'Pleased to meet you,' Cate said.

'I'm Rhonda. It's good of you to come up here with Adam for his big premiere. Will you be staying the night?'

'Of course she will, Mum.'

Rhonda looked faintly surprised. 'Well, Regina – that's Adam's little sister – will be very happy to meet you, too.'

Adam laughed. 'Happy? Is she still a goth?'

'They don't call them "goths" any more. I think she's an "emo".'

'I'm a *scene girl*,' came an acid voice from inside the house. A teenage girl appeared in the doorway, tossing her multicoloured hair.

'Hey, Gina,' Adam said.

She folded her arms across her black T-shirt. 'It's Darkwing Ravencloud.'

'On Tumblr, perhaps,' he teased.

'I bet everyone in town's pleased to see *you* back.'

'Hi! I'm Cate.'

Regina gave her a cool look. 'Good to know.'

'Are you coming to the film festival tonight?' Adam said.

'So I can watch all those dorks worship you? No thanks.'

'Got plans with your goth friends?'

'Ugh, they're not *goths*!'

Adam enfolded his sister in a hug. 'It's good to see you.'

She squirmed and huffed in protest, but Cate noticed that over Adam's shoulder, Regina was smiling.

They'd only just taken their bags out of the car – Cate had the clothes, Adam the film gear – when a horn started blaring from the road behind them. They turned to see a ute pulling into the driveway, blocking their car in. 'Adam!' a man shouted from the ute. Adam carefully put his bag down; only Cate was close enough to see him rolling his eyes.

'Wow, that was quick,' said Cate.

'News travels fast in this hick town,' Regina said, already heading back into the house.

At least three people had spilled out of the ute's cabin, and more were climbing over the sides of the tray. They were all holding beer bottles, except for the ones holding bottles of rum. The driver, a burly, sandy-haired man in his early twenties, was the last to get out; he had a bottle of whiskey in each hand. He held out one to Adam. 'Welcome back, mate,' he said.

'Robbo,' Adam said, taking the bottle. 'Davo,' he added, nodding to the equally stocky man now standing beside Robbo. Adam pointed the bottle at the other five guys from the ute, who looked like dodgy photocopies of one another. 'Macca, Bluey, Wozza, Spooge, Jazz Hands.'

'Jazz Hands?' Cate mouthed. No one noticed. They were all staring rapturously at Adam.

'Where are the girls?' Adam said.

'Like we'd let 'em near *you*, mate,' said one of the Secret Seven. Cate guessed it was Bluey, as he had red hair. 'They only settled for us once you left town.'

'Yeah, right,' Adam said, laughing. 'I didn't stand a chance against Bluey.'

One of the blond guys cheered.

'Wait,' Cate said. The men stared at her like she'd just fallen out of a passing UFO. 'Isn't Bluey the redheaded guy?'

They all guffawed.

'Nah,' Adam said, 'Bluey's called Bluey 'cause he blew his load in year eight rubbing up against the sander in woodwork class.'

'Ewww,' Cate said. She pointed at the red-haired guy. 'So which one are you?'

'I'm Spooge,' he said. 'I blew my load in woodwork class too.'

'Yeah, two weeks later,' said Robbo.

Cate shook her head. 'Which one of you is Jazz Hands?'

'Hi!' said the tallest of the bunch, waving enthusiastically.

'So,' Cate said, 'when are the girls getting here?'

'They're all off setting up the film stuff,' said Robbo.

'More like they're getting wasted,' said Davo, taking a swig from a beer.

'I might go give them a hand,' Cate said, giving Adam a peck on the cheek. Adam looked stricken. 'Have fun with your mates,' she said lightly, walking back down the driveway.

'Wait!' Adam called. She turned. He said urgently, 'I'll meet you in –'

'He's not goin' anywhere!' Bluey yelled.

'I'll meet you down the shops in an hour,' Cate said, and headed on her way.

Behind her the guys started talking loudly; Adam watched her go, then took a swig from the bottle in his hand.

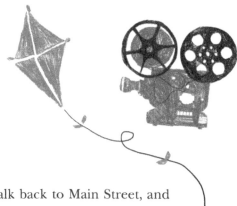

22

It took Cate twenty minutes to walk back to Main Street, and another five to find the hall where the film festival was being set up. Uncharacteristically, she used that time to worry. She knew Adam's mum had been joking when they arrived, but it had brought to the surface a vague but persistent concern she'd had over the last week: was she more invested in the relationship than Adam? It wasn't that he'd lost interest; more that she was really starting to feel things for him, instead of just feeling him up. And she wasn't sure that he was feeling the same way.

Sure, he was an attentive boyfriend. He listened to her. He was kind. He didn't mind when she ran her hands over his broad chest. None of this had changed in the time they'd been together. But the longer Cate spent with him, the more she realised that Adam would be just as nice to any girl he was with. She was looking for signs that she was more than just a casual thing to him. Hopefully, this trip back to his hometown would reveal if this relationship was becoming something special to both of them.

Ladbroke Community Centre was your standard local hall. Various banners and pennants around the walls, in between old photos of sports teams and honour rolls of men sent off to war. A framed picture of the Queen, so faded by time and sunlight that her skin looked blue. A serving hatch to the kitchen at one end. A stage at the other end, with a screen pulled down in front of velvet curtains; whatever projector they were going to use hadn't been set up yet, and the folding chairs were still stacked up the back.

'Hello?' Cate said. 'Anyone here?'

'Hey.' A woman in her mid-twenties, her hair swept up in a messy ponytail, emerged from a side door wiping her hands on a tea towel. 'Sorry, everyone else is having lunch. Can I help you?'

'I'm Cate,' she said, 'I just wanted to make sure I was at the right place for the film festival.'

'Madison,' the woman said with a friendly smile. 'And yes, this is the place. Are you coming tonight?'

I sure hope so. Cate fought back a smirk. 'Oh yes,' she said. 'My boyfriend's got a film in competition.'

The temperature seemed to drop ten degrees. 'Oh, really?' Madison said. She wasn't smiling now. 'Who's your boyfriend?'

'He's a local boy, Adam –'

Madison cut her off. 'Oh, right,' she said, almost sneeringly, 'he's your *boyfriend*, is he?'

'Well, yeah,' said Cate, 'We came up here together and –'

'Yeah, well, gotta go,' Madison said, turning on her heel.

'See you tonight?' Cate called after her, not sure what was happening. Madison didn't answer. Her ponytail swished as she stomped back to the kitchen. *What did I say?* Cate thought. Madison slammed the door behind her. On the other side, Cate could hear muffled angry voices. She shrugged and headed for the exit. What was *her* problem?

Whatever it was, it seemed to be spreading. As Cate walked back along Main Street, she noticed the locals now stared as she passed. Did she have chocolate on her face, or maybe one of her shirt buttons had come undone? Was it just paranoia? Or was it something more sinister? Ladbroke was starting to creep her out.

An idea began to form at the back of her mind. Could that Madison chick have been... no, it was silly. But what if Madison *was* in the League? Of course they'd have members in Adam's hometown. That might even be how this whole Hot Guy thing had started.

Then again, maybe it was just a regular small town where new folks attracted attention. She looked across the road at a sign in a shop window that said 'WE'RE SLASHING PRICES'. Nothing sinister about that. Under it was another sign that said, 'DISCOUNTS TO DIE FOR'. That seemed a little over-enthusiastic. The sign under that said, 'I WILL KILL AGAIN'. Taped over that was a piece of paper with the handwritten advice, 'Back in 10 Minutes', plus a smiley face.

Cate felt someone tap her on the shoulder. Barely stifling a squeal, she spun around to encounter a sweet-looking old lady. 'You gonna die,' said the crone.

'What?'

'I said, you want a pie?'

Cate realised she was standing outside a bakery.

'Best pies in town. We make 'em outta strangers.'

'*What?*'

'I said, we ain't got no... dangers?

'I don't think that's what you said.' Cate began to back away. The old lady held up a pie, then slowly squeezed it until the pastry cracked and gravy ran thick through her fingers. Cate took another step backwards... and felt muscular arms enfolding her. She drew in a breath to scream. The man holding her spun her around.

'Adam!' she said, far too loudly.

'Mrs Doogue,' Adam said sternly, 'are you trying to sell my girlfriend a pie?'

The old lady cackled.

'Mrs Doogue makes the best pies in town,' Adam said.

'Her sales manner leaves a lot to be desired,' Cate said, still shaken.

'Yeah. That discount butcher across the road has given everyone some funny ideas about sales techniques.'

'They should film *Midsomer Murders* here!' Mrs Doogue said.

'Can we go?' Cate whispered.

'Bye, Mrs Doogue,' Adam said loudly.

'If I'd known *you* were going to be in town, young man,' she called as they hurried away, 'I would have got my special pie ready.'

'Special pie,' Cate said, 'Ewwwwww.'

'It's a perfectly innocent pie,' he said. 'It's really tasty too.'

'Ewwwwww.'

'She makes this special gravy.'

'I'll bet she does,' Cate said. 'That's quite impressive at her age.'

'Oh, I get it,' Adam said. 'Ewwwwww.'

Behind them, someone yelled out 'Adam!' Cate sighed; Adam turned. From the unguarded delight on his face, it was someone he was pleased to see.

'Hey, Ugly Joe!' he yelled back, waving enthusiastically. 'It's Ugly Joe,' he said to Cate.

'I guessed,' said Cate. She didn't turn around. 'Isn't he the park ranger guy?'

'Yep,' Adam said, still waving.

With a name like that, Cate wondered just how hideous Joe must be. Maybe that was why he'd become a park ranger, hiding out in the bush where his hideous visage frightened campers and sparked rumours of Bigfoot – or worse. Maybe he was wearing a mask on this rare visit to town – no, a pillow case, with crude, lopsided eyeholes, the fabric fluttering in and out wetly as he sucked in each tortured breath through lips mangled by the cruelty of a negligent god.

Out of the corner of her eye she saw Adam embrace a vaguely humanoid shape. Did he have a hump? A grotesque, bulging forehead? A giant nose? No nose at all?

'Cate,' Adam said, 'this is my best friend, Ugly Joe.'

There was no avoiding it. She took a deep breath, steeling

herself for the nightmare to come. She turned, then gasped.

'But Ugly Joe...' she blurted, 'you're beautiful!'

He smiled. His teeth were as perfect as the rest of his features. 'Thank you,' he said, clearly a little taken aback.

'So... why on earth would they call you Ugly Joe?' He really was seriously good-looking, in a rough-hewn, outdoorsy way.

'Well, I started hanging out with Adam when we were kids. We were inseparable, and it just sort of stuck.'

'When he was younger,' Adam said, 'they called him Ugly Kid Joe.'

'What can I say? It was the '90s,' he laughed. 'Now I'm older, it's just plain old Ugly Joe. My name's not even Joe,' he added. 'It's Tim.'

'Nice to meet you, Tim,' Cate said.

'Nah, just call me Joe. Everyone does now, even my wife.'

'Where is Debra?' Adam said. Something about the way he said her name made Cate's ears prick up.

'Here she is now,' Joe said, looking over Adam's shoulder. Cate saw Adam's expression darken for an instant. Then he was turning to Debra, a fixed smile on his face.

'Hi Adam,' Debra said brightly. She was a petite woman with a smattering of freckles across her nose, and a rosy-pink complexion that made her look cheerful even when she was frowning. Which she was doing now.

'Back for the festival?' she said.

Adam nodded.

'Because you wouldn't come back to see your friends?'

'It's not like that,' he said.

'Joe's been working on this for months, and you show up on the day to collect your prize.'

'What makes you think I'm going to win?'

She sighed. 'Don't be naive, Adam. I hoped living in the city would have helped you grow up a little.'

'Hey Cate,' Joe said loudly, 'why don't I show you the, uh... historical car park?' He took her by the arm and led her a short distance down the street.

'Shouldn't we wait?' she said.

'This is an old argument,' Joe said, 'I've heard it before, and you don't need to hear it now.'

Behind her, Cate heard Debra shout, 'When are you going to start living in the real world?'

'Why should I? You'd just find something else to have a go at me about!' Adam shouted back.

'So,' Joe said, 'how'd you manage to get Adam all to yourself?'

'I wonder that too sometimes,' she said. 'He seems to find my complete social ineptitude charming.'

Joe didn't seem to know what to say to that.

'Oh, I don't know,' she went on. 'Who knows why anyone falls in love?'

'Debra knows,' Joe said admiringly. 'She's got it all planned out.'

'And you like that?'

'Yeah, takes the weight off. I've got my hands full at work. It's nice to be with someone who takes care of that side of things at home.'

'What side of things?'

'You know... she's always thinking long term. She's got me taking evening classes so I can step up into a manager's job in a year or two. You need that kind of money if you're going to start a family.'

'I guess,' said Cate. This had literally never occurred to her. Babies needed money? What did babies spend money on? Mink nappies? Diamond teething rings? Platinum rims for their prams? She imagined a baby wearing gold chains, saying, 'Welcome to my crib.'

'What about you?' Joe said. 'You and Adam making plans?'

'We're just taking it as it comes,' she said.

'Yeah, that sounds like Adam,' Joe said, with a rueful smile. 'He's always been a dreamer.'

Adam stomped over to them, leaving Debra behind. Her arms were folded, her face furious. 'Let's go,' Adam said, looking upset.

'Nice to meet you, Joe,' Cate said, hurrying after Adam as he walked away.

'See you tonight, Joe,' Adam said, without turning around.

'What was *that* all about?' Cate said.

'Nothing,' Adam said. 'She's just really good at making me feel like shit.'

'Oh,' Cate said. She wanted to ask more, but this didn't seem the time. Anything she said would only make things worse, anyway. She'd never seen him so upset and she wasn't sure how to deal with it.

She took his hand and looked up at him. He gave her a small, tight smile. Cate relaxed a little; whatever was happening here, it wasn't between them.

'You want to get some lunch?'

'Sure,' Adam said, 'I had to drink half a bottle of Bundy before those guys would let me come get you.' He burped. 'I feel like one of Mrs Doogue's pies.'

'What, sloppy and overdone?' The attempt to lighten the mood was met with silence; he didn't even crack a smile. Cate tried again. 'Um, let's get a burger instead,' she said.

23

Cate was surprised by just how many people had turned out for a small-town film festival. The hall didn't have a seat spare, and there were people milling around the back, ready to pounce the moment someone got up to go to the bathroom. Maybe, she thought, they were here because they knew the filmmakers or were in the films. But then she saw how they reacted to Adam's arrival, and she could lie to herself no longer. He was the star attraction, they were his adoring fans and she was... what? She might as well have been invisible.

'Hi Regina,' she called out. Having been separated from Adam by the crowd, she was relieved to locate his sister up the back of the hall. Regina didn't look around. She was deep in conversation with a sketchy, fidgety guy whose grubby T-shirt showed off his neck tattoos. He was constantly scanning the room, and when Cate started towards them, he bolted.

'Fuck yiz!' he said over his shoulder.

'Good one, Cate,' Regina said. 'That guy owes me five grand.'

'Five grand what?' Cate said.

'Dollars, you idiot. Do you know how hard it is to find a place in this town where you're not being watched?'

'But the place is full,' Cate said.

'And who are they all looking at? Not me. Not when Mr Hollywood's in town. It's been almost impossible to keep my business running without him around to pull all the attention.'

'Your business?'

'Here's a clue: it's not a paper round.'

'Drugs?'

'Jesus,' Regina sighed, 'what exactly is it that Adam sees in you? Do you make him feel smart?'

'I just didn't expect Adam's younger sister to be a drug lord.'

She narrowed her lavishly made-up eyes. 'You grow up with a brother like Adam, you soon realise the way the world works. People like me don't get anything handed to them for free.'

'People like you?'

'Normal people,' Regina said. 'People who don't look like Adam.'

Cate couldn't say anything to that. She wondered what it must have been like growing up with Adam grabbing all the attention. Always being in the shadows, having people only interested in you to get to your brother...

Regina laughed. 'Are you imagining my harsh upbringing? Always in the shadow cast by Adam's good looks and that kind of shit?'

Cate shook her head unconvincingly.

'What makes you think I want people in this dead-end town looking at me? You can have a lot more fun when no one's paying attention. And it's a lot more lucrative.'

'But selling drugs...' Cate said.

'Who said anything about drugs?' Regina said. 'I'm selling these chumps genuine Adam relics. Old photos, mostly, but anything is good for a few bucks. School essays, school uniform... once I sold a pair of his used undies for a hundred bucks.'

'Eww,' Cate said.

'They weren't really his. I just bought a pack of Y-fronts, painted on a few artistic stains with coffee, and put them through the wash a bunch of times. The girls at my school will buy anything they think he's worn, even if it's got skidmarks.' She wrinkled her nose. '*Especially* if it does.'

Cate realised her mouth was hanging open.

'What'd you sell the guy who owes you five grand? A jar of Adam's blood?'

'Dad sold him Adam's old car when I said I didn't want it. I don't get the money until he pays Dad.'

'Ahhhh,' Cate said.

Regina shook her head. 'You really have no idea what you've gotten yourself into. Adam's my big brother; he's been part of my life since I was born. He's never made a thing of it, but I've seen people go crazy around him.'

Cate thought back to the stadium riot. 'I know.'

'Do you?' Regina said. 'If you really knew, you wouldn't be here with him. It won't be easy seeing everyone in town pushing you out of the way to get to him.'

'Not everyone,' Cate said. 'Debra doesn't seem to have a lot of love in her heart for Adam.'

'Debra's one of the coolest people you'll ever meet,' Regina said. 'And you know how sweet Adam is. But he broke her heart without even trying.'

'They were a couple?' Cate said.

But before Regina could answer, a blare of music and flickering lights signalled the film festival was about to begin. A cheer went up from the audience. Cate turned towards the screen; when she looked back, Regina was gone.

She searched the darkened room for Adam. He was seated in a roped-off section down the front with a bunch of other people she assumed were fellow competitors. There didn't seem to be any spare seats anywhere near him. Or anywhere else in the hall; she had to watch standing up the back with the rest of the town rejects.

The first film was some action footage of the local high school footy team, set to stomach-churningly loud guitar music. It was verging on artistic, Cate supposed, this hypnotic experience of watching a series of essentially very similar goals and tackles in slow motion, repeated again and again, getting slower and slower. Each one drew cheers from the crowd, while the lack of story passed unmentioned.

The next film depicted some local kids doing skateboard tricks to a soundtrack of Aussie hip-hop. 'I got some durries and minimum chips,' rapped a broad yet somehow whiny voice, 'Fuck John Howard!' A couple of the oldies tutted; Cate liked to think it was for the poor rhyming and unimaginative sound production, rather than the swears.

The third film turned out to be an earnest New Age parable made by the local burnt-out hippie. She also had the starring role as a protester trying to save some woodland (which looked a lot like someone's backyard) from evil loggers, who helpfully wore shirts with 'LOGGER' written across the back. The ending was a bit of a downer: as a tree was chopped down, fake blood gushed from the protester's neck, spurting arterially across the ground to spell out 'WE ARE ALL ONE'.

The message was blunted somewhat by being splashed on a patch of concrete that was clearly a driveway. A forest floor was not the most screen-legible place to write in fake blood. And the 'blood' was obviously tomato sauce squirted from a bottle just out of frame. Still, Cate thought, the clumsy intercutting between the blood splatters and the hippie theatrically clutching her neck was kind of effective.

The second-last film starred a cat wearing sunglasses and eating salad. It looked vaguely familiar to Cate; she wondered if the filmmaker had ripped off some viral video. Then the cat shook its head, dislodging the sunglasses, and the realisation hit her. 'Oh my god, that's Salad Cat!'

Everyone close by looked at Cate like she was an idiot. 'Well, it is,' she said. Salad Cat was an internet sensation – the video had gone around Cate's office half a dozen times, and even Ursula had cracked a smile at the adorable antics of the cat that couldn't get enough salad.

Despite its leafy diet, the cat was very fat. The offscreen

owner tried to take away the salad, but the cat yowled in dismay, strands of rocket dangling from between its whiskers. 'What, you want your salad?' an offscreen voice said, putting the bowl back in front of the cat, which happily returned to munching the greenery. The audience laughed fondly.

How could Adam possibly beat Salad Cat? That cat had its own line of salad servers. Maybe someone from Ladbroke had simply taken one of the original videos offline and claimed it was their own work. But no. Sitting next to Adam at the front of the room was a bulky, shaven-headed biker wearing a jacket covered in patches, and resting over his shoulder was Salad Cat, looking contentedly back at her fans. As the video finished and the crowd burst into cheers, he raised Salad Cat aloft to bask in the glory her salad-eating antics had earned her.

The cat let out a disgruntled yowl, identical to the one from when her salad had been taken away. The crowd laughed uproariously. Cate sighed. Poor Adam.

Now it was Adam's turn. Cate was suddenly glad she wasn't sitting with him. She wasn't sure she could hide her reaction if *Metadata* turned out badly. And at first, it seemed like it was going to be a mess. Filmed in black and white, and with lots of arty angles, it was a confusing look at life in a totalitarian surveillance state. It was shot like an old-fashioned noir detective film, but set in a high-tech world...Tech-noir?

The audience only perked up when Adam was onscreen. He was playing a spy, or maybe a bureaucrat, his hair slicked and glistening, his face illuminated by the glow of the flatscreen monitor he was staring into. The lighting caressed the angles of his brows, cheekbones and jaw, and made his irises glow; Cate supposed this was Orson's doing. No wonder that weirdo wanted Adam to be in his ridiculous baby movie. Adam had never looked more remote and glamorous.

The focus shifted. Now Cate was seeing what Adam was seeing: a youngish woman running down dark streets, hiding out in seedy hotel rooms, venetian blinds leaving charcoal shadows across her face. But she was some kind of hacker as well. Droning electro music throbbed on the soundtrack. Cate really hoped they weren't going to have sex.

The tension rose as Adam skilfully intercut between the two characters. At least he knew how to make it look like a proper movie, Cate thought. Events came to a head: the woman burst into the Adam-character's office, pointed forcefully at him and said, 'Stop following me!'

'Who are you?' Adam said, munching on a slice of pizza. The audience laughed.

'But,' she said, confused, 'haven't you been watching me?'

'Nuh,' Adam grunted, turning his monitor around to show a still of Salad Cat, her face buried in a big bowl of iceberg lettuce. The audience roared.

There was a crazy zoom into the heroine's face as she realised her fantasies of surveillance were just that – fantasies. Tears ran down her cheeks as she was left all alone in a world that didn't care what she did. The film faded between shots of her spinning face and the footage Adam had filmed at Sambo Stadium. It was so over-the-top it had to be intentional. Cate clapped louder than anyone as the end credits rolled, though she paused when her own name appeared in the 'thanks' section, for modesty's sake.

The lights came up, and Ugly Joe appeared on stage, mic in hand.

'Well done to all the entrants tonight!' he said expansively. 'This has been the best film festival Ladbroke's ever had.'

'It's the only film festival Ladbroke's ever had!' a heckler yelled. Cate thought it was Adam's mate Wozza. A ripple of laughter ran through the audience.

'I'd just like to thank our sponsors,' Ugly Joe said.

'Get to the winners!' Spooge ejaculated, and the crowd murmured in agreement.

'Okay, well then, the judges will now go and –'

'Get to Adam!' Macca yelled. The crowd cheered.

'Um,' Ugly Joe said. He looked over at the trio of judges, who were sitting behind a table to one side with clipboards in front of them. Their leader, the high school drama teacher, nodded.

'And the winner is Adam!' Ugly Joe shouted. The crowd exploded into raucous cheers. Adam could barely get to his feet for all the people leaning over to slap him on the back. Ugly Joe held a trophy aloft, then pressed it into Adam's hands. Cate was touched to see that Adam looked genuinely surprised and pleased to have won.

She didn't even try to make her way forward; she'd catch up with Adam outside. At least now she wouldn't have to lie about the quality of his film; she really hadn't expected the skill he'd shown. Especially as – to her, at least – it was clear that he'd come up with the ending at the last minute.

But those few final jokes had made the earnestness of the early scenes seem more knowing and light-hearted in retrospect; Adam had a real flair for comedy. Maybe that was something she'd brought out in him, she thought with a small stab of pride.

When Adam finally made it outside the hall, Cate was waiting for him. 'Look what I got,' he said boyishly, thrusting the trophy into her hands as well-wishers continued to cluster around him. Cate was interested to notice the trophy was already engraved with Adam's name.

'This is so great! Thank you so much,' he said, wrapping his arms around her and kissing the side of her face.

'What for?' she said, suddenly aware of the crowd pressing in around them.

'Everything.'

She laughed. 'You're making it sound like I gave you this trophy.'

His face was serious. 'I mean it,' he said. 'The film would have been a mess without you.'

'Adam,' she said, '*I'd* be a mess without *you.*'

They kissed. The crowd fell silent. The silence dragged.

'You comin' down the pub, Adam?' a notably belligerent voice called out.

'Yeah,' Adam said.

Cate stifled a groan.

'You guys go on ahead, I'll meet you there.'

The crowd slowly melted away. Cate kept her arms wrapped around Adam's waist as the occasional backslapper tried to push her aside to get a swing at Adam. She looked up: Debra was standing backlit in the doorway of the hall. Cate couldn't quite make out her expression, but something in her posture said she wasn't happy with what she was seeing.

'We're not going to the pub,' Cate said softly.

'No,' Adam said just as quietly. 'Let's go home.'

He put an arm around her shoulder as they walked toward the parked cars. As they drove away she noticed that Debra was still standing in the doorway. Her face was briefly illuminated by their headlights. Cate couldn't be sure, but she thought she saw tears shining on Debra's cheeks.

24

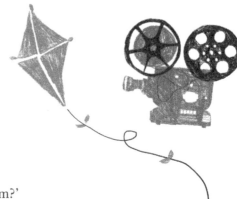

'This was your childhood bedroom?'

'Yep,' Adam said. 'Nothing's really changed since I moved out for uni.'

'It's a pretty big bed,' Cate said in amazement. 'Did you stick two queen-size mattresses together?'

Adam nodded. 'Plus we put a single across the end for more leg room.'

Cate looked at the quilt, which was clearly constructed from three regular quilts stitched together. 'Why did you need such a gigantic bed? There's no room in here for much else.'

Adam shrugged. 'Sometimes friends stayed over.'

'Is that why you have the fully equipped wet bar in the corner?' She looked up. 'And the mirror on the ceiling?'

'Yeah, the girls wanted all that,' Adam said. 'They said they liked watching me sleep.'

'I'm surprised there was any sleeping going on.'

'It wasn't like that,' Adam said. 'They were just friends.'

'Yeah,' Cate said, '*sexy sex* friends.'

Adam put the film festival trophy on a shelf already groaning with awards. 'You've got a dirty mind.'

'I thought that's what you liked about me.'

'I do,' he said. 'I just mean that...'

Cate was examining the awards. 'You won a state prize for woodchopping?'

Adam laughed. 'I didn't even enter,' he said. 'They said

they'd engraved my name on the trophy by mistake, so I might as well have it.'

'Does that happen a lot?' Cate considered the suspicious swiftness with which tonight's trophy had been engraved with Adam's name.

'It used to,' he said, 'but they realised after a while that I didn't care about winning. That's what I like about filmmaking. It's about the craft.'

'What about the Oscars?' Cate said.

Adam scoffed, 'The Oscars are just a promotional tool. The only films that win are commercial tearjerkers and blanded-out biopics.'

Cate said nothing. The last three Oscar-nominated films she'd watched had been *My Dead Baby, Oh No, Yoko: What Ringo Saw* and *The Caligula Diaries*. Adam was fussing with the trophy, clearing others away to give it more space on the shelf.

'This is the first thing I've won that's actually meant something to me,' he said, pride coming through in his voice. 'I know it's just a provincial festival, but now I can legitimately say I'm an award-winning director. It'll make a real difference when I apply to the bigger film festivals. And people pay attention to those. I might get a decent producer, and funding to make the feature-length version of *Metadata*...'

Cate couldn't follow Adam's film industry talk, but his passion was undeniable. Over the years, she'd heard plenty of guys talking big, but as Adam talked up his future, for once it seemed like something more than empty boasting. She'd viewed his filmmaking as just a hobby – a youthful phase he'd grow out of eventually. But it startled her now to realise how much she wanted Adam's dreams to come true. Not for her sake – she didn't care what he did for a living – but because she could see how happy it would make him.

She blurted, 'You do know I love you, right?'

His eyes widened and he smiled tenderly. It was like making God smile, she thought. 'Oh, Cate,' he said, reaching out for her. 'I love y–'

There was a loud scraping noise from outside. Cate let out a squeal.

Adam sighed. 'Don't worry,' he said. 'It's just Dad.' He pulled aside the curtain to reveal the top of a ladder being propped against the window frame. Cate hoisted the window open and peered outside.

'Oh, good,' came a voice from below. 'No problems opening the window, then?'

Standing on the lawn under Adam's window was a handsome silver-haired man in his fifties, wearing jeans and a flannel shirt and holding the base of the ladder.

'Hey there,' Cate said uncertainly. 'Um, thanks. I'm Cate, by the way.'

'No worries,' the handyman said. 'I'm Harris, Adam's dad.'

He gave the ladder a shake as if to check its sturdiness. 'I'll just leave this here. It's solid wood! And these solar lights are on motion sensors,' he added, gesturing down the drive. 'You can easily find your way to the front gate.' He put a pair of plugs into his ears. 'Okay, nighty-night.'

Cate turned to Adam. 'What the hell?'

Adam shrugged, looking embarrassed. 'Parents.'

Cate looked out the window again. 'Is that a taxi rank at the end of your drive?'

Adam nodded. 'The council put it there when I was in Year Twelve. Not sure why – there isn't much through traffic here. It's pretty convenient, though.'

She raised an eyebrow.

'Well, it is,' he said.

'I don't care,' she said, shaking her head. 'Come here.'

Adam smiled and pulled the curtain closed.

Sex with Adam had always been great. By now, they knew

each other so well that their bodies fell into an easy rhythm. While they were in bed, they couldn't be closer. But afterwards, when they were lying in each other's arms, Cate sometimes felt a distance between them.

At first she had just been enjoying sex with a really hot guy. And Adam didn't just rely on his hotness; he was a passionate, inventive, playful lover. But as her feelings for him deepened, so did her concerns. He'd been sleeping with so many women that it shouldn't have surprised her he was great in bed. What if there was nothing behind those skills? No real connection between them? What if he was showing her the same good time he would have shown anyone? Maybe Adam didn't feel what she was feeling. Maybe all they were having was really great sex, and there was nothing more to it than that.

But tonight, it was different. She looked into his eyes and saw he knew what was in her heart, because he felt it too: that what was between them meant more than just their bodies intertwining. They had abandoned themselves completely to one another, the sensations not so much passing between them as happening in a shared space that they both belonged to, a world for them alone.

25

It wasn't even daylight when Cate awoke. Someone was nudging her shoulder. 'Oh, Adam...' she mumbled, 'Again? Okay,' she rolled over, 'get on board.'

She blinked sleepily. Why was Adam standing beside the bed? And why were there two of him? Plus the one still asleep beside her? She let out a confused sound.

'Cate,' Adam's mum Rhonda whispered urgently, 'you fell asleep.'

'No der,' Cate replied automatically. 'That's why they call it a bed.' Then she realised who she was speaking to. 'Um, sorry? What? But – what are you two doing in here?'

Harris beckoned. 'Come on,' he said. 'Up you get. Quick quick.'

Cate rubbed her eyes. 'But... why?'

'Didn't you see the ladder?'

'Yes, but why am I leaving?'

Rhonda frowned. 'Why are you staying?'

'Because I'm his girlfriend,' she hissed. Adam usually slept like a log, but she didn't want him waking up to this.

'Girlfriend?' Harris said, as if the word were describing an exotic foreign custom he'd heard of, but never encountered in real life. 'Does Adam know this?'

'I'm pretty sure he does,' she said. 'We've been going out for almost two months.'

Adam's parents exchanged a look. 'Okay,' Rhonda said. 'Maybe we should talk downstairs.'

148

Five minutes later Cate padded down the stairs, wrapping herself in a robe. The kitchen was a cosy, rustic space, with timber-fronted cabinets and a slate floor. Adam's parents were sitting at a round wooden table. Rhonda was wearing a fuzzy pink dressing gown; Harris was already dressed in jeans and a worn grey jumper. They had a pot of tea waiting for her.

'Sorry about that,' Harris said, handing a steaming mug to Cate. 'You just caught us by surprise.'

'Most of Adam's lady friends don't stay the night,' said Rhonda.

'We try to make it easy for them,' said Harris.

Cate sipped her tea. 'That's nice of you,' she said carefully.

'It's better for everyone,' Rhonda said. 'It used to break Adam's heart, the lame excuses they'd make. If they weren't there when he woke up, he'd assume he'd catch up with them later. But it was so awkward when they'd try to explain why they were leaving...'

Harris rolled his eyes. 'You should have heard the crap they'd come out with. They'd drag it out. Then Adam would feel like crap. He'd mope around for the rest of the day trying to figure out what he did wrong. He didn't deserve that kind of bullshit. It was just easier for everyone if we got them out of here as painlessly as possible.'

'So, Adam had a *lot* of girls through here?'

His parents looked at each other. 'He was very... *popular* in school...' Harris began.

'Look,' Rhonda interrupted, 'we know exactly how good-looking he is. And I'm sure you do too. But we've tried our best not to draw attention to it. He was a cute kid, but it wasn't until he got to his teens that he –'

'The girls couldn't keep their hands off him!' said Harris.

'It wasn't *that* bad,' Rhonda said, 'but he was getting a lot of attention. Adam was always a sweet, sensitive boy, and these girls were just after one thing.'

'We're not prudes,' Harris said. 'We didn't have a problem with him… being with women. But we didn't want them treating him like crap once the novelty wore off.'

'What made you think they'd treat him like crap?' Cate said.

'Well, his looks are the first thing people notice about him,' said Harris. 'Sometimes that's the *only* thing people notice about him. We didn't want him to start thinking of himself that way.'

'We didn't want him to rely on his looks to get through life.'

'We wanted to bring Adam up as…'

'A decent person,' Rhonda said. 'Having the… *advantages* Adam has can go to a boy's head.'

'We didn't want to raise a complete dickhead,' added Harris.

Cate smiled. 'You didn't. He's great. I wouldn't be with him if all he had going for him were his looks.'

'Well,' Rhonda said, 'there's a first time for everything.'

'Seriously?' said Cate. 'He's never had a serious girlfriend?'

'Well, sometimes they do stay,' conceded Rhonda. 'Debra stayed.'

A meaningful look passed between the parents, which Cate caught but couldn't decode.

'Debra? Ugly Joe's wife?' asked Cate. 'What happened with them?' But at this moment Adam walked in, yawning.

'What are you guys talking about this early?'

'Oh, nothing,' said his parents in unison.

'Just family chit-chat,' Rhonda said.

'Want a cuppa?' said Harris.

Cate opened her mouth to speak, but thought better of it. She took another sip of tea instead.

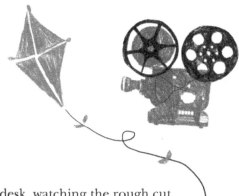

26

Monday morning saw Cate at her desk, watching the rough cut of Adam's corporate video. They'd got back to the city late the previous night, after Adam's parents had spent the day trying to fill the car with pieces of junk they wanted to offload. Adam had dropped her straight home, promising to email her the video in the morning. And now here was the download link.

She hovered her mouse over the link. Would it meet Brunner's high standards? Would it even meet her middling standards? Had Adam included enough about the turf? What if Cate's piece to camera made her look like a plank of wood? Or, worse – a complete buffoon? Would they have time to hire a replacement spokesmodel? Maybe they could just edit Cate out and say it in voice over? If this video didn't do the trick, Brunner would edit her out of Ursula's job.

Don't be silly – just watch the damn thing. Worry about it afterwards. For an instant, she fretted that Adam had filled the video with cheap shot transitions – star wipes, and spinning frames. What if he'd put a glowing love heart around her face? No – she'd seen Adam's film. He knew what he was doing. She was the weak link here.

She took a deep breath, and clicked the link.

It was reassuringly professional. Adam hadn't drawn attention to himself with flashy camera tricks. He'd conjured something simple and... heroic about Sambo Stadium. The video opened on a beautiful shot of the stadium exterior in the late afternoon, viewed from the ground. The setting sun was a corona outlining its bulk, tactfully obscuring the ugly brutalist concrete walls, as punters strolled towards the entrance. His camera roved around the arena, stopping just short of the most dilapidated parts, and lingering on groups of laughing spectators in the stands. Cate knew they were actually blind drunk, but here they looked thrilled… by sport. *Sport is not terrible at all,* the images seemed to say, *no, it is noble and brings the people together.*

The information about the stadium's features was presented in a straightforward yet dynamic fashion. Adam got to each point quickly, and then moved on smoothly to the next. Cate found herself appreciating how little waffling and padding there was – it instantly stood out from the corporate videos she'd winced her way through in meetings and at conferences.

And then she realised it was *her* voice holding it all together. Rather than reproducing her painstakingly composed script, Adam had drawn heavily on the second version of her voice over – the one where she'd told him, in her own words, what was so great about Sambo Stadium. 'Hey!' she said uneasily to herself, 'I worked hard on that stuff. He's cut out all the good bits! Those were gems! Or, at least, nuggets.'

But she had to admit the video was better for leaving those nuggets out. And – oh, god – there she was now on the screen. She cringed reflexively.

At first it seemed like another one of Cate's trademark awkward presentations. What was wrong with her arms? They just kind of *hung* there. Why did nobody *tell* her this? But the shot swiftly zoomed in, cropping out Cate's hesitant gestures. It began to dawn on her that, for once, her antics didn't seem inappropriately unprofessional. Instead, the camera saw her as fresh and sincere. She'd been afraid of looking silly, but instead she came across as likeable.

Adam had chosen the best parts of her original voice over script, and the best moments from her off-the-cuff explanation. She didn't look stupid, but she wasn't dry and boring either.

Adam had expertly navigated a middle path. He'd seen through her awkwardness and captured a warmth and enthusiasm that she hadn't realised she felt for this crap shack.

No, not the stadium. Sambo Stadium was a crumbling toilet that happened to host sporting events. Cate remembered how Adam had coached her to speak directly to him. Of course, that was it! The video worked so well because Adam was interested in what *she* had to say, because *she* was the one saying it. It wasn't anything as embarrassing as a love letter to her, but his affection was obvious in every frame.

The closing scenes blurred as her eyes welled with tears. She'd known in an abstract way that Adam loved her – he'd said as much. But plenty of guys had told her they loved her. She hadn't realised until now that someone might *like* her – for herself – and that she might be someone worthwhile.

Cate reached for the phone. She had to tell him what a wonderful thing he'd done.

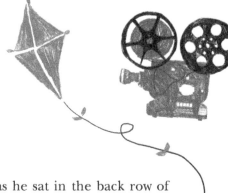

27

Adam's phone vibrated silently as he sat in the back row of Rafferty Cinema Eight. It had once been a maintenance room, and it still smelled faintly of bleach. But they'd dropped in twelve seats and a screen the size of a tabletop, and now it was the preview theatrette. During the day it was used to test the prints and preview upcoming films, and occasionally it was rented out for private functions.

Annoyingly, Renton's suggestion of *K-19: The Widowmaker* had been a raging success: Submarine Night had been the Rafferty's biggest-selling theme night all year. So, ahead of the forthcoming Australian film theme night, Renton was helping choose from the cinema's library of old movies. Today, he had all but dragged Adam into the cinema.

'You gotta see this one,' he urged. 'I think you'll find it's relevant to your interests.'

'It's not another one of your '70s sex comedies, is it?' Adam said warily. 'The last time was enough.'

'It's nothing like that,' Renton said. 'This one's from 1983. And it's a serious drama.'

'What's it called,' Adam scoffed, '*The Schlong Goodbye?*'

'It's called *Flames of Desire*,' said Renton. 'It's an Aussie cult classic about the horrors of war. It was adapted from a bestselling novel called *The Sculptor*. "He started out with clay. He ended up with wood." '

'That was the actual tagline?'

'If only!'

'This had better be good,' Adam said. 'I'm giving up a lunch date with Cate.'

Renton turned off the lights and started the projector. Adam's phone buzzed again, but it was a cinema rule that you never answered a call during a screening, out of respect for other cinemagoers – and for the integrity of the cinema experience. Plus, the only people who ever called him during the day were telemarketers; Cate always texted.

On the screen, a dashing young Australian man was falling in love with a young country girl, to an incongruous soundtrack of wailing saxophone.

'Strewth, your face is bonza,' said the woman in the film.

'Stone the crows,' the man said. 'I flamin' love ya.'

But then World War II came along and tore their budding romance apart. The handsome young man joined the air force; his sweetheart became a nurse. As he was about to ship out for Europe, and she was heading to the Pacific, they married in passionate haste.

'I didn't realise they had so much saxophone during the war,' Adam said.

'Sax and violence,' said Renton. 'Another possible tagline?'

Adam shook his head silently.

The young nurse was captured by the Japanese, and in an uncomfortably lurid sequence, was forced to service the soldiers as a comfort woman. Despite the '40s setting, these scenes looked as if they'd been filmed in an '80s Asian disco, and the captive nurse seemed rather implausibly to be enjoying her sexual servitude.

'They had to appeal to the sexploitation crowd back then,' Renton whispered.

Meanwhile, the hero was serving as a bomber pilot over Europe, and his handsome picture was being used to sell war bonds. His plane was shot down on a mission, and the captive pilot was presented to Adolf Hitler, who wanted to use him for propaganda purposes. The Australian pilot patriotically refused. Hitler raged, 'If I can't have your beautiful face, nobody can!' On the spot, horrifyingly, the pilot's face melted like a candle.

'I didn't know Hitler had face-melting powers,' Adam said. The special effects looked suspiciously like the ones from *Raiders of the Lost Ark.*

When the disfigured hero was sent back to the Allies, his commanding officer turned away in disgust, a single tear rolling down his cheek. The CO phoned Winston Churchill: 'Bloody hell, mate, his face looks like a burnt chop that a dog's been chewing on.'

Now a hideous freak, the hero travelled home from the war. On the troop ship, he met another soldier, who shyly revealed his ambition to be a sculptor. 'I used my hands to kill. Now I want to use them to create.' Sensing a fateful opportunity, the wounded hero invited the young soldier to stay with him and his wife – who had been blinded in Hiroshima – in their country town. There, the sculptor would model the husband's original face so that his wife could still feel the sculpture and love him for who he was, not the monster he had become.

There followed a lengthy montage of the hero running his hands obsessively over the sculpture in progress, demanding it be resculpted. 'More handsome. More beautiful.' As Adam and Renton watched, the sculptor began to fall for the hero, seeing beyond his ruined face to the beauty within. The saxophone hooted seductively on the soundtrack as the sculptor and his subject gradually discovered a tender love for one another, pushing the poor, bewildered wife away.

'After Hitler finished with my face, there wasn't much left,' the hero was lamenting.

'Hasn't Hitler done enough evil in the world?' snapped the sculptor. 'Now the mongrel wants to ruin our happiness!'

'Mate, Hitler made a mess of Europe. He even made a mess of my face. But if he hadn't ruined my face, we never would've got together. And when I feel the love between us – a love Hitler helped create – I can't help thinkin'... that Hitler bloke's all right.'

Adam looked speechlessly at Renton.

Renton shrugged. 'Most cuts don't have that line. This must be the director's cut.'

'Who directed it?'

Renton consulted the masking tape on the side of the film canister. 'Orson Reich.'

Onscreen, the wife had discovered her husband's infidelity by overhearing the two men's groans of passion. At this point the film's soundtrack seemed inappropriately loud. Adam looked at the exit; this would be an awkward moment for some wandering cinema patron to burst into the theatrette.

When he turned back to the screen, the wife was running tearfully across a moonlit paddock.

'No! Let her go, mate,' the sculptor was saying.

Adam said, 'He should go after her. She might trip over something. Isn't she blind?'

Renton nodded. 'I guess she's seen the truth now.'

Apparently not that bothered about his lost wife, the disfigured pilot adjourned with his sculptor lover to the local pub, arm in arm, as the music swelled triumphantly.

Inside, a local yelled out, 'Are youse blokes poofs?'

'We're in love!'

'Not according to the social mores of Fifties Australia, you ain't!'

Adam watched, appalled, as the two lovers were brutally bashed to death. 'Jesus!' he blurted.

Renton nodded in satisfaction. 'This film makes some really bold tonal shifts.'

When the wife – returned from her night lost in the bush – was called on to identify her dead husband, both he and his lover were so mangled that she couldn't tell them apart by touching

their faces. She decided to bury them in the same grave. 'He's...
he's beautiful,' she sobbed. 'They both are.'

In the film's grim coda, she visited their grave only to find
the headstone had been defaced. 'I'm sorry, missus,' said the
old cemetery groundskeeper, removing his battered bush hat
and holding it against his chest. 'We'll clean the graffiti off.'

'What does it say?' she said.

He paused, dramatically. 'Bum chums.' He looked away, a
tear rolling down his wizened face.

'No, leave it!' she said. 'I'm proud of what they were. They
were majestic.'

Fade to black, and an intertitle: 'Being a bum chum remained
illegal in Australia until 1983. This film is a plea for tolerance.'

Adam flipped on the house lights and turned to Renton.
'There is no fucking way we are screening that abomination
in public.'

'Don't you see? This is what's gonna happen to you!'

'Someone's going to write "bum chum" on my grave?'

'No! When you've got the gift of looks, it can be taken from
you at any moment.'

'I think I'm pretty safe from Hitler at this stage.'

'But anything could happen! Do you want to spend the rest
of your life like a fuggo, thinking of all the women you could've
banged?'

'I don't "bang" women.'

'Maybe that's the problem! You *should* be bangin' 'em!
Bangin' 'em 24/7! Bangin' 'em like a dunny door! Do you know
how embarrassing it is when people ask me about you? I have
to tell them, "He's bangin', but he doesn't bang," know what
I mean?'

'What is your point, Renton?' Adam checked his phone.
Three missed calls from Cate.

'The point is, you're a good-looking man and you should be
taking full advantage of those looks. Otherwise you'll end up

with a face like a burnt chop a dog's been chewing on, and the only one who'll touch you is some stupid sculptor who doesn't realise being gay is illegal in Fifties Australia.'

'That seems awfully specific.' Adam lifted his phone to his ear. 'Hi, Cate,' he said, getting up from his seat. 'Sorry I missed your calls. I've just been watching this ridiculous, offensive film. And you will *never* guess who directed it. How's your day going?'

As Adam walked out, Renton tried one last, desperate salvo. 'Ditch her and start having sex with other women!'

Adam looked back. 'No.'

28

'So what's the big news?' Cate said.

'In a second,' Kirsty said, rummaging in her handbag. She pulled out an empty white wine bottle and tossed it over her shoulder. She was aiming for the bin behind their usual corner table, but today, the bottle landed in a pram. A woman nursing a baby glared at Kirsty before pointedly removing the bottle.

'What the fuck are all these yummy mummies doing here?' Kirsty said, shaking her hair disdainfully. They didn't usually meet up at Café Nom Nom on weekdays, and it seemed their abandoned weekend hangout turned into a childcare centre during the week.

'Maybe they're trying to recapture their happy child-free days of the late aughts,' Cate said.

'Then why did they bring their kids?'

Vanessa was picking her way elegantly through the gridlock of prams and strollers. 'Sorry I'm late,' she said. 'What did I miss?'

'Okay, guys,' said Kirsty, her face serious, 'I wanted you to be the first to know... I'm going into rehab!'

'Oh, thank god!' Vanessa said.

'It's the right thing to do,' nodded Cate.

'Just joking!' Kirsty said. 'I'd rather die than live without booze.'

'Well, dreams do come true,' Vanessa said.

'Good one, Kirsty,' Cate said. 'So what's the real deal?'

'I got a promotion!' Kirsty said in triumph.

'That's great,' Cate said.

'Wonderful news,' said Vanessa.

'Yeah, it just came out of fucking nowhere,' said Kirsty. 'Now I'm officially Head of Strategic Capability.'

'What does that mean?' said Cate.

'More money. A bigger office. A hunkier assistant...'

'So...' Cate said, 'they just promoted you?'

'It was the weirdest fucking thing,' Kirsty said. 'I got an urgent email telling me to go up on the roof of my building with a walkie-talkie and wave either a red flag or a white flag, depending on what I was told on the walkie-talkie.'

'How did you even get to the roof of your building?' Vanessa said. 'I didn't think that skyscraper even had a roof – just a shiny, pointy thing.'

'Turns out there's a hatch on the side,' Kirsty said. 'It was all explained in the email. Anyway, I hung out there all afternoon in the wind, waving flags. And when I got back, there was a note on my desk saying I'd been promoted to Head of Strategic Capability.'

'Hmm...' said Cate.

'What kind of place do you work for?' Vanessa said.

'Your work is just the fucking same!' Kirsty retorted. 'Didn't you get a promotion once for emptying a vending machine?'

'I didn't empty the vending machine,' Vanessa said, tapping her nails on the table. 'I had to program in a fifteen-digit code, and the machine emptied itself. Then I had to put one can back.'

Cate frowned. 'How did you do that?'

'Believe me, it wasn't easy.'

'Mummy,' piped up a small child, pointing at Kirsty, 'why does that lady smell like Uncle Boozo?'

'Shh, we don't call him that name outside the house,' the mother replied. 'And Uncle Boozo smells like scotch. That woman smells more like Bacardi Breezer.'

'It's Bombay Sapphire!' said Kirsty, sniffing experimentally at the fabric of her dress as the woman pulled a protective arm

MEL CAMPBELL AND ANTHONY MORRIS

around her child. 'What kind of example is she setting for her kids?'

'Lay off the kid stuff,' Cate said, 'I really want to talk to you guys about something.'

'Are *you* going into rehab?' Kirsty said.

'I'm serious. Are you guys in the League?'

'What the fuck?' Kirsty looked confused.

'No!' Vanessa said. 'Why would you even think that?'

'I don't know,' said Cate. 'You organised a stadium riot to break up my relationship?'

'That was a spur-of-the-moment thing,' said Kirsty. 'Anyone could've done it.'

'The League are trying to break me and Adam up. You're trying to break us up. Join the dots.'

'It's totally different,' Vanessa said. 'We wanted you to break up because we didn't want you to get hurt. We're not part of some evil organisation trying to destroy your happiness.'

'What,' said Cate sarcastically, 'so you're not part of the League because you had good intentions?'

'Exactly,' Vanessa said. 'We want you to be happy. They don't. That's why they're evil and we're your besties.'

'Yeah, besties before testes!' added Kirsty.

Vanessa nodded. 'Well said, Kirsty.'

'But the League are women too...' Cate said, confused.

'Look, we want you to be happy!' Vanessa repeated. 'And a big part of happiness is not getting hurt.'

'By Adam's big part!' added Kirsty.

Vanessa rolled her eyes. 'Not helpful, Kirsty.'

'No, screw you, Vanessa,' Cate said. 'Kirsty's right.'

'That'd be a first!' Kirsty said.

'Adam's got a "big part"?' Vanessa said.

'His part is none of your business. But at least Kirsty's making jokes about it! She gets that Adam and I actually have a relationship. Why can't you? I'd rather you made fun of us than tried to break us up. At least if you were making jokes I'd know you accepted that we were together.'

Vanessa didn't answer.

'Look,' Cate said, 'I'm not stupid. I know Adam's amazingly good-looking –'

'Fuck yeah, he is,' Kirsty said. 'It's not even possible for someone to be that good-looking.'

'Not helping,' Vanessa said quietly.

'I know women throw themselves at him,' Cate continued, 'I've got an entire League of them trying to break us up. And I know I could get hurt. But isn't love about putting yourself out there?'

Kirsty laughed. 'Putting out is pretty important.'

'Shut up, Kirsty!' Cate looked pleadingly at Vanessa. 'Look, I need you guys to support me. I'm really freaking out about this League. You swear you're not involved?'

Vanessa raised her hand solemnly. 'I swear.'

Kirsty raised hers. 'Fuck!'

'Near enough,' Cate said, her lower lip trembling. 'I need you guys to have my back.'

'Hur hur! *Back.*'

'How is that even funny, Kirsty?'

'I'm just trying to be supportive.'

Vanessa was looking off into the distance, blinking fiercely. 'Are you crying?' Kirsty said.

'It's just this stupid mascara,' Vanessa said. 'It's irritating my eyes. I'm totally never buying it again.'

Cate held her arms out. Vanessa didn't quite fall into them, but their hug was definitely more emotional than usual.

'I know you were just looking out for me,' Cate said softly.

Vanessa nodded into her shoulder.

'Hug it out, bitches!' said Kirsty.

Vanessa carefully wiped her eyes. 'So, did you really spend your whole weekend away freaking out about the League?'

'Not the whole weekend,' Cate said. 'Adam had a good time. His film won first prize.'

'And did *you* have a good time?' said Kirsty.

'There was this one girl who kind of freaked me out,' Cate said. 'Debra. She was Adam's ex, I think, but I never got the full story. She might've been part of the League too.'

'A hometown ex! Of course,' Vanessa said. 'Was she pissed off that he dumped her?'

'That's what I thought at first,' said Cate, 'but now I think she might have dumped him.'

'Inconceivable!' Kirsty said. 'Was she even hotter than him?'

'She just looked... normal,' Cate said. 'Pretty, I guess. Basically, she was really mean.'

'Mean to you?'

'To Adam. She didn't care about me. Nobody in that town did.'

'Sounds like a pretty crap weekend.'

Kirsty rapped her knuckles on the table. 'Let's get back to Debra,' she said. 'I just don't get why she would have dumped Adam. Is there something wrong with him you're not telling us about?'

'No,' Cate said. 'I don't get it either. Adam is... well... Adam. Wouldn't he be the one who ended all his relationships? Maybe I'm jumping to conclusions.'

'Maybe she's gay,' Vanessa suggested. 'Did she try and hit on you?'

'No! She's married. Not that that means anything. And she's married to Adam's best friend. He's almost as good-looking as Adam.'

'Didn't you say before you left that Adam's best friend was some guy named Ugly Joe?'

'Turns out everyone's ugly compared to Adam.'

29

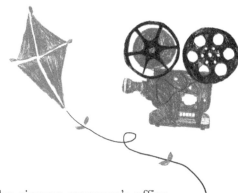

The phone rang. Adam was in the cinema manager's office, checking his roster for the next week. 'Rafferty Cinema, how can I help you?' he said.

The voice on the other end was confident and forthright. 'May I speak to the manager?'

'He's not in right now,' Adam said. 'Maybe I can help.'

'My name is Art Saunders,' he said. 'I'm calling on behalf of Edible Films.'

'Are you the same Art Saunders who works for the Aperture Film Festival?'

'Uh, yes...'

'I just sent you guys my film,' Adam said. 'It's called *Metadata.*'

'Yeah,' Art said. 'Don't get your hopes up. A lot of scenester wankers have made short films this year.'

'But are they any good?' countered Adam.

'Look,' Art said patiently, 'with this kind of festival, it's all about the big names. If nobody's heard of you, we're not the place to start.'

'Oh,' Adam said, deflated.

Art noticed his disappointment. 'That doesn't mean it won't get in,' he said, 'but it probably won't.'

'Well,' Adam said, 'on that cheery note, how can I help you?'

'We're scouting for locations for an upcoming feature film.'

'Isn't Edible Films the production company behind the *Consumption* movies?'

Art sighed. 'Look, keep that under your hat. We don't want the set mobbed by squealing teens.'

'Yes,' Adam said earnestly. 'I've been there.'

Art laughed.

'So, you need a cinema?' Adam said.

'We need a cinema and a lobby for a night.'

'Depends when, and I'll have to check with management,' Adam said, 'but I think that's doable. Maybe call back after three?'

'Sure, I'll do that. So,' he said, not unkindly, 'you fancy yourself a bit of a filmmaker, then?'

'I'm working on it,' said Adam.

'Well, if we do end up filming there, make sure you introduce yourself to me. We're always looking for runners and assistants.'

'Oh, okay,' said Adam, trying to hide his excitement. 'That'd be great, Art.'

The line went dead. Adam began to dial Cate's number, but paused. News like this was better delivered in person.

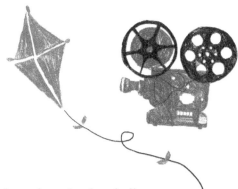

30

Cate was lying in bed thinking of Adam when the doorbell rang. Actually, she was thinking of Adam in a way that probably would have led to something more than thinking, so to say she was annoyed at the interruption would have been something of an understatement. She'd even started humming her special wanking song: the soundtrack to an artfully edited mental movie of Adam's greatest hits. 'Gettin' it on to a song, going strong and long,' she sang to herself. 'Down to get the friction on.'

'I can hear you!' came a voice muffled by the front door.

'Oh, shit!' Cate muttered to herself. Then, louder, 'I'm just doing... the vacuuming!'

'Can't hear a vacuum!' the voice said.

'Of course you can't! Sound doesn't travel in a vacuum,' Cate yelled back, hurriedly pulling on a pair of tracksuit pants.

'I don't think that's how science works.'

'That's how my vacuum works.'

'What did you say? That's how your *vibrator* works?'

Ugh, Cate thought. *Only one person would be that crude through my front door.* She flung it open and glared down at the idiot standing on her front step.

'Hello, Alistair.' Her eyes had trouble adjusting to the aggressively bland palette of his outfit, from the beige jumper draped over his shoulders to his even more beige chino pants. On reflection, the jumper was lemon, while a faint blue stripe on the beige shirt only accentuated how offensively neutral the whole ensemble was.

Seeing her checking out his clothes, he smirked. Cate was horrified to realise she was wearing the exact same outfit she'd been wearing when he saw her last. Defensively she folded her arms across her chest to hide the RUM PUNCH slogan.

'Sorry to interrupt,' Alistair said, still smirking. 'Going by that song, I'm guessing your current boyfriend is leaving you high and dry.' He raised an eyebrow. 'Well, maybe not *dry*...'

Cate rolled her eyes. 'Why are you here, Alistair? I thought you never wanted to see me again.'

'Well, maybe I was a little hasty. We had a good thing together. Maybe I was wrong to throw it away.'

From behind his back he pulled an ostentatious bouquet of roses. Cate ignored the flowers.

'We did not have a good thing together. And you were more than happy to throw it away.'

'Going by what I just heard, it doesn't sound like anyone's rushing to pick it up.'

'I'm perfectly happy with my boyfriend,' Cate said. 'Do I have to go there with the whole, "He's so much better in bed than you are" thing? I mean, he is. Way better than you. But it seems kind of mean to say that. I will, though, if you don't hurry up and tell me what you came here for.'

'I thought maybe we could go out. Coffee?' He shook the flowers in her face, as if they were a magic totem.

'We never went out for coffee. You never bought me flowers, either. What makes you think I would want to get back together with you?'

'I made a mistake. I shouldn't have been so... whatever. You know... that thing...'

'No. I don't know. What thing? Are you apologising?'

'Apologising for what?'

'For being a jerk? For making me feel like shit pretty much every second I spent with you? Like I was just a step on the ladder you were climbing?'

'But we can climb that ladder together, baby!'

Cate laughed. 'What, do you need a date for some event, and no woman in her right mind will lower herself to being your arm candy?'

'Oh, I've got no problem getting dates, baby.'

'Sure. And that's why you're stinking up my doorstep.'

'Those chicks don't mean anything to me! They were just jizz jars.'

Cate's mouth fell open. 'Oh my god.'

'You know what I mean! They're just for a good time. But you were for a long time.'

'Yeah. Every date felt like a thousand years.'

'See!' Alistair said. 'That's what I miss! That wit! Those zingers!'

'You hated my zingers. You hated my wit. You hated how I dressed. You hated how I looked. Come to think of it, there wasn't anything about me you didn't seem to hate. Why on earth would you possibly want me back now?'

He shrugged. 'Just accept that I do, babe.'

'Why should I?'

'It's a man's prerogative to change his mind.'

'No, it's a *woman's* prerogative to change her mind. I certainly have. I can't believe I even felt terrible for being dumped by you. I'm putting all that behind me. And that's not *all* I'm putting behind me.'

Alistair looked confused. 'I have a new boyfriend now,' Cate said, condescension dripping from her voice. 'We're having lots of sex all the time, and it's really good. Especially compared to the pathetic two minutes of flailing you used to call "making love". I have zero interest in whatever you're trying to do here, Alistair.'

She took a step back and prepared to shut the door. 'Wait!' he said desperately. Cate paused, with the door half closed. Alistair gestured desperately with the bouquet. 'Babe! I...' He turned to look at a bush in Cate's front yard. The bush shook violently. '... love you?'

The bush rustled approvingly. It was Cate's turn to raise a quizzical eyebrow. 'What's in the bush?'

'That depends,' he said, grinning. 'What would you *like* in the bush?'

Cate pushed him away and strode into her front yard. 'Out you get,' she said forcefully in the direction of the bushes.

For a few seconds, there was silence. Then, a petite blonde woman emerged sheepishly from behind the offending shrubbery. 'You!' Cate said dramatically.

'And me too,' said a taller woman, picking leaves out of her silky black hair.

'I should've known the League was behind this,' Cate said.

'You're right to fear us!' said the blonde.

'Yeah, nah,' Cate said. 'I should've known it was you because this scheme was rubbish.'

'Hey!' protested Alistair.

'Why did you think I wanted to get back with *him*?' Cate said, jerking her head contemptuously in Alistair's direction. 'He's rubbish too. Why would I dump Adam for this bag of crap?'

'Who truly understands the ways of the human heart?' the blonde said, folding her arms as she glared at Cate. 'You're the one who went out with him in the first place.'

'So what, you thought that I was still nursing a flame for *him*? After I'd been with Adam for months?'

'I'm standing right here,' Alistair said.

'Yeah, and seeing you again only reminds me of why I'm glad to be rid of you.'

She turned back to the blonde. 'I don't know why I spent a single solitary second worrying about what you had planned if this is the best you can do. Fuck off, and take your trained monkey with you.'

'So, am I still going to get the polo membership?' Alistair

said to the blonde. 'I totally carried out my side of things, right? It's hardly my fault if all her taste is in her mouth.'

'You shall get... nothing,' the blonde said. 'Results are all we are interested in.'

'What if you take a bunch of photos of me and her together?' Alistair said, scurrying over to stand by Cate, who winced in horror. 'Then you can send them to this guy you're obsessed with, make it look like we're back together, he'll dump her and I get my club membership.'

Cate laughed. 'You might be that stupid, but Adam isn't. You know, in a real relationship there's a little thing called trust.'

'You're fooling yourself if you think what you and the Hot Guy have is a real relationship,' the blonde said. 'He's a god, and you're...' she waved a hand limply in Cate's direction, 'you.'

'Yeah babe,' Alistair said, 'sometimes in life you've got to settle. That's why they call it "settling down".'

'You'll find out why they call it "throwing up" if you don't get away from me,' Cate said.

The brunette League lady looked to her leader. 'I think we should go.'

The blonde ignored her. 'You will never defeat us!'

'I think I just did,' Cate said. 'Taste the pain!'

'This was a waste of time from the start,' said the brunette. 'Anyone could tell she'd never give up the Hot Guy for this no-neck loser.'

Alistair defensively tugged the collar of his shirt away from his ears.

'I can't believe I was crouching in that bush for an hour,' the brunette said. 'I'm going to get a coffee.' She walked off.

Cate watched in satisfaction. 'Looks like your little secret society is falling apart.'

'Cut off one head and two shall take its place!' the blonde said defiantly.

'I'm not sure how that'll work,' said Cate. 'It's not like

Adam's going to be sleeping with anyone else. Without him as a recruitment tool, you won't get any more footsoldiers. And it looks like they're losing heart. Whereas the only thing I'm losing is the ability to sit down.'

Everyone winced. 'Too far?' said Cate.

'Just a little,' said Alistair.

The blonde tossed her hair. 'The Hot Guy's still a man,' she said ominously. 'How long do you think you can keep him interested when wave after wave of hot chicks are constantly crashing against him? Every woman in this town could be one of us. You'll never know who to trust. We'll penetrate the wall you throw up around him, don't worry about that. And once we do, you'll be nothing to him but a distant memory.'

Cate was silent. The blonde threw her head back and laughed triumphantly. 'You know it's true!'

'Sounds like a win to me,' said Alistair. 'Where's my polo membership?'

Ignoring him, the blonde walked away. Alistair held out the bouquet of roses imploringly. 'Lunch next week?' he said to Cate.

She shut the door in his face.

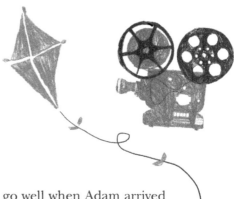

31

She knew the date wasn't going to go well when Adam arrived fifteen minutes late. He didn't even have a real excuse – he'd been held up talking to someone at a bus stop, and he hadn't even been catching the bus. She realised that not only was he almost always a few minutes late to everything, he also never seemed all that fussed about it.

They were seeing a movie. It was something they did a lot. Adam loved watching movies, and had to see a lot of them for his work. Cate was happy to tag along, even though most of the movies they saw weren't to her taste. Tonight they were seeing a film titled *Toxic Waste Gangster*, an Indian film Adam had been talking up to her all week. Cate was intrigued rather than excited; it seemed an odd title for a film full of dance numbers and brightly coloured saris, but maybe this was a Bollywood take on *West Side Story*? She'd find out soon enough.

'What's wrong?' Adam said as they queued for their tickets.

'You could have told me you were running late,' she said, annoyed at how petty she sounded.

'It was only fifteen minutes,' said Adam, sounding more confused than anything else. 'I didn't realise it was such a big deal.'

'Well, the movie starts at 7 p.m.,' she said. 'We want to get there in plenty of time to get a good seat.'

'And then we'd just be sitting around for fifteen minutes doing nothing.'

'Well, I was sitting around for fifteen minutes waiting for you.'

'Sorry,' he said, giving her shoulder a squeeze, 'I didn't realise. I'll do better next time.'

'Right,' Cate said. She didn't believe him. Everything about him said that he thought *she* was the one with the problem. *He's probably never had anyone annoyed to see him in his entire life*, she thought. He could turn up two hours late, and all he'd have to do was smile and it'd be forgotten. This was just part of who Adam was, and there was no point trying to change him. *It's not worth arguing about*, she thought. Then she realised one day they probably would have that argument, and she squeezed into his shoulder, feeling just a little older than before.

Adam bought the tickets from a blushing teenager. Cate couldn't help rolling her eyes at Adam's unconscious flirting. *Guess it worked on me.* Once you noticed it, Adam's flirting was a constant thing, a steady layer of charm he spread over every social interaction. It wasn't just that he was attractive physically; his personality was just as hot. He was attentive, with a genuine interest in other people, and he had a way of making you feel you were the centre of his world. Until he focused it all on someone else…

For the first time she realised exactly why her friends were worried for her. She knew it was silly, but seeing Adam flirt with the ticket teen made her feel mean and jealous – hurt that, even for an instant, there was someone else in his spotlight. She didn't like feeling this way, and she wondered how much worse it would be if he ever left her.

'You're going to love this,' Adam said as they walked over to the candy bar, 'It got five poo-splosions from BackedUpToilet.com.'

'What kind of website is that?' Cate said. 'Is it just for shit films?' Adam didn't answer. 'I still think we should have gone to that tear-jerker instead. I really liked the first one.'

'*My Dead Baby: Cradle 2 The Grave*?' Adam sighed. 'How good could it be? They've already started making *My Dead Baby 3: The Trouble With Triplets*.'

174

'Have they?' Cate said excitedly as Adam bought a pair of choc tops. 'How can one family have so much bad luck?'

'It's a time travel story now,' Adam said, 'they go back in time to save the first baby or something.'

'Aww,' Cate said, 'the first one was really good. I really felt for that dead baby.'

'Sure,' replied Adam, 'that was kind of the whole point. You don't win Oscars by being subtle.'

'And *Toxic Waste Gangster* is?'

'It's a multifaceted look at life in today's India!'

'Sounds great,' Cate said.

Adam sighed, not believing her for an instant. 'You'll see,' he said, as they walked into the cinema.

The cinema was dimly lit but not packed, and by the time they found their seats the first lot of commercials had begun. After the public service announcements and ads for local restaurants, there was a stern warning about the use of mobile phones during the screening.

'Threatening to decapitate us seems a bit much,' Cate stage-whispered.

'Shh,' said Adam, beating three other people to it.

'Jeez,' Cate muttered to herself, 'the movie hasn't even started yet.'

The first trailer they saw started with a hitchhiker standing by the side of the road, waiting. He was clearly meant to be poor, wearing shabby clothes while a stream of giant black SUVs roared past. Suddenly he flung himself into the path of one vehicle. Cate gasped in shock as the SUV turned the hitchhiker into mincemeat, mowing him down without slowing.

His backpack lay discarded by the side of the road. It was blue with white stars and, as they watched, rivulets of blood flowed towards it, forming a grotesque parody of the American flag. The screen went black; the word *America* appeared in huge white letters.

'What is it with these hippie films and blood?' Cate whispered.

'Shh,' Adam said.

The next trailer largely involved a well-preserved French actress (Catherine Deneuve? Cate wasn't sure) wandering around Tuscany ogling some studly farmhand who didn't seem to own a shirt. It was called *Autumn Flowers Bloom Twice*, everyone laughed at this and Cate didn't know why.

'I read,' Adam whispered, 'that in French the title is *Fuck Me Hard with Your Steel Plough.*'

'Oh,' Cate said, suddenly much more interested.

The final trailer looked like a grim British kitchen-sink drama that had been filmed with mud on the lens. Cate was surprised to find she recognised the male lead.

'That's Baird Parkhouse from *Toff Squad!*' she hissed excitedly, 'I loved their last single, it was –'

Onscreen, Baird suddenly had his teeth knocked out with a brick. 'Time to put that lovely-jubbly arse of yours to work,' a cockney gangster sneered as he kicked at the teeth scattered on the floor, 'the Tooth Fairy won't give you enough for those to keep your bruvva out of borstal.'

Onscreen the title came up: *Gums*. The trailer ended on a close-up of Parkhouse's mashed face while an old crone giggled, 'Cheer up, matey – givvus a smile.'

'That looks great,' said Adam.

'Yeah, if you're a dentist,' said Cate. The cinema darkened; the feature presentation began.

One hundred and ninety-five minutes later Cate staggered out of the cinema, with Adam close behind.

'What did you think?' he said carefully. Cate didn't answer, heading directly for the exit. He followed, waiting until they were on the street outside the cinema before speaking again. 'I thought it was really powerful.'

'Yeah, a really powerful laxative,' she muttered. He looked at her blankly. 'Because it gave me the shits,' she explained.

'I thought you'd really appreciate the way Mr Mukherjee struggled so hard to provide for his family in a climate of near-total corruption.'

'The film was called *Toxic Waste Gangster*,' Cate said.

'Yes,' Adam said, not sure where she was going with this. Around them the crowd leaving the cinema had thinned; soon they were the only people left on the footpath. 'Did you want to get a coffee?'

She shook her head. 'It was three hours of some weedy guy in an office filing paperwork!'

'To illegally dump toxic waste! He was doing it for his family!'

'But what about the part where he had a barrel left over so he had to take it home and his family ate it?'

'That was symbolic of the toxic taint of corruption. They thought it was curry!'

'Slurry curry?'

Adam smiled. 'Okay, they may have stretched the metaphor a bit far there.'

'And that ending, after he died – what did he even die from, shame or toxic waste?'

'His head exploding at the orphanage was a symbol of the corruption eating away at Indian society!'

'Whatever. Why did his whole family end up working at a call centre? Even the baby?'

'I guess you just don't get symbolism,' Adam said.

'I do when it symbolises a giant waste of time,' Cate said.

Adam looked up and down the empty street, looking for an excuse to change the subject. 'Sorry if you think hanging out with me is a waste of time,' he said.

'That movie certainly was.' Cate glared at him. The conversation was firing her up rather than releasing her tension. 'Did you even need me to come with you for this? We weren't spending time together, really. You didn't ask me if I wanted to see this film – you just announced we'd be seeing it tonight.'

'You said you were fine with seeing it,' Adam said.

'Because I trusted you to take me to something that wasn't shit. Are you even interested in anything that isn't a movie?'

'I'm interested in you,' he said.

'If you were really interested in me, you would've known that this kind of movie isn't anything I'd want to see.'

'Well, I know that now,' he said, then smiled apologetically. 'Look, I'm sorry. I thought you'd like it. You can pick the movie next time.'

'Good,' she said. Adam held her gaze. 'Good,' she said again, her anger slowly being replaced by embarrassment at her pettiness. 'I'm interested in you too.'

'And movies are part of who I am,' Adam said.

'Yeah, well, going to the toilet is part of who I am, but I don't invite you along every time.'

'Maybe this wasn't the best movie for us to see together,' Adam said.

'Sometimes after a long day I just want to relax and see something fun. That movie was hard work.' She looked at her watch. 'And I have to get up in eight hours.'

'Sorry,' Adam said, 'We'll see something more fun next time, promise.'

She nodded, and took a step closer to him. He smiled, just a little, and leant down to kiss her lightly on the lips. 'Was that our first fight?' he said.

'That was hardly a fight.'

'It felt like a fight to me,' Adam said.

'Aww,' Cate said, 'you must have had a sheltered childhood.'

As she said it, she realised it was true: despite his parents' best efforts, he must have grown up in some kind of… beauty-powered bubble. No one would have fought with him; no one would have disagreed with him. Who would want to see that face look sad?

'Adam,' she said, 'what's the deal with you and Debra?'

'Why?' he said, wincing at how defensive he sounded.

'I saw you two back at Ladbroke. You weren't afraid to fight with her.'

'You say that like fighting's a good thing.'

'It's not. But when I see you getting all worked up like that about a woman you're not even with, how am I supposed to feel?'

'Like I love you.' He took her hand. 'Like I never want to fight with you.'

Now was her chance to clear this up once and for all. 'Then tell me about Debra.'

'There's not much to say. We dated for a while. It didn't work out.'

That wasn't enough. 'If that's the whole story, you wouldn't have been fighting like that. Plus, she married your best friend! She's always going to be around.'

'That's not my decision.'

She had to put it out there. 'But surely after you dumped her –'

Adam interrupted. 'I didn't dump her.'

'But...' Cate said. 'I don't...'

'She dumped me,' Adam said.

'Okay, but...' Cate shook her head repeatedly. She'd suspected as much, but it was still a shock that someone could have dumped the Hot Guy. 'She... left... *you?*'

'Yeah,' Adam said. 'Debra's always known what she wanted out of life. It's a ladder you're always climbing, and I wasn't climbing fast enough for her. I wanted to make films. That didn't fit in with her plans. She just needed a guy with a steady job – and that wasn't me.'

'Wait,' Cate said, 'She dumped you because... you didn't make enough money?' She didn't want to say that anyone who looked like Adam could easily make a fortune as a model. Or a stripper. Or a stripper-slash-model. Maybe it was model-slash-stripper? And now she was thinking about Adam wearing those tearaway pants – oh wait, he'd started talking again.

'Well, not really,' Adam said. 'It was more that she couldn't understand how important filmmaking was to me. She'd work all day then come home and yell at me for doing nothing. But I'd been watching movies! For research!'

Cate could imagine herself yelling at Adam after a couple months of that. Suddenly she saw Adam through Debra's eyes: a man getting by on his looks, sitting around in PJs all day watching action movies and expecting to make up for it all with a smile.

'She kept calling me a shiftless loser,' Adam said, starting to sound like the younger, couch-bound version of himself. 'But if *she* was going out with a loser, wouldn't that make *her* the real loser? But then she dumped me. Then she became a winner.'

'She married a guy named Ugly Joe,' Cate said. 'She's not that big a winner.'

'Nah, they're good together,' Adam said. 'But every time I see Debra, it's like she brings it all back. I'm happy for her and Joe. Why can't she be happy for me?'

'What does she say?'

'Ah, you know. Keeps asking if I've got a proper job, am I saving money, have I met anyone serious. Why does she even care? She's the one that dumped me.'

'That doesn't mean she doesn't care about you,' Cate said. 'It just sounds like you were on different paths.'

'I guess,' Adam said. 'She was so serious about the future.'

'Aren't you?'

'Of course I am. I want to make movies! My whole life has been working towards that. But that wasn't a serious career to her. She kept talking about backup plans.'

'So,' Cate said, distractedly, 'you're not interested in serious girls?'

'I'm interested in you,' Adam said with a smile.

'That's not an answer,' Cate said. She hesitated before continuing. 'Do you take me seriously?'

Adam realised that what he said next was going to be very important. 'Sure I do,' he began, unsure of where the traps were in this conversation. 'You're my girlfriend. I see who you are, and I love you for it.'

'But do you see me as the kind of person that you could take seriously?'

'Of course,' he said, grabbing at the lifeline she had thrown him. 'Our relationship is –'

'No, not the relationship,' she said, annoyed. 'Me. Am I a person you take seriously, or am I just some silly ditz who makes stupid jokes and acts like an idiot?'

'Is that how you see yourself?'

'Sometimes I worry that, deep down...'

'I take you really seriously,' he said.

'Really?' she said, wanting to believe him.

'Really,' he said. 'And your jokes aren't stupid. They're really funny.'

'I just worry,' she said. 'I worry that people don't respect me. Just because I like making jokes, it doesn't mean I want to be one.'

'I don't think you're a joke,' Adam said, pulling her close and hugging her. After a moment she hugged him back.

'Thank you,' she said. 'I know it's silly, but I just wanted to hear you say that.'

'Why are you worried that people don't take you seriously?' he said. 'You know so much about your work.'

'I make a point of knowing everything. I want to be good at my job. That way no one can say I'm a ditz.'

'Who would call you a ditz?' he said. 'Do your friends call you one?'

'No,' she said, surprised. 'Why would you think that?'

'Well, I've never met them,' he said. 'For all I know they're the ones treating you like shit.'

'No!' she said. 'They're very supportive. Well, they're very

181

supportive now – for a while there they thought you were just going to use me and break my heart.'

'What?' Adam said. 'I would never do anything like that.'

'They didn't know you,' Cate said.

'They still don't,' he said.

'We'll have to change that. It's my fault; I've been so preoccupied with doing Ursula's job on top of my own. But I really want you guys to get together, I think you'll really like them. And you should bring your friends.'

Adam looked like he'd just eaten a toxic waste curry. 'Uh, maybe not,' he said. 'They can be a bit much.'

'Not the Ladbroke lads. I meant those guys from the cinema,' she said. 'They seemed... okay?'

'They kept telling me to break up with you.'

'Why?' Cate looked worried. 'Do you think they were right?'

'Renton's never been right. He thinks the Teenage Mutant Ninja Turtles sank the *Titanic*.'

Cate laughed. 'Don't worry, I don't want to be besties with them. I just think it'd be nice to meet them properly. They're part of your life, and so am I.'

'Sure, let's organise something some weekend. Bring your friends to the movies, that's a safe introduction. Wait, do they like movies?'

'Not if they're like *Toxic Waste Gangster*... I know!' Cate said excitedly, 'Vanessa loves the *Consumption* series.'

'Uh, okay,' Adam said. 'We're still showing *Consumption 2: Combustion* on the weekends...'

'Great,' Cate said. 'We'll have to watch the first film to get caught up.'

Adam sighed.

'Aw, c'mon,' she said with a laugh. 'Are you too cool to watch a chick flick?'

'I love chick flicks. I love all cinema. But...'

'But you'd rather watch a *good* film?' She laughed. 'Maybe it'll turn out to be a good film?'

'Not likely.'

'Maybe,' Cate said playfully, 'you'll end up making a *Consumption* film! There are still two more books in the series.'

Adam groaned. 'Not likely.'

'Why not?' Cate said. 'It's about a love beyond love.'

'What? That makes no sense.'

'Well, they love each other, and... I guess they just... keep going?'

'Isn't it enough to just love someone?'

'Aw,' Cate said, touched. 'You old softie.'

He kissed her. 'Love you,' he said.

'Love you too.'

32

The lights came up in the boardroom. 'And there you have it,' Cate said. 'This is an opportunity to stake your claim to the place that brings the whole city together.'

A murmur of approval rippled around the table. Even the oldest, greyest bankers seemed more lively after Cate's spirited presentation.

'Gentlemen,' John Brunner said smugly, 'If you need more time to think about it –'

'We don't,' said the lead banker, who had the bulging eyes and lipless smirk of a salamander.

'– too bad,' Brunner continued. Everyone laughed. 'No, seriously, we need to know today.'

'We're on board,' the lead banker said, leaning across the table to shake Brunner's hand. Brunner's wince at the clammy reptilian grasp was barely noticeable. 'Send the contracts over,' said the banker, 'and we'll get them back to you by end of business.'

'Sounds good,' Brunner said, standing. 'Gentlemen, lunch is on me.'

'Sounds messy,' said Cate. Everyone laughed, even Brunner – eventually.

With the bankers gone, it was just Cate, Isaac and Hugo left around the table.

'That was really impressive work,' Hugo said.

'Thanks,' Cate said. 'The video did most of the heavy lifting.'

Isaac shook his head sadly. 'Yeah, the video didn't suck,' he said.

'Thanks,' Cate said, surprised that he was complimenting her.

'It's not a compliment,' he said. 'This place should be a temple to sport, not some banker's plaything.'

'It is a temple,' Hugo said. 'One of those shitty Greek ones that fell down.'

'There'd be nowhere to play your precious sports without the money those bankers are going to give us,' Cate said. 'Not that we need to bother with sport now anyway.'

'We don't?' Isaac said.

'Once we can afford to fix up the toilets and the collapsed stand, we can get re-licensed to hold serious concerts,' said Cate expansively. 'A few of them and we can renovate all the stands, then we can start holding big public events, live arena spectaculars, the Dalai Lama... the Pope... Jamie Oliver...'

'Gladiators?' Isaac snorted.

'Isaac,' Cate said heavily, 'no one likes sport.'

Hugo laughed.

'It's a sports stadium,' Isaac shouted.

'*Was* a sports stadium,' Cate said. 'The future is big spectacular events, not some guys kicking a ball around.'

'The future,' Isaac said. 'You're talking a lot about the future for someone who has no future.'

'What?'

'Ursula's back any day now. The future's her job. *Your* future'll be all about making sure the corporate boxes have got enough wine.'

'And your future will be the same as always: selling what Ursula and I give you to sell.'

'I'm the one who has to deal with the public,' Isaac snapped. 'People in the real world do like sport.'

'Well, they don't want to come here for it. Great job, Isaac.'

'That's not my fault. If we invest properly in sport, the fans will reward us. If we build it, they will come.'

'If we fix the toilets they'll come,' Hugo said.

'Look,' Cate said. 'We needed sponsors, I got us sponsors. End of story.'

'Did you ever find out how to pronounce their name?' Hugo said.

'Didn't have to. Turns out they changed it last week. Now they're Cash Money Brothers Financial Services.'

'Cash Money Stadium,' Isaac groaned. 'Fuck me.'

'No thanks,' Cate said, 'I've got a boyfriend. Whom I really should be calling to thank for his work on the video.'

'He did do a good job,' Hugo said. Even Isaac nodded.

Cate took out her phone. 'Ooh, an email,' she said excitedly, tapping it open. 'It's from the bank... blah blah blah... I'm awesome... Oh! They want Adam's details – they want to offer him some corporate promotion work to go with their rebranding...'

She stood. 'Pardon me if I go outside and make the kissy noises to my boyfriend in private.' She walked out the door and down the corridor towards her office for her jacket. She probably wasn't going to make kissy noises to Adam, but she was really excited about what had just happened – both for her and for him – and the last thing she wanted was any of her co-workers listening in.

It wasn't like she could get any privacy inside; she could hear someone messing around in her office. She slowed her pace, not wanting to barge in if it was Brunner, pissed off if it was anyone else. But the snazzy stilettos resting on her desk pretty much ruled him out – the shapely legs wearing them confirmed it.

'Ursula,' Cate said.

'Glad to hear you remember my name,' Cate's boss said, standing up and moving in for a hug. 'What did I miss?' she said, kissing Cate on both cheeks.

'Well,' Cate said, putting her phone on her desk, 'we just had a big meeting with a –'

'Bo-ring,' Ursula said. 'What did I miss with you? Did you get over your shit boyfriend?'

'Who, Alistair? He's history. Ancient history. Dinosaurs ate him.'

'Good to hear. You can tell me all about it over drinks tonight.'

'Tonight? Sorry, I can't. I'm meeting my new boyfriend – I was just about to call him.'

'New boyfriend? You move fast.'

'It's been two months.'

'Has it?' Ursula shook her head. 'They didn't even have clocks where I was.'

'They don't have clocks in Monaco?'

'They don't have clocks at the pokies. Just joking,' she said, seeing Cate's horrified expression. 'But the time did fly.'

'Well, I'm glad you're back.'

'No, you're not.' Ursula smiled. 'You're about to go back to being the assistant. And just when you've brought in the biggest sponsor this stadium's ever had.'

'Why didn't you come into the meeting?' Cate said.

'You didn't need me. I just came in to get my stuff.'

Cate frowned. 'Aren't you back yet?'

'I'm not coming back at all. I was just using up my holidays before I quit this dump.'

'Quit? That's great!'

Ursula laughed.

'I mean, great for you.' Cate grabbed Ursula's hand. 'What are you going to do now?'

'I lined up a job with Ilyn Payne, the headhunters. Turns out I'm really good at bringing people together.'

'You can say that again,' Cate said.

'What?'

'Oh, nothing,' said Cate. 'So when are you finishing up?'

'Already finished,' Ursula said. 'I gave my notice two weeks ago. Didn't they tell you?'

'Obviously not,' Cate said, thinking of the one hundred and twelve unread work emails in her account.

'Well, now you know. Something else you need to know: I'm totally going to recommend they give you my job.'

'Wow, really? Thanks.'

'You've basically been doing it for the last year anyway,' Ursula pointed a finger slyly at Cate, 'don't think I didn't notice. You're the most capable person here.'

'What, more than Darren the Jumbotron guy?'

'I'm serious,' Ursula said. 'You do good work, and you should be rewarded for it.'

'Thank you,' Cate said. 'That means a lot, coming from you. Want to get lunch?'

'I'd love to,' Ursula said, 'but I've got to wrap things up here. If I can get it all done today, I'm outta here.'

'No worries,' Cate said, 'I've got to call my boyfriend anyway. But we're definitely having farewell drinks.'

'Already arranged it, Friday night at Bar Up.'

'Oh god,' said Cate, 'I never want to go back to that meat market.'

'No boyfriends allowed – no, wait, bring your boyfriend, I want to meet him.' She smiled. 'Sounds like we've got a lot to get caught up on.'

33

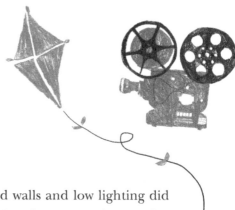

Bar Up was a dump. Black-painted walls and low lighting did little to disguise the dirt and stains that covered every flat surface. Rumour said it had once been a disused underground public toilet that the council had concreted over, but demented hipsters had tunnelled into it from the basement of the burnt-out shopfront across the road. The music was loud and the booze was cheap – well, cheap if it really was what it said on the walls; expensive if it was the turps everything tasted like. You could pick up someone without seeing their face or hearing their voice. Ursula had been coming here on and off for the last five years.

It was open all night until 9 a.m., but Cate wasn't going to last that long. She'd be lucky to last until 9 p.m; even with Vanessa and Kirsty running drinks from the bar to the corner where she was holed up with Adam, this bar was not her idea of fun.

'Where did you find out about this place?' Adam shouted. 'It's pretty dark in here.' Cate nodded; that was actually one of the few things she liked about Bar Up. It was so badly lit that the other patrons couldn't see how hot Adam was, which meant they all left him alone. Well, almost all: a bright burst of light illuminated Adam's face as Vanessa held up her phone.

'Look at those cheekbones,' she said loudly to Kirsty. 'You could butter bread with those.'

'Yeah, his butt's great,' Kirsty shouted back. 'So are his cheekbones.'

'I'd totally bone him too,' Vanessa yelled. 'He's so hot.'

'Guys, can you chill the fuck out?' Cate said, looking around furtively. 'Don't call him the Hot Guy. If I can hear you, so can Adam. Plus, Ursula doesn't know.'

'Is Ursula even here?' Kirsty said.

'I think she might be out the back.'

'She's scoring smack?' Vanessa said, just as there was a lull in the music. 'Is Scozza here?'

'Who's Scozza?' asked Adam.

'Fuck no,' Cate said under her breath.

Vanessa's face grew wistful. 'When I first saw him here, under the lights – well, there weren't any lights, but I saw his outline as the kitchen caught fire – Scozza took my breath away. And my purse. I ran after him, but he was waiting for me... Well, he was passed out in the gutter. But he looked so beautiful once I cleared away the vomit...'

'Why couldn't the music have drowned that out?' Cate sighed, scanning the room again for Ursula while Adam rested his hand on hers. She hadn't realised until now that he was still just 'the Hot Guy' to her friends.

'Next round's on me!' Cate said. Maybe giving them some time alone together would get Adam and her friends talking.

'Try and get my drink spiked!' Kirsty said.

'Kirsty!' said Cate, shocked.

'What? This stuff's weak as piss! And may very well *be* piss.'

'I will not get your drink spiked for you.'

'Wait 'til Scozza gets here,' Vanessa said. 'Then you can spike your own drink.'

The next track kicked in, loud enough to send glasses jumping on the tables. The room was crowded with black-clad students and the occasional dishevelled office worker, all yelling to be heard. Shoving her way through the throng, Cate approached the bar. It was a solid slab that, upon closer inspection, seemed to be a chunk of wall scavenged from a building site. She stood there patiently, staring intently at the bartender, hoping some kind of psychic connection would form that would tell him to look her way and take her order.

'You're gonna have to do more than that, babe,' said a voice next to her.

'Sorry?' she said. The speaker was a rugged, outdoorsy-looking type, with red, roughened skin and blindingly white teeth. He wasn't bad-looking for a guy in his forties, she thought, and briefly wondered how Adam would age. Would he fall apart? Would his heat fade as he grew fat, turning from a bright yellow sun to a bloated red giant? That astronomy class she'd taken in high school was still paying off.

'You got to work it,' said the outdoorsy type. 'Shake what your mama gave you.'

'My rape alarm?'

He laughed. 'Might as well set it off. I've been waiting here ten minutes.'

She rummaged in her purse. The outdoorsy type watched closely. 'Guess this'll have to do,' she said, taking out a reddish rubber object that – once she flattened it out – was obviously a whoopee cushion. 'What?' she said, seeing his surprised look. 'I bought it to put on my boss's chair but then I chickened out.'

'Was it a rubber chicken?' he said. Cate groaned.

'I don't usually do this in front of strangers,' she said, blowing into the rubber balloon. Once it was inflated she held it up. 'Ready?' He nodded. She brought her hands together around the cushion. It let out a satisfyingly prolonged facsimile of a fart.

'Jesus,' shouted someone at the other end of the bar, 'who dropped their guts?'

The bartender turned. 'It was her,' the outdoorsy type said, pointing firmly at Cate.

'Gee, thanks,' she sighed.

The bartender glared at them, waving a hand in front of his face as he shook his head. 'Guess I didn't really think this through,' she said. 'Maybe a fart isn't the best way to get a guy to come over.' She quickly held up the whoopee cushion. The bartender didn't look impressed, but shuffled down their end of the bar. She put in her order; the outdoorsy type ordered a rum and coke.

'Don't worry, darl,' the outdoorsy type said as the bartender turned his back on them with a sneer, 'I wouldn't kick you out of bed.'

'You'd never get me in bed.'

'More of a back alley type? I can dig it.'

'Sorry, I don't date older men.'

'I'm twenty-four!'

'Jesus,' she muttered.

'It's a tough life down at the plant,' he said. 'We had three spills in the last month. And that's just on me!'

'Um, okay. Where do you work?'

'ToxCo,' he said with pride. 'You know the stuff they use to get rid of bodies at murder scenes? We make that!'

Cate wondered if he meant it was used to clean up at murder scenes, or whether it was the stuff murderers used to dissolve corpses. She decided not to ask.

'We also make Nature's Kiss Pure Health Water,' he said. 'I drink it every day.'

'If you're that health-conscious, I'm surprised you come here.'

'Are you kidding? This place is like a detox.' The bartender dropped a rum and coke in front of him, the thin greenish fluid sloshing onto the bar.

'Aaaah,' he sighed, tipping the glass's contents down his throat. 'That hit the spot. You wan' another?'

'Sorry,' Cate said, collecting the drinks the bartender had just placed in front of her. 'I've got to get these back to my friends.'

'Sure, sure,' he said. 'Look, if you ever want me to sniff ya farts for real –'

'No,' Cate said firmly.

'– here's my card,' he continued, as if she hadn't spoken. He held up a greasy business card. Cate shrugged – her hands were clearly full – but before she could turn away he stuffed the card down her cleavage, as if swiping it in an EFTPOS machine.

Unable to dislodge the card without dropping the drinks, and with the outdoorsy type staring bluntly at her cleavage to see what she'd do, she turned and said loudly, 'I hope they can cure your penis leprosy in time.'

Several patrons turned their heads.

'My dad had that,' someone said. 'Now he's me mum.'

'That's horribly transphobic,' said a young student type.

Cate didn't look back. Weaving her way through the crowd, she managed to deliver the drinks to her table largely intact. The music was even louder in the corner; Cate handed out the drinks without speaking, and if anyone got the wrong one they didn't seem to mind.

This time she sat at the other end of the group, next to Kirsty, discreetly slipping the card out from her cleavage as she sat. 'Hey, have you been talking to Adam?' she said. 'I really want you guys to get to know each other.'

'Have we been stalking Adam?' said Kirsty, frowning.

'No! I want you to talk to Adam. It's really important to me that you get along.'

'Get a bong?' Vanessa said. 'Maybe Scozza can sort us out later.'

'No!' Cate said. 'You've got to get past seeing him as just "the Hot Guy". There's so much more to him than his looks.'

'He's a sook?'

'Scozza's not a crook!'

'Listen to me!' Cate shouted. 'I've never told him that a group of women on the internet call him the Hot Guy! He's got no idea! His parents were crazy people who never treated him differently because he was hot!'

'He's got a yacht?' Vanessa seemed impressed. 'It just keeps on getting better.'

'He's a really nice guy!' She glanced towards Adam at the far end of the table. 'He'd be horrified if he found out that women were just using him for his hotness! Please don't say anything about what we were doing in that bar. I really love him!'

Everyone looked at Cate. The music had cut out – presumably someone had spilled their drink in the jukebox again – just as Cate had declared her love. She turned to Adam, who was smiling sweetly at her.

'Aw,' he said, 'I love you too, sweetheart.' He got up and walked over, sat down beside her, and they kissed.

Kirsty threw up noisily into her handbag. 'That's not a comment on your relationship, guys,' she said, wiping at the corner of her mouth. 'Well, maybe a little.'

'I'm pretty sure the drinks here are a mixture of methylated spirits and antifreeze,' Vanessa said reassuringly. 'Don't take it personally, Adam.'

Adam was still staring into Cate's eyes. He brushed a strand of hair from her face. 'I don't want anything to come between us,' he told her softly.

'You don't want anything to come out of your penis?'

'Kirsty,' Vanessa said, 'we can all hear them clearly now.'

Cate wasn't even paying attention. 'We'll be together forever,' she told Adam, stroking his cheek. 'Nothing can come between us.'

'Hey ladies,' said Ursula, appearing suddenly from out of the gloom, 'which one of you invited the Hot Guy?'

'Who's the hot guy?' said Adam.

'Uhhh... just some joke... from... around the office...' stammered Cate. 'Forget it. It's nothing. Ursula's drunk. And a bit crazy.'

'Ursula?' The name seemed familiar to Adam. He studied Ursula's face, then smiled. 'Ursula!' he said, more confidently.

'How's your mum? You said you had to go... repair her? Because she was... a robot?'

'Silly boy,' Ursula said. 'I just said that to spare your feelings.'

'Okaygreatthanksbye,' said Cate.

'Why did you have to spare my feelings?' said Adam.

Ursula looked at him with pity. 'I didn't want you getting attached – it wouldn't be fair to the next girl.'

'Next girl?'

'Well, the next girl who wanted to hook up with the Hot Guy.'

Adam looked at Cate. 'Weren't you talking about a Hot Guy before?'

Cate's mouth opened, but she had no idea what to say.

'C'mon,' said Ursula in a world-weary tone, 'we both know why you're at that cinema bar every Friday night. And we're grateful, really we are. You're performing a wonderful service for womankind.'

'Maybe dudes too,' Kirsty slurred.

'No, just ladies,' Vanessa said. 'I asked Cate.'

'Did everyone know this?' Adam said. 'That I was providing a... "service"?'

Everyone except Cate nodded.

Adam turned to Cate. 'Is that all I was to you?' he said. 'A... service provider?'

'We used to call you the ISP,' Ursula said. 'Intercourse Service Provider.'

'No!' Cate said. 'I mean, maybe at first, when I went to the bar – but then I –'

'You used me,' Adam said grimly. 'You all used me.'

'I didn't,' said Kirsty. 'I mean, I was gonna... when Cate had finished with you. But she never did.'

'And what, you all just see me as some kind of dumb stud?' said Adam. He turned to his horrified girlfriend. 'Cate, were you ever going to tell me about any of this?'

'I didn't want to hurt you,' she said. 'Once I got to know

MEL CAMPBELL AND ANTHONY MORRIS

you, I knew there was so much more to you than that. I didn't want you to find out –'

'Find out what? That everyone's talking about me behind my back, like I'm a… hunk of meat?'

'Hunk is right,' said Kirsty. Vanessa elbowed her in the ribs.

Adam's expression had hardened. 'Like I'm just a *thing* you could play with then throw away.'

'What does it matter how we got together?' Cate said. 'We're together now.'

'No. No, we're not.' Adam looked around, his face a mask of disgust. 'I've got to go save the president,' he snarled.

'What?'

Adam didn't answer and he didn't look back.

'Thanks, Obama,' Kirsty said.

'I hate to see you go, but I love to watch you leave,' Ursula said dryly.

'Fuck you guys,' Cate said through tears. 'Adam was right.'

'Obama's not even the president any more,' Vanessa said, putting an arm around Cate. 'Good one, Kirsty.'

'He'll get over it,' Ursula said, 'he's just enjoying the chance to be the one doing the walking out.'

'No,' Cate said sadly. 'You don't know him at all.'

34

Adam stomped down the street, furious and humiliated. It wasn't just that Cate had lied to him. His entire world had been turned upside down. When strange women would reach out to touch him as he walked past, he'd assumed that was a touchy-feely thing city women did. But now he realised they just wanted a piece of the Hot Guy. His extremely reasonably priced rent suddenly seemed suspicious. So did that huge discount on his new couch. What about all those old ladies who stood up for *him* on public transport? Or that time a politician dropped a baby to kiss him? On the mouth, too. He'd just thought the guy was passionate about his policies.

'Hey babe, wanna party?' A bottle-blonde woman was standing in the pool of light beneath a street lamp, her makeup twenty years younger than her face. She was wearing hotpants, boots, a fur jacket, and smoking a cigarette.

'No thanks,' Adam said.

'It's a freebie, hon,' she offered.

Adam shook his head and kept walking.

'I'll pay you!' she shouted behind him.

Once, this might have been flattering, or even amusing, but now it was like a knife in his heart. Had his whole life been a lie? What privileges had his looks bought him? Free drinks in bars? Free drinks in cafés? Free drinks at the movies? Free drinks at church? Free drinks at the service station?

He walked past a busker who was strumming some sad, noodly indie-rock song and keening disconsolately. As soon as he spotted Adam, however, the busker began to bust out lewd guitar licks, thrusting his hips and dropping suggestive lyrics. 'Shake it!' he expostulated. 'Grind that pepper!'

A local wino, slumped on a park bench, sat up and began to fan himself. 'Good gracious!' he growled. 'That ass is bodacious!'

'Shut up!' Adam yelled.

Even a day ago, he would have been charmed by the colourful street life of the big city, but now he realised they were only responding animalistically to his hotness. He'd always known society valued good-looking people, and he wasn't stupid – he knew he was better-looking than average. But he'd figured he had more to offer the world than just a pleasant face. He'd seen himself as just one of countless attractive guys in the city. Now he knew he was *the* guy. The Hot Guy. He ran all the way home.

An hour later Adam finally opened his front door. He could have got a taxi – seven or eight had stopped at random, asking if he needed a lift – but even they were just reminders of the burden he was cursed to carry. The burden... of hotness.

Maybe now he could lose himself in a good movie. He cast an eye over his DVD collection. He was among friends here. At least they wouldn't judge him on his looks. Movies respected him for who he was inside. He grabbed a movie at random. '*Some Like It Hot?* Ugh!' He tossed it aside.

As Adam scanned the shelves, other titles leapt tauntingly out at him. *Hot Fuzz. Wet Hot American Summer. Heat. Hot Rod. The Hot Spot. White Heat. Hot Shots. Cat on a Hot Tin Roof. Hot Pursuit. Hot Tub Time Machine.* '*Hot Tub Time Machine 2?*' he groaned. 'Oh, man.'

His phone rang again. He didn't need to look at it to know it was Cate. She'd called four times already on his walk home, and he had no intention of speaking to her. Briefly he tried to imagine a time when he would speak to her again. Everyone was wearing jetpacks and living in bubbles under the sea. It was the far distant future. Even then, he was still mad at Cate.

How could she have done this to him? He'd thought they'd grown so close, but she'd never even told him the real story of how they met. He thought their meeting had been a happy chance, but her creepy friends had set it all up, stalking him for who knew how long. How many women were part of their sick, twisted club, monitoring his every move?

He buried his face – his horrible, gorgeous, irresistible face – in his hands. How could he know anything about their relationship any more? Surely if what they'd had together had been real, she would have at least *mentioned* the fact that he was the Hot Guy? Why hadn't she told him why she'd come to the cinema bar? She must have known that being known across town as the Hot Guy would be a huge deal to him. Why had she let them live in a house of lies, with a door made of falsehoods, and windows that looked out onto a sham?

Adam sat down heavily on the couch. Why was he being so flippant? That was something Cate would do. Everything was a joke to her, he mused bitterly. He hadn't registered until now just how much he'd taken on her silly way of looking at the world. He felt like shit, and there wasn't anything funny about that.

He wanted to talk to someone. Maybe not Renton and Steve – they'd just laugh, and probably fist-pump and high-five, and then say 'Pew pew pew,' and then talk about comic-book superheroes, and ask when Adam was going to come out on the town with them again. He wasn't up for that. Not yet. He started to dial Ugly Joe's number, but even seeing the words 'Ugly Joe' on his screen made him flinch. Joe wasn't ugly. Thanks to Adam, his best friend had been given a cruel nickname – and he'd never realised exactly why it was cruel until now.

Adam had never felt so lonely. There were hundreds of movies on his shelves that had nothing to do with hotness. Adam grabbed one at random and looked at the cover. *Better Off Dead*, it said over a picture of a young, befuddled John Cusack. *How appropriate*, Adam thought as he shoved it into the DVD player and 'Savage' Steve Holland's directorial debut began to play. It was just noise in the background, but at least it was better than being alone.

35

Cate downed her seventh margarita of the night. 'I love you, Adam!' she sobbed.

Kirsty looked worried. 'I think you'd better slow down,' she said.

'I think your *face* had better slow down!'

'Come on,' said Ursula. 'Let's get you home.'

'Nooooo, I've gotta call Adam again!'

'I don't think he's gonna pick up,' Vanessa said.

'He probably *has* picked up,' Cate shouted, 'some slut.'

'Adam wouldn't do that to you,' Kirsty said, rubbing Cate's back soothingly.

'You wouldn't know what Adam would do to me – he did heaps!' Cate said. 'And I loved every second of it! I want everyone to know about our love. We did butt stuff.'

A couple of hipsters at the bar looked over with interest.

'Time to go,' Ursula said firmly, taking Cate's arm. Kirsty took the other arm, while Vanessa nudged Cate from behind. She was so drunk she could barely put one foot in front of the other. They ended up dragging her out the front door.

'Taxi!' shouted Ursula once they were standing on the street. She sighed. 'This would be much easier if Adam were here. Taxi drivers love him.'

'I love him!' Cate moaned.

At last a cab pulled up to the kerb. Kirsty got in first and guided Cate inside. Vanessa climbed in after her, while Ursula took the front seat.

'Where to, ladies?' The driver was an older woman.

'Adam's house!' Cate blurted.

'Not Adam's house,' Ursula said firmly.

'You wouldn't want to interrupt him while he's banging,' said Kirsty helpfully.

'Nooooo!'

'Shut up, Kirsty!' said Vanessa.

'Well, it's true.'

'Darl, let him blow off some steam,' Ursula said.

'Among other things!' Kirsty said.

Vanessa opened her mouth. 'I know,' Kirsty went on, 'I should shut up.'

'Have you worked out where you want to go yet?' said the taxi driver, not unkindly.

'Back in time!' Cate shouted.

'Can someone who's not drunk please give me directions?'

Vanessa gave her Cate's home address. 'We'll be making three more stops after that.'

Ursula twisted in her seat. 'Cate, the best thing you can do right now is go to bed.'

'With Adam?' she said hopefully.

'No, hon. With a big glass of water. Maybe a couple of painkillers. Just pretend this whole night never happened.'

Cate was beginning to snuffle quietly. Kirsty stroked her friend's hair, then, absently, her own. 'Can you make Adam forget, too?'

Her friends exchanged a worried glance. 'Do you really want him to see you like this?'

She whimpered again. 'I just want to see him,' she said in a small, choked voice.

'You will,' soothed Vanessa. 'I promise, things will look much better tomorrow.'

Cate closed her eyes, resting her head on Kirsty's shoulder. After a minute, she began to snore.

'Is your friend all right?' asked the driver.

'She broke up with her boyfriend tonight,' Ursula said, over the soft noises of Cate crying in her sleep.

'Men,' scoffed the taxi driver. 'They're only good for one thing.'

'What's that?' said Kirsty excitedly.

'Opening jars.'

Kirsty nodded solemnly. 'I haven't had a guy open my jar in weeks.'

Vanessa leaned forward. 'Do you think it was our fault? At least a little bit?'

Ursula shook her head. 'Absolutely not. Cate knew the deal. She really should have mentioned the whole Hot Guy thing to Adam months ago. He probably would have thought it was funny.'

'We warned her this would happen,' said Vanessa.

'She's a big girl,' Ursula said. 'She can handle this. Now she's had the Hot Guy, she can have anyone she wants.'

'I think,' Vanessa said, 'that she just wants Adam.'

'Back of the queue!' said Ursula. 'She was a fool to think he was ever hers. No one woman can expect to own a guy like that.'

'You might see it that way,' Vanessa said, 'but Adam didn't think he was the Hot Guy. He was just a guy. And I think he was really in love with Cate. You could just tell.'

'Ugh.' Ursula rolled her eyes. 'Love is like... bad medicine.'

Cate stirred in her sleep. 'But bad medicine is what I need,' she muttered.

'See?' Vanessa said. 'They're in love!'

'Love means nothing. It's just an excuse for throwing your life away,' said Ursula in exasperation. 'You think I didn't have feelings for the Hot Guy? We all did. He's awesome. But we knew the deal. We knew that if we gave him our hearts, he wouldn't even mean to break them. But he would. That kind of hotness... it's a force of nature. It's like a tidal wave. You just ride it once, and then you get the hell out of the way.'

'No,' countered Vanessa. 'Adam wanted a real relationship. It's sad to think all these women just used him for sex. Cate was the only one who saw him as a person. She never even talked about his looks.'

Kirsty scoffed.

'Well, no more than usual. She wasn't obsessed with them. It was all kindness this...'

'... and giant penis that...' chipped in Kirsty.

Ignoring her, Vanessa continued. 'I think she's shattered. It just makes me really sad thinking they won't be together anymore.'

'Maybe they'll get back together,' volunteered Kirsty.

'Nup,' Ursula said. 'That Humpty Dumpty's never getting back on that wall. He's so smashed they're serving him as an omelette at the Heartbreak Hotel.'

'You almost sound pleased,' Vanessa said.

Ursula shrugged. 'Better it end now, rather than in two years when she's got a hot bun in the oven, and Adam's frolicking with five bikini babes off the coast of Ibiza. What kind of life is that, being the single mum of a hot baby?'

'Adam wasn't like that,' Kirsty said. 'He had no idea he was even regular hot, let alone super hot.'

'And it wasn't just that she'd managed to hook a hot guy,' added Vanessa. 'They were really in love. Both of them, with each other. I mean, her face used to light up just thinking about him. And he was so good to her...' she trailed off wistfully.

'You know what I think?' said the old lady taxi driver.

They all nodded.

'I think we're letting too many Muslims into the country.'

'Um, you can let us out here,' said Ursula.

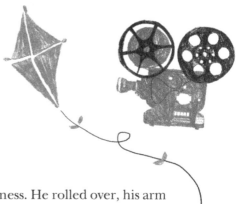

36

Adam drifted slowly into consciousness. He rolled over, his arm stretching into the space Cate should have been occupying. *Where is she?*, he wondered fuzzily. Then it all came crashing back. The bar. Cate's friends. Her betrayal.

He squeezed his eyes shut again. He knew if he looked around, everything would remind him of her. He couldn't face that, not yet. Last night he'd been furious at Cate, but now all he felt was a dull weight in his chest. He hadn't been this low since his break-up with Debra. But it was worse this time. It had come out of nowhere, and destroyed everything he and Cate had.

And yeah, it was worse this time, because he was the Hot Guy. Everyone had known except him. Humiliation flooded through Adam as he imagined all the conversations those women had been having about him, the way they'd deliberately converged on the cinema bar with only one thing on their minds. He'd been having innocent knock-off drinks with his friends while they'd been sizing him up, sharing lurid descriptions of what they could expect, and comparing the sordid details afterwards. And when he met each one of them, he'd stupidly thought he might be meeting someone he could share his life with. Every time, he'd thought *she* could be the one.

He'd thought Cate could be the one.

All the terrible excuses women had lobbed at him over these past months were running through his head now.

'I've got to save the president!'

'I just found out my mum's a robot!'

'I've only got five minutes to live, and I don't want to leave you with my corpse!'

'I have to go buy some oranges!'

'I don't know how to read, and I've gotta go learn!'

'My cat has become a mysterious stud!'

With a groan, Adam got out of bed. He caught sight of his reflection in the mirror on the back of the bedroom door, and paused, trying to see himself through someone else's eyes. *I'm not that good-looking*, he thought indignantly. *I mean, look at those earlobes!* He tugged on one. *Well, I guess they're all right.* He ran a hand through his hair. *Look at this! What a mess*, he thought. *It's so thick, it sticks up everywhere.* And his skin didn't look so crash-hot, either. *Remember when I used to get pimples?* Adam thought. *Well, it was just the one zit. And that was when I was twelve.*

He turned away in disgust. His face had always been his friend, but now he didn't recognise the person staring back at him from the mirror. Not a person, even – a *thing*, a prize to be won. A conquest to be boasted about. Had anyone ever seen *him*?

What must his parents have thought? Thinking back over his childhood, Adam didn't recall they'd given him any special treatment. Maybe they hadn't realised how hot he was. But then… the way his parents had constantly been going on about how it was important not to judge people by their looks? All those girls hanging around? He'd known he was popular, but having his mates basically live at his place hadn't seemed over the top at the time. He'd thought people liked him because he was a good person. But now he knew they'd never looked past his face.

He wanted to talk it over with somebody. Not Steve or Renton – he'd be seeing them at work tonight. And everybody else he knew in the city had tried to stroke his face at least once. Ugly Joe would understand. No – Joe. No! Tim. He picked up his phone.

'Hello?'

'Oh – hi, Debra, it's Adam. Is Joe, uh, Tim there?'

She laughed. 'Tim? What happened to you? Did you get hit on the head or something?'

'Something like that,' he said wistfully.

'Well, I'm sorry,' Debra said, '*Tim* is out. Doing his job. It's the weekend.'

'Okay, I'll try back later, I guess.'

'Right,' she said briskly, 'I'll tell him you called –'

'Wait!' he said. 'Do you… When we were…'

'*What*, Adam?'

'When we started going out, did you just like me for my looks?'

She sighed. 'Why are we going over this?'

'I just want to know… What did you like about me?'

There was a pause. 'Well,' she said, 'it wasn't like I had to put a bag over your head…'

'Whatever,' Adam said. He took the phone from his ear, though he could hear the buzzing of Debra trying to explain herself. Dully, he stabbed at the phone to end the call.

He wasn't going to get any help from other people. The phone rang in his hand. Ugh, it was Cate again. He flipped it to silent mode. He had nothing to say to her. And her apologies would be empty words, of course – she just wanted another chance to look at him. *Take a photo*, he thought bitterly, *it'll last longer.* Then he remembered all the photos Cate had taken of him. At the time he'd thought it was cute. But now it was just another sign of the fraud their relationship had been, right from the very start.

37

Cate put her phone down. In a way, she was glad Adam hadn't picked up. She was in too delicate a state to have that conversation just yet. But she knew they needed to talk. The longer this went on, the more serious it would get.

She groaned and slumped back against her pillows. On the other side of the bed, Kirsty lowered the book she was reading. The night before, she'd decided to crash at Cate's place to look after her drunken friend, although Cate did not remember agreeing to this. Cate did not remember much of anything after Adam had walked out.

'How are you holding up?' Kirsty said.

'I wish I was dead,' Cate replied flatly. 'And that's just the hangover.'

'You drank seven margaritas,' said Kirsty. 'And I think they made that fucking tequila out of brake fluid and potato skins.'

Cate groaned again. 'Can you get me something to dull the pain?'

Kirsty rattled her hip flask. 'Hair of the dog?'

'God, no,' Cate said, putting her head in her hands.

Kirsty patted her on the shoulder. 'I'll get you some painkillers.'

'They're in the bathroom cupboard.'

Kirsty went to investigate, leaving her book on the bed. Cate glanced at its front cover. 'What the fuck?' she said, picking up the chunky, well-thumbed paperback. '*The Fur Chronicles: Four Legs Good?*'

'It's the omnibus edition of books one to four, plus a bonus collection of the original online fanfic that started the whole thing,' Kirsty called out. 'It's got everything to get you up to speed for the second omnibus volume.'

'What's that called?' Cate jeered, '*Two Legs Bad?*'

'How did you know?' said Kirsty. 'It's fucking amazing.'

'Amazingly bad,' Cate said. 'Is this one of your terrible cat porn books?'

'Look,' said Kirsty, returning to the bedroom with two painkillers and a glass of water, 'these are light-years ahead of those rubbishy *Consumption* novels Vanessa reads. *The Fur Chronicles* is an epic fantasy series following the erotic adventures of humans and the silky cats they yearn to bone.'

'Uhhh...'

'Right now I'm up to the bit where Doctor Meowstophiles has been exiled from the Kingdom of the Cats, just as his evil rival Lord Bright Eyes has seized power and is about to plunge them into a war that none of them can win.'

Cate's eyebrows shot up as she scanned the contents page. '*The Fur Chronicles: First Litter?*'

'That's where it all began,' Kirsty said. 'I've gotta say, though, they're a bit different from what I thought they'd be.'

Incredulously, Cate read out the title of the first story. ' "Help! My Cat Has Become A Mysterious Stud..."?'

Kirsty looked embarrassed.

Cate opened the book to the beginning of this story.

Ellie 'Mittens' Murphy awoke and rolled over with a start. 'Morning, Tom!' she said to her cat, Tom.

She gasped! That wasn't her cat! It was a man in her bed. He was tall and handsome, in a sexy way. But where was Tom? And why was the man purring?

The man opened his eyes. They were the same bright emerald green colour as Tom's. Come to think of it, his bushy hair was the same shiny black colour as Tom's, too. She reached out her hand, and the man butted his head against it, just like Tom did.

It was Tom! He had somehow become human! She lifted the blankets. Human in every way!

Cate skipped ahead. 'This is just filth,' she said.

She was rubbing his tummy, but this time there was more... So much more to rub...

Paging forwards, Cate recited some more story titles: ' "Cat Scratch Fever, Be My Litterbox, Grooming the Bride..." ' She looked up with an expression of distress. ' "Fur Balls..." '

'For fuck's sake, they're not that bad,' Kirsty said defensively.

Cate put her face in her hands. 'They're so bad. Why are you even reading this?'

'It gets better...' Kirsty said.

'It would have to,' said Cate.

'Yeah, it turns into this epic fantasy. There are swords, and magic and stuff. Sure, at first there's the stuff with the other cats. And the litter box – that didn't do anything for me – and then the tragedy of Mr Waffles.'

'What happened to Mr Waffles?'

Kirsty shook her head sadly. 'Neutered.'

'Well, I guess I can't talk,' said Cate. 'Vanessa ended up getting me hooked on those *Consumption* books.'

'And these are so much better! *Consumption* is creepy and weird; these are just about people having sex with cats!'

'At least they're having sex,' Cate said bitterly. 'I'm never gonna have sex again.'

'Don't say that!' said Kirsty. 'There are plenty of mysterious studs out there.'

'I don't want a mysterious stud – I want Adam.' She started to cry.

Kirsty looked worried.

'Just hug me, you idiot,' Cate sniffed. Kirsty scooted over on the bed and put an arm around her friend.

Cate mumbled something.

'I'm here,' Kirsty said, putting her other arm around her. 'I'm here.'

38

Adam looked at his phone. It had been fifteen minutes since Cate's last – unanswered – call. *Typical,* he thought. *She's given up on us already. Clearly I meant nothing to her.*

He could just imagine Renton laughing. 'As if you were even going to answer the phone, dude.'

'I would have,' Adam muttered. 'Eventually.'

Renton shook his head sadly. 'No, you wouldn't. You overreacted last night, and you're overreacting now.'

'I wasn't overreacting! She lied to me!'

'What kind of lie was it – that she secretly thought you were really hot? Sick burn there, dude.'

'What would you know? The only relationship you've ever been in is with your hand!'

'You do realise you're talking to yourself, right?'

'Shit,' Adam said. 'Renton's the voice of my conscience.'

'It would've been Cate,' not-Renton said, 'but you dumped her. Now I'm all you've got.'

'Pfft,' Adam said. 'I'm the Hot Guy. I can get any woman I want.'

'Weren't you just complaining about that? Isn't calling you hot the worst thing Cate ever did to you?'

'No,' Adam said firmly. 'Lying to me was the worst thing she ever did.'

'There are worse things to lie about.'

'She shouldn't have lied at all.'

'What should she have done, then? Told you the next morning she'd only slept with you to get over her old boyfriend?

Like that's the first time that's ever happened in the history of the world.'

'It's not that.'

'What was it, then? Should she have told you when you met that her friends thought you were hot? That's not exactly a crime, either.'

'She wasn't honest with me. Our whole relationship was built on a lie.'

Not-Renton laughed. 'Listen to yourself, dude. She didn't give you the full story when you met – so what? Are you seriously saying everything after that was a lie?'

'It feels like it,' Adam said sadly.

Not-Renton didn't answer. When Adam looked around, he was gone. 'Thank god,' Adam sighed. It'd be bad enough seeing the real Renton tonight at work. And tonight was another one of those awful theme nights. He'd been dreading this one for weeks: they were showing a bunch of fairytale films under the banner of 'Handsome Prince Night'.

Adam's costume was as half-arsed as he thought he could get away with: a shapeless shirt with puffy sleeves and a pair of brightly coloured pants. Looking at the costume now, it seemed laughably modest. That was the old Adam; now he was the Hot Guy.

The first thing he did was tear off all the buttons on the shirt. 'Won't be needing these,' he said. Next to go were the pants; he had a pair that had shrunk in the wash, which would be far more suitable. He'd been meaning to throw them away; the one time Cate had suggested he try them on he'd literally blushed at how skin-tight they were.

Looking at himself in the mirror, he looked more like a slutty pirate than a member of a royal family. 'Eh, near enough for the Hot Guy,' he said. His back story would be that he was the black sheep of the family who'd run away to sea to have sex with mermaids, or something.

The more he looked, the more exposed he felt. Which was the point after all, but still. Maybe embracing his extreme hotness was going to take more than a single day. He went back to the cupboard and took out a blue bedsheet, fashioning it into a cape. Princes wore capes, didn't they? Plus he could sweep it around to hide his front if need be.

He looked at his phone. No new calls from Cate, and it was time to go to work.

He took one last look in the mirror. 'I look like an idiot,' he said.

'You sure do,' Not-Renton's voice said.

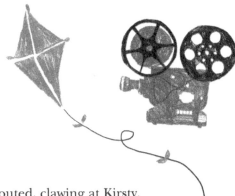

39

'Gimme back my phone!' Cate shouted, clawing at Kirsty.

Kirsty shook her head and scrambled down towards the foot of Cate's bed. 'It's for your own fucking good,' she said once she was safely out of reach. 'He knows you want to get in touch. Now it's up to him to return your...' she looked at the phone, 'seventeen calls? Jeez, show some fucking self-respect.'

'You don't understand,' Cate wailed. 'Adam is really hot!'

'No duh,' Kirsty said.

'But I never realised what that means!'

'Um, we did try to tell you. That stadium riot was a bit of a fucking giveaway.'

'But when I was with him I never thought of him that way.'

'Never?'

'Okay, maybe a bit at first. But being with him, he was just so loving... I never had to think about him going off with someone else.'

'Well, maybe you should've,' Kirsty said.

'But he wouldn't have! I felt so safe with him. He never even looked at other women.'

'Fuck, we were looking at him.'

'I mean, I know he *noticed* other women, but there was never anything lustful about it. He just likes women. And he loved me.'

Kirsty shook her head. 'He still loves you.'

'No,' Cate said, 'you saw his face last night. I've ruined everything.'

'Hardly.'

'I'm serious,' Cate said loudly. 'He's amazingly hot, women stare at him every time he leaves the house, and now he's got no reason to say no every time some slut tries to throw herself at him.'

'Like you did,' Kirsty said under her breath.

'Only because you guys told me to!'

'Well, he hasn't been "the Hot Guy" for a few months now. Maybe everyone's forgotten about him.'

Cate stared hopefully at Kirsty.

'Okay, maybe not. But he's not going to have hooked up right away. Is he working tonight?'

'Yes,' Cate sobbed. 'And it's Handsome Prince Night at the cinema!'

'Oh,' Kirsty said. 'That's not good.'

'He is going to be covered in women,' Cate wailed. 'He'll have forgotten I ever existed by midnight. I'll have turned back into a pumpkin.'

'You were never a fucking pumpkin,' Kirsty said. 'And he's going to be *working*. He'll find it pretty hard to do his job if he's covered in women.'

Cate sniffed.

'Plus, you know the kind of women who go to a cinema for Handsome Prince Night? Little kids, middle-aged women having a girls' night out, and sad spinsters.'

'Like me?' Cate sighed.

'Don't be fucking stupid. I'm saying that even if Adam wanted to move on, there's not going to be anyone there half as good as you.'

'You're saying Adam wants to move on?'

'I'm saying you're safe, at least for tonight. So stop calling him. And don't even think about going to the fucking cinema looking for him tonight.'

'But he's so hot,' Cate said.

'He'll still be hot on Sunday.'

'I don't want to risk it.'

'It's more of a risk if you do go there tonight. What are you saying to him – that you don't trust him alone for twenty-four hours? What kind of relationship are you going to have after that? And if he does cheat on you after one night apart, then maybe he isn't so hot after all.'

'But I want him back.'

'Give him time to want you back too.'

'I guess,' Cate said, not sounding convinced.

'Look,' Kirsty said, leaning over to where *The Fur Chronicles* lay discarded on Cate's bed. 'How about I make you a cup of tea before I go, and you can spend the night curled up in bed with a good book?'

Cate laughed bitterly. ' "Good" might be stretching it.'

But she took the book from Kirsty's outstretched hand as she left for the kitchen, opened it and began to read.

40

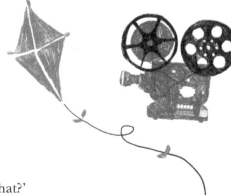

'What the fuck,' Renton said, 'is that?'

'What?' Adam said, stuffing his bag in his staff locker at the cinema.

Renton pointed at Adam's costume. 'It's Handsome Prince Night, not Homeless Prince.'

'At least I came as *a* prince,' retorted Adam, gesturing at Renton's purple crushed-velvet jumpsuit and frilly white shirt, 'not *the* Prince.'

Renton adjusted his pompadour of Jheri curls. 'Hey, Prince *was* a handsome guy.'

'And that wig looks like a dog that got run over while having sex with another dog.'

'You can talk! What have you even got on? Is that a… bedsheet?'

'It's my cape,' Adam said defensively.

'What happened to the buttons on your shirt?'

'Tore 'em off.'

'And those pants don't even fit.'

'They show off my junk,' Adam said.

'They make your junk look *like* junk.'

Steve Rogers swanned into the storeroom, wearing a ridiculously elaborate eighteenth-century military uniform that featured at least three sashes, enormous epaulettes and kilometres of gold braid. Two swords thumped against the buff-coloured breeches that clung to his thighs.

'Ladies, please!' Steve said mildly. 'Control yourselves. You're meant to be princes.' His expansive gaze settled uncertainly on

Adam. 'At least... *is* that your costume? I'm guessing your realm is yet to invent buttons.'

'Whereas your kingdom is...' Adam looked more closely at Steve's chest. 'Are you actually wearing a high-school sports trophy?'

Steve's hand went protectively to a small statuette of a footballer. 'Princes always wear medals,' he said. 'Everyone knows that.'

'Under-fifteens best and fairest?'

Steve nodded proudly. 'Yes, I was the fairest of them all.'

'This says runner-up,' Renton pointed out.

'That's not the point!' Steve said. 'We were talking about why Adam has come dressed as a sexy hobo.'

Renton gasped. 'Sexy? You're back on the market!'

Adam looked away.

'I knew it!' crowed Renton. 'That's why you're putting your junk out there. Because you're putting your junk out there!'

'Someone's hoping it's hard rubbish day,' Steve said.

'Get fucked,' Adam said. 'Can't a man be proud of his... body?'

'Well, you've never cared about that stuff before,' Steve reasoned. 'Every time I've brought up the value of good grooming, you've shut me down.'

'So you *have* dumped her?' Renton persisted. 'We're totally going out clubbing after this.'

'I didn't dump her,' Adam said. 'Well, I did, but it's not like that.'

'But you have broken up?' Steve said.

'Yes.'

'And you did the breaking up?'

'Well, yes.'

'So you did dump her.'

'It's not like that!'

'Um, dude,' Renton said, 'it totally is.' He fist-pumped.

'So, you're single,' said Steve.

Adam sighed. 'I suppose I am,' he said.

'Yesssss…' said Renton, still fist-pumping.

Steve studied Adam's expression. 'Hey, don't worry about it,' he said. 'You're hot enough to make that costume work.'

Adam scowled, but said nothing.

Steve folded his arms across his metal-strewn chest with a loud clang. 'Yeah, you'll be fighting the babes off tonight,' he said. 'The rest of us might as well have stayed at home.'

'Hey!' said Renton. 'This is my time to shine! I was going to do my Batdance!'

'Huh?' said Steve.

'You know,' Renton continued, 'from Tim Burton's *Batman.* It's the original and the best!'

Adam frowned. 'Um, it's neither the original nor the best.'

'Is that all you've got, Renton?' Steve said. 'Prince has other songs, you know. "Little Red Corvette"?'

'"Raspberry Beret",' Adam said. '"1999"? "When Doves Cry"? A thousand more sex jams?'

'Oh,' Renton said. 'I just thought he was the guy who did the *Batman* soundtrack.'

Steve and Adam looked at each other, and then shook their heads.

'Seriously though, mate,' Steve said, 'is this your idea of dressing for the ladies?'

'I don't know,' Adam said. 'Maybe? I've never thought about how I dress. I just thought that now I'm… single, I should, I dunno, make more of an effort?'

Renton laughed. 'And this is what happens when you make an effort?'

'It's Handsome Prince Night!' Adam said. 'I had to dress up somehow.'

'And he's dressing sexy, cos he's gonna get some sex!' Renton said.

Steve looked thoughtful. 'You never bothered before, even before whatsername.'

'Cate,' Adam said automatically.

'Uh-huh. What did she say to you when you broke up?'

Adam sighed. 'Some rubbish story, I dunno. They were all talking about me behind my back.'

'They?'

'Her. Her friends. All the single ladies.'

'All the single ladies?'

'All the single ladies!'

Renton put his hand up. 'Did she want you to put a ring on it?'

Steve shook his head. 'You're getting ahead of yourself, Renton.'

'They all knew about me,' Adam said. 'They knew to come to the bar on Friday nights. They called me... ah, it's silly...'

'What?' chorused Steve and Renton.

'They called me the Hot Guy.'

Steve gasped. 'That was you?'

'Oh god...' Adam said.

'What?' said Renton.

'This guy,' Steve said to Renton, 'is the one every woman in town wanted. I kept hearing about this guy, this mysterious stud. Wondering how I'd ever live up to his reputation.'

'Shit,' Adam said, 'did *everyone* know except me?'

'I didn't,' Renton said loyally.

'Did everyone who was having sex know?'

'Awww...' Renton said.

'I never knew it was *you*,' Steve said admiringly. 'Wow, dude. The famous Hot Guy. I can't believe he was right under my nose this whole time.'

'Yeah, me neither,' said Adam bitterly.

'So we've gotta take this act on the road!' said Renton.

Ignoring him, Steve said, 'You never even suspected?'

Adam shrugged. 'What, that I was the hottest guy in town? What kind of dickhead would think that?'

Everyone looked at Renton.

'What?' Renton said. 'Even I wouldn't think that.'

'But surely growing up,' Steve said, 'you had some kind of an inkling.'

'Well, my parents never said anything,' said Adam. 'That would've been weird.'

'But you were growing hotter!' Renton said. 'Hotter every day!'

'Hotter than the light of a thousand suns,' agreed Steve. 'His father would sit at the dinner table saying, "I am become Death, destroyer of worlds." '

'Well, he *did* say that,' Adam said, 'but I never made the connection.'

'Seriously?' said Renton. Steve looked at Adam, who shook his head.

'Well come on then,' Steve said. 'The ladies out there are hungry for prime princely meat.'

A queue was already forming at the ticket booth. 'These aren't the princesses we're looking for,' said Renton.

A small child pointed at him and started to cry. 'What's wrong, darling?' asked the kid's mother.

'That bad man is disrespecting Prince!' squeaked the child.

'Shhh,' the mother soothed. 'We can listen to *Purple Rain* when we get home.'

'Oh man,' Renton said.

The next punter in line looked at Adam in derision. 'What kingdom are *you* the prince of? The tip?'

'That's not a kingdom,' Adam said.

'And *that* guy's got a sports trophy pinned to his front.'

'At least I won a trophy,' said Steve.

'It says runner-up.'

'Cinema's open!' Adam yelled. The crowd surged past, waving their tickets.

'I thought you said there'd be babes,' Adam said.

'How was I to know only parents and kids would want to see *Prince Wonderful and the Legend of Sparkle Valley*?'

'Because it's about a dude called Prince Wonderful?' Steve said.

'Yeah, but Sparkle Valley,' said Renton, 'that sounds kinda sexy.'

An old lady approached Adam shyly, patting him on the arm. She stared into his eyes. 'Young man,' she said, 'are you cold, love?'

Adam recoiled. 'I don't want to sleep with you!'

She looked confused. 'I just thought you might be cold in that skimpy outfit.'

'No, no, the cinema's heated,' Adam said, embarrassed.

'Well, you rug up on your way home,' she said. 'You don't want to catch your death.' She tottered off towards Cinema One.

'That was a close shave!' Steve laughed. 'The babes are throwing themselves at you tonight.'

'Whatever,' Adam said. 'I've got to clean up Cinema Three.'

A cinema was a depressing place to be when the cleaning lights were on; they revealed every sordid stain. After five hours of sweeping up discarded popcorn and gingerly collecting half-empty drink cups – you never knew whether they contained melted ice, or other things the punters had... added – Adam didn't feel particularly hot. In fact, his costume was making it more difficult to do his work; he could hardly bend over in these too-tight pants.

Maybe that was where he'd gone wrong. What if being hot wasn't just about looks? He felt like a dickhead in this stupid outfit. What on earth had all these women even seen in him?

Renton stuck his head around the door. 'You finished here?'

'Yep, this is the last one,' Adam said.

'Great,' said Renton, 'time to hit the clubs!'

'Traditionally,' said Adam, 'the clubs hit you.'

Renton shook his head. 'When did you get so lame?'

'It's these pants,' Adam said. 'They're cutting off the circulation to my legs.'

'You may mock my ableist banter,' Renton said, 'but as long as the blood's still flowing where it counts…'

'If we could go the rest of the night without you referring to my junk, it would be nice,' said Adam.

'So lame!' Renton said.

Adam carried the final bag of garbage past the closed-down candy bar. By the time he'd retrieved his belongings from his locker, Steve and Renton were waiting for him by the front door.

'Time to hit the clubs!' said Steve.

'Don't,' Adam said.

'But dude! Nobody's going to care about your terrible outfit in a dark nightclub,' Steve said.

'I'm not in the mood,' Adam said. 'Not tonight.'

'What?' Renton said. 'You've got to make up for lost time.'

'I don't care about lost time.'

'But what about *my* lost time? I've been waiting for this for months.'

'So you can wait another month,' Adam said.

'*Month*!' Renton said. 'Think of all the babes you'll have missed in a month.'

'They'll still be there in a month.'

'But they'll be a month older!' said Renton.

'Deal with it, Renton; he doesn't want to go out,' Steve said. 'More babes for us.'

'More babes for you!' Renton said. 'I'm getting nothin'. We need that high-powered Adam wattage to bring the moths to the flame.'

'That makes no sense,' said Adam, hefting the garbage bag.

'I'm throwing this in the dumpster, and then I'm done. Good night.'

Outside by the dumpster, Adam checked his phone. No calls from Cate.

41

Cate shut her laptop in disgust. 'He's not even *on* social media!' she said. 'How am I supposed to stalk him?'

Sitting beside her on the couch, Vanessa shook her head sadly. 'You just have to deal with him face to face.'

'His face is what got us into this mess,' said Cate. 'Even now, I can't stop seeing it when I close my eyes.'

'Mmm,' Vanessa said, closing her own eyes, 'I can see it too.'

'Stop fantasising about my boyfriend!'

'But didn't you say you guys had broken up?' Vanessa smiled, her eyes still closed.

'Didn't you come over to make me feel better?'

'Sorry,' Vanessa said, looking at Cate again. 'I shouldn't joke.'

'That's right. I'm depressed. Cheer me up!'

'Well, at least you don't have to watch Adam on social media, getting hit on by other women.'

'His hotness isn't virtual!' Cate said. 'It's real life I've got to worry about.'

'Well, what's he doing now? He doesn't go out to nightclubs, does he? He'll just be sitting at home, watching some boring arty movie and thinking about how stupid he's been.'

Cate frowned. 'He's at work. It's Handsome Prince Night.'

'Oh.'

'He's the handsome prince.'

'I guessed.'

'He's gonna be balls-deep in princesses. For all I know,

there'll be real princesses there. I'll turn on the news next week and he'll be King of Sweden.'

'That's not gonna happen,' Vanessa said. 'There already is a King of Sweden. Worst-case scenario, he'll be fourth in line to the throne.'

'Not helping,' said Cate. 'I'm not even a millionth in line to any throne. And what if it's not princesses? What about actresses? Or models? Or any professionally sexy women? I can't compete with them!'

'You're plenty sexy,' said Vanessa.

'I don't feel sexy,' said Cate. 'I feel like someone who got dumped, and it's all my fault, and I've ruined the best thing I've ever had, and what's the point of life, and –'

'Let me get you a cup of tea.'

Vanessa got up off the couch and headed to the kitchen.

'Am I doing the right thing, not getting in touch?' Cate called after her.

'Well, you called him during the day and he didn't answer,' Vanessa's voice floated back. 'It's not gonna hurt for him to think you're out having a wild night, getting your freak on at some crazy party. How do you have your tea again?'

'White with none,' Cate said, and hung her head. 'Just like me.'

'I said a crazy party, not a pity party,' said Vanessa.

'Shut up,' said Cate. 'I feel awful. I really think I've lost him.'

'You'll work it out,' Vanessa said.

'You saw his face last night,' said Cate. 'He looked really hurt.'

'He just needs time.'

'Yeah, and while I'm giving him time, someone else is gonna swoop in and give him *her* time.'

Vanessa came back into the living room, bearing two mugs of tea. 'This'll cheer you up,' she said.

'Thanks, Nanna,' Cate said, taking the offered mug.

'Mark my words,' Vanessa said, 'You'll wake up tomorrow,

and there'll be a dozen missed calls from him, wondering what you've been up to.'

'I don't think I'll get any sleep tonight,' Cate said. 'I'm way too stressed. All I want to do is cry.'

'Aww,' Vanessa said, slinging an arm around her friend's shoulders. 'Adam's not stupid enough to let you get away. He's just angry with you right now. All you can do is wait for it to blow over. I mean,' she rubbed Cate's shoulder, 'you're pretty awesome. And he knows it.'

Cate didn't answer. She bowed her head over her tea mug. Vanessa noticed the tears rolling down her cheeks.

'Hey,' Vanessa said, 'what's this? I thought you were reading *Consumption*.' She held up the fat paperback that was lying open on the coffee table.

'Kirsty left it here,' Cate said, wiping her face. 'She thought it'd make me feel better. But it's just people having sex with cats! I don't want to have sex with cats!'

'You don't have to have sex with cats if you don't want to,' said Vanessa. 'The cats won't mind.'

'I can't believe Kirsty reads this stuff,' Cate said. 'It's kind of creepy.'

'Kind of!'

'Not like *Consumption*,' said Cate. 'Those people just have sex with... monsters. And zombies. And ghosts.'

'Mmm-hmm,' said Vanessa. 'The Vapours are super hot.'

'Maybe we shouldn't judge,' said Cate. 'Whatever gets you through a dry spell.'

'You're not in a dry spell!' Vanessa said. 'He'll be back tomorrow. Then you'll be, uh...'

Cate laughed.

'I didn't think that through,' Vanessa said.

'No, I needed a laugh.' She sighed. 'Maybe I should try and sleep.'

'If only you'd told me! Scozza could've given me something.'

'What – herpes?'

'That's harsh,' said Vanessa, 'but fair.'

'I'm sorry for being mean,' Cate said. 'I'm cranky. I should just go to bed.'

'Do you want me to stay?'

'No, I'll be all right. Well, no, I'm just going to lie awake, imagining Adam boning every attractive woman in the state. But you don't need to be here for that.'

'I guess not,' Vanessa said. 'I did say to Scozza I'd go to his gig.'

'Oh, he got a gig? That's really good!'

'Yeah, I'm pretty excited. He's playing at Artisanal Jam.'

Cate frowned. 'The jam festival?'

'No, it's a music festival.'

'I'm pretty sure it's an event where hipsters show off their home-made preserves. The bartender at Auberon's Moustache was going to enter his foraged blackberry ram jam.'

Vanessa had a panicked expression. 'Oh no, Scozza doesn't know the first thing about jam.'

'I'll be fine,' Cate said. 'You go get him out of that jam.'

Vanessa groaned, then hugged Cate. 'I'll call you tomorrow.'

'Thanks for being here,' Cate said. 'I'll be fine.'

It wasn't until she heard Vanessa's car drive away that Cate let herself sob. 'Shit,' she said, wiping her eyes. She looked around the empty room. The clock said 8.45 p.m. 'Guess it's bedtime,' Cate said. She hadn't got out of her pyjamas all day. *Perfect*, she thought, and crawled into bed.

Though she'd expected to lie awake all night, it was already morning when Cate opened her eyes. She fumbled for her phone. No messages from Adam.

42

Cate pounded on the glass doors of the Rafferty Cinema. Inside, people stared.

Steve Rogers left the candy bar and opened the door for her. 'We're open, you know,' he said.

'Where's Adam?'

'Sorry, no Adam here,' said Steve, a little too quickly. 'Maybe you're thinking of the Royal Regal across town.'

'You're Steve, right?' said Cate. 'I'm his girlfriend.'

'Yeah, a lot of women think they're Adam's girlfriend.'

She sighed. 'We've been going out for the last two months.'

A look of realisation dawned on Steve's face. 'You're Cate.'

She nodded. 'Where's Adam?'

Before Steve could reply, Renton appeared at his side. 'Who's your lady friend, Steve?'

'Renton, this is Cate.'

Renton seized her hand and kissed it, with a bit too much tongue. 'Charmed, m'lady.'

Steve cleared his throat. 'This is *the* Cate.'

Renton dropped her hand as if it were a cold fish. 'Oh,' he said. '*You.*'

'Where's Adam?' Cate said.

'I'm Steve,' said Steve, 'and this is Renton.'

'You're wearing name tags,' Cate said. 'Where's Adam?'

'You know, you really broke his heart. That poor guy was really hurting last night.'

'Yeah, he was shattered,' said Renton. 'It took a whole five minutes to persuade him to hit the clubs after work. And in that prince outfit,' he sent Steve a sly glance, 'hoo boy...'

Cate ignored him. 'Where's Adam?'

'What?' Renton said in mock distress. 'He didn't call you? Something must have happened to him last night. I hope those women he was with didn't get him in trouble.'

'Give it a rest, Renton,' Steve said. 'Adam's not here today. He's working on the *Consumption* film set.'

'Bullshit,' Cate said. 'Where's Adam?'

'No, seriously,' said Steve. 'They were filming here last week, and then they rang on Friday, asking him to come down to the Harbour Studios. Dunno what for.'

Cate looked puzzled.

Renton cackled unpleasantly. 'What, he didn't tell you?'

'He definitely told me that you're a jerk,' Cate snapped.

'Hey, don't get mad at me. You're the one who wanted a hot boyfriend.'

'I didn't care that he was hot, I – ugh, why am I even explaining myself to you?' She turned to Steve. 'Make sure you tell him that I came by.'

'Sure,' Steve said unconvincingly.

'We're not your message service,' Renton said. 'Call him yourself – oh wait, he's not taking your calls.'

'You can go to hell,' Cate said, turning on her heel and walking out.

She felt the tears welling up when she was halfway back to her car. By the time she reached it, they were running down her cheeks. She sat behind the wheel and let the sobs come. Adam's friends were idiots, but that didn't mean they were wrong. Maybe she was never in Adam's league. These last few months had meant everything to her; had they meant anything to him at all?

She tried not to imagine him on the movie set, but it was all too easy to see the makeup artists and script girls fawning over him while the actresses held back, biding their time. Working on a Hollywood movie was what he'd always wanted, and now it was beginning to happen for him. He was leaving her behind. She tried to tell herself it was for the best: it was better that he'd left her before he became famous, so people wouldn't pity her for being the dumped average girlfriend of a glamorous blockbuster movie director. But the tears kept falling, and she cried for a long, long time.

43

Adam took his phone out of his pocket. No new calls. Having it on silent was killing him, but you weren't even supposed to have phones on set, and he needed to know if Cate –

'Excuse me, handsome guy? Can you stop fidgeting?'

'Sorry,' Adam said, smiling apologetically at the production assistant. Her glare dissolved in an instant.

'Not your fault,' she said. 'We'll let you know when we need you.' She smiled. Was that a wink?

Her attention just made him feel sad. He didn't want her; the way he was feeling, he didn't want anyone.

He'd been so excited when, after they'd spent Friday shooting at the cinema, they'd asked him to come down to the main set at Harbour Studios over the weekend. It was his first time on a big-budget set, and he was determined to show them that he was a hard worker and keen to learn. But now he was here, all he could think about was how excited Cate would have been for him. He hadn't even had time to tell her about it on Friday night.

Waking up that morning, he'd hoped being on the set would distract him from his problems. It turned out that a movie set was pretty much the worst place to be when you had something on your mind. So far his job had been to stand in the corner and wait while everyone else scurried around him; at first all the activity had distracted him from Cate, but now all he had was time to think. Too much time.

It might have been easier if they were actually filming something, but as far as he could tell they were only setting up for some special effects shots. The 'set' was just a corner of the warehouse-like space that had a huge, curved green sheet draped across the walls. There was a green sheet across the floor too, and where that ended there was a tangle of cables and wiring taped to the concrete. A good half an hour ago, someone had walked across the green corner holding up a tennis ball on a stick; since then everyone had been staring at various monitors, watching what they'd shot over and over again.

'Hey! You!'

Adam looked around, confused.

'Yeah, you! Handsome.'

Adam sighed. 'Yes?'

Another assistant was waving at him. 'Over here!' she said.

Adam walked over to where she was standing against the back wall of the studio. 'Here I am,' he said.

'Follow me. We've got to get you to makeup.'

'Makeup?'

'Well, a guy with a bucket of green paint.'

'Paint?'

She seemed exasperated. 'Didn't they tell you? You're doing Vapours motion capture today.'

'Does that mean I have to run around with ping-pong balls stuck to me?'

'No. It's just your face they want today.' She suppressed a smirk. 'They'll be back for your bod later.'

He frowned, but only for a moment. Six months ago he would have been flattered – hell, six *days* ago this would have been a great opportunity. He couldn't let his feelings about Cate get in the way of his big break. Visual effects weren't really Adam's thing – he'd never thought this would be his way into the business. But, he reasoned, once you were in, it didn't matter how you'd got there. From here, he could make his own way.

Adam followed the production assistant to a room that

looked like an ordinary office. He'd been expecting mirrors ringed with lights, and a gaggle of well-groomed female makeup artists wielding tiny brushes. What he got was a hairy, middle-aged guy in a singlet and grimy jeans, actually holding a bucket of green paint.

'Get ya shirt off,' the painter said.

Adam looked at the production assistant. She winked.

This is how you get ahead, Adam reminded himself as he pulled his shirt over his head.

Three hours later, a shirtless, green-torsoed creature received a text from Renton.

'*HULK SMASH!*' it said.

'I knew I shouldn't have sent him that selfie,' Adam said to himself. He was going to text back but then decided to call. He didn't want Renton texting him if he was suddenly called back on set.

He was standing against the back wall while the crew checked the last take. They'd shot six takes so far, and after each one the crew would spend twenty minutes crowded around the monitors, muttering to each other. The first time this had happened, Adam had joined them, but most of the discussion had revolved around how hot he was. So he'd decided to stand as far away as possible between takes. That hadn't stopped the crew from turning their heads between him and the monitors, like a crowd at a tennis match.

'Why didn't they paint your face?' was the first thing Renton said when he answered the phone.

'Hello to you, too,' Adam said. 'My face is the bit they're filming; the green paint is to block out the rest of me.'

'What are they gonna do with your face?' Renton said. 'Are you gonna be a giant... killer... Kong... thing?'

Adam sighed. 'I'm a ghost. Technically, a Vapour. Have you read the *Consumption* books?'

'Shit no,' said Renton. 'Aren't they for chicks?'

'They're not really my thing either,' said Adam. 'All I know is that there are ghosts, and I'm one.'

'So they just want you for your face?'

'They might want my body as well, later on,' Adam said.

Renton's mocking laughter was so loud in his ear he nearly dropped his phone. 'Look,' Adam continued, 'if that's what it takes to meet the right people, I don't mind getting my gear off.'

This time Renton's laughter was so loud that a crew member shushed Adam from across the room. 'Quiet on set!'

'So when are you filming your big sex scene?' Renton said.

'Ghosts don't have sex,' said Adam. 'I don't even have a body. They're only filming my face.'

'Is someone gonna sit on it?'

'You can't sit on a ghost's face.'

'Well, what do you do in the movie?'

'I dunno,' said Adam, 'waft around? The Vapours are, like, a ghost gang, and they fight some guy called Dropsy.'

'Dropsy and the Vapours?' Renton said. 'That's like a name for a shit band. Are you sure you're not gonna be playing guitars?'

'Like I said, I don't have hands.'

'So, basically,' Renton said, 'they just want to look at you.'

'That's what acting is.'

'But you're not acting. You're just a pretty face.' Renton laughed. 'The Hot Guy is moving up to the big screen!'

'This is different!' Adam said.

'Nah, that's totally it!' said Renton. 'They're exploiting your hotness, just for one day.'

'No they aren't! I got this job because I was willing to put... put in... ah, shut up!'

'Just make sure you don't get all precious and walk out in a huff,' Renton said.

'I don't get precious about my looks,' Adam said.

'Sure you don't,' said Renton.

'Hey! Hot stuff! We're ready for you again,' shouted the unit director.

'Gotta go,' Adam told Renton, and hung up without waiting for an answer. *I really am in a movie now*, he thought.

Walking back across the set, he wondered if Renton was right. It seemed unlikely – Renton still had KFC confused with KGB, and whenever they tried to correct him, he'd retort, 'Why is it run by a colonel, then?' But he couldn't deny that the special effects crew were objectifying him. And how was that different to the way Cate had done it when they first met? The obvious answer was that he'd chosen this, whereas Cate hadn't given him the choice. But wouldn't that mean that he was okay with being treated as a sex object under *some* circumstances? And didn't that mean maybe he *had* overreacted with Cate, just a little?

'Okay, can you stand on your mark and...' the director waved his hand, '... scowl or something?'

Behind him, one of the technicians interjected, 'Computer's still reading his hotness levels at 110 per cent. The system can't handle that!'

'Hmmm,' the director said. 'Maybe close one eye?'

44

'Hope I wasn't interrupting anything when I asked you to come over,' Cate said sarcastically from the couch, as her friends walked through her open front door and into her lounge room. 'Did you guys meet up before, to plot what you were going to tell me?'

'I was scared to come in on my own,' Kirsty said.

'Yeah, you sounded really angry on the phone,' said Vanessa.

'That's because I was,' said Cate. 'Angry, that is. Wait, let me start again – FUCK YOU.'

'Huh?' chorused Kirsty and Vanessa.

Cate stared at them. She'd clearly been crying, but her expression now was one of thinly concealed rage. 'I've had some time to think about it now. And I know what you did.'

Vanessa and Kirsty looked at each other, clearly puzzled.

'I thought you were my friends.'

Kirsty shook her head. 'This is not getting any clearer.'

'You betrayed me! You were in league! With the League.'

'What are you talking about?' Vanessa said.

'The League were trying to break me and Adam up,' Cate said coldly. 'Ursula broke us up. Ursula was part of the League. Connect the dots.'

'The dots don't connect to us,' Vanessa said.

'Are we one of the dots?' added Kirsty.

'You guys were there the night Ursula brought me to that bar. You knew all about Adam before I did. You never wanted me to be with him in the first place. And now you've got what

238

you want. You and the League – I hope you're happy.' She drew in a ragged, sobbing breath. 'Because I'm not.'

'Oh, Cate.' Vanessa sat on the couch beside her distraught friend. 'What do you think we did?'

'You broke me and Adam up.'

'No we didn't,' said Kirsty, sitting down on Cate's other side. 'You know that. You were there.'

'What about that time at the park? You guys ran off together – it was all suspicious. Kirsty, you said you had... things to do?'

'Yeah, I went home to drink,' Kirsty said, her hair rippling like seaweed stroked by a gentle ocean current. 'I didn't want to share the good stuff with you losers.'

Vanessa shot her a pitying look. 'Kirsty, a six-litre goon bag is not "the good stuff".'

'It is when you get it for ten bucks.'

Cate was still angry. 'It can't have been random... We can't have broken up by accident.'

'We thought the League was just a silly Facebook group,' Vanessa said.

'You know, a bunch of women joking about some guy they saw in a fucking bar,' said Kirsty. 'We didn't think they'd, like, *kidnap* people.'

'Well, they kidnapped me!' Cate said. 'They kidnapped me, and they tried to break up my relationship, and they, and they succeeded!' Her voice broke. 'I've got nothing.'

'You've got us,' Vanessa said.

'I've got nothing!'

'You've got –'

'NOTHING!'

'I know you're hurting,' Vanessa said. 'Maybe we should leave you alone.'

'That's right!' Cate said. 'You've got what you wanted now.'

'We never wanted you to be unhappy,' Kirsty said. 'We

thought Adam would be bad for you, that's all. But once we saw how much he loved you...'

'You only met him on the night we broke up!'

'Once we saw how happy he was *making you*,' Vanessa said firmly, glaring at Kirsty, 'we'd never have tried to break you guys up. We love you.'

'But there *must* have been a scheme,' Cate said, despairingly. 'We can't have just broken up like that. What we had was this love story. We were writing this story together, and we were the leads. And it was epic. It was bigger than both of us. It was a story that was changing our *lives*. And it can't have just ended on this... sad trombone.'

Vanessa shrugged. 'Sometimes that's just how it goes.'

'It can't have!' Cate insisted. 'We had evil forces actually trying to break us up. Real ones. They ate my pizza.'

'Is that a metaphor?' Kirsty said.

Cate was staring into space. 'Well, if you guys didn't break us up, and the League didn't break us up... We had all this love. It was so strong between us, and now it's just... gone. How could it just *end?*'

Kirsty rubbed the back of Cate's neck. 'It's hasn't ended yet,' she said. 'Those goon bags are still on sale.'

Cate began to cry.

45

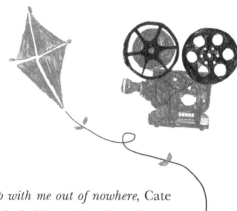

At least work isn't going to break up with me out of nowhere, Cate thought as she parked her car at Cash Money Brothers Sports Stadium. Workers were already taking down the Sambo branding and replacing it with a huge LED sign advertising the stadium's new sponsor. Cate frowned as she noticed the 'S' in 'Sports' was now a dollar sign. This was something she'd have to change once she was in her new job. They hadn't said anything officially, but Ursula's recommendation would have to carry some weight. And after all, Cate was the one who'd landed the stadium-saving sponsorship deal.

Yep, if sport could distract Cate from the ruins of her personal life, it was a great day for it. 'I love sport,' she said to the protesters who were permanently camped outside the stadium entrance.

'Yeah, well I love communism,' said a stringy-haired man in a buckskin jacket, carrying a sign that said, 'NO TOLERANCE FOR CAPITALISM.'

'Fair enough, Gareth,' Cate said. 'See you this afternoon.'

'See you, Cate!' he said, as she drove in.

'I love sport!' she announced to Dave the car park attendant.

He didn't look up. He was watching a replay of yesterday's game on his phone.

'I love sport!' Cate said to Isobelle, the receptionist. Isobelle didn't turn around. She was hanging another framed football jumper on the wall behind the front desk.

'I love sport!' she said to Mary, the office admin, when she stepped out of the elevator on the executive floor.

'Who doesn't?' Mary said. 'Coffee?'

Cate frowned. 'We have coffee?'

'You didn't bring me coffee?'

'Why would I bring coffee in to work?'

'I sent an email saying the machine was broken.'

'I know. That's why I asked if we had coffee.'

'I sent the email so you'd bring me some coffee.'

'Oh,' Cate said. 'I got dumped on the weekend.'

'And your boyfriend has my coffee?'

'I'm going to go cry in my office.'

Mary turned back to her computer. 'Better look for my coffee while you're in there.'

Nothing ever changes around here, Cate thought gloomily. But all that was about to change. Hugo was roaming the floor, shouting like a town crier, 'Staff meeting, boardroom, in five minutes!'

Cate straightened her jacket and checked it was free of toast crumbs. This was it – the meeting where her promotion would be made official. And in front of the whole office. Finally, these chumps would show her some respect.

It looked as if the entire stadium workforce was crowded into the boardroom. As well as the admin, marketing, accounts and legal teams, there were some uniformed groundskeepers, the security staff, even Darren the Jumbotron guy, squinting in the unaccustomed light. 'They only let me out once a year,' she heard him say excitedly, clutching the grimy hem of his T-shirt. 'This is like Christmas to me.'

Cate allowed herself a smile. This was all for her? Brunner must have been really impressed with her corporate video. Then her smile faltered. *Adam's* video. Well, she wasn't going to let him ruin her big day. This was about her, and her success, and her well-deserved rise to the top, and her –

'Excuse me!' John Brunner yelled. He was standing on the far side of the room, with his back to the window overlooking the arena. The crowd fell silent. 'We're all here today to welcome our new Head of Publicity –' Cate began to move towards the front of the crowd, 'Harry Harrison!'

The crowd erupted in applause. 'Go Harry!' someone shouted. A tall man in his mid-thirties bounded up to stand beside Brunner, slapping him comradely on the shoulder.

'Thanks John, everyone,' he said with the slickness of a media-trained sportsman. 'Some of the best days of my playing career were at this stadium, and I can't tell you how excited I am to be heading up the crew that tells everyone just how awesome this stadium is. We've got a lot of big games coming up, and we're expecting some big crowds. And I want a big effort from all of you guys to really bring home just how great this stadium can be!'

The onlookers cheered. Harry Harrison clasped his hands over his head and shook them in triumph.

'Sport!' the stadium employees began to chant. 'Sport! Sport! Sport! Sport!'

Cate's face was a mask, her smile curdling. Someone slapped her on the back. 'Isn't it great we got Harry? I can remember seeing him win the Dorfman five years back!'

'Dorfman?' Cate said numbly. The word was meaningless.

'Harry's gonna turn this place around!' the stranger continued. 'No more bullshit like land swimming! Back to real sport!'

'Real sport,' Cate said. 'Sounds great.'

Everyone was too busy hugging, back-slapping and waving sports memorabilia around to notice her leave.

Back in her office, Cate turned on her computer to check her emails. What the hell was going on in this place? On Friday it had been a normal office. Now everyone at this sports stadium seemed to have gone crazy about... *sport*.

According to an all-office memo, the usual Monday morning publicity work-in-progress meeting had been cancelled while they got Harry up to speed. He was currently being toured around the various departments, no doubt being greeted by showers of confetti and ticker tape. *No*, Cate thought, *grass. They'll be throwing handfuls of Brunner's precious turf at the new golden boy.*

She couldn't just sit there staring at her computer screen all morning. What she needed right now was some kind of stimulant. Surely performance-enhancing drugs couldn't be hard to find in a sports stadium.

Cate was rifling through the kitchen cupboards when Isaac swaggered into the room, swathed in head-to-toe football regalia: beanie, scarf, jumper. Even Cate could tell they were all in different teams' colours. Thankfully he'd drawn the line at wearing shorts, although Cate had to check twice that he wasn't wearing football boots.

'So, how about that big game last night?' he said.

'There wasn't a game last night, Isaac,' Cate said.

'Uh, I meant Saturday night,' he said.

'You know less about sport than I do, Isaac. Stop sucking up to the new regime.'

His eyes widened. 'Oh, there's a new regime? I thought this was *always* a sports stadium.'

'Don't kid yourself,' Cate said. 'This place is still going to need big, spectacular events.'

'Yeah,' said Isaac, 'big, spectacular *sporting* events. Harry's already talking about winning back the Obernewtyn Cup.'

'Did he actually say "Obernewtyn"?'

'He called it the Obie.'

She rolled her eyes. 'I bet he did.'

'Don't worry,' Isaac said, 'I'm sure you've still got a bright future here, getting the wine for the corporate boxes.'

'Dunno why. You're the expert on whining.'

Isaac smiled ruefully. 'I'm not sure if you've noticed, but things have changed around here. Your new boss? He likes sport. He played sport. He knows sport. The future is sport!'

'Did someone say sport?'

Mary came around the corner with a big smile on her face. 'Isn't it exciting that we've finally got a publicity director who actually knows about sport?'

'Is there any coffee in here?' Cate said. 'Any tea? Cola?'

'I told you the machine was broken,' said Mary.

'It's always broken,' Cate said. 'Can't we do anything right around here?'

'We got a publicist who knows about sport,' Isaac said cheerfully.

Cate glared at him.

'Harry's such a lovely guy, too,' Mary said. 'He's so nice to all the admin staff. And even when he was a player, you never heard about him raping anyone.'

'What a feminist,' Cate said.

'He's already talking about making some big changes, bringing in more staff with sports backgrounds,' Mary continued. 'It's so exciting.'

'I'm excited!' Isaac said.

'You should be,' Mary said.

'No you shouldn't!' said Cate. 'What about when I landed the big sponsorship deal?'

'Stop resting on your laurels – that was ages ago,' Isaac said.

'What?' said Cate. 'It was last week!'

'A week is a long time,' Isaac said, 'in football.'

'He shoots, he scores!' Mary said, holding up a hand for Isaac to high-five.

'Is this what it's going to be like here now,' Cate said, 'showboating after every point?'

At this point, Hugo walked in. ''Sup, losers!' he said. 'Is this where the B-team hangs out?'

'Weren't you taking Harry on the tour?' said Isaac.

'Nah,' said Hugo. 'He wanted to glad-hand the groundskeepers personally. They'll be talking about fertiliser till lunch.'

'Shame you're not there, Isaac,' said Cate. 'You've always

been good at talking… fertiliser.' She held her hand up for a high five. Everyone stared at her blankly. After a moment, Cate high-fived the fridge instead.

'So, tell us, Hugo,' Mary gushed, 'what's Harry really like? Is it true that if you listen closely when he breathes, you can hear the roar of the crowd?'

Cate smirked, already anticipating the pithy smackdown Hugo would serve up to this stupidity.

'As far as I can tell,' Hugo said, 'he's really on the ball.'

He graciously accepted Isaac's high-five.

'Oh, come on!' Cate said.

'Yeah, he's got some good ideas,' Hugo said. 'I was expecting some meathead jock, but he's really sharp. It'll be a change to have someone around here worth paying attention to.'

'But Hugo, you hate sport!' said Cate. 'We've spent more time at work talking about the Spice Girls than sport.'

He shrugged. 'What can I say? My favourite Spice Girl? Sporty Spice.'

Cate stormed out of the kitchen, making a beeline for Brunner's office. She stomped past Hugo's empty desk and flung open Brunner's door. Inside, the stadium chief was behind his desk, peering intently at a patch of turf he'd had transplanted from the arena into a small pot.

'When were you going to tell me you hired Harry Harrison?' Cate said loudly.

Brunner appeared unruffled. 'It's not my job to keep you apprised of staff changes,' he said. 'Don't you read your emails?'

Cate thought of her overstuffed inbox. 'But someone should have told me personally. He's my new boss.'

'That's Ursula's job, not mine,' Brunner said.

'Ursula told me she'd recommended *me* for this job.'

'She did,' said Brunner, 'and we thought about it. But this is a sports stadium, and to be honest, the Head of Publicity needs to have an enthusiastic approach to sport.'

'I can be enthusiastic about sport!'

'Well, maybe when Harry moves on, we'll keep you in mind then.'

'He'll never move on! This is his spiritual home! In a few weeks it might be his actual home! They've already got his clothes hanging up in the lobby.'

'That's his guernsey.'

'I knew that!' Cate said.

Brunner looked at her steadily, petting his potted grass.

'Well, all right – I didn't know that!' Cate admitted. 'But sport is shit! You know it's true!'

'I know,' Brunner said. 'All it does is mess up the turf. But I can afford to hate sport. I'm the boss. I need people working for me who can deal with these sports people. And after all, it does say Cash Money Brothers Sports Stadium on the door.'

'Yeah,' Cate said, 'thanks to me.'

'And we were all very impressed,' Brunner said. 'We really did consider you seriously for this position. You've done a great job keeping the doors open.'

'Isn't that enough?'

'Well, no,' he said. 'You have a lot of great ideas. But a lot of them don't fit with what we do here. Ursula was good at applying your ideas to our business. But if she isn't here, who's going to do that now?'

'Me!' said Cate. 'I would do that, automatically, as part of the service.'

Brunner shrugged. 'You've still got a chance to prove yourself,' he said. 'But the board didn't feel you were in the right place.'

'I was here! In this place! I'm a public relations professional, and Harry's just some sports...' she struggled for words, 'jock!'

'Look,' Brunner said, 'since we announced his appointment, sponsors have been calling *us* wanting to come on board. And he hasn't even sat down at his desk yet. He's got the clout, but you've got the brains. You'll make a great team, and who knows where we'll be in a few years.'

'I'll tell you where *I'll* be!' Cate said. 'Working somewhere else! Because I quit!'

Brunner put down the grass. 'Now, Cate,' he said, 'don't be hasty.'

'I'm not being hasty,' she said. 'I'm not being impetuous. I'm not some silly little girl throwing a tantrum because I didn't get my way. I've just realised that if my job is going to be working for a sports guy, selling sport, at a sports stadium, then it's best I move on. I can't do a job I don't believe in.'

'Is this about money?' Brunner said. 'We can give you a 5 per cent raise, spread over the next seven years.'

'That's a pay cut!'

'We're going to need money for sports equipment.'

'And that *right there* is why I'm leaving.'

'You know you owe us two weeks' notice.'

'And I've got three weeks' sick leave stored up,' Cate said.

'You don't have to leave, Cate,' Brunner said.

'I really do,' she said. 'I hate sport.'

46

It was that time on a Wednesday afternoon when Chicken Shaq was practically deserted. All the kids who usually hung out there were in school. The mums' groups had long since finished their Shaqqe Lattes and wheeled their prams away. The drunks hadn't even woken up for the day.

'What's the point?' Cate muttered to herself. 'I'm supposed to be better than this. That job was just a stepping stone. How did I end up being the one who got stepped on?' She sighed. 'I might as well eat Cluckers until the end of time. At least a Clucker won't leave me. A Clucker won't play sport.'

She looked down at the congealed lump of breaded, processed meat on the tray in front of her, making a dark stain of grease on its paper napkin. 'And you're not even a Clucker,' Cate said to her half-eaten Smacker burger.

'I thought I'd find you here.' A familiar petite blonde figure slid into the booth opposite Cate.

'You!' hissed Cate, rearing back in her seat as if a snake had appeared in front of her. 'Come to gloat, have you? Now you've got everything you wanted? Have you fucked Adam yet?'

The blonde laughed bitterly. 'You've poisoned *that* well,' she said.

'What do you mean?' Cate said.

'Once we heard the Hot Guy was back on the market, the League went all out,' said the blonde, with a thousand-yard stare. 'We threw everything we had at him. We were covering the bar round the clock. Annabella ate so many bananas in front of him at the supermarket she got potassium poisoning. Roxy even went to his house disguised as a door-to-door lingerie saleswoman. Nothing. He just wasn't interested.'

Cate looked up. She realised the blonde was looking worse for wear – was that a pimple beginning to show beneath the makeup caked on her chin? 'What, he couldn't find a root among your *hundreds* of members?'

The blonde looked at the floor. 'We've had something of a talent drain these last few weeks. A lot of members didn't think the Hot Guy would ever come back on the market.'

'Well, who's left?'

'Those fools lost faith. But I never did,' the blonde continued, ignoring Cate. 'I knew this day would come. This day of triumph. Well, not exactly, because he wouldn't sleep with me. Maybe that was because I grabbed his butt on a bus. But he will. Oh yes, he will. Victory shall be mine.'

Cate only just managed to conceal a smile. 'You're the only one left, aren't you?'

For a moment the blonde was silent. Then she burst into tears. 'I couldn't even score off the rebound. The Hot Guy didn't want me. He's never gonna want me. Everybody else just walked away – they didn't care. But he was my life! He was my everything!'

'Aren't I supposed to be saying this?' Cate said, frowning. 'I was the one who was actually going out with him.'

'That's why I came here!' the blonde said. She reached across the table to take Cate's hand, which Cate quickly snatched away. 'I'm not crazy. I know I'll never have a real relationship with the Hot Guy, but that's not what I wanted. I just wanted him for one night.'

'Why were you running an organisation devoted to Adam when you didn't want to date him?'

The blonde leaned forward. 'Well, I'd broken up with my boyfriend, and I heard about this Hot Guy. This magical dude who could get you over that bad time in your life, give you confidence again. I guess I just really loved that idea. I thought it would be healthy, you know, to get involved in a group that helped people get over their exes. I thought I was dealing with my issue. Rather than, I dunno, taking up crochet, or getting a cat.'

Cate looked dubious. 'I guess that makes sense…'

'No it doesn't!' said the blonde. 'I was just using the Hot Guy to avoid my heartbreak! I wasn't getting over my ex – the Hot Guy was a distraction. And now I look back at the comments in our Facebook group, it wasn't like the Hot Guy was this magic bullet. Some women came away from their night with him feeling great, feeling like their best selves. But there were some who just… It was just another one-night stand to them. And sometimes those make you feel shitty.'

Cate nodded. 'Well, sure. That's why I didn't want a one-night stand with Adam.'

'But you get what I'm saying, right?' The blonde reached for Cate's hand again. This time Cate was slightly slower to pull away. 'You can't go into a relationship thinking you're going to use the other person to solve your problems.'

'Is *that* what you thought I was doing?' Cate said. 'That wasn't it at all. It wasn't some coping mechanism. I wasn't sitting there thinking I had *control* over Adam! I was with him because I liked him, and I wanted to be with him. Not because I couldn't be with Alistair.'

The blonde didn't say anything.

'I don't know what you think we're meant to have in common here,' Cate said, tears starting to form in the corners of her eyes. 'But I just broke up with my real boyfriend, not some… fantasy date scheme you and your nutty pals had going on. You didn't even know Adam, and I'm not going to sit here and pretend that whatever it is you're feeling is anything like what I'm going through.' She looked down. The blonde had taken her hand and was squeezing it. This time Cate didn't pull away.

'I just wanted you to know you're not alone,' the blonde said, not unkindly. 'The Hot Guy – Adam – is really special. We all knew that. I mean,' she laughed, 'he did have a couple hundred women on social media plotting to sleep with him.'

'You're not making things better,' Cate sniffed, wiping her eyes.

'You know what I mean, though,' the blonde said, looking intently at Cate. 'We wouldn't have wanted him if all he had going on was his looks. There are plenty of handsome dirtbags out there for that. It wasn't just that he was a hot guy – he was a sweet guy.'

'He was,' Cate said, and burst into tears.

'Uh, okay,' the blonde said, leaning back in her seat. 'Let it out.'

'I can't believe I'm crying in front of you,' Cate said. 'You know you had me really scared for a while there.'

'Yeah, sorry about that whole kidnapping thing.'

'The threats kind of sucked, too.' Cate took a tissue out of her bag and gave her nose a mighty blow. 'I spent weeks worrying you guys were going to steal Adam away.'

The blonde laughed, a girlish sound that seemed come from a much younger version of the woman sitting across from Cate. 'He was never going to leave you,' she said, then realised her mistake. 'Sorry.'

'No, you're right,' Cate said. 'He never would have. I'm the one who drove him away.'

'Can't you try and win him back?'

Cate smiled, no joy in it. 'That's up to Adam. He knows how I feel.'

'You don't have to tell me how hard it is to change his mind.'

'I don't want to know,' Cate said, staring firmly at the blonde.

'For what it's worth, he wasn't acting like a man who was glad to be single,' the blonde said. 'I think the door's still open for you.'

'He's the one who has to walk through it now.'

'I guess.' The blonde stood, and slid out from behind the table. 'Anyway, I just wanted to let you know we're done. The Hot Guy is over. Adam's a free man.'

'Thank you,' Cate said quietly, not looking up. A thought crossed her mind. 'Hey,' she said.

The blonde turned, already halfway towards the Chicken Shaq's greasy automated doors.

'What's your name?' Cate said.

'Call me... Eve,' the blonde said.

Cate laughed. 'Really?'

'Nah, it's Mackaylah.'

Cate smiled. 'It's always nice to know someone's real name,' she said. 'Makes them seem more human.'

47

Steve was restocking the drink cups when a bearded figure approached the candy bar. *Wow*, Steve thought, *this guy's even hotter than Adam.*

'Hey Steve,' the bearded man said.

'Oh, hi Adam. Nice face fuzz. How long has it been, three days?'

'I dunno,' Adam said. 'Couldn't be bothered. It's one less thing to do in the morning.'

'I thought Cate was the one less thing you had to do in the morning.'

Adam looked at him. 'Too soon,' he said.

'You've gotta get over her, bro.'

'It hasn't even been a week.'

'I can't hold Renton back much longer,' Steve said. 'It's Thursday now. Tomorrow night he'll be wanting to hit the clubs.'

'Well, he can hit them without me,' Adam said. 'Anyway, they wouldn't let me in, looking like this. I look like a bum.'

'So, you grew that to put off the ladies?'

'Yes.'

'How's that working out for you?'

Adam shook his head. 'It's a nightmare. Turns out beards are in. A lot of ladies are into bearded men. A lot of *men* are into bearded men.'

'So... you've got a lot of dates lined up this weekend?'

'I don't plan to leave the house.'

'Wow, that's a lot of dates.'

'You know I meant the complete opposite of that.'

'So, you've finished filming, then?' Steve said.

'Yeah, for now,' Adam said. 'But they want me back.'

Steve smirked. 'Oh, so you messed up?'

'No,' Adam said, 'for the next movie. They've cast me as the lead Vapour.'

'You're Haze Volante, leader of the Vapours?' said Renton, walking behind the counter with a box of choc tops in his arms. 'Shit, man, that's huge!'

'Weren't you just a ghost in this movie?' Steve said.

'Nah, man,' Renton chirped up. 'Vapours *are* the ghosts. I looked up *Consumption* on Wikipedia. They're just ectoplasm in *Consumption 3: Conflagration,* but in *Consumption 4: Consummation,* they cast a spell on Haze and he turns into a real guy. He gets it on with the best friend.'

'I do?' Adam said.

'Everyone gets it on with everyone in the fourth book,' Renton said. 'Rumour has it the author finally got laid after the third book and threw away all the prudish stuff. Supposedly the fourth book's been banned in fifty-one US states.'

'Um, Renton...'

'Puerto Rico had to become a state so they could ban it.'

'Do you think any of that's true?' Adam said to Steve, who shrugged.

'You're the actor,' Steve sniffed. 'Why don't you read your script?'

'They haven't given me a script.'

'Well then, read the book!' Steve said, and stomped off.

'What's with him?' Adam said.

'He's just pissed off that you're living his dream,' said Renton. 'He's been working out like a motherfucker so he's buff enough to be on camera, and you just fell into it.'

'But that's not my fault!' Adam said. 'I didn't ask for the job. I just wanted to be on a film set for a day.'

'That's how it starts,' Renton said darkly. 'You just want to make out with a girl once, and then you end up married.'

'Since when did you ever make out with a girl?'

'I've made out with more girls than you have this week,' Renton said. 'And even I'm appalled. This isn't the way the world should be! What happened to you, man?'

'I just broke up with my girlfriend!' said Adam. 'Not even a week ago.'

'You've gotta be make out-ready!' Renton said. 'Have you *looked* at this actress you're going to be ghost-boning in *Consummation*?'

Renton tapped on his phone, then held it up to Adam. Onscreen was a picture of a generically pouting young woman.

'I've seen her sex tape!' said Renton. 'But the way you're talking right now, they'll just end up CGI-ing your face onto the sex tape dude's body.'

'Sounds fine to me,' Adam said.

'No, you idiot!' Renton said. 'People are gonna want to live their dreams through you! And what's your dream? Pining after some chick who's already moved on?'

'Moved on?' Adam said. 'She hasn't moved on!'

'You dumped her,' Renton said. 'Why would she stick around?'

Adam was silent for a moment.

'Well,' said Steve, returning to the candy bar with a cask of postmix drink syrup, 'have you heard from her?'

'No,' Adam said. 'She tried to ring me for a bit, and I didn't answer, and then she stopped.'

'Well, there you go,' Renton said confidently. 'Proof positive.'

'I thought she might have come past here,' Adam said.

Renton laughed, a little too heartily. 'Why would she do a crazy thing like that? Only a weird stalker would come to your place of work. You dumped her. Obviously she accepts it's over.'

There was an incoherent shout from across the foyer.

'Oh god,' Adam groaned.

Steve squinted. 'Is that...?'

'Hi, Orson!' said Renton, walking towards the boho hobo who had just pushed open the cinema doors. 'Great outfit!'

'Is that... a car-seat cover?' Steve muttered to Adam, who shook his head in despair.

'I think it's a toilet-seat cover. Or one of those blankets they put under old people so they don't get bedsores.'

'Those come in black?' Steve said.

'They do once you've been sitting on them long enough.'

Renton had reached Orson and was shaking his hand enthusiastically. Orson let go in a hurry and wiped his hand on a rag he produced from a pocket somewhere. Renton didn't seem to notice.

'So, did you get my email about the internship?'

Orson sighed. 'Email is a left-wing conspiracy invented by feminists to spread their penis-stifling ideology,' he said. 'You ever wondered why so much spam is about your dick? Feminists, man. Just trying to make you insecure.'

'You should make a film about that,' enthused Renton. 'It could be a game-changer.'

'The only games I play,' Orson said ominously, 'are my own.'

Adam stood up from behind the cash register. 'What the fuck does that even mean?'

'Oh, there you are, dear boy!' Orson said. 'I love the beard. Very Hemingway. Why, soon you'll look positively Papa-esque. Perfect for shooting *Baby Shoes.*'

'Orson, I told you I wasn't interested in being in your movie.'

'I've got to get you in on the ground floor,' Orson went on, as if Adam hadn't said anything. 'Now that my spies tell me you've been making quite a name for yourself. Or should I say... quite a *face* for yourself.'

'We're really busy today, Orson. Can I call you later?'

'You know I don't have a phone. It's a phallocentric device

invented by the homosexuals. They just want you to put a big dick up next to your ear.'

Everyone stared at him speechlessly.

Renton was first to recover. 'Speaking of homosexuals,' he said, 'we recently had a screening here of your movie *Flames of Desire*.'

'Oh,' said Orson dismissively. 'I've disowned that. Brad made me do it. Brad made me do a *lot* of things back then.'

'I'm guessing some of those things were drugs,' Adam said.

'Well, we did do a massive amount of amyl,' Orson said. 'One morning I woke up and I'd directed a film.'

'And what a film!' Renton said. 'So audacious, so ahead of its time.'

'Trash!' Orson barked. 'Don't ever speak of it again. Those who understand my oeuvre know that my true masterpiece is *And Then The Bag Came Off*.'

Steve frowned. 'I don't think I've ever heard –'

'No, Steve, no!' Adam said. 'Don't get him started.'

But he was too late. 'Picture it,' Orson said expansively. He'd clearly pitched this many times. 'A grey, windswept beach. Bergman was my inspiration. A callow youth wanders aimlessly, symbolising the pointlessness of our struggle. He sees a queue of men and realises he cannot resist the pull of society. He takes his place among them. Looking ahead, he sees the men are waiting their turn to service a spread-eagled woman, naked but for a bag over her head...'

'I've heard enough,' said Steve.

But Orson wouldn't be denied. 'Under the rolling gunmetal skies, the men shuffle forward – a poignant symbol of the dehumanising forces that compel us to move through our empty, mechanical lives. It's almost... Beckett-like in its formalist absurdity. Eventually our hero reaches the head of the queue. It's his turn to mount the woman. But no sooner has he begun his thrusting –'

Adam was frantically waving his hands, trying to prevent the horrible, inevitable punchline. 'Orson, what do you want?' he said. 'Why are you here?'

'And then the bag came off!' Orson said in a voice of triumph. 'And it was his mum!'

Silence filled the cinema foyer. Then Renton began a slow, steady clapping, his face alight with admiration. 'Bravo!'

'How do we know it was his mum?' Steve whispered to Adam.

'Don't make me remember,' Adam replied. 'It went for three hours. God, those facial expressions…'

'And that kind of artistic triumph could be yours!' Orson said. 'But instead you've sold yourself to those Hollywood whores.'

'Yeah Adam,' said Steve, 'that could be you having sex with your mum.'

'Wait, why am I selling myself to whores?' Adam said. 'Shouldn't I be selling myself to pimps? Or johns?'

'Either way, you're selling yourself!' Orson said. 'Didn't you want to use film to make a statement? Now you just want to make money.'

'If I'd stuck with you, I wouldn't make either.'

'Then take me with you!' Orson said urgently. 'You need a manager – someone who knows the ins and outs of this industry.'

'And nobody knows ins and outs better than Orson Reich,' Renton said reverently.

'This place is so provincial,' Orson continued. 'In Hollywood, they respect people with big ideas. People like you… and me!'

'Um, I'm not looking for representation at this time. I already have an agent.'

'But I'm the one who found you!' Orson said.

'I wasn't lost,' Adam said.

A sly expression crept over Orson's weather-beaten face. 'Weren't you?'

'No,' Adam said.

'Just a little bit?'

'Not even.'

'But without me you wouldn't have got your big break. I was your midwife into the world of cinema.'

'Ew,' Steve said.

'And now all you're leaving me with is the afterbirth.' Orson looked pointedly at Renton.

Adam sighed. 'I'll always be grateful, Orson. But this *Consumption* thing really had nothing to do with you. They came here to the cinema, and they were the ones who asked me to work for them.'

'And now you're just going to move on, and leave everyone behind, and lose touch with your artistic roots. You'll just be another pretty face – and those are a dime a dozen in Hollywood.'

'Well then,' retorted Adam, 'you'll have no trouble buying a new star for your baby gangster... Hemingway... yakuza movie.'

'You don't understand,' said Orson. 'Bland hunks are easy to find. But you've got a spark – an inner light the camera loves. That people love! There's something decent, something wholesome, something...' he groped for the unaccustomed word, '*good* about you.'

Adam scowled. 'Guess you got that wrong, then. Because a good guy wouldn't tell you to *fuck off.*'

Orson took a step back in shock.

'You're a terrible director, a horrible person and your ideas are morally repugnant. And you smell bad too!'

None of these accusations seemed to surprise Orson, who shook his head sorrowfully. 'You've changed.'

'Well, sometimes life *makes* you change,' snapped Adam. 'You've got to leave the past behind. No matter how kind it was. No matter how loving, and thoughtful, and caring, and funny, and sweet that past was.'

Everyone looked puzzled.

'What are we talking about?' said Orson.

'Get out!' Adam said. 'You're being disruptive. There are

people here who actually want to watch a movie today.'

He was right. A small queue was building up at the box office. Orson gathered his dignity and began to stalk away. 'You'll keep,' he shouted over his shoulder. 'I'll still be waiting when you slink back here in defeat. Only the good die young.'

Adam turned to the first person in the queue. 'I'm so sorry about that,' he said.

'That's okay,' said the young woman at the counter. 'You're going to laugh, but... one ticket to *Deto-Nation*, thanks.' She blushed. 'I like action movies.'

'Just one?' Adam said with a winning smile. 'A pretty girl like you shouldn't be seeing movies alone.'

Her own smile faded. She looked hurt. 'I like seeing movies on my own,' she said.

'So do I,' Adam said. 'Maybe sometime we could watch a movie alone... *together*.'

'Uh, doesn't that kind of defeat the purpose?'

'Well, maybe we could do something else together. I can think of a few things we'd both enjoy.'

She raised her eyebrows. 'I can't think of anything I'd enjoy doing with you,' she said. 'Apart from you giving me my movie ticket.'

'I'll give you your ticket all right.'

'That's not a euphemism.'

'So... you won't go out with me?' Adam said, confused.

'No.'

Adam sketched his face with a finger. 'Uh... are you sure?'

'Why would I? You seem like a jerk!'

'Oh,' Adam said. 'Okay.' He handed over the ticket. 'I'm sorry.'

She snatched it from his hand. 'Loser.'

'Oh man,' Steve said. 'That was brutal.'

'It was like watching a car crash,' said Renton. 'What happened?'

MEL CAMPBELL AND ANTHONY MORRIS

'I don't know,' Adam said, mechanically taking the next customer's money and dispensing more tickets. 'Aren't I the Hot Guy? I shouldn't have to work at this stuff. Isn't the deal that women are instantly attracted to me?'

'Welcome to the mortal world,' Steve said. 'Suffer in your jocks. Which are staying on your butt. Because you're not getting laid.'

Renton was shaking his head. 'Man, you've totally lost it. The golden age is over.'

'You're certainly not the man you used to be,' Steve said.

'Don't worry,' said Renton. 'You'll find some chick who doesn't care about your lame antics. She'll love you for your face. And then you'll go to Hollywood and be surrounded by hot babes, and it won't matter what you say to them. No one will even care what you say. That's what scriptwriters are for.'

Adam looked crestfallen. 'Maybe I've made a mistake.'

48

It was glorious kite-flying weather that Sunday in the park. Young families were picnicking under the trees, their rugs parked strategically to make the most of the river views. A jogger padded past; she was wearing all the latest fitness gear, and devouring a wedge of cheese.

On the oval, against a cloudless sky, Cate watched Kirsty's batwing wheel overhead, while Vanessa's drone darted in figures-of-eight, the sunlight glinting on its fuselage.

'Come on! Get it up there!' said Vanessa, gesturing at the diamond-shaped kite Cate was holding.

'That's what she said,' Kirsty said.

'I will,' Cate said, 'in a minute.' She fiddled with the tail of her kite.

'Is this a metaphor for your reluctance to get back in the dating pool?' said Vanessa.

'Course not,' said Cate. 'That's ridiculous.'

'Well, you haven't really been getting back into the swing of things,' Kirsty said. 'You refuse to go out. That kite's not going anywhere. And have you even fucking tried to look for a new job?'

'Yes,' said Cate. 'I sent off an expression-of-interest email to ToxCo just the other day.'

Kirsty took several steps back, her eyes on her kite. 'ToxCo? Didn't they own that ship full of toxic waste that ran aground into a kindergarten?'

Cate nodded. 'That's why they need good PR.'

'You can do better than that, Cate,' Kirsty said. 'You're really great at what you do. The stadium didn't know what they had.'

'Yeah, but none of the decent companies have PR openings. Good companies sell themselves through word of mouth – it's only the shitty ones that need me to clean up after them.'

'They're still cleaning up after that tanker ran aground,' Vanessa said. 'I heard some of the kids still glow in the dark.'

'You never would have heard that if they'd hired me,' Cate said. 'And if you had, I would've spun it as a cool new night light. All the kids would've wanted to glow in the dark! Human glowsticks!'

'That is pretty good,' Kirsty said. 'So, you haven't had any offers?'

'Nope,' said Cate. 'And I've tried the best of the worst. That disgraced charity Cuddle the Children... The Smoke Bloke... Doctors Without Boundaries... Extreme Prejudice Business Solutions...'

'Extreme Prejudice?' said Kirsty excitedly. 'We contract out a bunch of stuff to them. Do you want me to put in a good word for you?'

'That's okay,' Cate said, 'I think I might be over the whole PR thing. I feel like I need to make a clean break, you know? From everything?'

Her friends exchanged a look. 'Don't go rushing into anything,' Vanessa said.

'I don't know. I feel really burnt out by that stadium,' Cate said. 'I hated the work but I still put so much into that place. And then it turned out that none of it mattered – I was just wasting my time. I think I want to do something different. Not just another office job.'

'I feel you,' said Kirsty. 'If I wasn't getting paid a fucking fortune to go down to the docks and shine a torch on and off at a yacht moored in international waters, I'd quit in a flash.'

'See, that sounds interesting,' Cate said.

'It's all pointless bureaucracy,' Kirsty sighed. 'The last five guys I had to run checks on, they all died the day after I filed my report. Assessing their performance was a complete waste of time.'

'What did they die of?' said Cate.

'Uh, lead poisoning? There's some bad plumbing in our Infrastructure Hygiene department.'

'Maybe I should have applied to your work,' Cate said. 'Are there any PR jobs going?'

'Good luck,' said Kirsty. 'I don't even know what the place is called. They changed the name four times in a week, and then stopped telling us.'

Cate turned to Vanessa, who was wrestling with her drone's controls. It dipped overhead, then resumed its circling. 'Don't look at me,' she said. 'My work doesn't tell me anything either. Our last corporate retreat was a tree-planting session.'

'See, that sounds okay...' Cate said.

'They bussed us out to some remote property and made us dig these really deep holes. They must have been putting in established trees. We didn't even get to see them before they herded us back on the bus.'

49

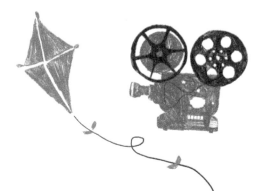

Adam stood on the footpath outside the address on Clive's business card. 'It's a Chicken Shaq,' he said.

'Sure is,' said a girl pushing past him as she walked out the door, a bag of chicken in hand. Maybe Clive had moved? But his phone number hadn't changed. Adam took out his phone and called him.

'Adam,' his agent said, surprised. 'What's going on?'

'Well, I'm out the front of your office, only your office seems to be a Chicken Shaq.'

'Come on up,' Clive said, and hung up.

'Up where?' Adam said to his phone. He looked at the business card again; there was a small 'level one' above the address, but the entire front of the building was taken up by the Chicken Shaq. The only stairs he could see were the ones that went to the upstairs dining area.

With a shrug, Adam went inside and climbed the stairs. Isolated from the busy downstairs, this area was the domain of delinquent teens, with the occasional hard-living hobo huddled in a corner booth. Aside from bolted-down tables and chairs, and a couple of sparrows pecking at abandoned fries, there wasn't much to look at here; the only doors led to the restrooms.

Wait – no they didn't. Right in the far corner was an old-fashioned wooden door, with a glass panel that had something hand-lettered on it in gold paint. Adam walked over and took a closer look. 'Clive and –' the next word had been crudely scratched out. That was good enough. Adam reached out, turned the handle and went in.

The tiny space seemed as if it had once been a cleaning cupboard, but a desk was jammed into the corner. Looking even more massively fat than he remembered, Clive was wedged behind it in a way that reminded Adam of a cork in a bottle. Papers were piled on every flat space, including the keyboard of an ancient computer that had probably been taken out by Y2K.

'Adam!' Clive said, waving his arms in a fashion that was presumably intended to be welcoming, but made him look like he was drowning. 'Can I get you something?'

'Um...'

'Coke? Fries? A Smacker?' He flashed a crafty smile. 'A Clucker?'

'I don't even know what that is.'

'Stacy,' Clive said, pressing a button on an intercom covered in papers, 'can we get two Cluckers in here, thanks?'

'Of course,' came the young woman's voice. 'That'll be twenty-two forty.'

'Get them to put it on my tab,' Clive said with a smile.

'Uh, I've been told to say you have to pay upfront,' Stacy said.

He glared at the intercom. 'That's not the arrangement,' he said, glancing at Adam before turning the speaker off.

'So, Adam,' Clive said, 'congratulations on the *Consumption* role.'

'That's what I'm here to talk to you about,' Adam said. 'I'm not sure it's a good move for me.'

'Oh, it's a terrible move,' Clive said. 'If you don't like money!'

Adam did not laugh.

'But, uh, if you're...' Clive gave up. 'Why wouldn't you want to do it?'

'I don't know,' Adam said. 'I'm just not sure it feels right. I want to direct. You know I've never wanted to be on camera.'

'Well, you're a natural,' Clive said. 'The *Consumption* guys were really happy with you. They were calling me up every day just to tell me how great you were.'

'Really?'

'Would I lie to you?'

'You told me you were a directing agent.'

'Would I lie to you today?'

Adam frowned.

'Look,' Clive said, 'do you have any idea just how huge this franchise is? The trades have been speculating for a year about who's going to be playing Haze Volante, and now they've gone with a total unknown. The fans are going to lose their shit over you.'

'That doesn't sound good,' said Adam.

'Consider it a springboard for whatever you want to do in Hollywood,' Clive said. 'You're going to be meeting loads of people who can help you in your career.'

'Well, who's going to be directing it, then? No one seems to know – and they want me in LA in six weeks.'

'All I know is, it's some European. Meant to be very old-school. You've probably heard of him, you like all that old crap.' Clive's face lit up. 'He's just like you – he's doing this to make a buck and get a foot in the door in Hollywood.'

'Has he done anything I would have seen?'

'*Parental Absence Party? Whores of War?* I think they're his.'

Whores of War, Adam thought. Hadn't he seen that at an actual film festival? It had been surprisingly arty for a slasher film about lingerie-clad sex slaves killing people with household items. The final kill had involved the head of the human trafficking ring fleeing through an apple orchard while the War Whores chased him with hammers; the final cut from a hammer coming down on his face to an exploding apple had been...

'Mnmskmo!' Adam said.

'Gesundheit,' Clive said automatically.

I guess everyone ends up selling out eventually, Adam thought.

The world only needs so many nine-hour yurt films. And if Mnmskmo couldn't make it work on his own terms, what hope did Adam have? Maybe he was just being too precious about the whole thing; for all he knew, Mnmskmo liked making slasher films and teen sex romps. The money had to be decent, at least.

And now Adam was going to be working with him. Imagine what he could learn from the master – there was a lifetime of experience here, just waiting for Adam to tap into. It'd be insane to pass up an opportunity like this.

'Okay,' Adam said. 'I'll do it.'

'Excellent,' Clive said, struggling to lean over his desk to shake Adam's hand.

There was a knock on the door. 'Enter,' Clive barked.

A teenage girl in a Chicken Shaq uniform came in holding a pair of paper bags, a wireless headset over her baseball cap. 'Here are your Smackers!'

'Stacy,' Clive said, 'we ordered Cluckers.' He eyed off the paper bags. 'And we ordered them to eat in.'

'We don't make Cluckers any more. And my manager said that technically, this is takeaway.' Stacy dropped the bags on the desk. 'That'll be twenty-two forty.'

Clive made a remarkably unconvincing show of patting his pockets. 'Oh darn,' he said, 'I seem to have left my wallet at home.'

Adam looked at the wallet sitting on the desk. Clive elbowed it under a stack of papers, already foraging in one of the paper bags. 'You'll be able to afford all the Smackers you like once you're in Hollywood.'

Adam sighed and paid for the burgers. Weren't business lunches meant to work the other way around? This should have been the most exciting day of his life. Why did he feel so empty?

50

'I need a fresh start,' Cate said, fidgeting with the kite in her hands.

'Well, what sort of job *do* you want?' said Vanessa.

'Maybe,' said Kirsty, 'you could have your own internet startup!'

'What would I be starting up?' said Cate.

'It doesn't even matter!' Kirsty said, tugging on her left set of strings to bring the kite around in an arc. 'That's the beauty of internet startups. Just start a website of some sort. An app... or a bot... maybe a butt bot... a crap app... butt app? I know! It could be called Crappr! And it could tell you when you have to go to the toilet.'

'I think my body already does that,' said Cate.

'It's a standard feature among humans,' said Vanessa.

'My body tells me when I'm hungry, but there are still heaps of apps about restaurants,' Kirsty said defensively.

'Maybe it could be a social network where people share their poos,' said Vanessa. 'Some people love talking about that shit.'

'Um, how did we get here?' Cate said. 'I'm not working on a butt app.'

'Maybe you could start up a quirky shop that sells delightful bespoke merchandise,' Vanessa said. 'Like antiquarian books about animals, or hand-printed wrapping paper, or organic cupcakes in the shape of other things, or personalised greeting cards, or old plastic children's toys with cute little cactuses planted in them.'

Cate looked at her in disgust. 'Do you even know me?'

'You're a zany single gal in the big city,' said Kirsty. 'How else will a man walk into your life if you don't run a pointless novelty shop?'

'Why not open an art gallery?' Vanessa said. 'A sophisticated little space in a converted loft downtown, painted white. And you can wear all black, and put your hair in a chignon, and walk around thoughtfully wearing stilettos, making quiet little tock, tock, tock sounds.'

'That sounds... specific.'

'And you can invite us all to your exhibition openings,' Vanessa continued dreamily. 'And there'll be champagne, and we'll meet all kinds of creative people, and have witty conversations...'

'Yeah, about your new butt app,' Kirsty said. 'That's how you're paying for all this highfalutin crap, isn't it?'

'Why am I getting the feeling that these are your particular dreams?' Cate said. 'Aren't we supposed to be taking care of my problems?'

'Well, we've given you lots of job suggestions,' Kirsty said. 'What else do you need?'

Vanessa smirked. 'Do you want us to fix you up with a guy?'

'Yeah, because that worked out so well last time.'

'Well, that wasn't our fault,' Vanessa said.

'Yes it was!' Cate said. 'If you hadn't sold Adam as the Hot Guy, and we'd just met normally, none of this would have happened.'

'Would you ever have spoken to him normally?' Vanessa said. 'The whole point of the Hot Guy is that it gives you permission to approach a guy who's out of your league.'

'You guys keep saying "the whole point of the Hot Guy", like he was a process,' she said. 'Some kind of theme park ride, or a training course you go through. But Adam's a person. And he wasn't out of my league.'

They looked at her.

'Well, maybe just one league above,' Cate said. 'I'm at the top of *my* league.'

'Of course you are, babe,' Vanessa said.

'Ugh, I don't even want to hear the word "league",' said Cate. 'Those crazy women on Facebook...'

'You know, I saw Adam during the week,' Kirsty said, casually tweaking her kite strings.

Cate jerked to face her. 'And you didn't tell me? Where? How did he look? Was he with someone – wait, I don't want to know.'

'Well, he was all alone,' Kirsty said, 'except for his new beard.'

'Ew,' said Vanessa loyally.

'Yeah, he looked like Saddam Hussein. Or, more like –' Kirsty glanced around to be sure they were paying attention, 'Sad Adam Insane.'

'Didn't Saddam Hussein have a moustache?' Vanessa said.

'It was like when he was in the hole!' Kirsty said.

'How long were you workshopping that joke?' Vanessa said.

Kirsty shrugged. 'It just came to me.'

'Sure it did,' said Vanessa.

'How much beard could he have grown in a week?' said Cate.

'Look, my point is,' Kirsty said, 'he looked really broken up.'

'Poor Adam,' Cate said softly.

'Have you called him this week?' Vanessa said.

Cate sighed. 'I wanted to,' she said, 'but I went past his work last weekend and left a message with his friends. And he knows I've been trying to call him. I can't do anything more.' She wiped away a tear. 'I really can't.'

Vanessa took one hand from her controls to rub Cate's shoulder consolingly. Overhead, the drone began to dive.

'I mean,' Cate continued, 'if he hasn't got back to me by now, I don't know what to think. Is he over me? Should I just... let it go? I don't want to let it go. But if I push it, won't I push him away?'

'You're right,' Vanessa said, righting her drone moments

before it would have collided with Kirsty's mass of hair and, eventually, Kirsty's head. 'You've done everything you could to show him you're sorry and you want him back.'

'Maybe you could try just one more time,' Kirsty said, 'if you really do miss him.'

'It's not really worth thinking about now,' Cate said dismissively. 'I don't want him to ruin a lovely day.'

She set off at a run along the grass, holding her kite above her head and paying out the line. She always felt a little stupid during this part. But today the wind was on Cate's side. It tugged on the kite and she fed it more string, feeling the nylon slip through her fingers. The breeze lifted the kite high, sending it to join her friends' flying machines.

Relief filled Cate as she tweaked the string and saw the kite respond. It was such a simple object, needing nothing more than a breeze and a flick of the wrist to send it curving through the air with fluid grace. And she was the one determining its path. Keeping it aloft required a constant concentration that emptied her mind of everything else. Cate felt the burdens of her life fall away – the breakup with Adam, her work worries. It was just her and the kite.

She hadn't felt this pure sense of purpose since her early days in PR. That, she realised, was what she needed now in her work. She needed to think smaller. She'd been applying for jobs at big companies thinking that was the way to advance her career. But now she knew those were places where even the most successful PR campaigns would have next to no impact. Maybe if she went somewhere smaller... somewhere more agile... somewhere that offered more direct control over her work...

Cate looked up at the brightly coloured diamond with its undulating tail. What if she could help other people have this same feeling? A horrible image swam into her mind of her waving the kite in some naff self-help seminar. It would have been all right if the seminar room were packed... but even in

Cate's dreams, nobody had shown up to learn about the mental health benefits of kite-flying.

Well, at least that was a good angle to help sell kites. She wondered who actually made them. She'd bought hers from a hobby shop, but she had no idea where they'd got it from. Did they make them out the back? Was there a kite factory? Maybe it was worth approaching these places, and offering her skills to promote kite-flying. There might be some money in it, and it would keep her occupied until she found a real job.

'Hey, guys – do you know who makes kites?' she called to Kirsty and Vanessa. 'Where do they come from?'

Kirsty frowned. 'Do they grow on trees? I've seen trees before with kites hanging from them.'

'Um, Kirsty...' said Cate.

'Why do you want to know?' said Vanessa.

'Oh, nothing,' said Cate. 'I've just had an idea. Hey, we should do this more often. It's really...'

Vanessa nodded. 'Really...'

'Yeah,' said Kirsty, 'really fun!'

'I was going to say it's really soothing,' Vanessa said. 'We've got so much going on in our lives, sometimes it's just nice to focus on something simple.'

'Exactly!' said Cate.

'And speaking of simple, now that Adam's gone...' Kirsty said.

Vanessa shook her head. 'Too soon?'

'Just a little,' Cate said. 'But I am feeling better. And I want to thank you guys for being there for me.'

'Where else would we be?' said Vanessa.

'We could be down the pub,' Kirsty suggested.

Cate checked her watch. 'Well, it is lunchtime,' she said, 'and I could go a drink. What about you, Vanessa?'

She shrugged. 'Fine by me. Let me just land this thing.'

'Why didn't anyone ask me?' Kirsty said.

'We didn't have to, Kirsty,' Cate said.

Vanessa's drone dropped rapidly and scudded to a stop on the grass.

'Nice landing,' Kirsty said, reeling in her kite.

With a sharp tug on the string, Cate began to bring her own kite back to earth. It thudded against the ground a few metres away. Walking over, she picked it up and looked for any clue to its manufacturer. According to a label on the underside, her kite was a Breezemaster 2000, by Thompson Novelties.

She'd give them a call in the morning.

51

A limp string of Australian flags behind the ticket counter was the only outward sign that tonight was Australian Film Night at the Rafferty Cinema. Showing in Cinema One was a double feature of period melodrama *Waiting for Jack* and its somewhat harder-edged sequel *Jack Never Came Back*, while Cinema Two was showing the low-budget, all-indigenous Quentin Tarantino ripoff, *Armed Corroboree*. In Cinema Three, meanwhile, was the multi-AFI Award-winning drama *A Torturous Limbo at the Woollahra Abattoir.*

The cinema was deserted.

Adam was manning the ticket counter when Steve approached, wearing photocopied twenty-dollar notes pinned all over his clothing. 'What are you supposed to be?' Adam said.

'I'm a stack of taxpayers' money.' Steve gestured at Adam, whose costume consisted of an oversized garbage bag with holes cut for his arms and legs. His head was protruding from the drawstring opening of the bag. 'What are you?'

'I'm a pile of rubbish,' Adam said.

Steve nodded thoughtfully. 'Theme-appropriate.'

'I think we've both nailed it tonight.'

'Look at this pathetic turnout!' came Renton's aggrieved voice. 'If we'd shown *Flames of Desire*, we would've been packing them into the aisles!'

Steve and Adam turned, and laughed in horror as Renton strutted towards them, naked but for a pair of alarmingly tight red Speedos and a red-and-yellow lifeguard's cap.

'And what are *you* meant to be?' Steve said. 'Something no one wants to see?'

With great dignity and an audible snap of elastic, Renton unwedged his swimmers from between his butt-cheeks. 'I'm *The Coolangatta Gold*,' he said.

'More like the fool-in-datta outfit,' Steve retorted.

'*You're* always stripping off for these theme nights,' Renton said.

'That's because my body actually attracts customers.'

'You don't get many blind customers at a cinema,' countered Renton.

'Guys,' Adam said. 'Can't we all be united in our love of Australian film?'

They paused, then laughed heartily.

Customers were beginning to drift in now, even if many of them seemed confused about where they were.

'Am I in the right place for the Austrian film festival?' asked one middle-aged lady, her amber beads clanking.

Renton nodded enthusiastically. 'You sure are!' he said. 'Yodel-ay-hee-hoo!'

'I didn't know Tarzan was Austrian,' the lady said. 'But sure, one ticket please.'

A drunk girl leered at Adam. 'You look just like Heath Ledger!' she gushed.

'Really?' he said, bemused. This was a new one.

'Totally!' she said. 'And you know what my favourite Heath Ledger movie is?'

He shook his head.

She lunged towards him, arms outstretched. '*Two Hands!*'

Steve caught her before she could make contact. 'You know what *my* favourite Heath Ledger movie is?' he told her, steering her away from the ticket counter. '*Ten Things I Hate About You.*'

Renton chimed in from the candy bar. 'I think Ledger was

really great in *The Imaginarium of Doctor Parnassus*,' he said. He shook his head sorrowfully. 'Gone too soon.'

She cast a scornful glance at Renton's crotch. 'Well, there's one Heath Ledger movie I wish I hadn't seen...'

He brightened.

'*Monster's Ball!*' she shouted.

Renton discreetly looked down and adjusted his Speedos, as the girl wove back across the foyer in the direction of the cinema bar.

'Thanks for nothing, guys,' Renton said. 'I was totally in there.'

'Yeah,' Steve said, 'in trouble. Surely it's a food hygiene violation to have you on the candy bar.'

'Stop cock-blocking us, Steve!' Renton said. 'Adam and I are single, and looking to mingle.'

'Dude, there's not much blocking your cock in that costume,' Steve said.

'I'm not mingling anything with you,' Adam said, handing a ticket to a latecomer for *Armed Corroboree*. *Waiting for Jack* had started ten minutes earlier; the foyer was now completely empty.

'You're not mingling anything with anyone, Adam,' said Steve. 'Have you even got your dick wet since you ditched Cate?'

'Jesus, Steve, lay off,' Adam said. 'Look, I'm trying to get past Cate, but what can I do? I can't stop thinking about her. She moved on just fine. And I'm left behind.'

'Weren't you the one who left *her*?' Steve said.

'Well, yeah, but I was an idiot. Why did I make such a big fuss about this Hot Guy thing? She didn't like me just because I was the Hot Guy.'

'It didn't hurt,' Renton said.

'Yeah,' Adam said, 'but it's not like she was spending all day staring at my face.' He smirked. 'Sometimes she stared at my butt.'

Renton nodded. 'It is a nice butt.'

'I was mad at her. That's why I didn't answer her calls,' Adam said, 'but I thought at least she'd try to meet me face to face.' He shrugged. 'Maybe she just wasn't into me. Maybe she didn't really care.'

Steve and Renton exchanged a look.

'Um,' Steve said, 'we've got good news and bad news. The good news: Cate did come by here looking for you.'

'The bad news,' said Renton, 'is that it was a week ago. When you were off on the film set.'

'What?' Adam said. 'Why didn't you tell me?'

'Because she was a *bitch*,' said Renton. 'And we thought you were better off without her.'

'You dumped her. We thought you wouldn't want to talk to her,' Steve said.

'What made you think that?'

'Those times you said, "I don't want to talk to her"?'

'Shit,' Adam said. 'Did she leave a message?'

'She just wanted you to know that she was looking for you,' Steve said. 'And we figured you already knew that, what with her ringing every five seconds.'

'Well, she's not ringing now!' Adam said, exasperated.

'Do you want her to ring?' Renton said. 'I thought we were going out tonight.'

'What's the point?' Adam said. 'All I want is Cate.'

Steve and Renton looked at each other. 'Shit man, I'm sorry,' Steve said. 'We just thought you were wasting your time.'

'Don't I get to decide if I'm wasting my time?'

Renton couldn't help himself. 'But why would someone who looks like you want to be tied down?' He paused. 'Unless you *wanted* to be tied down. Did she tie you down?'

'No,' Adam said. 'Well, maybe once. Look, that's not the point.' He ran his hands through his hair, frustratedly. 'I liked spending time with her. She was interested in me, not just my face. She was smart. She was funny, even when she didn't think she was being funny. She was... *fun.*'

Adam was struggling to explain himself to his friends. 'Love is this big force that, like, makes you do things that you don't want to do, but you do want to do, because you're part of a story – you and her, and it's your story. Your story together. And I never thought our story would be like this. That we'd just drift apart, just fade away. I mean, she was my life, and I didn't think it'd just drain away through my fingers. I thought we'd end it in some dramatic way – a big fight or something. But it's just nothing. How can it be nothing? She was everything to me, and now what am I supposed to do? I don't know what to do. I was so mad at her, but it's like being mad at a part of yourself. It's like being mad at your hand.'

Renton sniggered. 'Yeah, I get it, though,' he said. 'It's like being mad at your dick. It brings you so much pleasure, but sometimes,' Renton shook his head, 'it lets you down.'

'So,' Steve said, 'I'm confused. Is she your hand?'

'She was part of me,' insisted Adam. 'I let her in, and then she became part of me, and then I thought I could just throw all that away. But she's part of me. And it hurts to lose a part of yourself.'

'Yeah,' said Steve, 'like that scene in *Armed Corroboree* where the guy loses his nose to the rabid wallabies. His story was all downhill from here.'

'There wasn't even a second act to our story,' said Adam. 'We'd only just got started.'

'Well, maybe you'll start over,' Renton said excitedly. 'Like a reboot.'

'They never work,' Adam said. 'Name one good sequel.'

'*Godfather II*,' Steve said.

'Everyone says *Godfather II*,' Adam said. 'And that's a prequel. Love stories don't have sequels. There's no *When Harry Met Sally II*.'

280

'What about *Bridget Jones: The Edge of Reason?*' Renton said to himself.

'No one says your story's over,' Steve said. 'You can still go after her.'

'What if she's decided it's over?'

'What have you got to lose?' said Steve.

'Everything! Nothing! It doesn't feel like I've got anything without her. I've got nothing to lose because she was my everything.'

'Oh man,' Steve groaned, 'and we thought you'd be right after a couple of days of boozing on.'

'Booze isn't the glue that holds together a broken heart,' said Adam.

'What, are you writing country songs now?' Renton said.

'I'm serious,' Adam said. 'I meant everything I said just now.'

'Well,' Steve said, 'why don't you tell her that?'

'Fuck it, I will,' said Adam, taking out his phone. The seconds it took for his call to connect seemed long and terrible.

'The number you have called is not connected or has been changed. Please check the number before calling again.'

Adam stared at his phone in disbelief.

'What?' Renton said.

'Straight to voicemail?' said Steve.

'She changed her number,' Adam said numbly.

'Oh man,' said Renton. 'She ghosted. Harsh.'

Adam was still staring at the screen. 'It's only been two weeks.'

'You must have really messed with her,' Steve said.

'There must be something wrong with her phone,' Adam said. 'Maybe she forgot to pay the bill or something... She can't have deliberately changed it...'

Steve looked at Renton, who was shaking his head. 'Dude,' Renton said carefully, 'you know... you can't just...'

'Adam, it was cool when you were coming out drinking with us,' Steve interrupted, 'and women would come up to us, and you weren't interested. And even when you were hooking up with those chicks who'd run off the next day. Y'know, that was fine. But if you're gonna start having proper relationships, you've gotta realise –'

'Dude, you're really hot!' Renton blurted. 'Seriously.'

Adam laughed. 'What?'

Steve's face was solemn. 'You've got to get serious about the way you treat people. They go crazy for you. Women, dudes too. And you need to respect that. You can't go around thinking you can just walk out on someone and they won't care. You're a great guy, but with great hotness comes great responsibility.'

'I've seen it,' said Renton. You just *look* at some girl and it's made her night. What do you think's gonna happen if you start a real relationship?'

'But I didn't mean to hurt Cate! She hurt me!'

'Man, get over it,' Renton said.

Steve nodded. 'You're the one who dumped her.'

'I didn't *dump* her! I thought we'd...'

'She was in love with you, and you pushed her away!' Renton said. 'What did you think she was going to do?'

'I didn't think she'd change her phone number!'

'Guess that means you're still coming out with us tonight.' Renton yelped as Steve punched him in the arm.

'Ring her work, then,' Steve said.

'I can't wait till Monday! I'll have to go round to her house.'

'Maybe she'll be out,' said Renton. A loud slap followed. 'Owww.'

'That's a good point,' Steve said. 'It's Friday night.'

'But I can't stand here and do nothing!' Adam said.

'Um, technically you're being paid to be here,' Renton said.

'We'll cover for you,' said Steve. 'I'm more concerned about the fact that you're trying to have your big romantic reunion wearing a garbage bag.'

'There's hardly anyone here tonight anyway,' Renton said.

'You never know,' Steve said, 'there might be a late surge of interest in Australian film.'

They all laughed.

'We've totally got you covered, bro,' Renton said.

'Go get her,' Steve said. 'Fight for love.'

Adam pushed open the glass doors of the cinema, and didn't look back.

There were lights on at Cate's house. Someone was home. Adam marched up the front path, his garbage-bag costume billowing and rustling dramatically, and leaned on the doorbell. He waited. Nothing happened.

He looked up. Cate's bedroom was the front upstairs room, he knew – and while the window was lit up, he couldn't see any movement from inside. He pressed the doorbell again.

Adam was about to yell out when he thought, *What if she's in there with someone?* He had a sudden flash of insight into how stupid his grand romantic gesture would look if she'd already got over him. Rummaging in his bag, he found a pen and a notebook.

Dear Cate,

I'm sorry I was an idiot! I should never have pushed you away. I've made a terrible mistake. Please call me!

I love you,

Adam

He folded the note and slid it into Cate's mailbox. But instead of the reassuring thud of it hitting bare metal, Adam heard it land with a soft rustle. He peered through the slot and saw his note sitting atop a thick stack of mail, along with a few dead leaves. How long had it been since Cate checked her mail? Would she even read his heartfelt declaration?

Adam briefly considered leaving the note under her front door instead, but then dismissed it. Maybe he was being too dramatic. Cate might clear her mail on weekends. He couldn't plaster notes all over her house. It'd end up looking like Steve's

Australian film costume. Adam decided that if he hadn't heard from her by Monday, he'd call her at work.

He was standing at the kerb, trying to hail a taxi, when a grizzled man in a stained, moth-eaten jacket shuffled past, gripping a bottle in a crumpled paper bag. With rheumy eyes, the man looked Adam up and down and shook his head sadly. Adam smiled, warmed by the brief moment of empathy between them.

'Man,' the wino said, gesturing at Adam's costume, 'that's a real shame, when folks be throwing away a perfectly good white boy like that.'

'Ah, *Better Off Dead*,' Adam said, nodding. 'Nice work on the classic movie reference, but, "white boy"? C'mon!' He looked down at himself. 'You can't even see my skin under all this garbage.'

The man shook his head, took a big swig from his bottle and started walking back up the road.

'Wait a second,' Adam said as an idea slowly dawned, 'I think I recognise you! Are you Savage Steve Holland, director of the '80s cult classic *Better Off Dead*?'

The man started to run.

'And its under-appreciated quasi-sequel *One Crazy Summer*?' Adam shouted as the man disappeared into the night.

'Geez,' Adam said as he watched him go. 'It's not like I mentioned *Legally Blondes* or anything.'

52

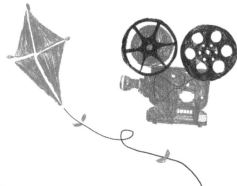

The Royal Regal Cinema, Cate thought, was everything the Rafferty was not. For one thing, the staff were polite and competent. She was sitting on a velvet couch in its plush foyer, surrounded by potted plants and deco-style lighting. A luxuriously appointed chrome bar stretched along the entire far wall, holding a coffee machine and a glass-fronted display cabinet of cakes.

Cate was on the phone to Kirsty. 'It was so weird,' she said. 'Someone kept ringing my doorbell, but when I looked out the window all I could see was a bag of garbage. And then when I went out the front, it was gone.'

'Sounds like a prank,' Kirsty said.

'A pretty stupid prank,' Cate said. 'What happened to the garbage? It had, like, an old rug sticking out the top. I'm glad they took it away.'

'So, who's your hot date?'

'Some guy Vanessa works with. She said he's into movies.'

'Doesn't sound like much of a basis for –'

'Look, I've got to start somewhere. I can't wait for Adam forever.'

'Is he there yet?' Kirsty said. 'Is he hot?'

'I'm done with hot guys,' Cate said. 'Oh, he's just walked in. Gotta go.'

An earnest young man had walked into the foyer and was hesitating, glancing around him. He had a wholesome look, as if his face had been freshly scrubbed. And he was wearing the kind of smart casual clothes that suggested he'd come straight from work, but that he worked somewhere hip and innovative. He had the most fastidiously polished shoes Cate had ever seen.

'Cate? Hi, I'm Albert.'

Cate shook his proffered hand. 'Hi, I'm Cate,' she said. 'I mean, yes, that's me. Do we have time for a coffee before the movie?'

'Sure,' he said. 'I'll get it.'

Cate's thoughts wandered as Albert went over to the bar. She didn't want to compare him to Adam, but she couldn't help herself. Adam was hot; this guy was more like reheated. He was handsome, she supposed, but... A shiver of fear ran down her spine as she thought, *Maybe Adam's ruined me for other men.*

No, she thought, and set her jaw determinedly. She was going to make this work. Or at the very least, have a good time. She watched Albert's butt as he stood at the bar, and sighed. Not *that* good a time.

He turned to head back, holding two black coffees and a small jug of milk. 'Sorry, I forgot to ask what sort of coffee you drink,' he said, placing the cups on the table in front of Cate. 'Sugar?'

'No, you're sweet enough,' she said, smiling at him.

He stared back blankly. The moment dragged.

'Um, I mean... no thanks,' she said, unable to hide her disappointment that he hadn't got her joke.

Albert didn't seem to notice. 'Would you like some water?' he said.

Cate smirked. 'Why – do I look *thirsty* to you?'

Now he actually seemed bewildered. 'What do you mean?'

Clearly it was too early for smutty jokes. 'Uh...' she said, 'I... don't know.'

'Interesting,' Albert said, in a way that suggested it was anything but.

'You know,' Cate forged on gamely, 'I've always felt you can divide cafés into two groups. Ones that bring you a glass of water, and ones that bring you a bottle of water.'

'Uh-huh,' Albert said. 'Do you want me to get some water?'

She nodded mutely, and he got up from the sofa and went back over to the bar. Cate squeezed her eyes shut. This date was off to a great start.

He was back with a bottle of water and two glasses. 'I wasn't sure if you wanted a bottle or a glass,' he said, 'so I brought both.' He filled a glass and handed it to Cate.

She took a sip. 'Mmmm,' she said. 'Really lives up to the hype.'

'Hype?'

'Well, you know, we were talking about it before, and... Never mind.'

He gulped from his own glass. 'I'm really looking forward to this movie.'

'Yes,' Cate said with relief, 'Vanessa told me you're something of a movie buff.'

'I wouldn't say that,' Albert said, 'but I have seen all six *Fart Knocker* films.'

'What – even *Fart Knocker VI: Steer Into The Skid*? That didn't even make it into cinemas here.'

Albert looked uncertain. 'Maybe I haven't seen that one.'

'It was just a wacky races knock-off, except it was about a fart-powered car.'

'That doesn't sound very likely,' he said.

'And the fart-powered blimp in *Fart Knocker IV: Stench of Evil* was?' Cate countered. 'Not that I'm an expert.'

'Well, what kind of films *do* you like?'

'Oh, all kinds,' Cate said. 'I used to watch films all the time with my last boyfriend.'

'Oh,' Albert said.

The pause stretched. Cate wished someone would break the tension, even if it were by breaking wind. Where was Bud

MEL CAMPBELL AND ANTHONY MORRIS

'Buttocks' Brown, star of the *Fart Knocker* films, when you needed him?

'Cinema Three is now open for the 9.30 session of *The Orange Peeler: The Man Who Peeled The Orange*,' called an usher.

'Sounds like he gave that orange a real going over,' Cate said.

Albert looked faintly dismayed. 'I thought you might like it. I heard it had some positive reviews.'

'No, no, it sounds great,' Cate said, quietly dying inside. These were jokes! Why was this date so hard going?

They took their seats in the cinema during a warning about the use of mobile phones during screenings.

'Setting us on fire seems a bit much,' Cate said.

'Yeah, the flames would be a worse distraction than the phone,' Albert said.

Cate smiled. Maybe this would work out after all.

The first film trailer was for a stoner detective comedy, and featured a humorous voiceover. 'From the makers of *James and the Giant Blunt* and *Thomas the Dank Engine* comes an outrageous new film!' chuckled the narrator. 'Everyone knew the Titanic was unsinkable. But they never said it was... unsmokeable.'

'What?' Cate said loudly. Then the film title came up onscreen: *BLAZE THE TITANIC*. An unseemly bark of laughter escaped Cate, and she swiftly disguised it as a cough.

It seemed that in this context, the Titanic was a legendarily enormous joint that various wacky characters were trying to track down. Evil government scientists wanted to extract the DNA from its unusual THC strain, while a meth dealer known as the Iceberg wanted it off the streets. But the film's shaggy heroes just wanted to smoke it: 'We gotta save the Titanic from the Iceberg.'

Cate giggled as the trailer showed a sign that read, '420 Spliff Street'. Albert shot her a confused look in the darkness.

'It's funny!' she said.

'Uh, no it isn't.'

She didn't want to contradict him. He'd had enough of

her dumb sense of humour for one night. The jolly voiceover returned: '*Rolling* into cinemas on April 20th!'

The trailer that followed was advertising a broad Australian comedy titled *What Have I Written?* It involved a middle-aged man who'd awoken from a coma with severe memory loss and promptly done something silly. The man – played by Aussie screen legend Barry Otto – was engaging in all manner of quirky antics as he struggled to understand why everyone was so angry at him. Text faded up on a black screen: 'The long-awaited sequel to the arthouse classic *What I Have Written.*'

The trailer ended with Otto shrugging pantomimishly, as a string of review quotes flashed up onscreen.

'The question on everyone's lips this winter will be... *What Have I Written?*' – David Stratton, *The Australian*

'Some movies make you laugh; others make you think. This one will make you wonder why' – @renton69, *BackedUpToilet.com*

'It... was... really... good' – Pauline Kael, *WikiOuija*

The final trailer showed a young South American woman running through a cornfield. The cornstalks crackled atmospherically as she brushed past – the only sound apart from her ragged breathing and the thump of her bare feet against the earth. Cate waited for something else to happen, but the trailer was just shot after shot of the same girl running through the corn. It seemed to go on forever.

At last, the title melted slowly onto the screen. *Maize Runner: The Starch Trials.*

'Oh, I really want to see that!' Cate said excitedly. 'The first one was really good, according to... Adam...' She trailed off.

'Who's Adam?'

'Oh, no one,' she said. 'I won't be seeing it with him.'

Thankfully, the feature began. *The Orange Peeler: The Man Who Peeled The Orange* was a Spanish drama set on a family farm. A long-lost son had returned to claim his inheritance. He devoured a succession of oranges with gusto, juice streaming down his handsome face as he stared lustily at a young woman who was playing the castanets.

Meanwhile, an old drifter had shown up at the farm to peel oranges with his trusty knife. But it felt to Cate like he had other plans for that knife, considering he kept stabbing the oranges while glaring at various characters.

'When the sun rises, it is red, but then it becomes orange,' said the subtitles. 'The orangest of oranges. Oranges are orange, but also the colour of an orange is orange. Orange we see, and orange we eat. Orange is of the eyes and of the heart. The orange of the sun fathers the orange of the trees.'

It took several minutes for all this to display on the screen.

'I'm pretty sure that's not what she just said,' Cate hissed.

'Mmm,' Albert said.

'Her lips weren't even moving that much.'

'Uh-huh.'

'And she was eating an orange for half of it.'

As the sultry señorita embarked on a passionate flamenco solo, the excessively detailed subtitles kept running. 'Orange orange orange orange orange...' The subtitles began moving across the screen like a news ticker. 'Orangeorangeorangeora nge...'

Cate zoned out. She dimly registered that there was an orange fight. Someone's house was painted orange. At one point Cate thought she saw a man's head turn into an orange, then fall off and roll away. Was this a dream sequence? Was *she* dreaming?

The film climaxed as the young man, frantically trying to escape the demons of his orange farming past, drove his car wildly down a dirt track. The car fishtailed and crashed into a large tree. The man began moving – he'd survived the crash! – but then oranges started to fall from the tree, pelting the man as he tried to stagger away from the twisted wreck.

In the final shot, the old orange peeler, now riding a donkey, slowly approached the car. By now it was completely buried under a mountain of oranges – more, Cate thought, than could possibly have fallen from one tree. The only trace of the young man was an arm protruding limply from the orange pyramid. In his hand was a single orange. Enigmatically, the old man took the fruit and began to peel. The scene faded to black.

'Sponsored by the Spanish Orange Board!' Cate scoffed in the foyer afterwards. 'What a shock!'

'Oh well,' Albert said. 'Do you want to get something to eat?'

'As long as it's not orange,' Cate said. 'I think I've had my Vitamin C intake for the day.'

Albert nodded. 'There's a little Korean dumpling place down the road.'

'What about that bit where the village was crushed by the giant orange? Was that for real, or was it just a metaphor?'

'Their fried dumplings are great.'

Cate frowned. 'Don't you even want to talk about what we just saw? That was insane!'

'Not really,' Albert said apologetically. 'I was bored, mainly.'

'Oh,' she said. *Adam would have wanted to talk*, she thought, and realised she hadn't stopped thinking about Adam all night. She'd somehow convinced herself that if Albert liked movies, he might be like Adam in other ways, too. But Adam liked to *discuss* movies. Adam liked to talk to *her*. And he listened. They had actual *conversations*. Albert wasn't at all like Adam, Cate realised – and Adam was all she could think about.

'Maybe I'm a bit too tired to eat right now,' she said. 'I might just head home. Thanks for a lovely evening.'

'We could do dumplings another time, maybe?'

'Sure,' she said, knowing it would never happen.

53

A bell tinkled as Cate pushed open the door of Up In The Air.

'Can I help you?' asked a bearded hipster shop assistant, who was wearing an apron.

'Just looking,' said Cate.

The shop was filled with kites. They hung from the ceiling and lined the walls, in a dizzying variety of shapes and colours. Basic diamonds, like Cate's own kite; batwings in sizes up to a few metres across. Striped and patterned kites; kites with giant eyes and military roundels painted on their wings. Three-dimensional kites in the shapes of planes, butterflies, dragons, frogs, penguins... *A penguin is a flightless bird*, Cate thought.

She picked her way through the festive chaos, past racks of kite-tail ribbons and multicoloured strings. She was dazzled. There had to be some kind of order underlying all this, but Cate couldn't see what it was. She turned around, and –

'Cate?'

'Mr Thompson! They've got you working on a Saturday?'

'The head of the company doesn't get any time off,' he replied. 'And what are you doing here? You don't start till Monday.'

'I just wanted to take a look around the store before I start,' she said. 'I'm not going to get much time once I'm in the office.'

'Well, it's a good thing you're here, then. I'm showing around one of our clients. He might have some input for you.'

'I haven't even started on the marketing yet,' said Cate.

'We only covered the bare outline of your business in the job interview.'

'Just come out the back and say hi, then,' Thompson said.

Cate nodded, and followed him towards the back of the store.

Behind the counter was a door that led to a corridor, which opened onto the Thompson Novelties factory floor. Sunlit through large skylights angled in the roof, the space was filled with huge wooden workbenches mounted with sewing machines, giant spools of nylon kite string, and other pieces of industrial equipment whose purpose was unclear to Cate.

'Do you have to work a lot on weekends?' Cate said.

Thompson laughed at the faint note of anxiety she'd been unable to conceal. 'No, this client has just started up his new hobby shop, and he's spending all week dealing with building contractors. Today was the only day he was free.'

The client was waiting for them at the roller doors that connected the factory to the laneway. He was in his mid-thirties, and handsome in a distracted, rumpled sort of way. He had his hands stuffed in the pockets of his outdoorsy canvas jacket.

'Oh, hello!' he said, stretching out a hand to greet them. 'Alan Dickson. Um, delighted to be, uh, to make your acquaintance.' His stammer should have been infuriating, but his English accent made it endearing. It also didn't hurt that he was easy on the eye, Cate thought.

'Alan!' said Thompson. 'Thanks for coming by on a Saturday. This is Cate, our new marketing manager.'

'I hope you, uh, didn't take time out of your no doubt busy schedule, that is to say, to meet me.'

'No,' Cate said, 'I was just passing by. So, you're stocking up your new shop, Alan?'

His nervous air vanished. 'Oh yes! Thompson Novelties has the best kites around – or, at least, that's what my dad always says. It's really his shop, you see. He's getting on now, and I'm sort of taking it over, if you like.'

'So, you're new to the hobby business?'

'Um, yes, actually. I'm a – professionally, that is – I'm a speech pathologist.'

Cate smirked. 'That's a coincidence,' she said, 'because I'm a pathological liar.'

Alan looked stricken. 'Is, um, is that true?'

'No!' she deadpanned, then shot her new boss a wink. To Alan, she said, 'It's just a joke.'

'I should've warned you, Cate's got a sense of humour on her,' Thompson said. 'You gotta keep it light when you're flying kites.'

'Oh, absolutely, of course,' Alan said. 'I can see why you've taken her on.'

He met her gaze, with an intensity she hadn't expected.

'Now,' said Thompson, 'let me show you our new range of 3D animal kites.'

'Are you, uh, coming, Cate?' Alan asked.

She knew it was probably a good idea to familiarise herself with the range of products she'd soon be in charge of marketing, but she found herself rooted to the spot by despair.

'I'll catch up,' she said, and saw the disappointment in Alan's eyes as she waved them away. Why was she suddenly feeling so awful the instant a man began to flirt with her? It wasn't as if she was cheating on Adam. He'd probably already forgotten her. She was just a face in his past by now, overwritten by a dozen others.

But Cate didn't want anyone else. She still wanted Adam.

'It was awful,' Cate told Vanessa over lunch at Café Nom Nom an hour later. 'This guy at my new work was just being nice, but I felt horrible. All I could think of was Adam.'

'Did you follow them around the warehouse?' Vanessa said

loudly. 'And is it just me, or is this place finally getting popular?'

'I guess 2009 is retro now,' said Cate, eyeing the faded *Avatar* poster behind the cash register. 'Anyway, once I pulled myself together it was okay, but how long is this going to go on? I can't feel like shit every time a nice guy flirts with me.'

'What about your hot date last night? Albert hasn't told me anything yet.'

'Nothing to tell,' said Cate. 'We didn't click. He seemed nice enough, but…'

Vanessa gave Cate a look. 'But he wasn't Adam?'

'I thought we started off okay,' Cate sighed. 'I didn't want to compare him to Adam, but he was so serious. He didn't get my jokes…'

'What, like 90 per cent of the human race?'

'Hey! My sense of humour is universal.'

'Just not in this universe,' Vanessa said pityingly.

'Maybe going out with Adam has spoiled me,' Cate said. 'And before you butt in with some comment about his looks, that wasn't it at all. With Albert, it was like throwing words down a well. I'd say something, and I'd get nothing back.'

'Adam hasn't spoiled you,' Vanessa said. 'You'll find someone soon. You've just gotta keep looking.'

'The thing with Adam was that he was attentive,' Cate said. 'He listened to me.'

'Well, maybe this new guy could be the same. What's his name – Alan? Is he one of your new colleagues?'

'No, but I'll be dealing with him a lot. He's a client.' She sighed. 'What am I going to do?'

Vanessa frowned. 'Oh, sweetie. You're in a bad way. We tried to warn you –'

'I know, I know,' Cate said. 'You told me the Hot Guy would ruin my life. And I'm trying to get it back together. I really like this job. I like Thompson. I might even like this Alan guy, if my brain would only give me the chance.'

'Maybe you should get back to killing it with alcohol,' Vanessa said. 'Worked for Kirsty.'

'I should give her a call,' said Cate. 'And speaking of killing your brain, what time are you meeting Scozza?'

'He should be here any minute,' Vanessa said. 'He probably *will* be here in the next couple of hours.'

'I should get going, then, unless…' Cate said, uncertainly, 'you want me to meet him?'

Vanessa considered this. 'Yeah,' she said at last, 'maybe you'd better get going. Unless you want to lend him twenty bucks.'

'I don't even have twenty bucks,' Cate said, getting up from the table. 'Call you later tonight?'

'You're not going out?'

'And set myself up for more depression? I'll be staying in with a bad movie and a bottle of whatever Kirsty left behind last time she was over.'

'She left a bottle behind? You're lucky.'

'Yeah, she passed out before –'

An unfamiliar man had walked through the café and was now standing directly behind Vanessa, a finger to his lips in a shushing gesture. Cate frowned. The man was a few years her junior, clean-cut-looking, wearing an expensively tailored business suit and shirt, with a spotted ascot tied around his throat. *Scozza won't like this*, Cate thought. Then the man reached down and held his hands over Vanessa's eyes.

'Is that you?' Vanessa said.

'I don't think it's… who you think,' Cate said, looking around in case a skinny junkie was staggering their way with a knife – or a syringe – in hand.

'It's me, darling,' the man said, in a voice even posher than his outfit.

Vanessa giggled, prising the hands from her eyes. 'Babe!' she said excitedly, using his hands to drag him down to her level.

They kissed: a long, graphic pash that involved far too much visible tongue and wandering hands. Trying to catch Vanessa's eye, Cate tugged at her collar while looking around frantically. Scozza could arrive at any moment, and he didn't sound like the kind of person who'd appreciate seeing his girl tongue-wrestling some snooty stranger.

'Vanessa,' she said firmly, 'isn't Scozza on his way?'

'My love,' he said, pulling back slightly to stare into Vanessa's adoring eyes, 'I thought that was *our* private nickname.'

'*Whaaat?*' Cate said, slumping back into her seat in shock.

Somewhere in the back of the café, a CD skipped.

Scozza handed Cate a business card. A tastefully plain rectangle: engraved letters on thick, creamy-white card. It had no address or phone number – just a name.

'Lord Scotherington XXIII, Baron or... Drouthvedges?' Cate read aloud, stumbling over the last word.

'It's an old Northumbrian name, pronounced "Drugs",' Scozza said.

'You're... a drug baron?' Cate said, befuddled.

'It's an obscure but ancient barony in the Lake District hills. It's the highest in England.'

'So Vanessa has told me,' said Cate.

'Darling, this is Cate,' said Vanessa.

'Charmed,' Scozza said, bending chivalrously over Cate's hand. 'I don't suppose either of you ladies happen to be... holding?'

'Sorry?'

'Would you know where one could procure...' he paused dramatically, '... drugs?'

'Cate's not into that,' said Vanessa.

'Oh,' he said. 'How disappointing. I'm rather,' he began scratching the inside of his tweed-clad elbow, 'rather strung out.'

'I should probably get going,' said Cate, reaching under the table for her bag.

'No, don't leave on my account,' Scozza said. 'Please, continue your conversation.'

'I was just giving Cate a pep talk about her love life,' Vanessa said, as Cate squirmed in embarrassment. 'She went on a date, but it didn't work out because she's still thinking about her ex.'

Scozza considered this with a serious face. Finally, he said, 'You've got to get back on the horse.'

'That's right!' Cate said. 'I should start dating again.'

'Um, yes. That too.' Scozza quickly hid the syringe and rubber tubing he had taken from a coat pocket.

'There's no point dating other people if you're only going to be thinking of Adam,' Vanessa said. 'You don't want to be one of those people who can only have sex while fantasising about someone else.'

'That's true,' Scozza said. 'I was once dating a young lady, but my mind was elsewhere.'

'On drugs?' said Vanessa.

'Yes – but my mind was also elsewhere. It was no good trying to repress those memories. I had to confront it. Work through it. And then I was able to get back to the love of my life.'

Vanessa's face softened.

'And also, the woman I was sleeping with.'

Cate looked at Vanessa, who shrugged. 'I'm not sure how that advice applies to me,' Cate said.

'You can't hide from your feelings,' Scozza said. Then he laughed. 'Well, obviously, with the right dealer you can.'

Vanessa interjected, 'I think what Scozza means is that you need to confront your feelings about Adam.'

'Well, what more can I do?' Cate said. 'I let him know I wanted to talk, and he never got back to me. I can't force him to talk to me.'

'I didn't know you needed to use drugs to hide from your feelings,' Vanessa said tenderly, gazing into Scozza's eyes.

'Ironically, I use drugs to hide from my feelings *for* drugs,' he said. 'I love drugs so much, only drugs can ease the pain of being without drugs.'

'I think that's called withdrawal,' said Cate.

'Call it what you will,' Scozza said, 'I call it the pain of a broken heart.'

'Who's got a broken heart?'

Cate looked up. Ursula was standing over her shoulder, wearing a dashingly oversized pair of sunglasses.

'Ursula! What are you doing here?'

Ursula removed her sunglasses with a flourish. 'I read about this place in the latest issue of *Thiefbook* magazine. Nom Nom is hot, hot, hot.'

'I thought Auberon's Moustache was the cool place,' Vanessa said.

'More like Hitler's moustache!' said Ursula. 'Darling, it's over.' She regarded Scozza appraisingly. 'Who's this stud?'

Scozza rose, buttoning his suit jacket. 'Scotherington,' he said, offering Ursula his hand. 'May I ask if you're... holding?'

'Right, that's it,' Vanessa said, getting to her feet and looping her arm through Scozza's. 'We have got to go find this man some drugs.'

'A pleasure,' Scozza said over his shoulder as Vanessa led him away.

Ursula sat down in Vanessa's empty seat. 'That was odd.'

'Yes, he likes drugs,' Cate said.

'Don't we all,' said Ursula. She studied Cate's face more closely. 'I hope you haven't got on the gear, after those idiots at the stadium let you go.'

'I quit!' Cate said indignantly.

'Jumped before you were pushed?' Ursula nodded. 'Good one.'

'They were going to push me?'

'Well, you were my number two, and you know what they do to number twos...'

'They flush them?'

'Not at Sambo Stadium. Unless they've fixed the toilets.'

'Well,' Cate said, 'I've got a new job. Doing PR for a kite company.'

Ursula raised an eyebrow. 'At least the Hot Guy will be bringing in the big bucks.'

'What do you mean?'

'Darl, the word's already out. The Hot Guy will soon be scorching up the screen in *Consumption 3: Conflagration* – which is something of an achievement for a ghost.'

'A Vapour,' Cate said automatically, trying to process what she was hearing.

'Whatever,' Ursula said. 'I hear he's already signed for the next movie. He gets his body back in that one. And what a body!' He fanned herself with her hand.

'He's... an actor now?'

'Doesn't he tell you anything?'

'Not anymore,' Cate said. 'We broke up the night of your drinks.'

'What? Really?' Ursula said. 'Over that? It was just a tiff! But I guess when you've got skin that smooth, it doesn't need to be thick.'

'I thought we'd get past it,' Cate said, 'but we haven't even talked since then. And it was two weeks ago. I've got to assume it's over.'

Ursula put her well-manicured hand on the table over Cate's. 'Oh, honey,' she said. 'Maybe it's time you came to my side of the street.'

Cate blushed. 'Ursula, I think you're getting the wrong idea. I'm not... not into...'

Ursula laughed. 'No, darl. Though to be fair, Adam could make any lesbian turn. I mean there's another bar, on the other side of the street from the Rafferty. And up the road a little bit. Anyway, it's where all the girls go after their dalliance with the Hot Guy.'

'Really?' Cate said. 'Another bar?'

'Well, they can't go back the cinema bar after they've done the deed. They have to leave the playing field free for the next batter.'

'It's not another pick-up joint, is it?'

Ursula shook her head. 'It's just women. Everyone's solo, and all about the YOLO.'

Cate brightened. 'Sounds like my kind of place.'

'Totally,' said Ursula. 'You've had your time with Adam – now you're ready to start life over, with that special burst of confidence that only the Hot Guy can give.'

'I don't feel that confident,' Cate said.

'That's because you stayed with him too long. You over-complicated this. Here's how it works: you sleep with the Hot Guy; you feel good; you move on. And this is the bar you move on to.'

'I guess,' Cate said. 'He's not coming back, is he?'

'It's for the best,' said Ursula. 'He's going to be a huge movie star soon. How can you compete with a hundred million fans, drawn like moths to his flame?'

'I guess,' Cate said. 'That would explain why he never called me back. He's got bigger fish to fry.'

'On his hot bod.'

'Thanks, Ursula.'

'Seriously. Let's go to this bar tonight. Believe me, it really helps.'

Cate saw the expression on her friend's face. Ursula's night with Adam must have been special, too.

'All right, I'll go,' she said. 'But I've got to go alone. This is something I have to do by myself.'

'Are you sure?'

'I've got to get over Adam. I can't keep going like this. I've got to draw a line under it. Make a clean break. I'll go to this bar tonight, and then that's it. He's dead to me. He could come crawling back tomorrow, and I wouldn't give him the time of day.'

'Yes, but are you sure you should be doing this on your own?'

'I have to. That was my problem in the first place – I was relying on other people to help me get over things. Now I've got to stop.'

'By going to a bar full of other people?'

'It's symbolic, bitch!'

54

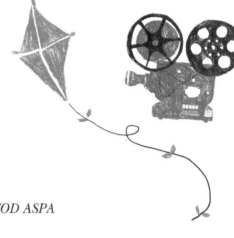

HAI ADAJM
   UR BIG STAR CUM 2 HOLYWOD ASPA
   THX
   LOOK 2 DA SKTYES
   STEVEN SPIELBURG

Adam read over the email one more time, hardly believing his eyes. When it had first arrived, he'd thought surely this was spam. Or Renton, trying to screw with him. But then he'd checked with his agent, Clive.

'It's legit,' Clive had said over the phone. 'Steven Spielberg really does want you to fly over to meet him.'

'He can't spell his own name?'

'Maybe he was typing in a hurry?'

'The guy who wrote *Close Encounters* can't spell "Hollywood"?'

'He makes movies, he doesn't write novels. Look, his people say there's like a three-day window where he's willing to fly you out – he's seen the footage from *Conflagration*, he knows you're locked in for the next one, and he wants to test you for *Munich 2: Freedom's Sweat.*'

'I don't...' Adam had shaken his head. 'Should I take it?'

'A free trip to Hollywood? Shit yeah. And if you say yes, my 10 per cent should get me to at least Christchurch.'

'I don't think it works that way.'

'Who's the agent here?'

'Fair enough. But if I go, I'm never going to come back, am I?'

'That's up to you,' Clive had said. 'But realistically, why would you? What's keeping you here?'

Adam couldn't answer him then, and as he closed his laptop now, he was no closer to an answer. He'd never wanted to be an actor, but getting a foot in the door over there would be a massive leap forward for his career – five years on Hollywood sets and he could do anything, make anything. It was everything he'd ever wanted, and on the other hand...

He checked his phone one more time. Cate still hadn't called. And there was Kirsty's number. She'd given it to him when they'd met on the street. 'If you ever want to talk...' she'd said, and winked.

'I don't think that would be fair to Cate,' Adam had said, and Kirsty had punched him in the arm.

'*Talk* talk, not sex talk.'

Adam had been strangely touched by her kindness. Maybe he should give her a call. She might have a different perspective from Steve and Renton. He couldn't stop thinking about Cate, couldn't help feeling he'd totally fucked it up. But how was he going to fix things? Cate's old phone was disconnected. If she'd wanted to talk to him, she would have given him her new number. She clearly thought he was a dickhead. He *was* a dickhead. And she wouldn't go out with a dickhead. But he still wanted to let her know how he felt...

He looked at his watch as he dialled Kirsty. It was 6.30 p.m.; he hoped Kirsty wasn't out somewhere.

'Hello?'

'Hi Kirsty, it's Adam.'

He suddenly had a thought: *What if she's with Cate?* He'd been hoping Kirsty would say Cate was waiting for his call. But he needed time to figure out what to say to Cate.

'Cate's not there, is she?'

'Have you been trying to call her? You know she had to hand back her phone when she quit her job.'

'She quit her job?'

'Uh-huh,' Kirsty said. 'They wanted to play sport at the sports stadium.'

'Ugh. That's a bad idea.'

'Tell me about it. I hate sport.'

There was a pause. 'So,' Kirsty said, 'are you still pissed off about being the Hot Guy?'

'I'm not in love with the idea, but what am I going to do?' Adam said. 'Now I know about it, it's over anyway.'

'So what? Are you going to become a professional stud?'

'Yep, that's exactly why I want to get in touch with Cate – to bill her for my services.'

Kirsty laughed. 'That cinema's going to go broke if you quit to go pro.'

'Well, I'm quitting the cinema job anyway,' Adam said. 'Haven't you heard? Hollywood's calling.'

'I've heard fuck-all,' Kirsty said. 'Why didn't you tell me? Why didn't you tell Cate?'

'It's all happened really suddenly,' he said. 'And I've tried to call Cate, but I guess she hasn't been getting my calls.'

'Not if you've been calling her old number.'

'Well, what's her new number?'

Kirsty paused. 'Um, I'm not sure if I should give you that.'

'Why?' Adam's heart lurched. 'Is she... Is there...?'

'No,' Kirsty sighed. 'She's not seeing anyone. Yet.'

'Then what's the problem?'

'Tonight, she's going to a bar,' Kirsty said.

'So?'

'It's a bar where women go to get over you.'

'What?'

'You know that bar up the road from the Rafferty? After a woman's spent the night with you, she can't very well go back to the cinema bar, because that's where you are. So all the women you've slept with, from that bar, they go to the bar up the road.

That way they don't have to see you. They can hang out, compare notes. They've all got something in common.'

'Hang on,' Adam said. 'Do you mean that place with the front window that opens onto the street? I always thought it was a lesbian bar.'

'You should be flattered,' Kirsty said.

'So, why is she going there?'

'Do you really need me to spell it out to you?' she said. 'This is how she proves to herself that she's over you! Forever! No more Adam and Cate.'

Adam was puzzled. 'She has to go to a bar to do this?'

'You have no idea how crushed she was when you dumped her. She was totes devo.'

'But I didn't dump her! I just said the relationship was over and walked away!'

'Yeah,' Kirsty said, 'I can totally see how she got the wrong impression.'

'I didn't – I was just so mad! Sure, I overreacted, but what would *you* do if someone said you were the Hot Girl? Don't answer that.'

'I wouldn't run off and sulk for a week.'

'I was only sulking for three days. Four days! Five days, max.'

'It was long enough for you to lose Cate.'

Adam said, plaintively, 'I've lost her?'

'I dunno, Einstein. She's going to a gay bar.'

'She can't go to that bar!' Adam said. 'We've still got so much to say!'

'Well, once she's in the bar I don't think she's going to want to hear it.'

'No!'

'I don't think she'll be able to hear you over all the Indigo Girls songs.'

'But we've gotta talk! I've got to tell her…'

'She's not there yet,' Kirsty said. 'If you hurry, maybe you can catch her.'

'Shit!' Adam said. 'Shit shit shit!'

'Good luck,' Kirsty said, as Adam hung up. 'You crazy kids are gonna need it.'

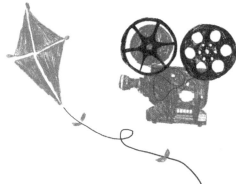

55

Cate stood on the footpath outside the bar. The windows were open, and she could see people inside. Well, women. Ursula was right – there didn't seem to be any male patrons. *This must be the place*, she thought, looking up the street towards the Rafferty. A small, tasteful sign advertised the bar name: The Icebox.

Do I really want to do this? she thought. It was silly, she knew, but it really did feel as if going into the bar would be crossing a threshold. While she stayed on the street, there was still a chance to go back to the life she'd shared with Adam. *Not that Adam seems interested*, she thought, and the weight of their failed relationship settled back on her like a shroud.

What's the point of dragging this out? Cate thought. But then she tried to imagine a life without Adam, and she still couldn't. Two weeks was nowhere near long enough. But how long would it take? Would she be on her deathbed, her loving husband and children by her side, still calling out with her final breath for Adam?

She could see it now: 'Darling, I've always loved you,' her conventionally attractive husband would tell her, tenderly cradling her withered, veiny old hand. 'I can't let go without hearing your voice one last time.'

'AD-AM,' Cate would croak.

'What was that, dear?' her husband would say, leaning closer.

'I WANT AD-AM!'

Why am I talking like a Dalek on my own deathbed? she thought, shaking her head to clear the nightmarish vision. *No*, she thought, *now is the time to move on. If Adam doesn't want me, then I don't want him.*

She took a step towards the bar entrance. Suddenly, all her doubts crowded back in. Going into the bar didn't really mean anything, she knew, but she wasn't sure if she was ready to write off everything she'd had with Adam. If she went in here, it felt like she would be throwing all their time together in the bin. She'd be going back to the start – saying that everything that had happened since Alistair had dumped her had meant nothing.

Her face was suddenly wet. She looked up – was it raining? The sky was grey. She looked down at the footpath. No raindrops there. *It's just me,* she thought, wiping away the tears from her cheeks. Then as she stood with her head downcast, she saw the first fat drops of rain begin to fall.

Guess that's that, then, she thought. The only thing more stupid than loitering out the front of a bar would be loitering out the front in the rain. She knew it was silly, but she had to say his name one last time.

'Adam...' she murmured. 'Why did you leave me?'

'I was a fool.'

Ugh, her imagination was telling her what she wanted to hear. 'Why didn't you call me?' she said.

'I tried. But I didn't have your number.'

Wow, she had a pretty vivid imagination. 'Why did you let that stop you?'

'I didn't.' She felt a hand on her shoulder. A warm, familiar hand. She closed her eyes, remembering. Hoping.

'Adam?'

The hand turned her around. 'Oh, Cate,' Adam said. She was surprised to realise that for once Kirsty had been right: his beard only made him look hotter.

'Adam!' she said. 'How did you find me?'

'I called Kirsty,' he said. 'Also, I just live around the corner.'

'Oh yeah, right,' Cate said, unable to suppress a grin.

'Cate,' he said, grabbing her hand. 'I'm an idiot. I don't know why I made such a big deal of everything.'

'I should have told you,' she said. 'I didn't want to ruin what we had.'

'You didn't,' he said. 'I did that. I messed it all up.'

'How do you say to your boyfriend that every woman in town thinks he's the hottest guy alive?' She shook her head. 'It's more than that. When they first told me about you, I thought you'd be some arrogant, sleazy pick-up artist. I thought it was okay to use a guy who was just going to be using me, but you were so sweet and lovely and you cared about me.'

There was water running down her cheeks and she didn't know if it was tears or the rain. 'I couldn't bring it up because…' she tried to brush her damp hair off her face, '… the guy they brought me to meet, that wasn't you. You're not the Hot Guy. You're Adam, and I love you.'

A wet chunk of hair flopped down over her eyes. She laughed. 'I must look fucking awful.'

'Don't worry,' Adam said with a smirk, 'I'm good-looking enough for the both of us.'

Cate loosened her grip on Adam's hand and looked over her shoulder at the bar. The rain didn't seem to be slowing the partying down. She'd never stopped to think that Adam might actually embrace being the Hot Guy. What if he liked being the centre of attention? What if in these few weeks apart he'd become everything her friends had warned her about?

Adam reached over and brushed the hair out of her eyes. 'All the better to see me with,' he said, and this time Cate saw he was joking – or, at least, trying to make a joke. The smirk was still there on his lips, but in his eyes she saw a look that was almost beseeching. It wasn't a joke he was making – it was a peace offering.

'Hey,' she said, 'I thought I was meant to be the funny one.'

'There's more to you than telling jokes,' he said.

'So what, you want to swap?' she said. 'You be the funny one, and I'll be –'

'You always were the good-looking one,' he said.

He leant down to kiss her and she knew it was coming, and yet when his lips met hers it was better than she'd dared hope. For a second it felt strange and new with his beard brushing against her cheek, but then she felt the familiar comfort of his arms around her, and it was like the last three weeks had been nothing. She knew that this was where she wanted to be, now and for always.

From behind her Cate heard a cheer erupt. She pulled back, not wanting the kiss to end, but the noise was too loud to ignore. Turning, she saw the open front window of The Icebox was now lined with women cheering, clapping and punching the air. They were all women from Adam's past, she realised. Some she recognised from the League. Others were strangers. But they all wore the same happy grin. And when she looked up at Adam he was blushing.

'You go girl!' yelled Mackaylah, the former League leader.

'About time you settled down, Adam,' said another woman.

'I should have let the President die,' shouted a dark-haired girl wearing glasses.

'Do you still want to go in?' Adam said, a note of hesitation in his voice.

'Only if you come with me,' she said.

Hand in hand, they walked in out of the rain.

THE END

ACKNOWLEDGEMENTS

Mel and Anthony thank:

Our commissioning editor Angela Meyer, whose enthusiasm for our book was infectious, and who gratifyingly laughed at many of our jokes.

Our supportive agent, Alex Adsett.

The capable and enthusiastic team who brought the book into being: our diligent copy-editor Nicola Williams; Echo marketing sages Kirstin Corcoran and Sabita Naheswaran; and Alissa Dinallo for our eye-catching cover design.

All our early manuscript readers, especially Lee Zachariah, Lisa Dempster and Alison Bean.

Our friends in the Secret Film Critics Thread and the Westside Writers Group.

All the places where we wrote and discussed the book: Panini Bar, Jungle Juice Bar, Trotters, Lygon Food Store, Tre Bicchieri, Cremorne Hotel, Hells Kitchen, Le Cirque Fine Foods at Spencer Outlet Centre, the food courts at Emporium Melbourne and Melbourne Central, and the air-conditioned lobby of the Telstra building on Lonsdale Street.

Jo Case, Rochelle Siemienowicz, Jess Lomas and Myke Bartlett, for advice on writing and guidance on the publishing industry.

... and all the movie hot guys.

Anthony thanks:

My mother Lois and my sister Angela, both of whom are perhaps the only people I know who would read this book even if I hadn't written half of it.

Aileen Smith, Guy Davis, Thomas Caldwell, Greg and Andrew Jarman, Melissa Cranenburgh, Rebecca Harkins-Cross, Anna Hoskin, and everyone else who had to hear me testing out the many bad jokes and poor one-liners that eventually found their way into this novel.

Daniel Baker, who first told me the "Then the bag came off" joke 25 years ago and we've been laughing about it ever since. I've been doing most of the laughing, but still.

The various science-fiction novels stacked by my bedside, the authors of which provided the names for Cate's workmates.

And of course I'd like to thank the charming and erudite Mel 'Smell Hamwell' Campbell for editing out most of my excesses, putting up with my repeated demands to dumb things down, and generally adding class and polish to what otherwise would just have been a collection of grunts and farting noises with the occasional World War II reference thrown in. She's a far better writer than me, and all the good parts of this book come from her.

Mel thanks:

My parents and family – especially my youngest brother Matt, whose childhood teddy bear Poly (alias 'Captain Horny') I stole and gave to Adam. My cat Graham was no help whatsoever in writing this novel. He gets no thanks from me.

My dear pals in the PLC crew and in the Crimp, Book Club, Dinner Club, Holiday Club and Period Club. I've taken such joy and solace from their company on mini-breaks to bucolic holiday houses that Anthony cruelly calls 'murder shacks'. This is because he is jealous of what we have. I'd especially like to thank Paulina Olszanka, some of whose absurd everyday encounters found their way into the book. You *do* have charisma, Paulina!

My *Rereaders* colleagues, and my collegial communities of fellow writers and critics on Twitter and Facebook.

And of course I'd like to thank Anthony 'Mongo Schlong' Morris, my co-conspirator and comrade, constant provider of moral support and weeper with laughter at his own dreadful jokes. It has meant a great deal to have his sardonic presence just a text message away at any time of the day or night, but especially at 4.20pm.